WELL IT'S PLAIN TO SEE YOU
WERE MEANT FOR ME
YEAH, I'M YOUR BOY,
YOUR 20TH CENTURY TOY
—T. Rex

image

ROCK

ROCKSTARS, VOL. 1: NATIVITY IN BLACKLIGHT First printing. June 2017. Published by Image Comics, Inc. Office of publication: 2701 NW Vaughn St., Ste. 780, Portland, OR 97210. Copyright © 2017 JOE HARRIS and MEGAN HUTCHISON. All rights reserved. Contains material originally published in single magazine form as ROCKSTARS #1-5. ROCKSTARS™ (including all prominent characters featured herein), its logo and all character likenesses are trademarks of Joe Harris and Megan Hutchison, unless otherwise noted. Image Comics® and its logos are registered trademarks of Image Comics, Inc. No part of this publication may be reproduced or transmitted, in any form or by any means (except short excerpts for review purposes) without express written permission of Image Comics, Inc. All names, characters, events and locales in this publication are entirely fictional. Any resemblance to actual living persons (living or dead), events or places, without satiric intent, is coincidental. Printed in the U.S.A. For more information regarding the CPSIA on this printed material call: 203-595-3636 and provide reference # RICH - 738676.
ISBN: 978-1-5343-0190-0   Third Eye Exclusive Variant ISBN: 978-1-5343-0416-1
For international rights, contact: foreignlicensing@imagecomics.com

Joe Harris	Writer
Megan Hutchison	Artist
Kelly Fitzpatrick	Colorist
Tom Muller	Designer
Michael David Thomas	Letterer
Shawna Gore	Editor

STARS

VOL. 1
NATIVITY IN BLACKLIGHT

Originally published as ROCKSTARS 1-5

IMAGE COMICS, INC: Robert Kirkman: Chief Operating Officer / Erik Larsen: Chief Financial Officer / Todd McFarlane: President / Marc Silvestri: Chief Executive Officer / Jim Valentino: Vice-President / Eric Stephenson: Publisher / Corey Murphy: Director of Sales / Jeff Boison: Director of Publishing Planning & Book Trade Sales / Chris Ross: Director of Digital Sales / Jeff Stang: Director of Specialty Sales / Kat Salazar: Director of PR & Marketing / Branwyn Bigglestone: Controller / Sue Korpela: Accounts Manager / Drew Gill: Art Director / Brett Warnock: Production Manager / Meredith Wallace: Print Manager / Tricia Ramos: Traffic Manager / Briah Skelly: Publicist / Aly Hoffman: Events & Conventions Coordinator / Sasha Head: Sales & Marketing Production Designer / David Brothers: Branding Manager / Melissa Gifford: Content Manager / Drew Fitzgerald: Publicity Assistant / Vincent Kukua: Production Artist / Erika Schnatz: Production Artist / Ryan Brewer: Production Artist / Shanna Matuszak: Production Artist / Carey Hall: Production Artist / Esther Kim: Direct Market Sales Representative / Emilio Bautista: Digital Sales Representative / Leanna Caunter: Accounting Assistant / Chloe Ramos-Peterson: Library Market Sales Representative / Maria Eizik: Administrative Assistant / **IMAGECOMICS.COM**

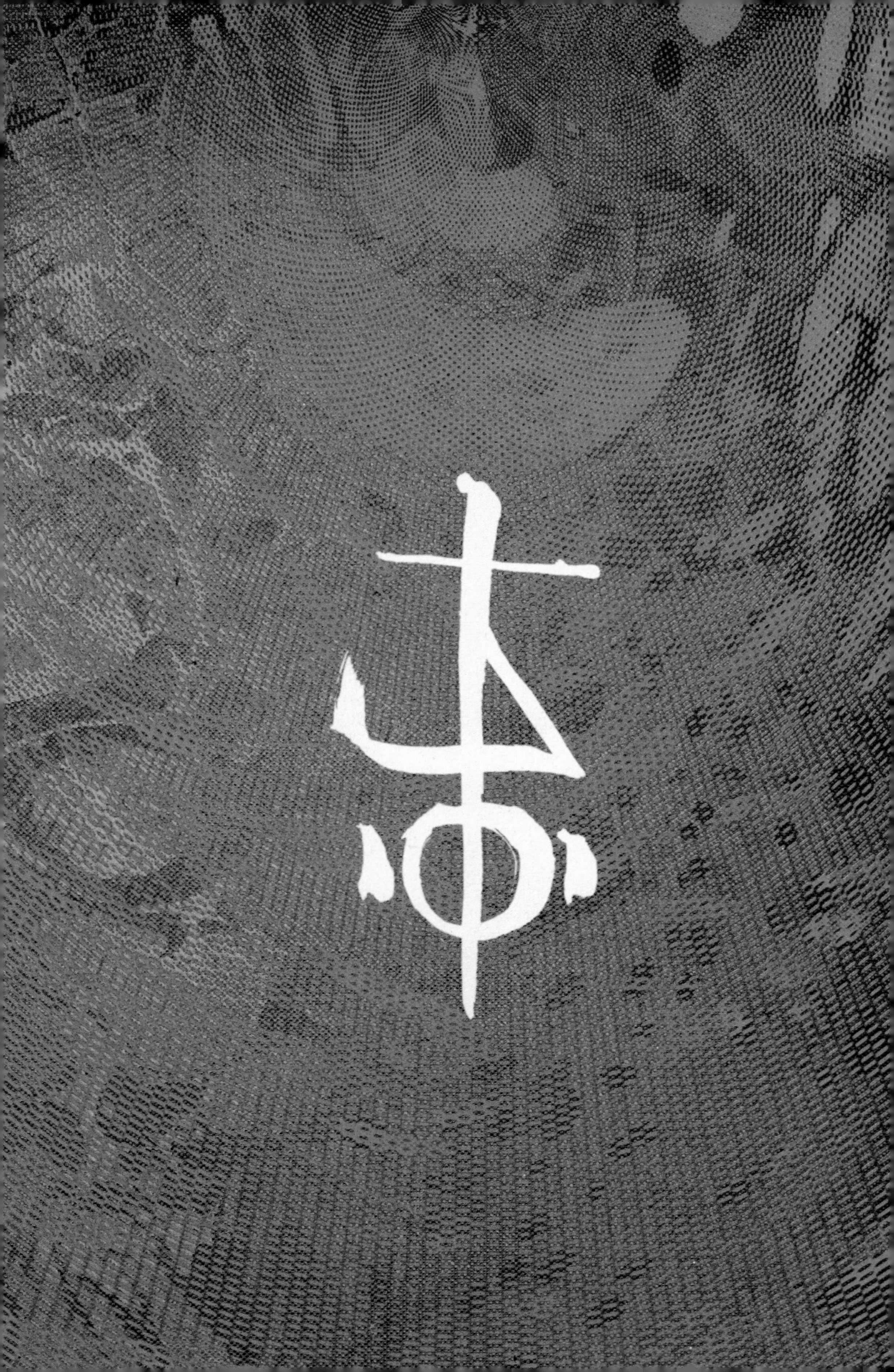

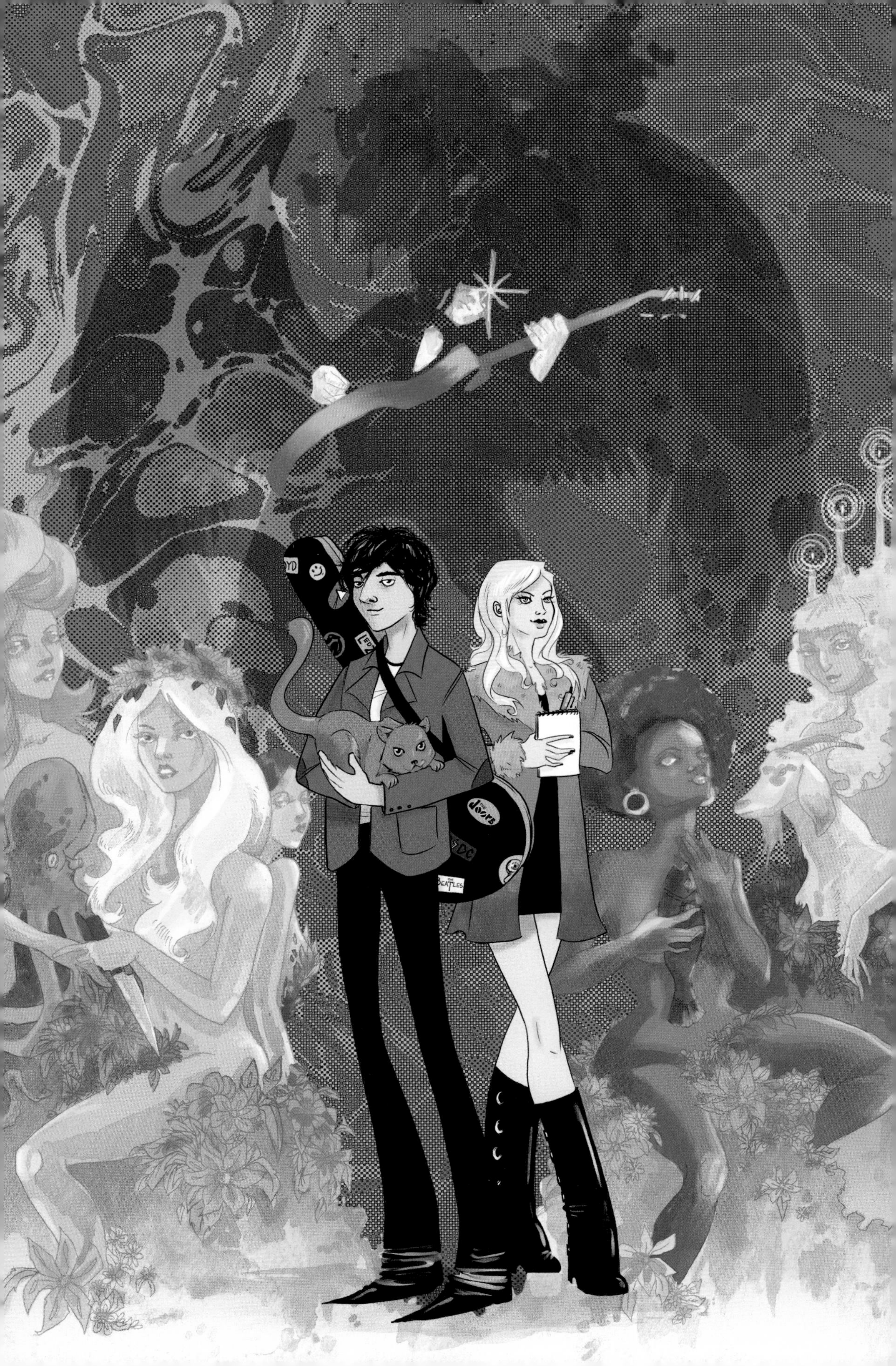
BEATLES

Jackie Mayer knows what's actually hidden behind the music and what the backwards messages really say... but he's not the only one listening.

ROCKSTARS

SIDE # 1		Track 1
FULL COLOR		

NATIVITY IN BLACKLIGHT

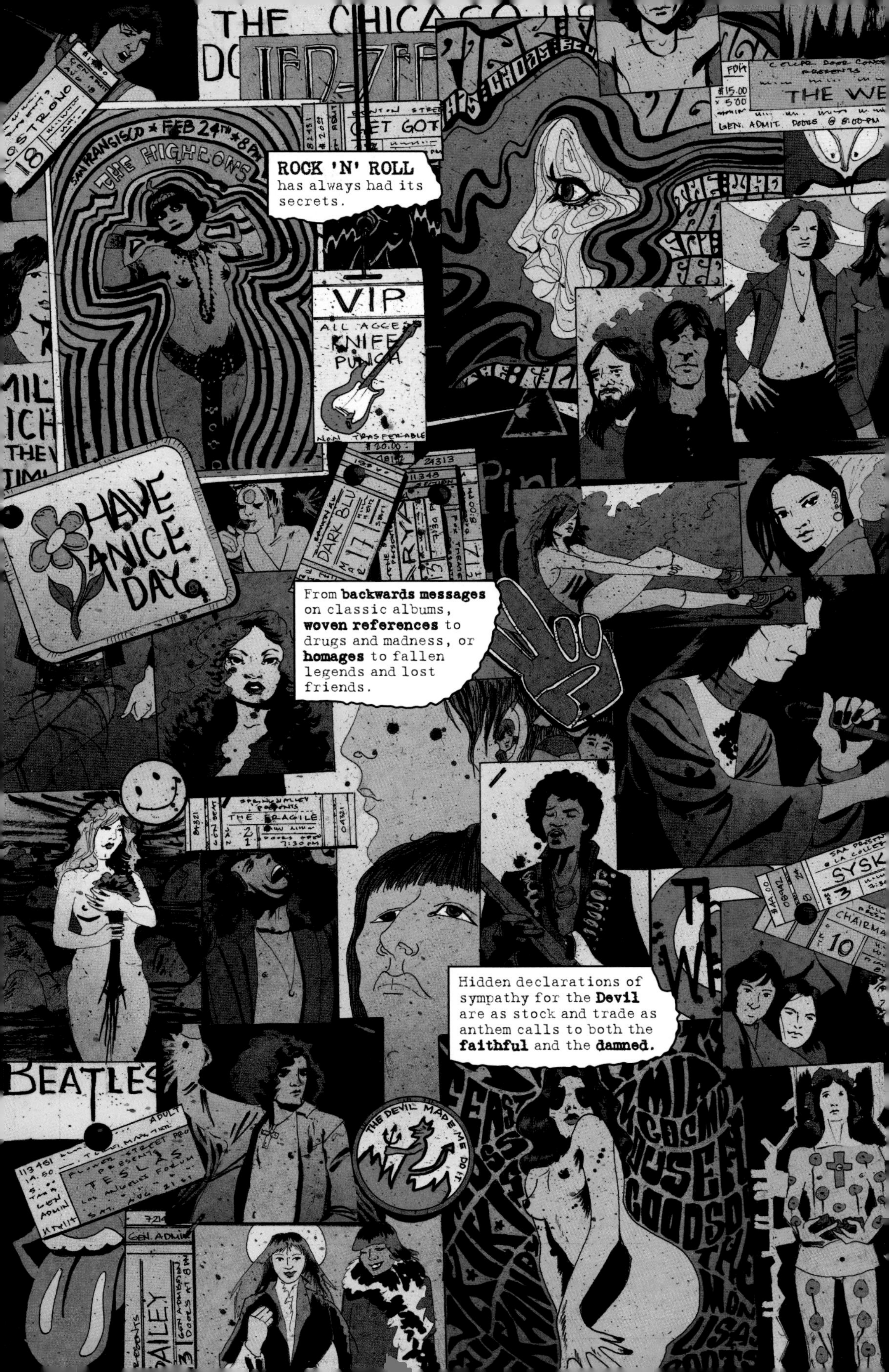
ROCK 'N' ROLL has always had its secrets.
From **backwards messages** on classic albums, **woven references** to drugs and madness, or **homages** to fallen legends and lost friends.
Hidden declarations of sympathy for the **Devil** are as stock and trade as anthem calls to both the **faithful** and the **damned.**
VIP
HAVE A NICE DAY
BEATLES
THE DEVIL MADE ME DO IT

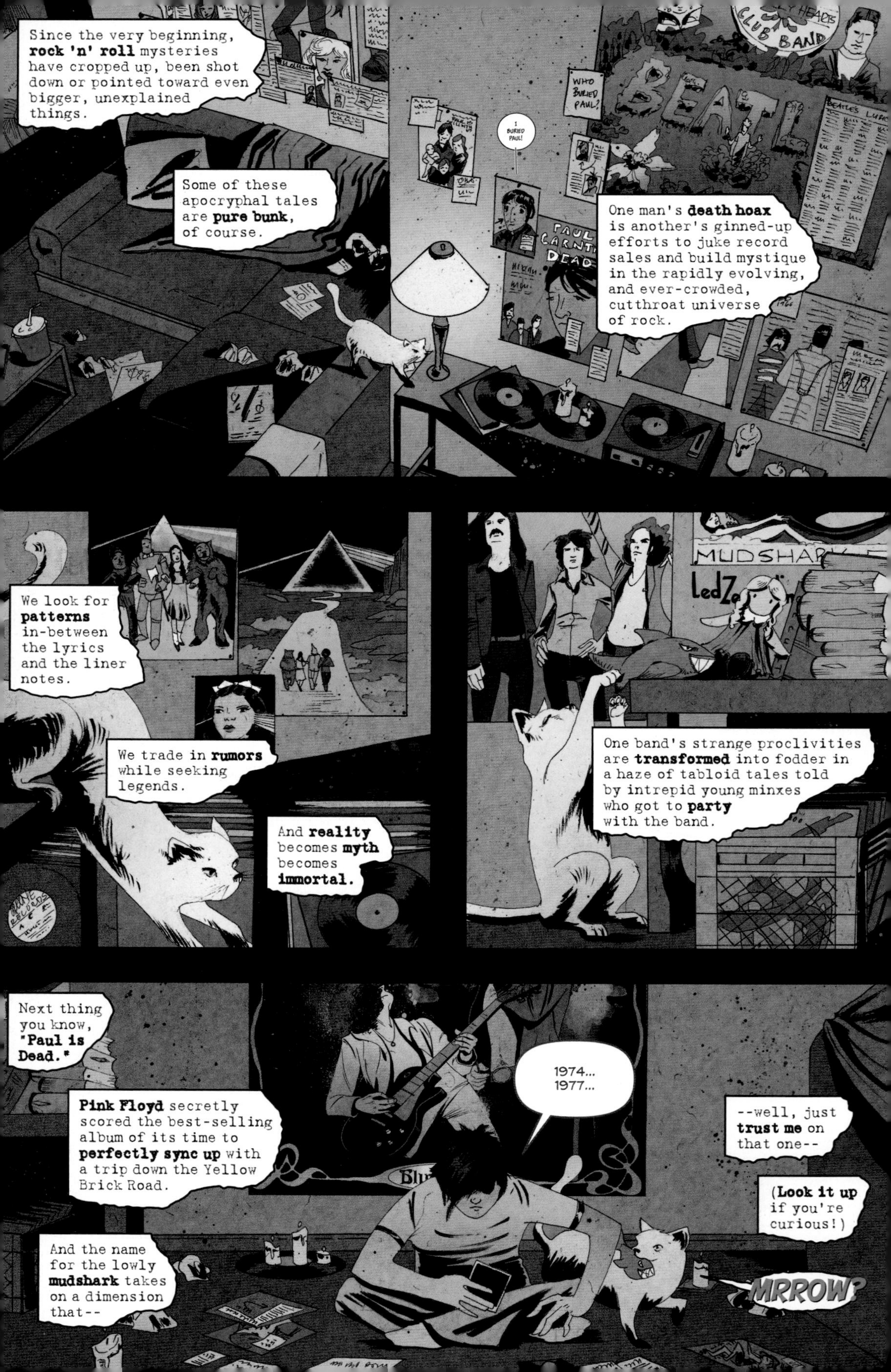

Since the very beginning, **rock 'n' roll** mysteries have cropped up, been shot down or pointed toward even bigger, unexplained things.
Some of these apocryphal tales are **pure bunk**, of course.
WHO BURIED PAUL?
I BURIED PAUL!
One man's **death hoax** is another's ginned-up efforts to juke record sales and build mystique in the rapidly evolving, and ever-crowded, cutthroat universe of rock.
We look for **patterns** in-between the lyrics and the liner notes.
We trade in **rumors** while seeking legends.
And **reality** becomes **myth** becomes **immortal.**
One band's strange proclivities are **transformed** into fodder in a haze of tabloid tales told by intrepid young minxes who got to **party** with the band.
Next thing you know, **"Paul is Dead."**
Pink Floyd secretly scored the best-selling album of its time to **perfectly sync up** with a trip down the Yellow Brick Road.
And the name for the lowly **mudshark** takes on a dimension that--
1974... 1977...
--well, just **trust me** on that one--
(**Look it up** if you're curious!)
MRROW?

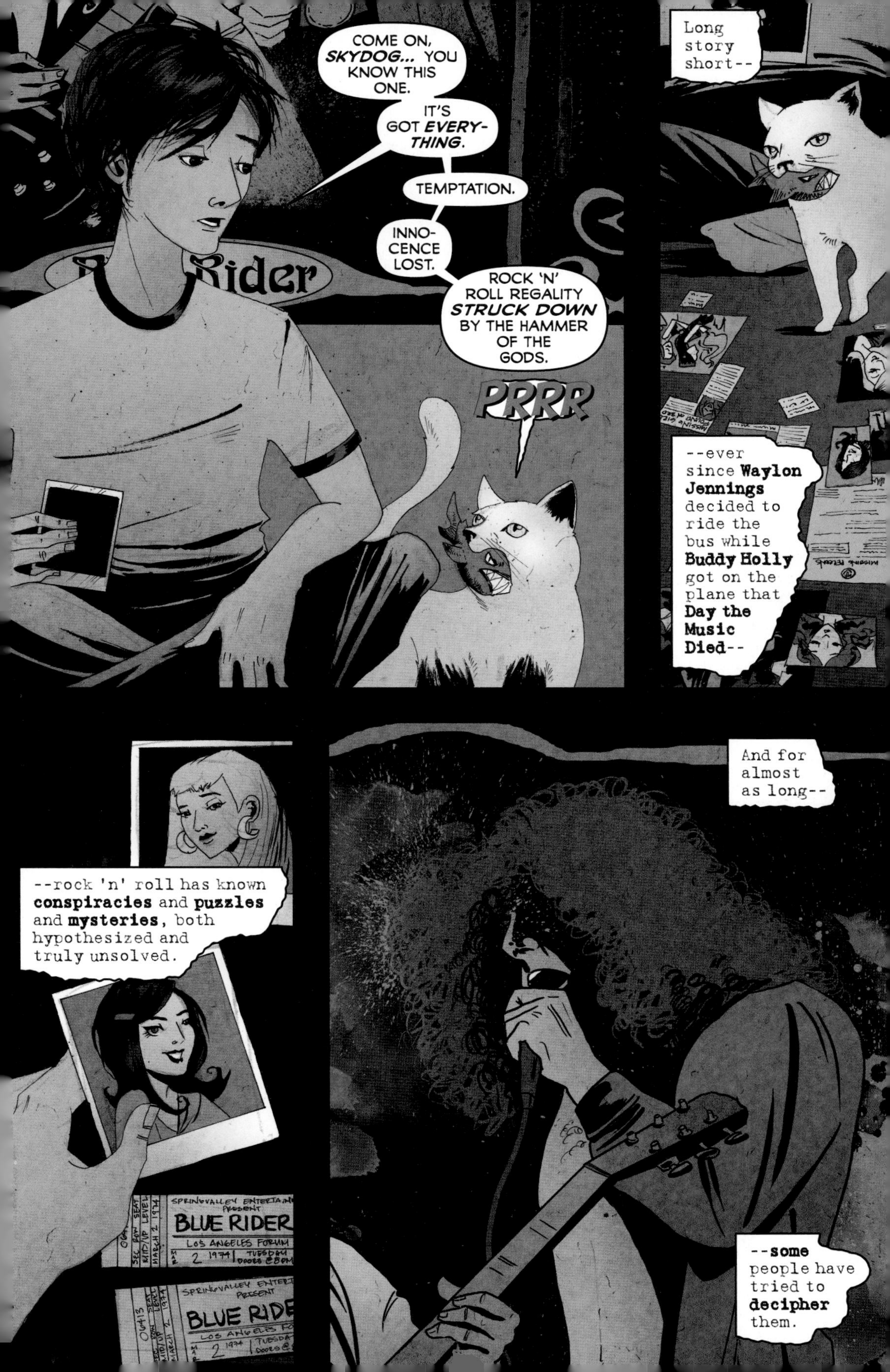

COME ON, *SKYDOG...* YOU KNOW THIS ONE.
IT'S GOT *EVERYTHING*.
TEMPTATION.
INNOCENCE LOST.
ROCK 'N' ROLL REGALITY *STRUCK DOWN* BY THE HAMMER OF THE GODS.
PRRR
Long story short--
--ever since **Waylon Jennings** decided to ride the bus while **Buddy Holly** got on the plane that **Day the Music Died**--
And for almost as long--
--rock 'n' roll has known **conspiracies** and **puzzles** and **mysteries**, both hypothesized and truly unsolved.
BLUE RIDER
LOS ANGELES FORUM
--**some** people have tried to **decipher** them.

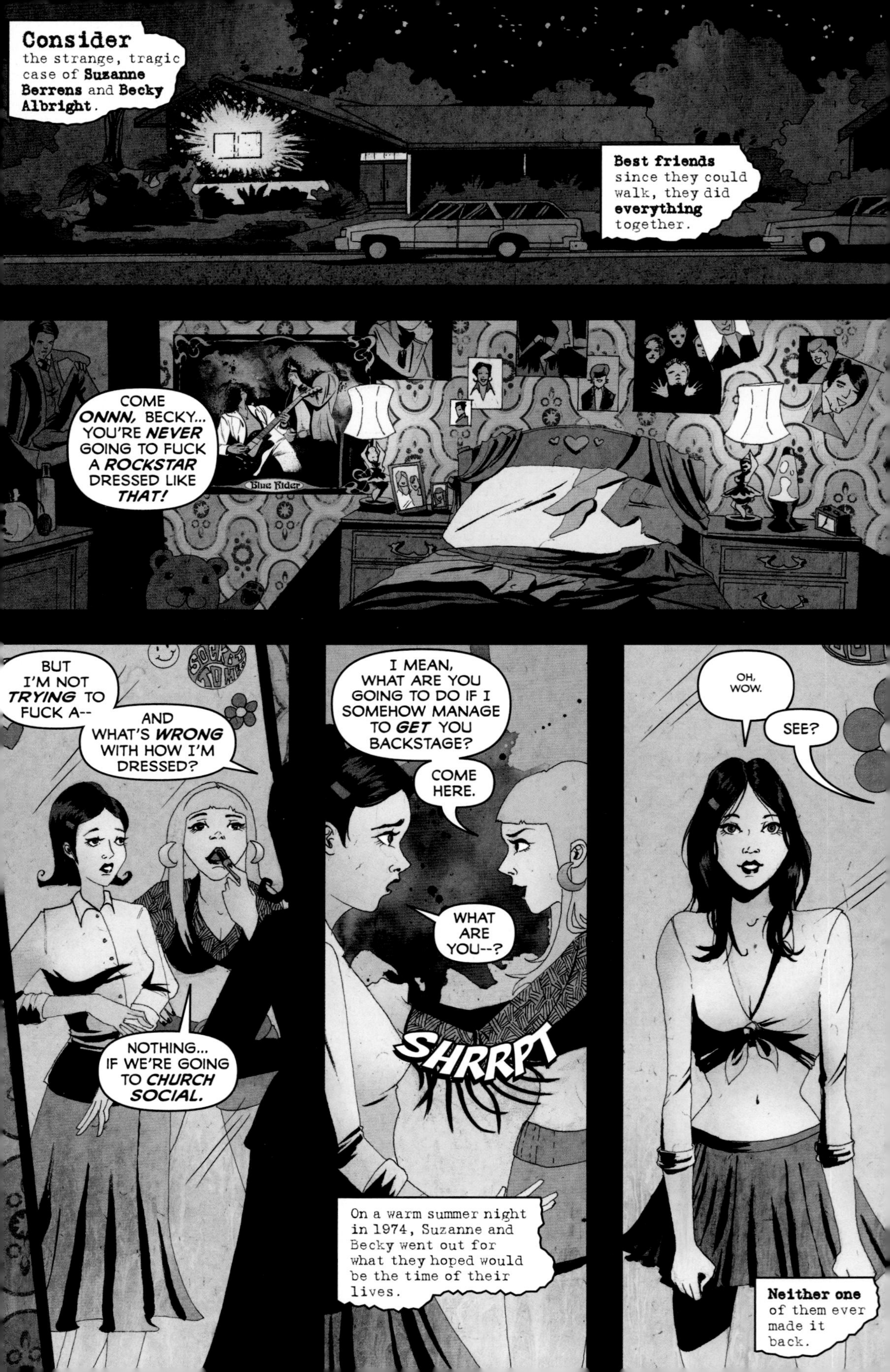
Consider the strange, tragic case of Suzanne Berrens and Becky Albright.
Best friends since they could walk, they did everything together.
COME ONNN, BECKY... YOU'RE NEVER GOING TO FUCK A ROCKSTAR DRESSED LIKE THAT!
Blue Rider
BUT I'M NOT TRYING TO FUCK A--
AND WHAT'S WRONG WITH HOW I'M DRESSED?
NOTHING... IF WE'RE GOING TO CHURCH SOCIAL.
I MEAN, WHAT ARE YOU GOING TO DO IF I SOMEHOW MANAGE TO GET YOU BACKSTAGE?
COME HERE.
WHAT ARE YOU--?
SHRRPT
On a warm summer night in 1974, Suzanne and Becky went out for what they hoped would be the time of their lives.
OH, WOW.
SEE?
Neither one of them ever made it back.

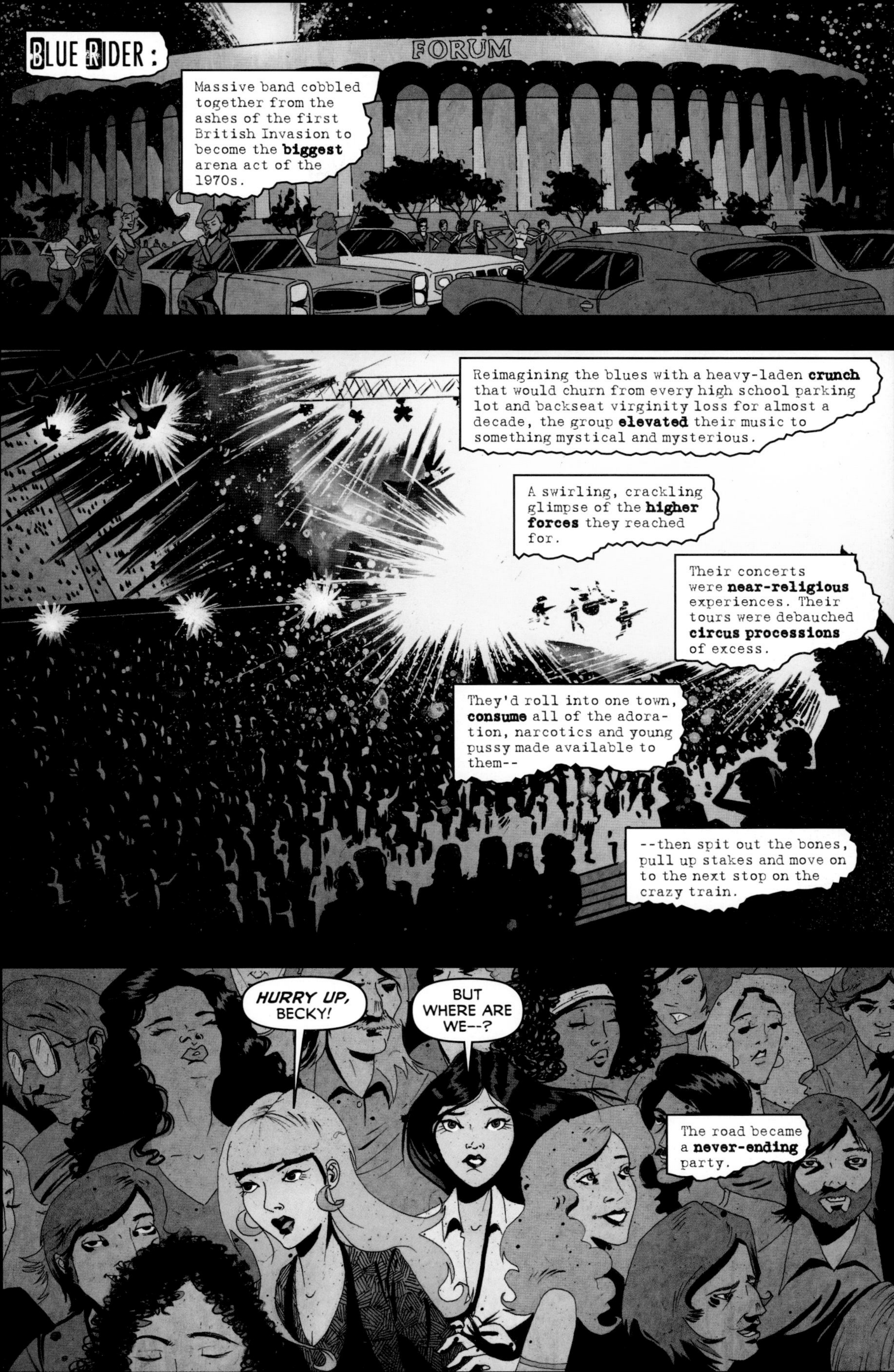
BLUE RIDER:
FORUM
Massive band cobbled together from the ashes of the first British Invasion to become the **biggest** arena act of the 1970s.
Reimagining the blues with a heavy-laden **crunch** that would churn from every high school parking lot and backseat virginity loss for almost a decade, the group **elevated** their music to something mystical and mysterious.
A swirling, crackling glimpse of the **higher forces** they reached for.
Their concerts were **near-religious** experiences. Their tours were debauched **circus processions** of excess.
They'd roll into one town, **consume** all of the adoration, narcotics and young pussy made available to them--
--then spit out the bones, pull up stakes and move on to the next stop on the crazy train.
HURRY UP, BECKY!
BUT WHERE ARE WE--?
The road became a **never-ending** party.

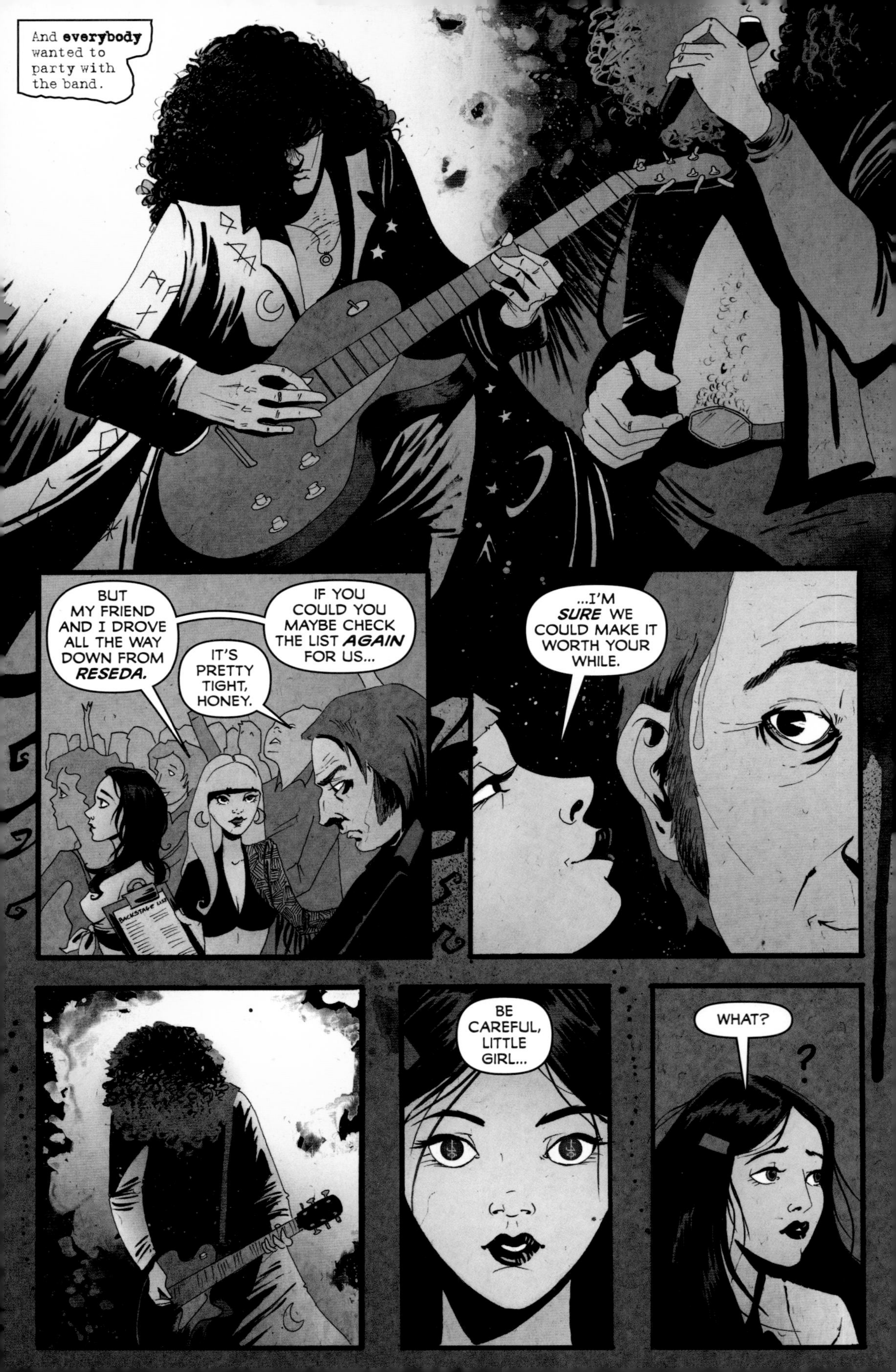
And **everybody** wanted to party with the band.
BUT MY FRIEND AND I DROVE ALL THE WAY DOWN FROM *RESEDA.*
IT'S PRETTY TIGHT, HONEY.
IF YOU COULD YOU MAYBE CHECK THE LIST *AGAIN* FOR US...
BACKSTAGE LIST
...I'M *SURE* WE COULD MAKE IT WORTH YOUR WHILE.
BE CAREFUL, LITTLE GIRL...
WHAT?
?

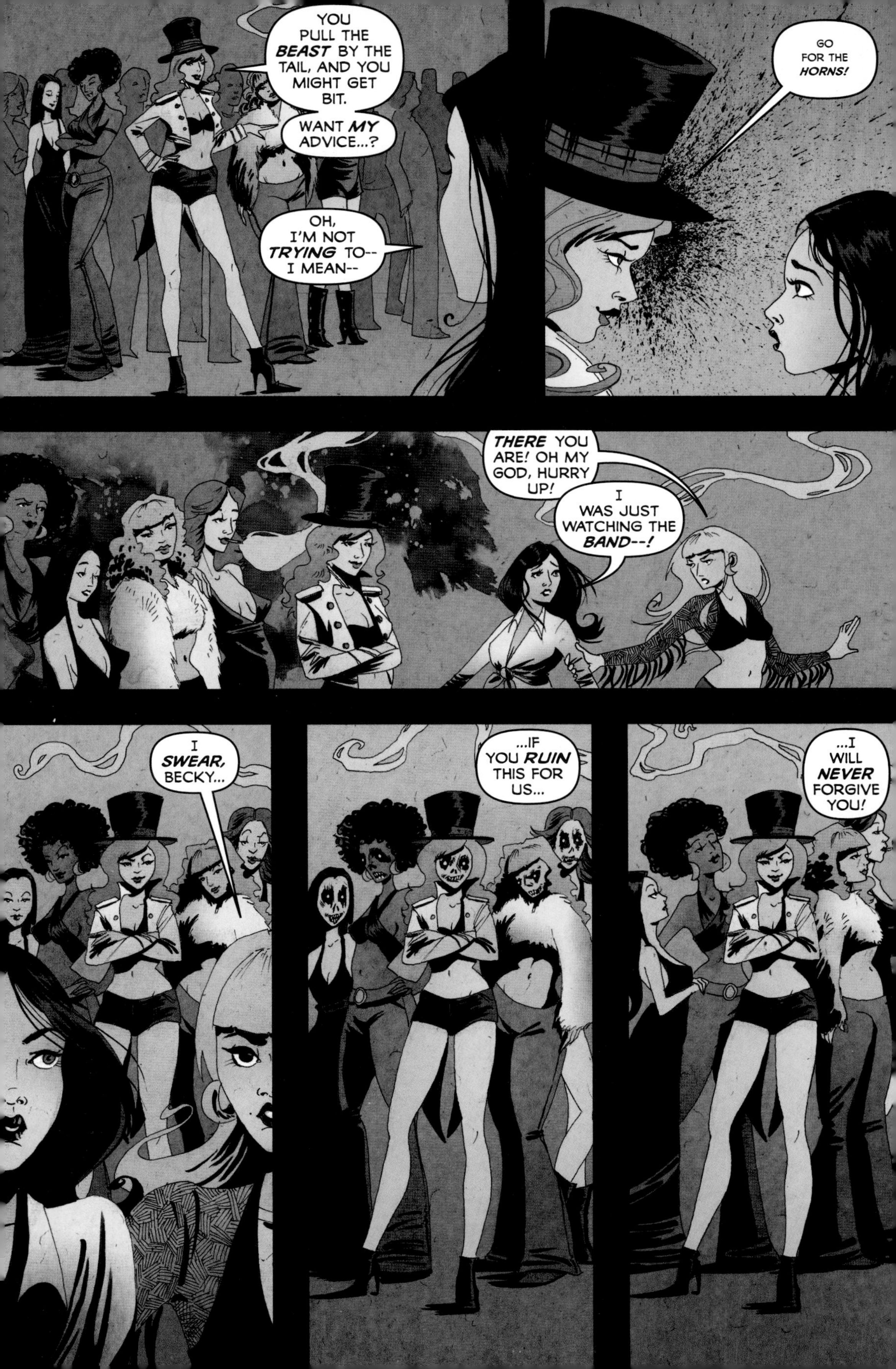
YOU PULL THE BEAST BY THE TAIL, AND YOU MIGHT GET BIT.
WANT MY ADVICE...?
OH, I'M NOT TRYING TO-- I MEAN--
GO FOR THE HORNS!
THERE YOU ARE! OH MY GOD, HURRY UP!
I WAS JUST WATCHING THE BAND--!
I SWEAR, BECKY...
...IF YOU RUIN THIS FOR US...
...I WILL NEVER FORGIVE YOU!

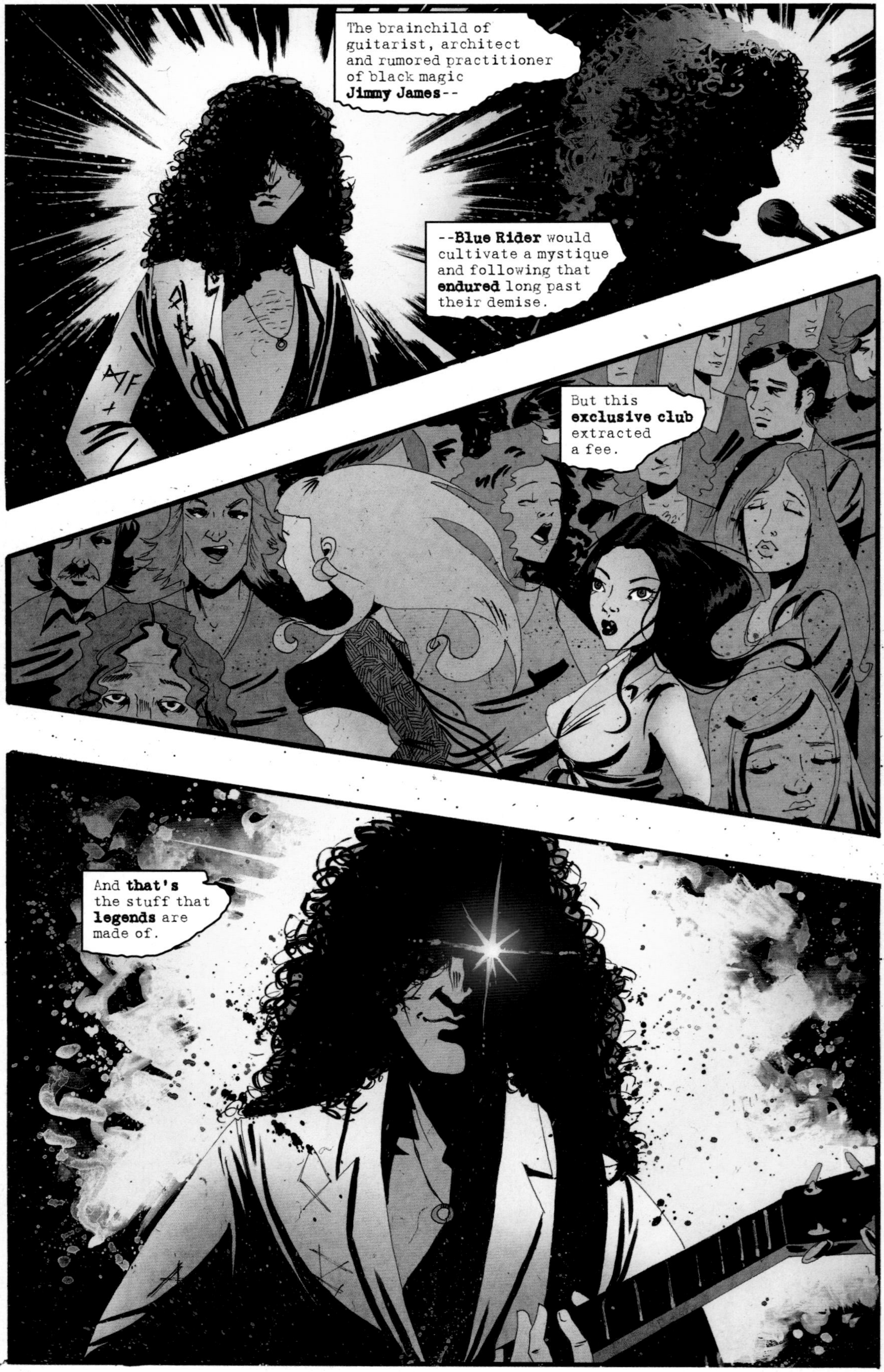
The brainchild of guitarist, architect and rumored practitioner of black magic **Jimmy James**--
--**Blue Rider** would cultivate a mystique and following that **endured** long past their demise.
But this **exclusive club** extracted a fee.
And **that's** the stuff that **legends** are made of.

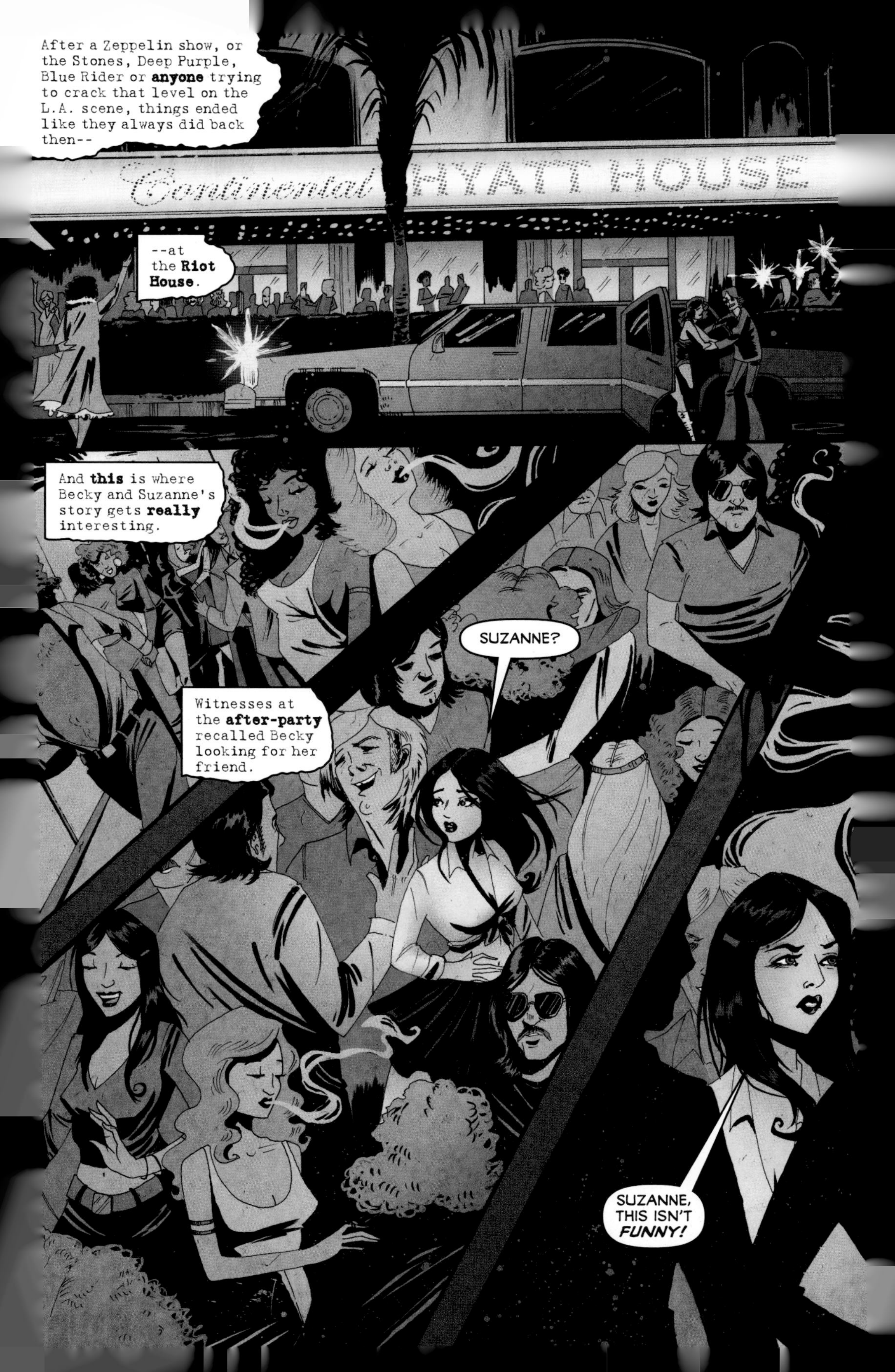
After a Zeppelin show, or the Stones, Deep Purple, Blue Rider or **anyone** trying to crack that level on the L.A. scene, things ended like they always did back then--
Continental HYATT HOUSE
--at the **Riot House**.
And **this** is where Becky and Suzanne's story gets **really** interesting.
SUZANNE?
Witnesses at the **after-party** recalled Becky looking for her friend.
SUZANNE, THIS ISN'T ***FUNNY!***

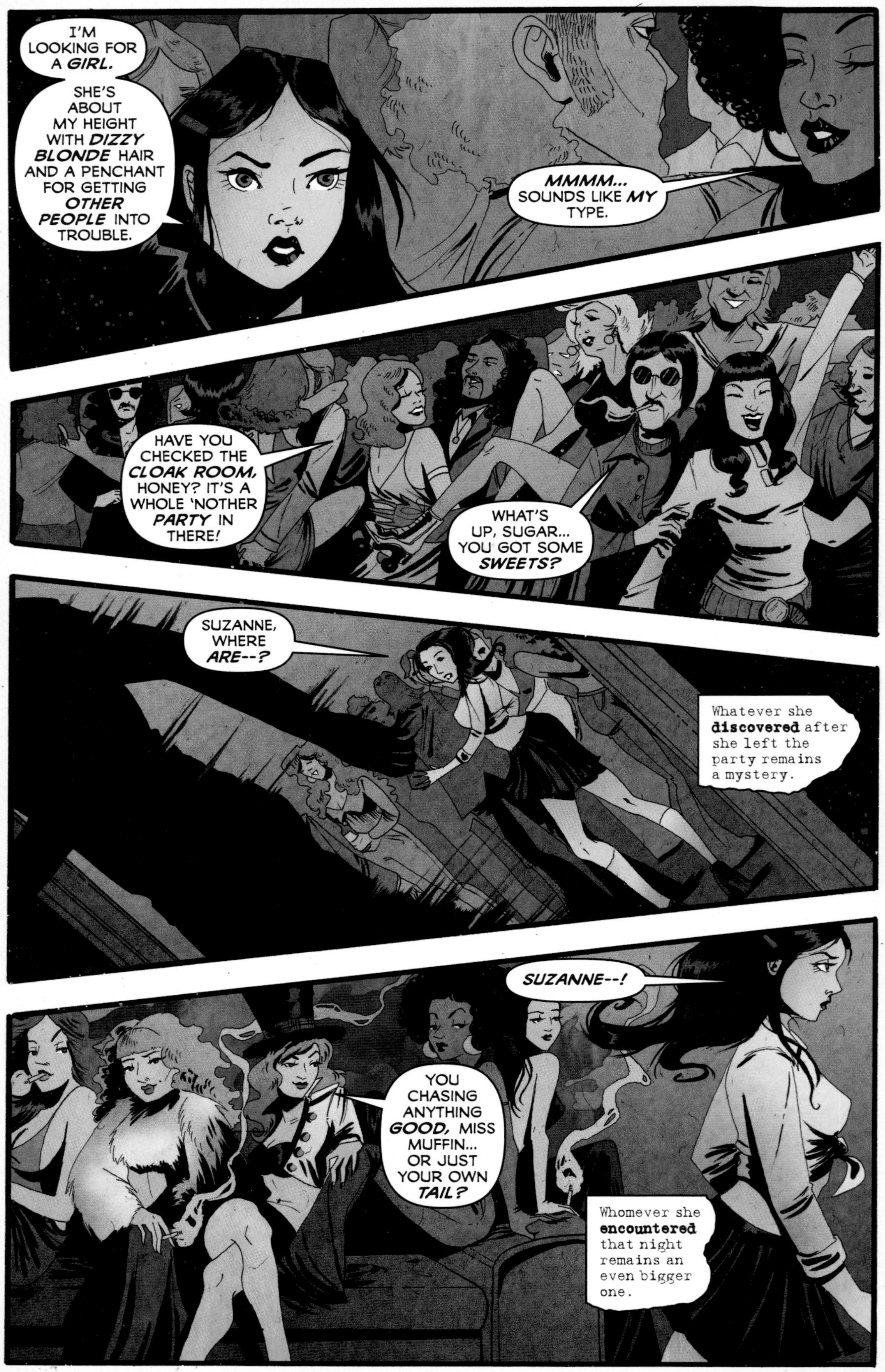
I'M LOOKING FOR A GIRL.
SHE'S ABOUT MY HEIGHT WITH DIZZY BLONDE HAIR AND A PENCHANT FOR GETTING OTHER PEOPLE INTO TROUBLE.
MMMM... SOUNDS LIKE MY TYPE.
HAVE YOU CHECKED THE CLOAK ROOM, HONEY? IT'S A WHOLE 'NOTHER PARTY IN THERE!
WHAT'S UP, SUGAR... YOU GOT SOME SWEETS?
SUZANNE, WHERE ARE--?
Whatever she discovered after she left the party remains a mystery.
SUZANNE--!
YOU CHASING ANYTHING GOOD, MISS MUFFIN... OR JUST YOUR OWN TAIL?
Whomever she encountered that night remains an even bigger one.

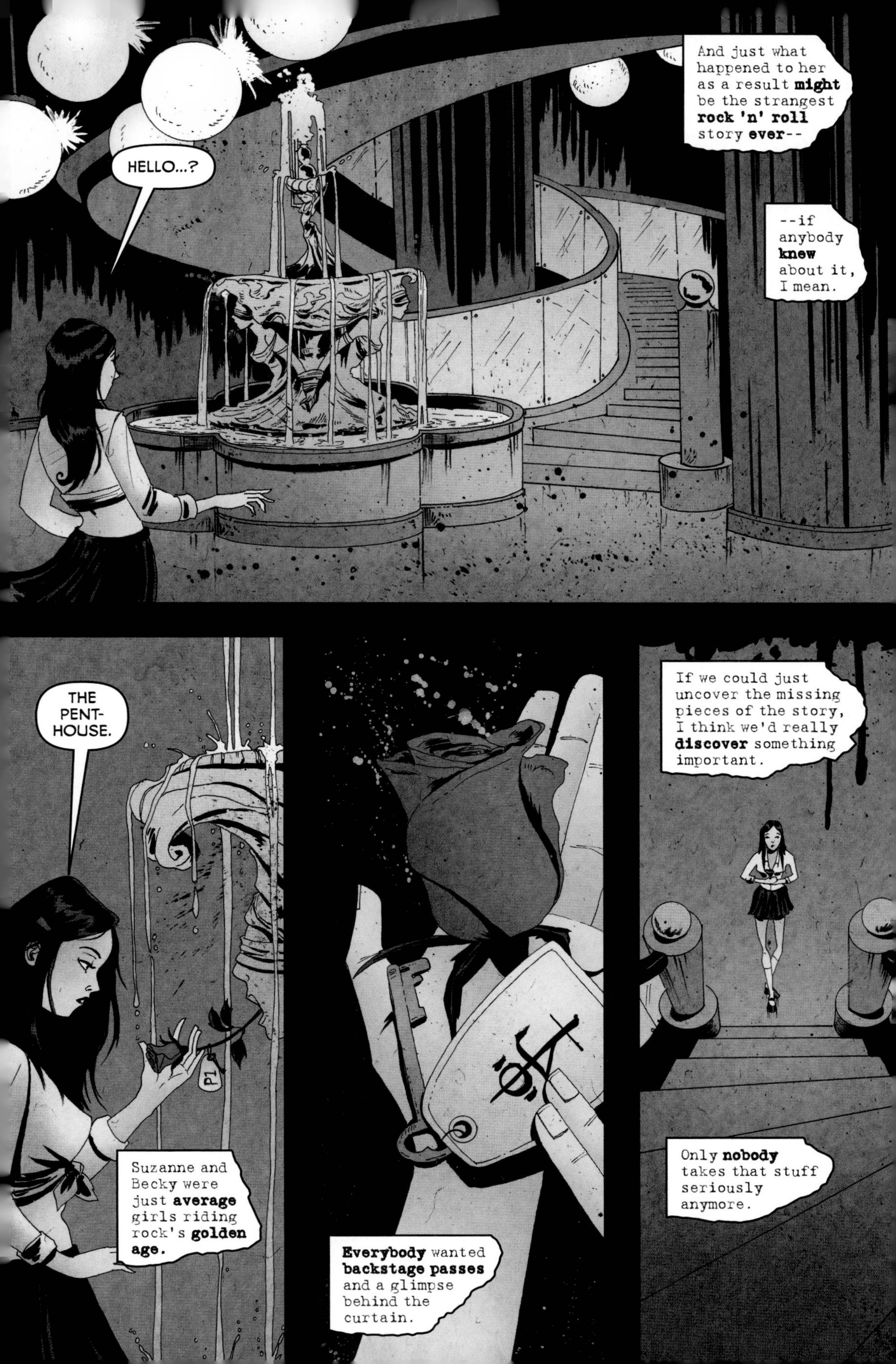
HELLO...?
And just what happened to her as a result **might** be the strangest **rock 'n' roll** story **ever**--
--if anybody **knew** about it, I mean.
THE PENT-HOUSE.
P1
Suzanne and Becky were just **average** girls riding rock's **golden age.**
Everybody wanted **backstage passes** and a glimpse behind the curtain.
If we could just uncover the missing pieces of the story, I think we'd really **discover** something important.
Only **nobody** takes that stuff seriously anymore.

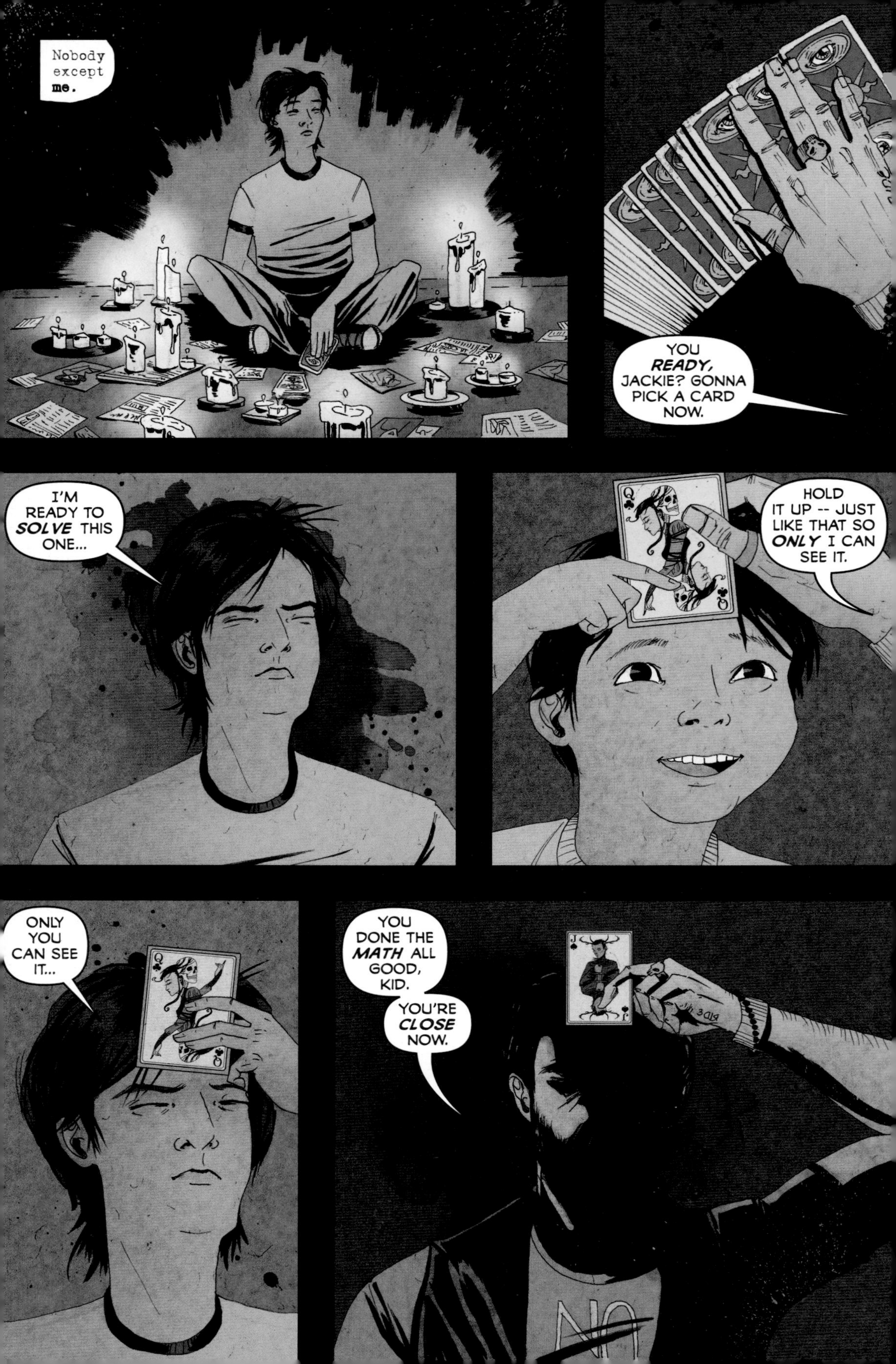
Nobody except me.
YOU READY, JACKIE? GONNA PICK A CARD NOW.
I'M READY TO SOLVE THIS ONE...
HOLD IT UP -- JUST LIKE THAT SO ONLY I CAN SEE IT.
ONLY YOU CAN SEE IT...
YOU DONE THE MATH ALL GOOD, KID.
YOU'RE CLOSE NOW.

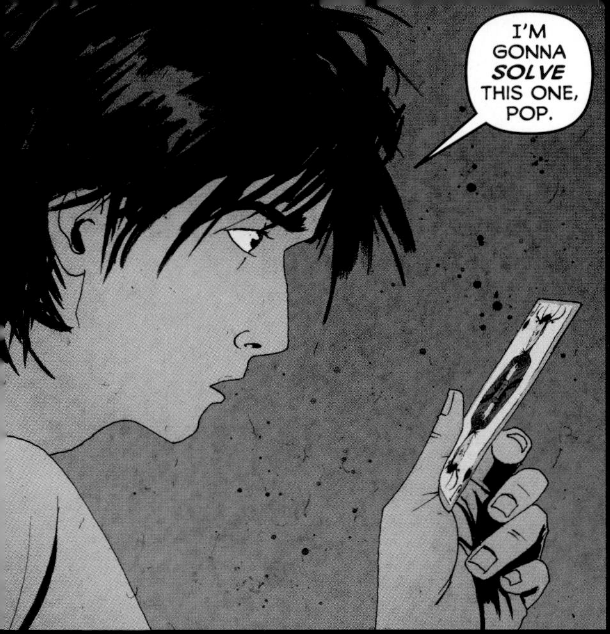
I'M GONNA *SOLVE* THIS ONE, POP.

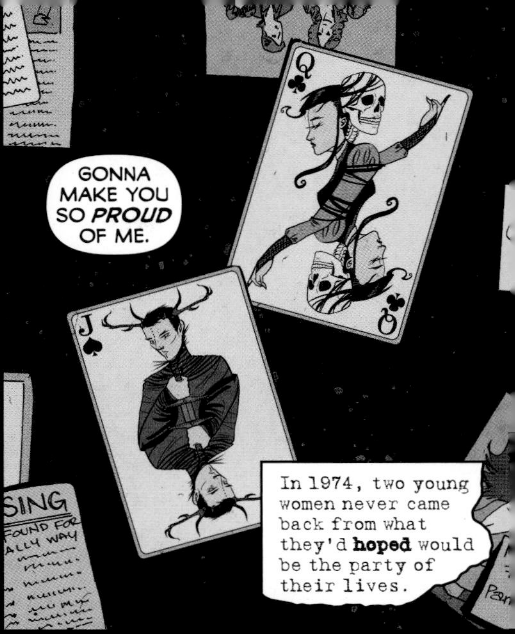
GONNA MAKE YOU SO *PROUD* OF ME.
In 1974, two young women never came back from what they'd **hoped** would be the party of their lives.

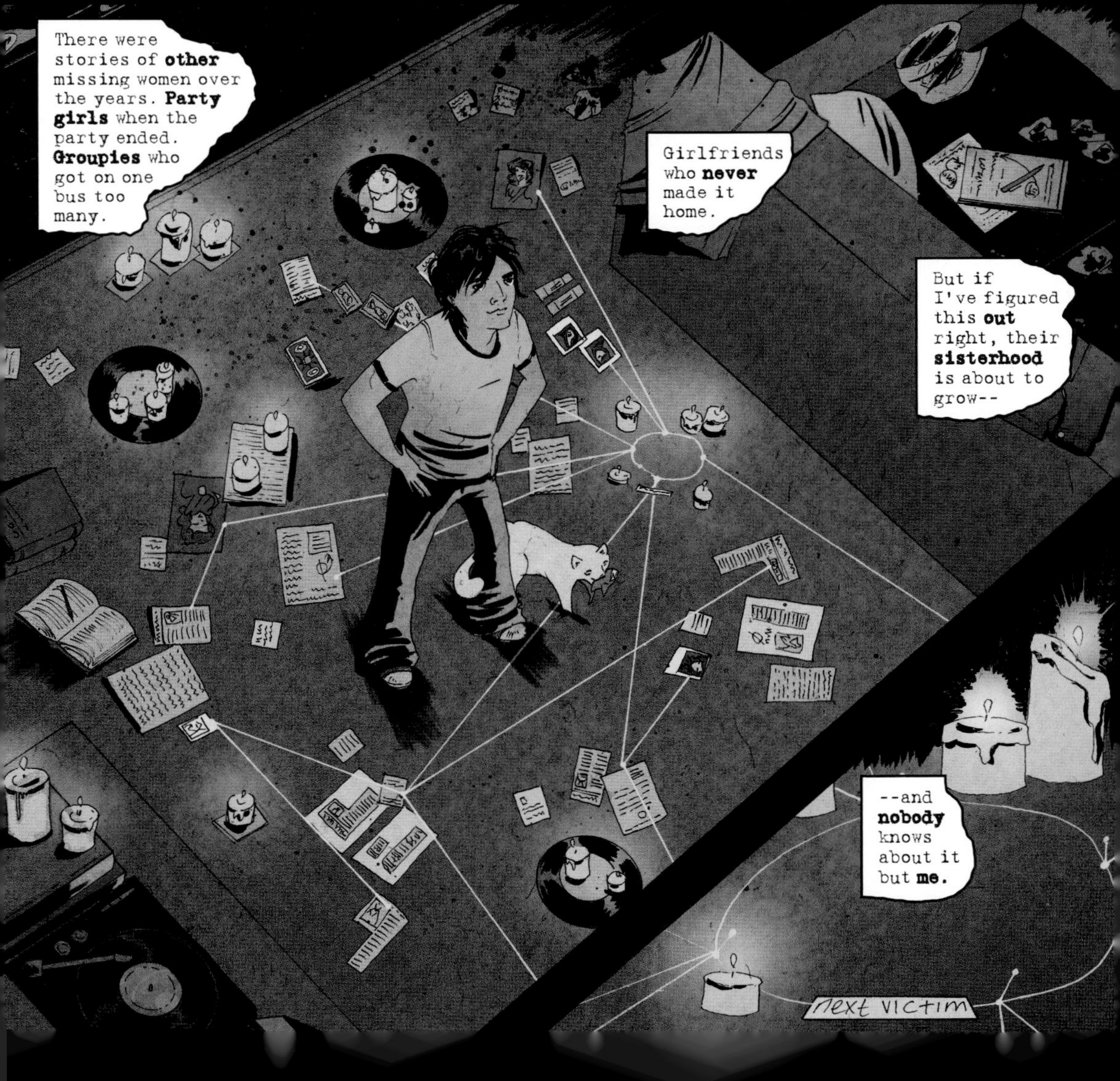
There were stories of **other** missing women over the years. **Party girls** when the party ended. **Groupies** who got on one bus too many.
Girlfriends who **never** made it home.
But if I've figured this **out** right, their **sisterhood** is about to grow--
--and **nobody** knows about it but **me.**
next victim

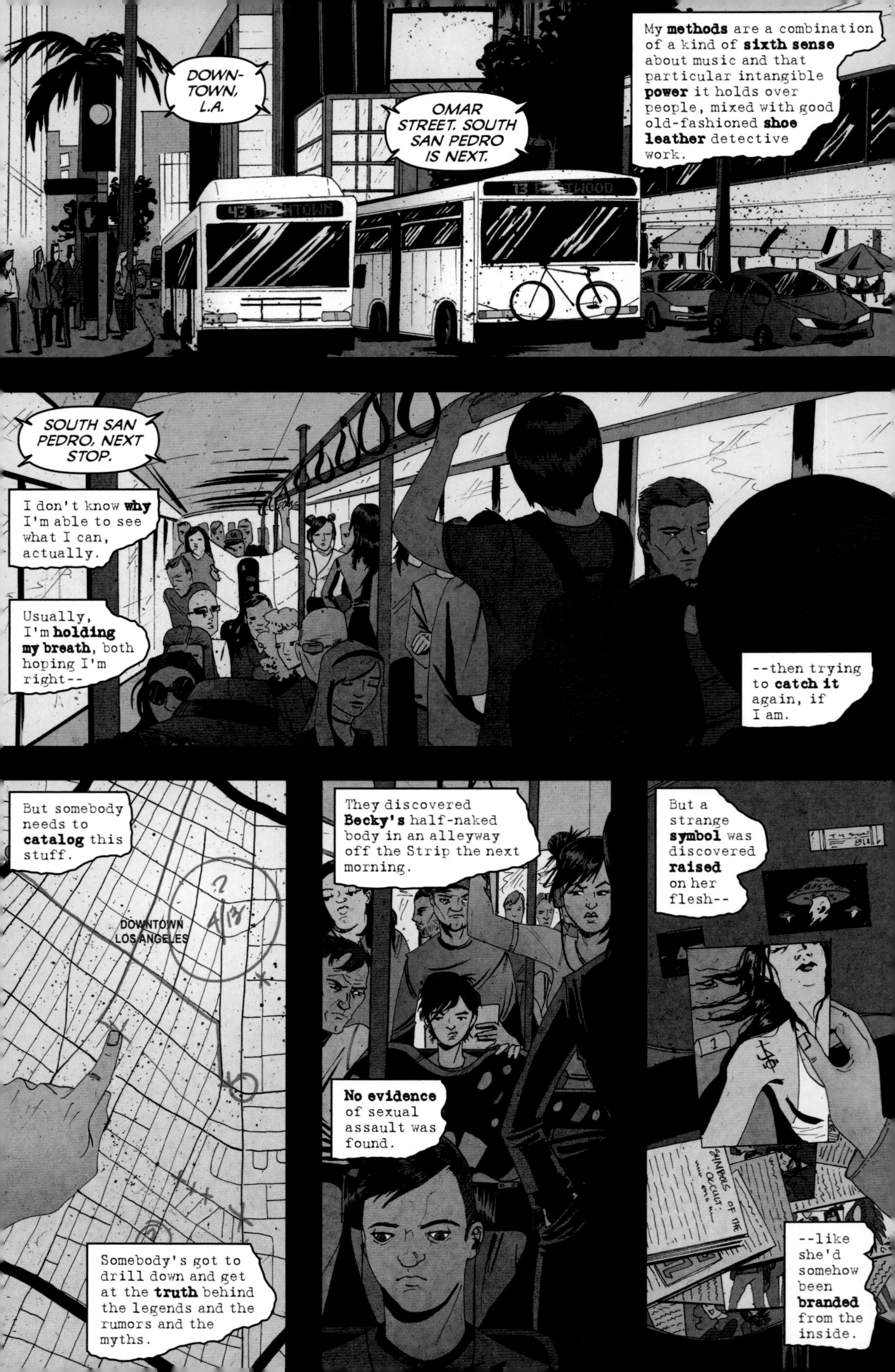
DOWN-TOWN, L.A.
OMAR STREET. SOUTH SAN PEDRO IS NEXT.
My methods are a combination of a kind of sixth sense about music and that particular intangible power it holds over people, mixed with good old-fashioned shoe leather detective work.
SOUTH SAN PEDRO, NEXT STOP.
I don't know why I'm able to see what I can, actually.
Usually, I'm holding my breath, both hoping I'm right--
--then trying to catch it again, if I am.
But somebody needs to catalog this stuff.
DOWNTOWN LOS ANGELES
Somebody's got to drill down and get at the truth behind the legends and the rumors and the myths.
They discovered Becky's half-naked body in an alleyway off the Strip the next morning.
No evidence of sexual assault was found.
But a strange symbol was discovered raised on her flesh--
--like she'd somehow been branded from the inside.

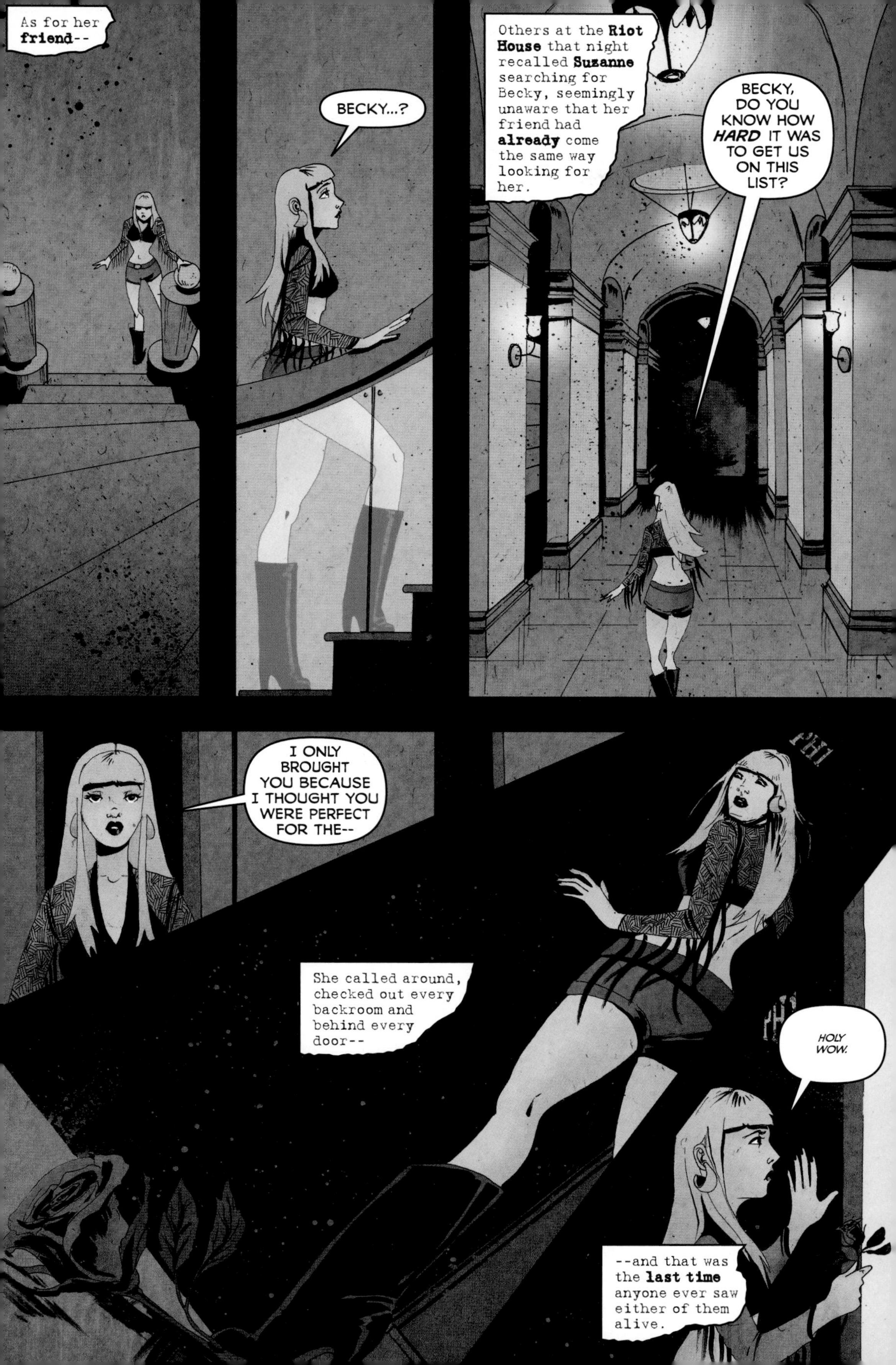
As for her **friend**--
BECKY...?
Others at the **Riot House** that night recalled **Suzanne** searching for Becky, seemingly unaware that her friend had **already** come the same way looking for her.
BECKY, DO YOU KNOW HOW *HARD* IT WAS TO GET US ON THIS LIST?
I ONLY BROUGHT YOU BECAUSE I THOUGHT YOU WERE PERFECT FOR THE--
She called around, checked out every backroom and behind every door--
HOLY WOW.
--and that was the **last time** anyone ever saw either of them alive.

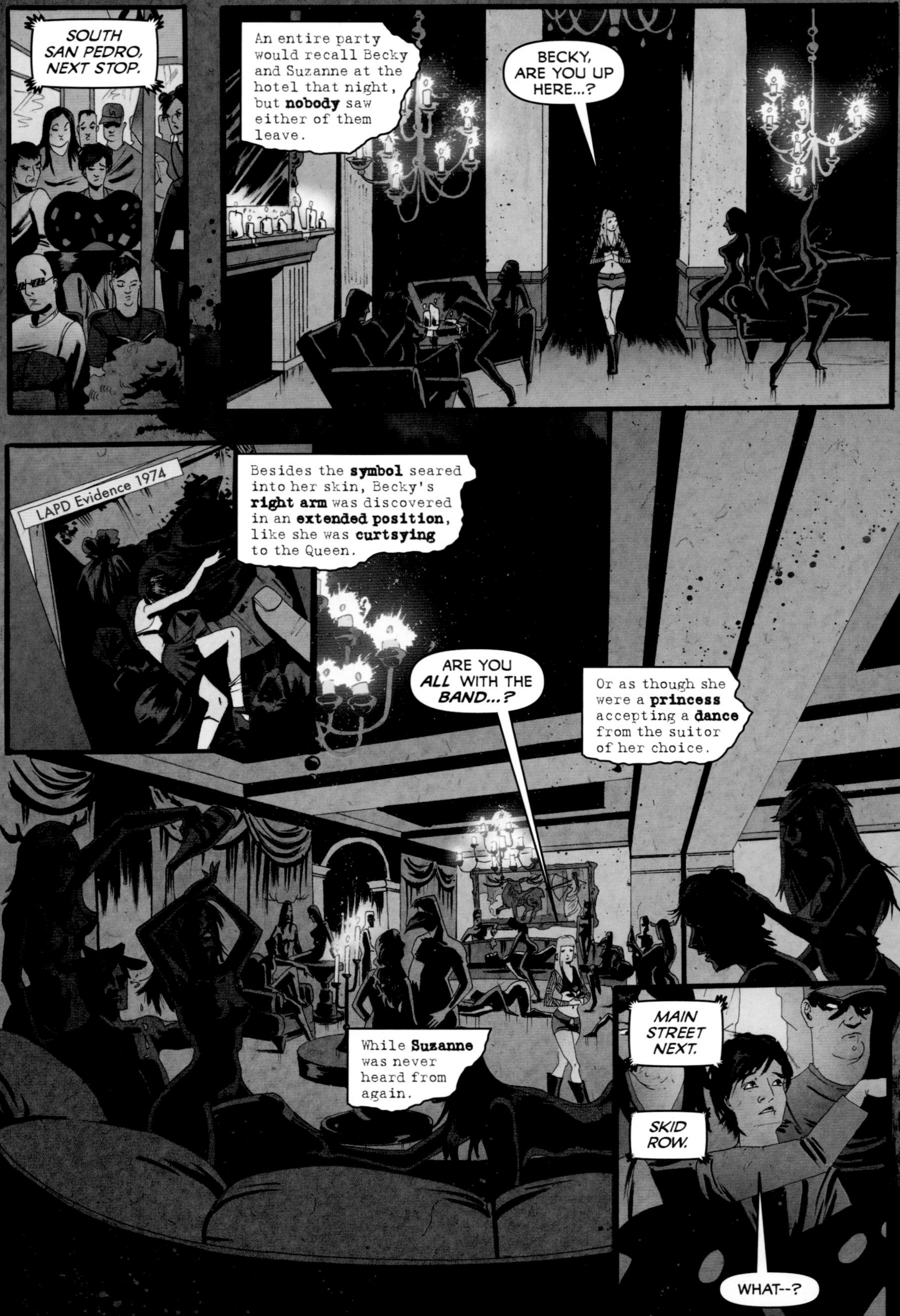
SOUTH SAN PEDRO, NEXT STOP.
An entire party would recall Becky and Suzanne at the hotel that night, but **nobody** saw either of them leave.
BECKY, ARE YOU UP HERE...?
LAPD Evidence 1974
Besides the **symbol** seared into her skin, Becky's **right arm** was discovered in an **extended position**, like she was **curtsying** to the Queen.
ARE YOU *ALL* WITH THE *BAND...?*
Or as though she were a **princess** accepting a **dance** from the suitor of her choice.
While **Suzanne** was never heard from again.
MAIN STREET NEXT.
SKID ROW.
WHAT--?

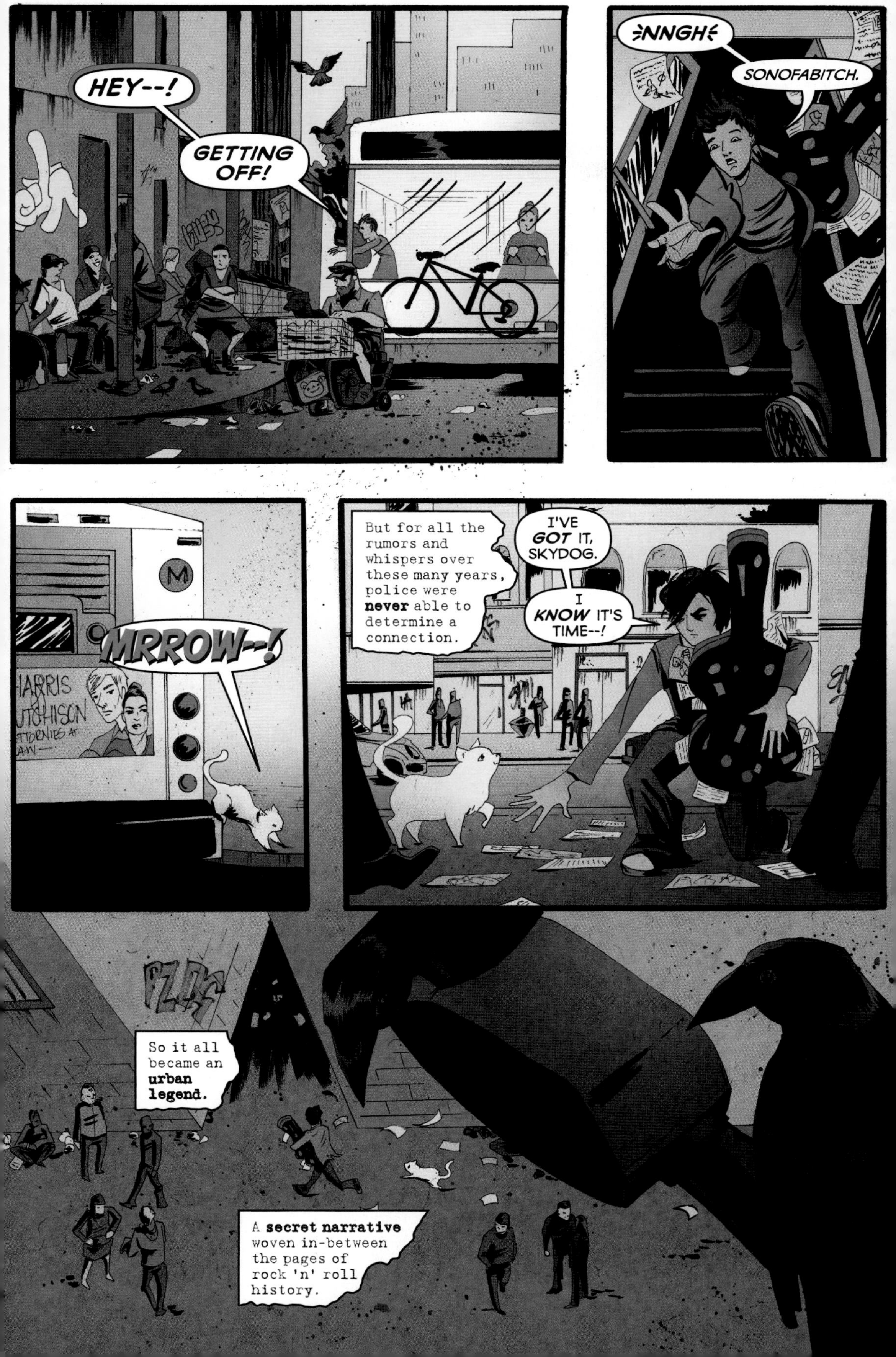
HEY--!
GETTING OFF!
NNGH
SONOFABITCH.
MRROW--!
But for all the rumors and whispers over these many years, police were **never** able to determine a connection.
I'VE *GOT* IT, SKYDOG.
I *KNOW* IT'S TIME--!
So it all became an **urban legend**.
A **secret narrative** woven in-between the pages of rock 'n' roll history.

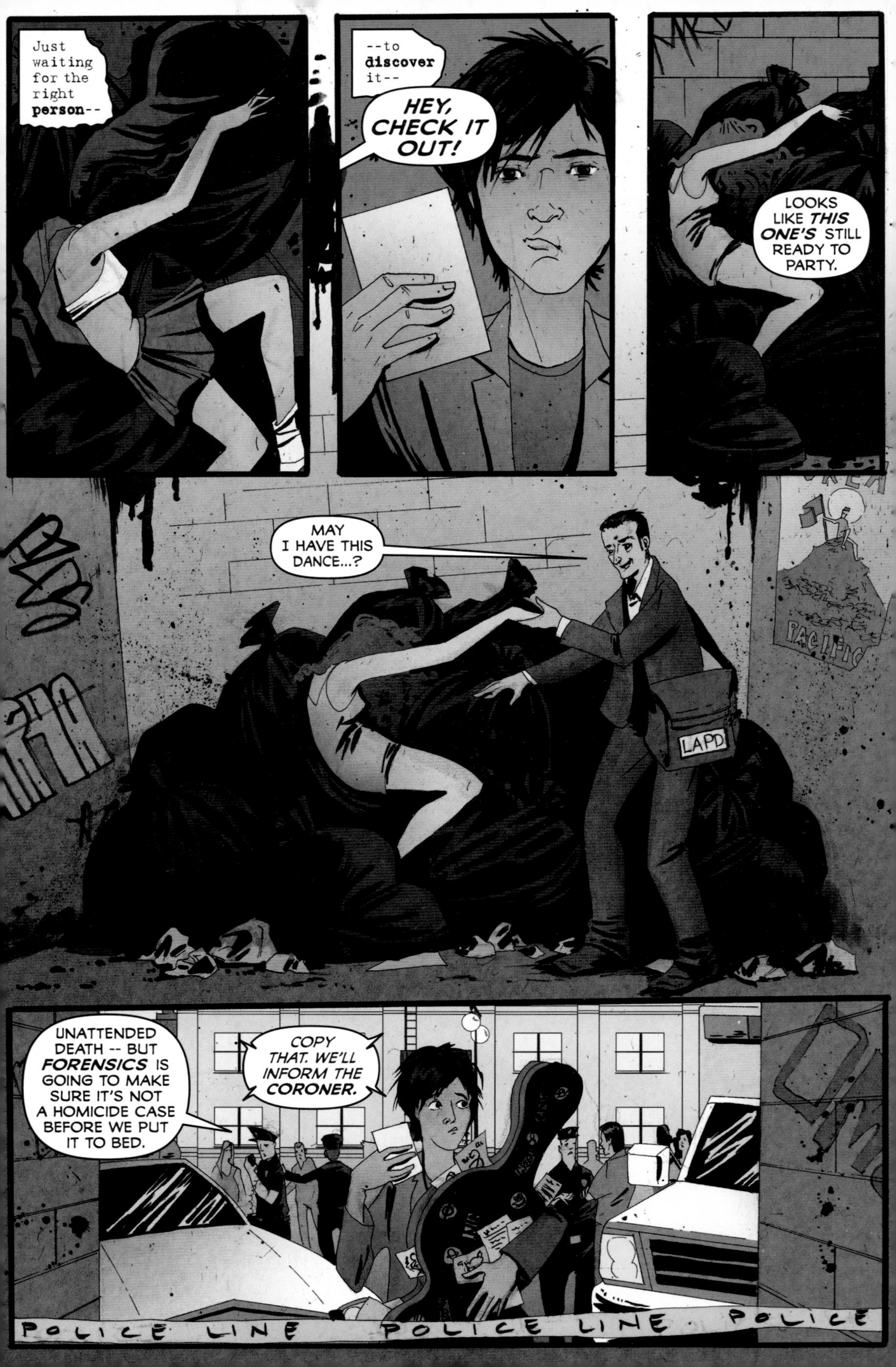
Just waiting for the right person--
--to discover it--
HEY, CHECK IT OUT!
LOOKS LIKE THIS ONE'S STILL READY TO PARTY.
MAY I HAVE THIS DANCE...?
LAPD
PACIFIC
UNATTENDED DEATH -- BUT FORENSICS IS GOING TO MAKE SURE IT'S NOT A HOMICIDE CASE BEFORE WE PUT IT TO BED.
COPY THAT. WE'LL INFORM THE CORONER.
POLICE LINE POLICE LINE POLICE

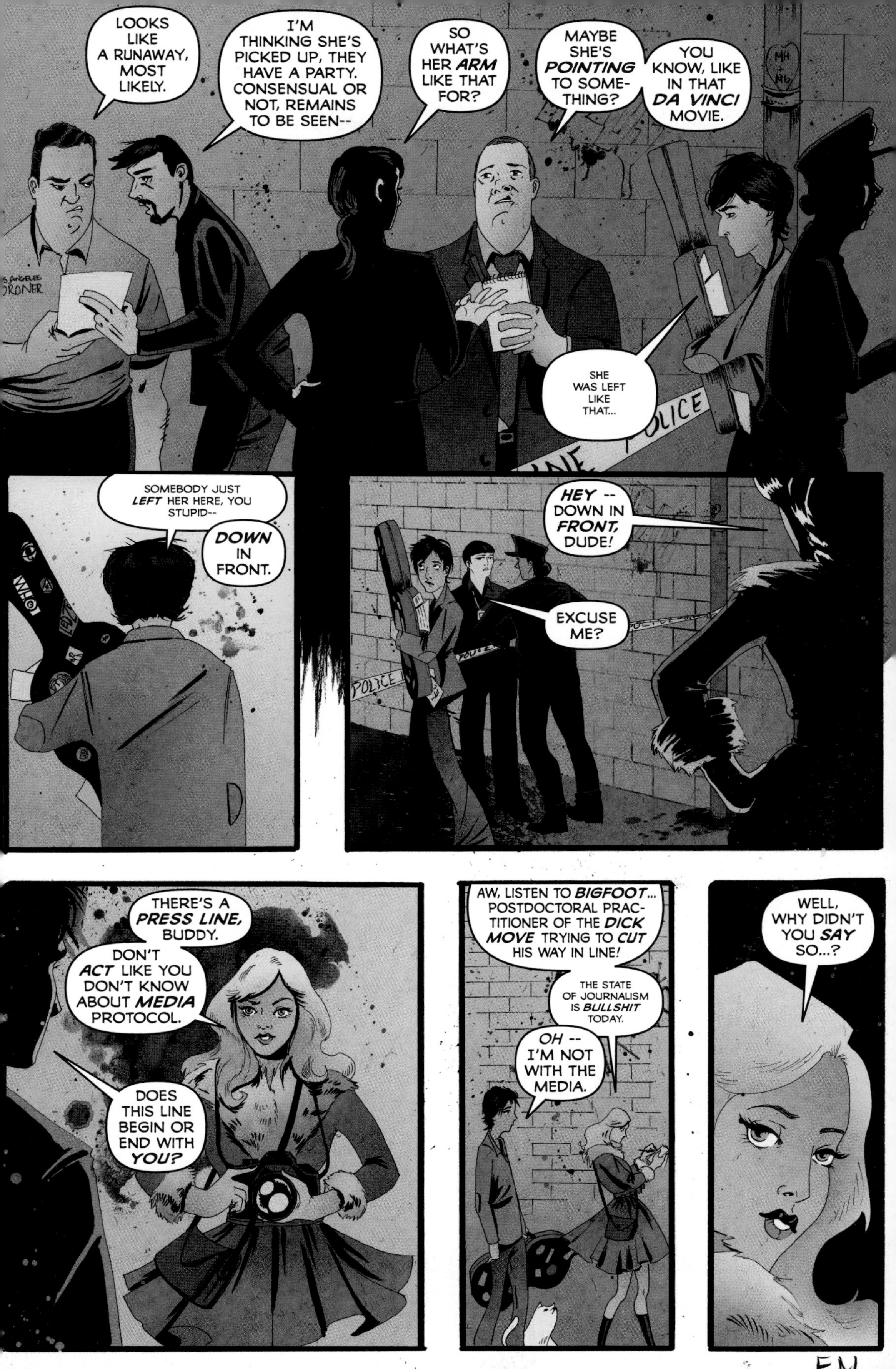
LOOKS LIKE A RUNAWAY, MOST LIKELY.
I'M THINKING SHE'S PICKED UP, THEY HAVE A PARTY. CONSENSUAL OR NOT, REMAINS TO BE SEEN--
SO WHAT'S HER ARM LIKE THAT FOR?
MAYBE SHE'S POINTING TO SOME-THING?
YOU KNOW, LIKE IN THAT DA VINCI MOVIE.
SHE WAS LEFT LIKE THAT...
SOMEBODY JUST LEFT HER HERE, YOU STUPID--
DOWN IN FRONT.
HEY -- DOWN IN FRONT, DUDE!
EXCUSE ME?
THERE'S A PRESS LINE, BUDDY.
DON'T ACT LIKE YOU DON'T KNOW ABOUT MEDIA PROTOCOL.
DOES THIS LINE BEGIN OR END WITH YOU?
AW, LISTEN TO BIGFOOT... POSTDOCTORAL PRAC-TITIONER OF THE DICK MOVE TRYING TO CUT HIS WAY IN LINE!
THE STATE OF JOURNALISM IS BULLSHIT TODAY.
OH -- I'M NOT WITH THE MEDIA.
WELL, WHY DIDN'T YOU SAY SO...?

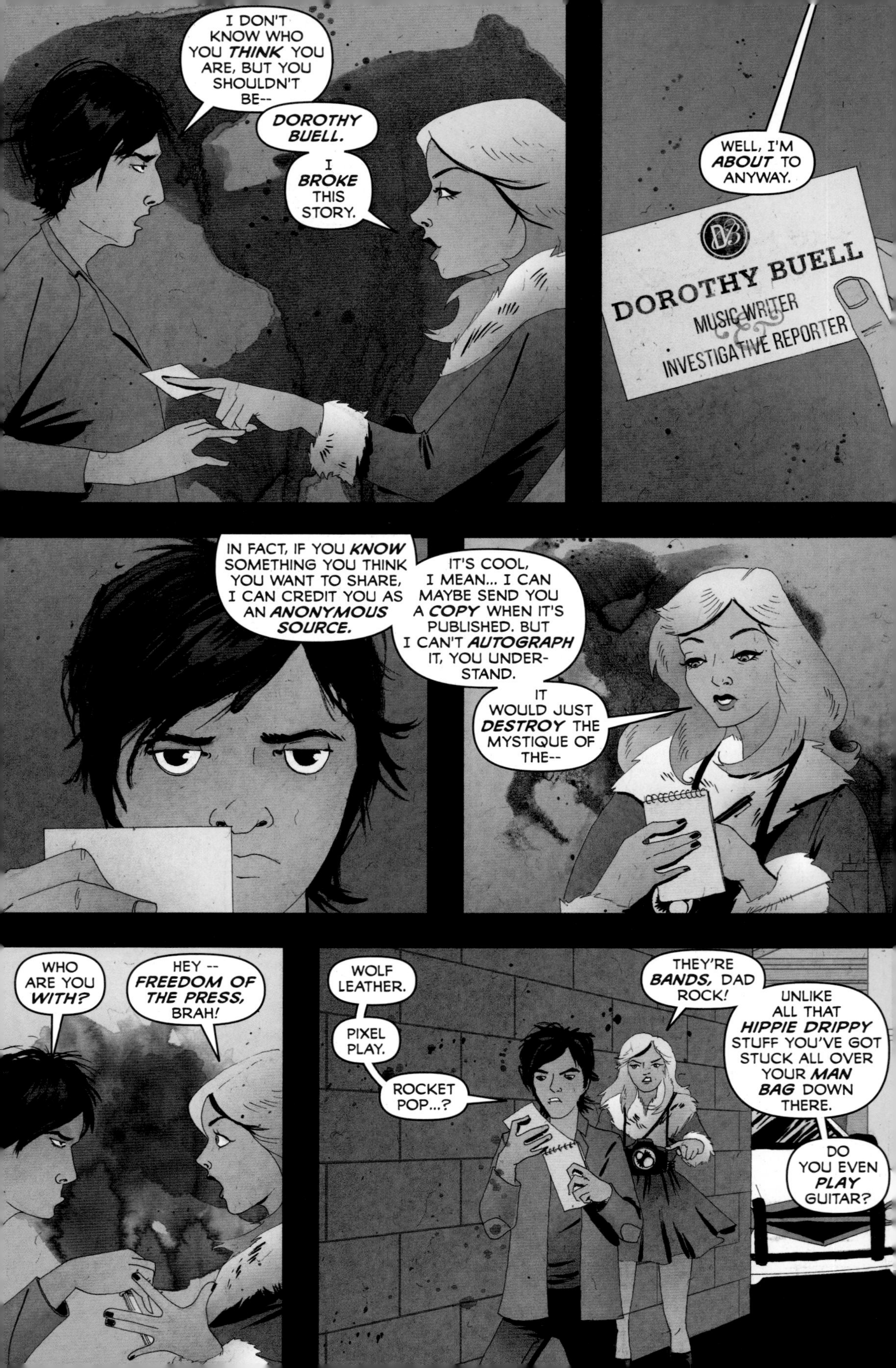
I DON'T KNOW WHO YOU *THINK* YOU ARE, BUT YOU SHOULDN'T BE--
DOROTHY BUELL.
I *BROKE* THIS STORY.
WELL, I'M *ABOUT* TO ANYWAY.
DB
DOROTHY BUELL
MUSIC WRITER & INVESTIGATIVE REPORTER
IN FACT, IF YOU *KNOW* SOMETHING YOU THINK YOU WANT TO SHARE, I CAN CREDIT YOU AS AN *ANONYMOUS SOURCE.*
IT'S COOL, I MEAN... I CAN MAYBE SEND YOU A *COPY* WHEN IT'S PUBLISHED. BUT I CAN'T *AUTOGRAPH* IT, YOU UNDER-STAND.
IT WOULD JUST *DESTROY* THE MYSTIQUE OF THE--
WHO ARE YOU *WITH?*
HEY -- *FREEDOM OF THE PRESS,* BRAH!
WOLF LEATHER.
PIXEL PLAY.
ROCKET POP...?
THEY'RE *BANDS,* DAD ROCK!
UNLIKE ALL THAT *HIPPIE DRIPPY* STUFF YOU'VE GOT STUCK ALL OVER YOUR *MAN BAG* DOWN THERE.
DO YOU EVEN *PLAY* GUITAR?

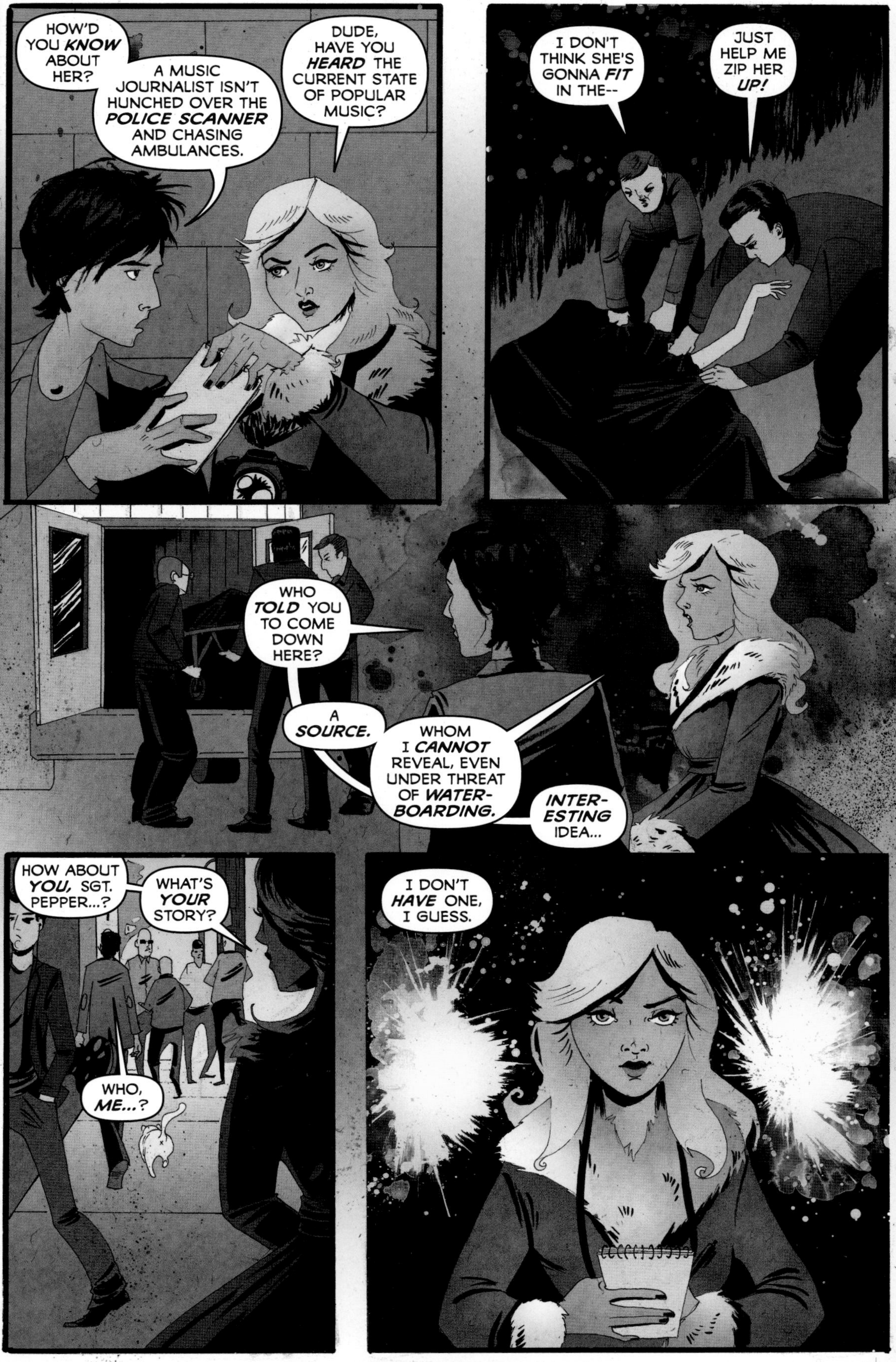
HOW'D YOU KNOW ABOUT HER?
A MUSIC JOURNALIST ISN'T HUNCHED OVER THE POLICE SCANNER AND CHASING AMBULANCES.
DUDE, HAVE YOU HEARD THE CURRENT STATE OF POPULAR MUSIC?
I DON'T THINK SHE'S GONNA FIT IN THE--
JUST HELP ME ZIP HER UP!
WHO TOLD YOU TO COME DOWN HERE?
A SOURCE.
WHOM I CANNOT REVEAL, EVEN UNDER THREAT OF WATER-BOARDING.
INTER-ESTING IDEA...
HOW ABOUT YOU, SGT. PEPPER...?
WHAT'S YOUR STORY?
WHO, ME...?
I DON'T HAVE ONE, I GUESS.

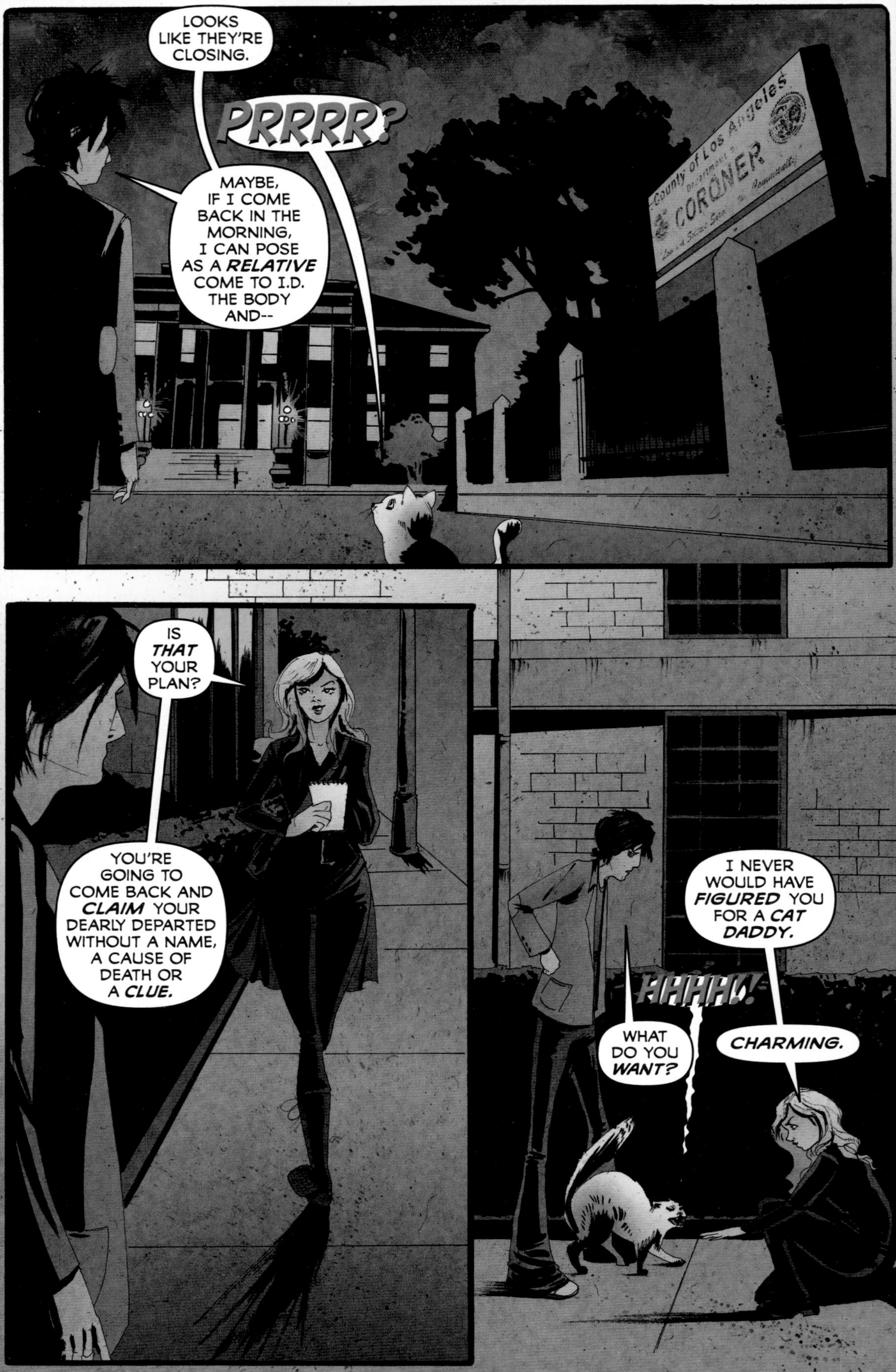
LOOKS LIKE THEY'RE CLOSING.
PRRRR?
MAYBE, IF I COME BACK IN THE MORNING, I CAN POSE AS A *RELATIVE* COME TO I.D. THE BODY AND--
County of Los Angeles
CORONER
IS *THAT* YOUR PLAN?
YOU'RE GOING TO COME BACK AND *CLAIM* YOUR DEARLY DEPARTED WITHOUT A NAME, A CAUSE OF DEATH OR A *CLUE.*
I NEVER WOULD HAVE *FIGURED* YOU FOR A *CAT DADDY.*
HHHH!
WHAT DO YOU *WANT?*
CHARMING.

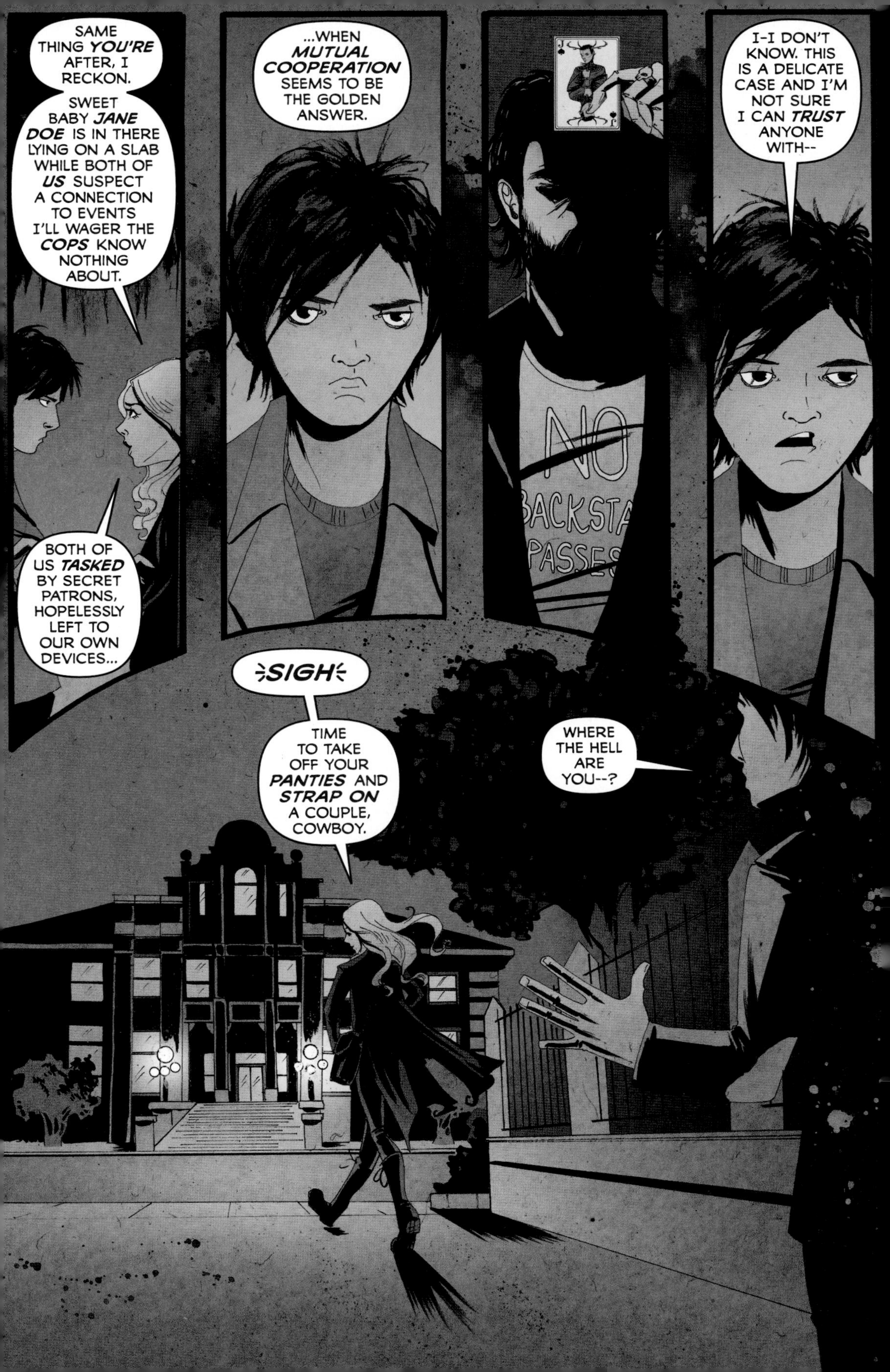
SAME THING YOU'RE AFTER, I RECKON.
SWEET BABY JANE DOE IS IN THERE LYING ON A SLAB WHILE BOTH OF US SUSPECT A CONNECTION TO EVENTS I'LL WAGER THE COPS KNOW NOTHING ABOUT.
BOTH OF US TASKED BY SECRET PATRONS, HOPELESSLY LEFT TO OUR OWN DEVICES...
...WHEN MUTUAL COOPERATION SEEMS TO BE THE GOLDEN ANSWER.
NO BACKSTA PASSES
I-I DON'T KNOW. THIS IS A DELICATE CASE AND I'M NOT SURE I CAN TRUST ANYONE WITH--
SIGH
TIME TO TAKE OFF YOUR PANTIES AND STRAP ON A COUPLE, COWBOY.
WHERE THE HELL ARE YOU--?

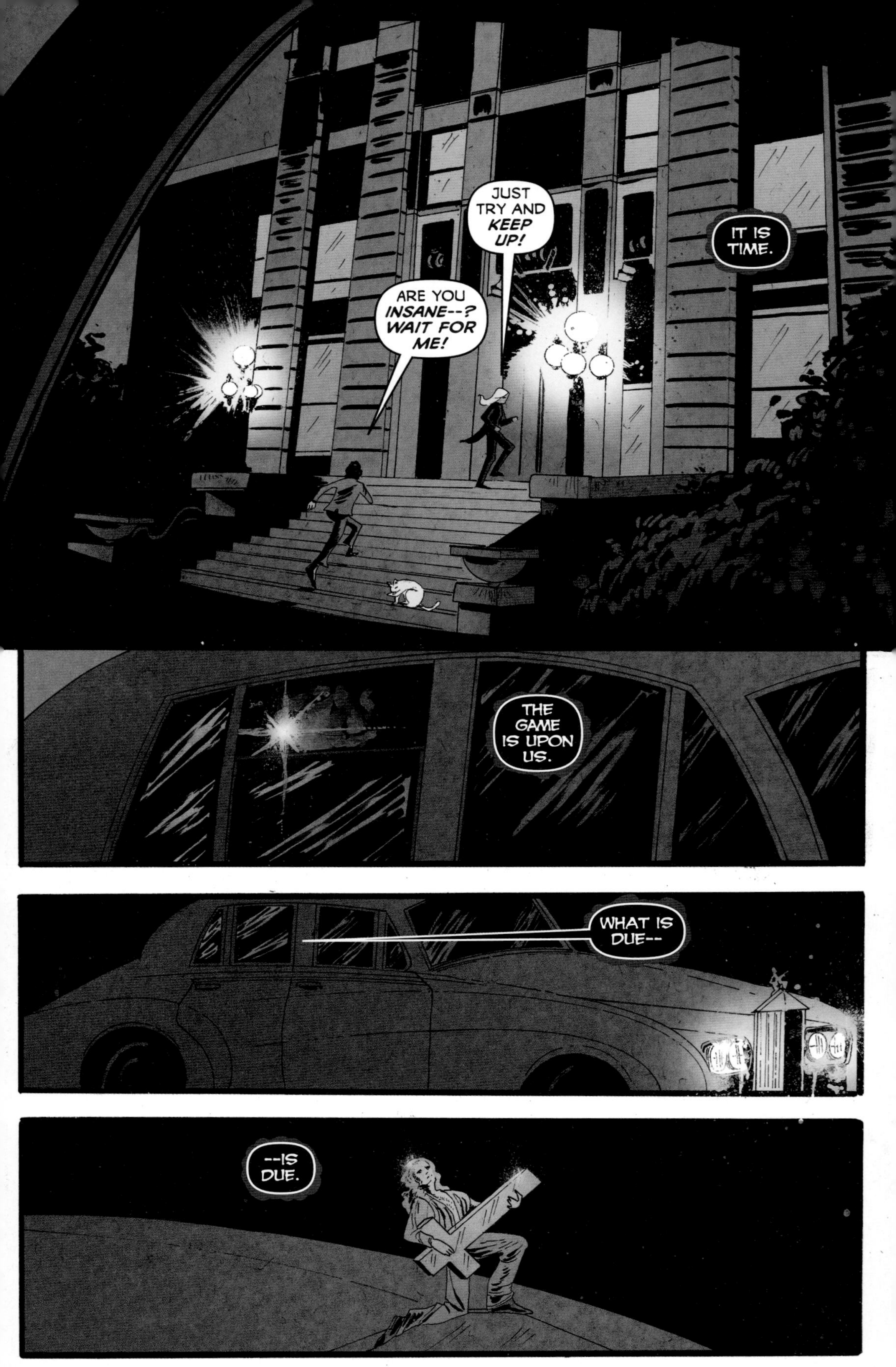
IT IS TIME.
JUST TRY AND KEEP UP!
ARE YOU INSANE--? WAIT FOR ME!
THE GAME IS UPON US.
WHAT IS DUE--
--IS DUE.

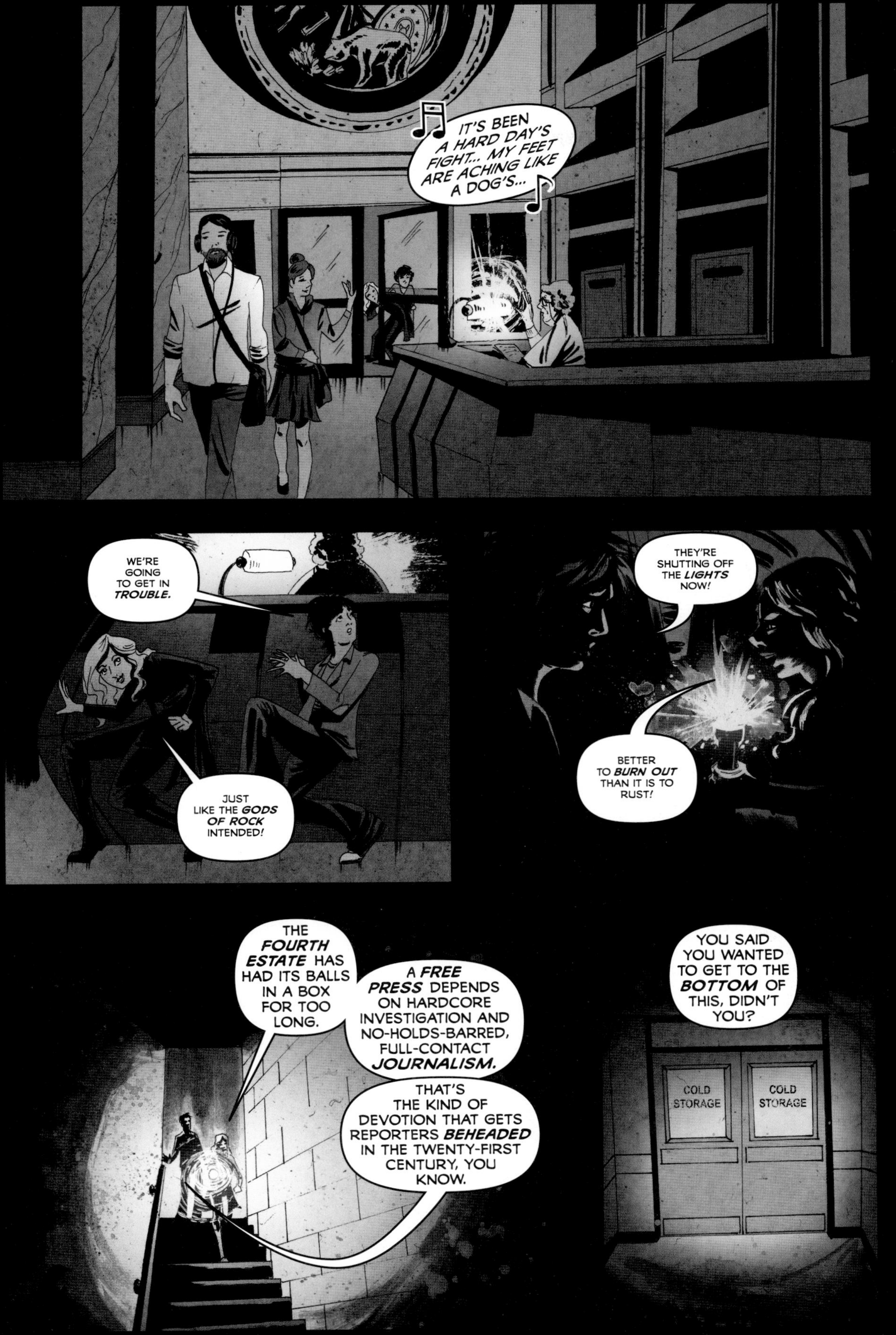
IT'S BEEN A HARD DAY'S FIGHT... MY FEET ARE ACHING LIKE A DOG'S...
WE'RE GOING TO GET IN TROUBLE.
JUST LIKE THE GODS OF ROCK INTENDED!
THEY'RE SHUTTING OFF THE LIGHTS NOW!
BETTER TO BURN OUT THAN IT IS TO RUST!
THE FOURTH ESTATE HAS HAD ITS BALLS IN A BOX FOR TOO LONG.
A FREE PRESS DEPENDS ON HARDCORE INVESTIGATION AND NO-HOLDS-BARRED, FULL-CONTACT JOURNALISM.
THAT'S THE KIND OF DEVOTION THAT GETS REPORTERS BEHEADED IN THE TWENTY-FIRST CENTURY, YOU KNOW.
YOU SAID YOU WANTED TO GET TO THE BOTTOM OF THIS, DIDN'T YOU?
COLD STORAGE
COLD STORAGE

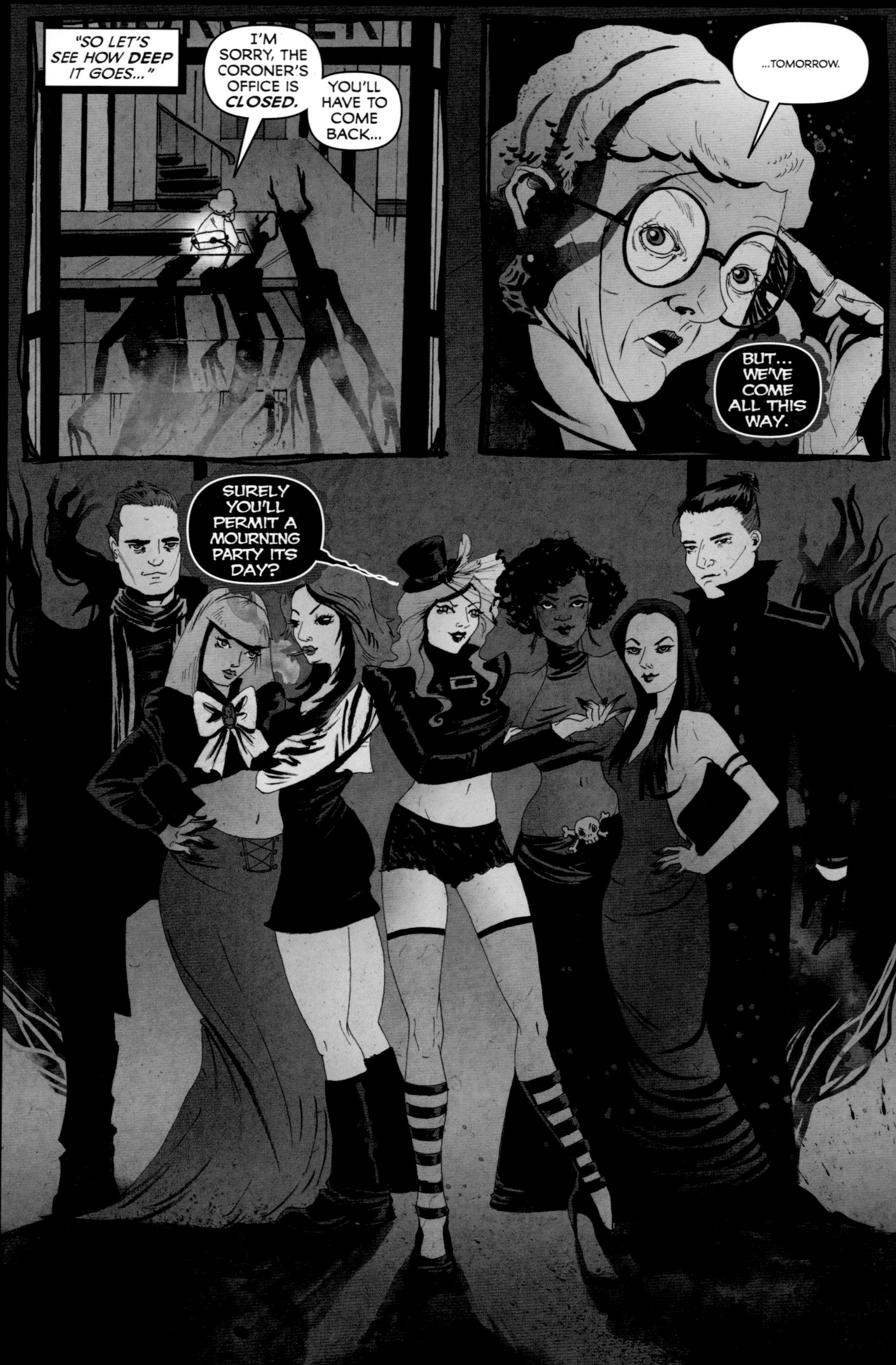
"SO LET'S SEE HOW DEEP IT GOES..."
I'M SORRY, THE CORONER'S OFFICE IS CLOSED.
YOU'LL HAVE TO COME BACK...
...TOMORROW.
BUT... WE'VE COME ALL THIS WAY.
SURELY YOU'LL PERMIT A MOURNING PARTY ITS DAY?

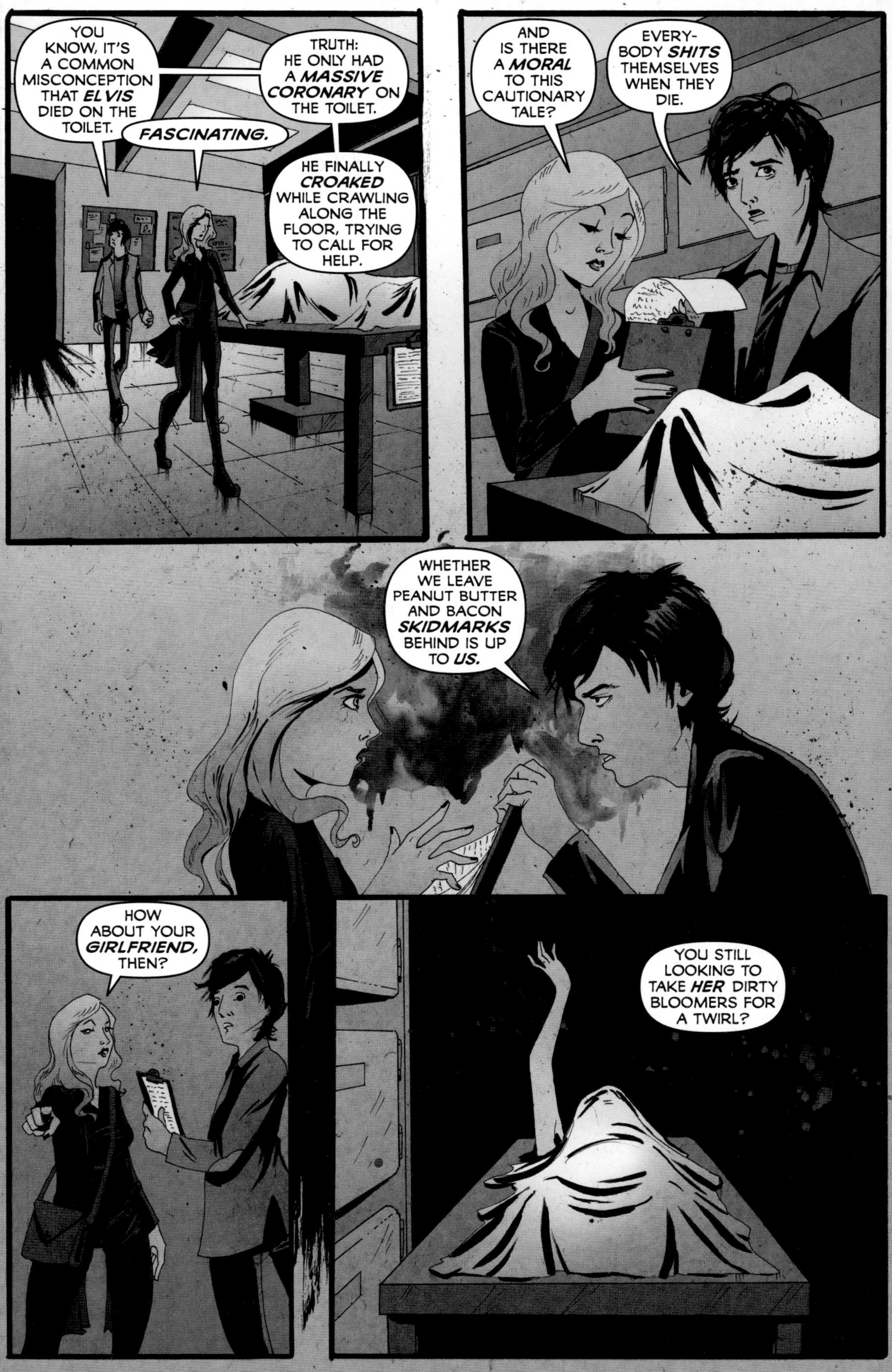
YOU KNOW, IT'S A COMMON MISCONCEPTION THAT ELVIS DIED ON THE TOILET.
FASCINATING.
TRUTH: HE ONLY HAD A MASSIVE CORONARY ON THE TOILET.
HE FINALLY CROAKED WHILE CRAWLING ALONG THE FLOOR, TRYING TO CALL FOR HELP.
AND IS THERE A MORAL TO THIS CAUTIONARY TALE?
EVERY-BODY SHITS THEMSELVES WHEN THEY DIE.
WHETHER WE LEAVE PEANUT BUTTER AND BACON SKIDMARKS BEHIND IS UP TO US.
HOW ABOUT YOUR GIRLFRIEND, THEN?
YOU STILL LOOKING TO TAKE HER DIRTY BLOOMERS FOR A TWIRL?

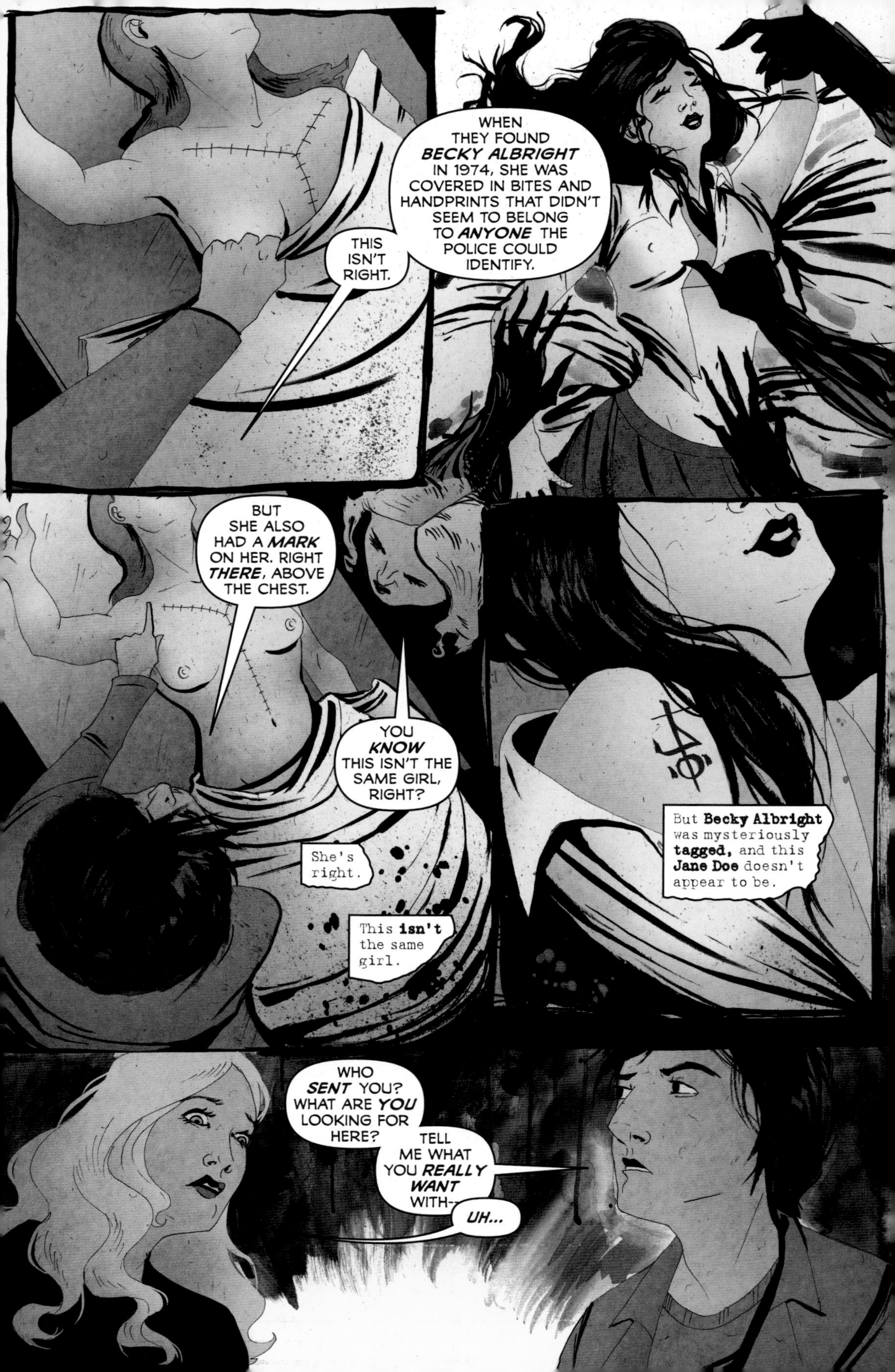
WHEN THEY FOUND BECKY ALBRIGHT IN 1974, SHE WAS COVERED IN BITES AND HANDPRINTS THAT DIDN'T SEEM TO BELONG TO ANYONE THE POLICE COULD IDENTIFY.
THIS ISN'T RIGHT.
BUT SHE ALSO HAD A MARK ON HER. RIGHT THERE, ABOVE THE CHEST.
YOU KNOW THIS ISN'T THE SAME GIRL, RIGHT?
She's right.
This isn't the same girl.
But Becky Albright was mysteriously tagged, and this Jane Doe doesn't appear to be.
WHO SENT YOU? WHAT ARE YOU LOOKING FOR HERE?
TELL ME WHAT YOU REALLY WANT WITH--
UH...

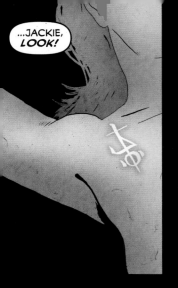

...JACKIE, LOOK!

HOLY BALLS!

DON'T BE A GROPER, DUDE!

YOU DON'T UNDERSTAND -- THAT'S THE MARK!

THE SAME ONE THEY FOUND ON--

JACKIE -- SHHH!

CREEEEEAK

WE HAVE COME.

THE TIME IS NOW.

WHAT IS DONE IS DONE.

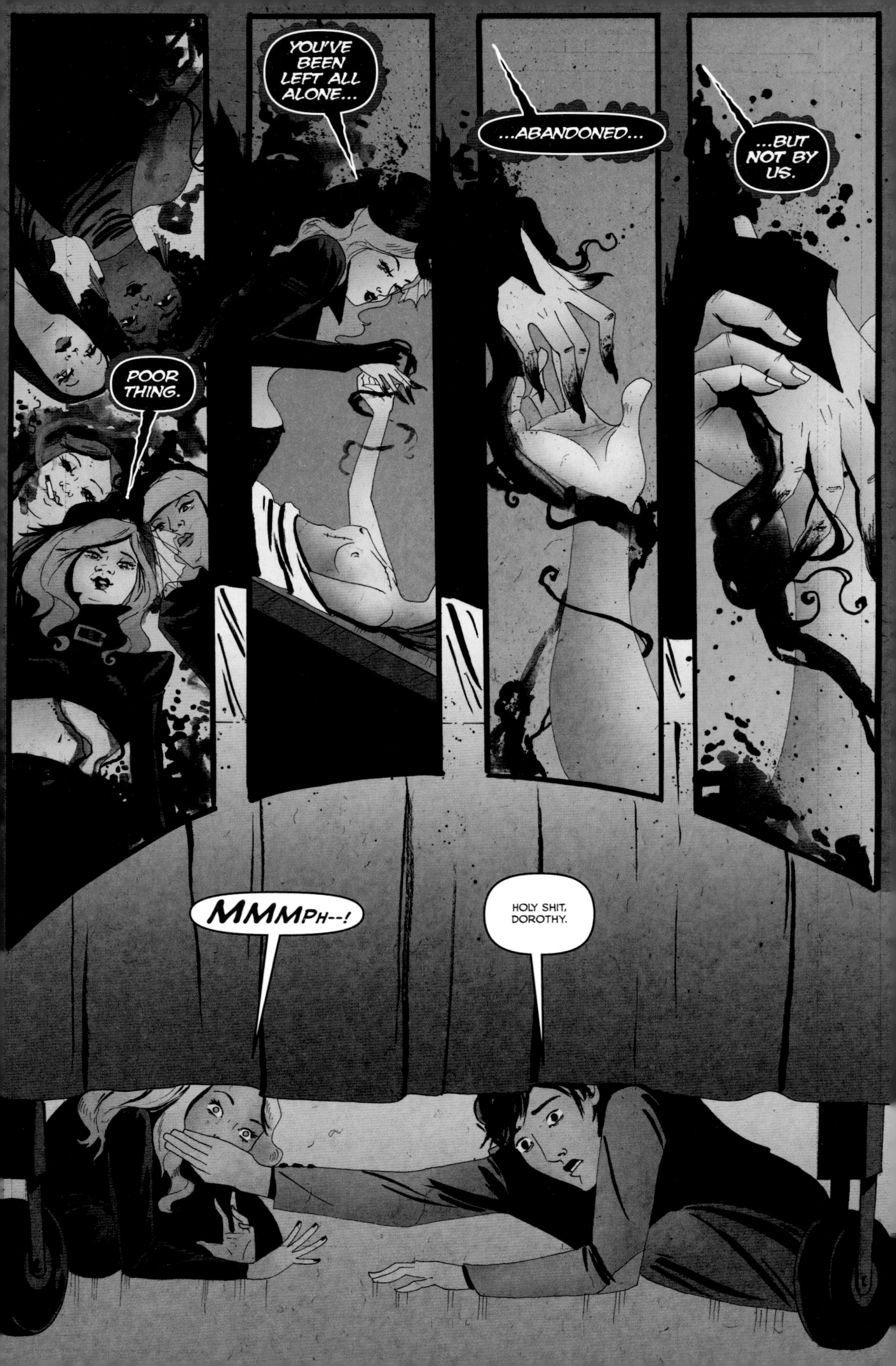
YOU'VE BEEN LEFT ALL ALONE...
POOR THING.
...ABANDONED...
...BUT NOT BY US.
MMMPH--!
HOLY SHIT, DOROTHY.

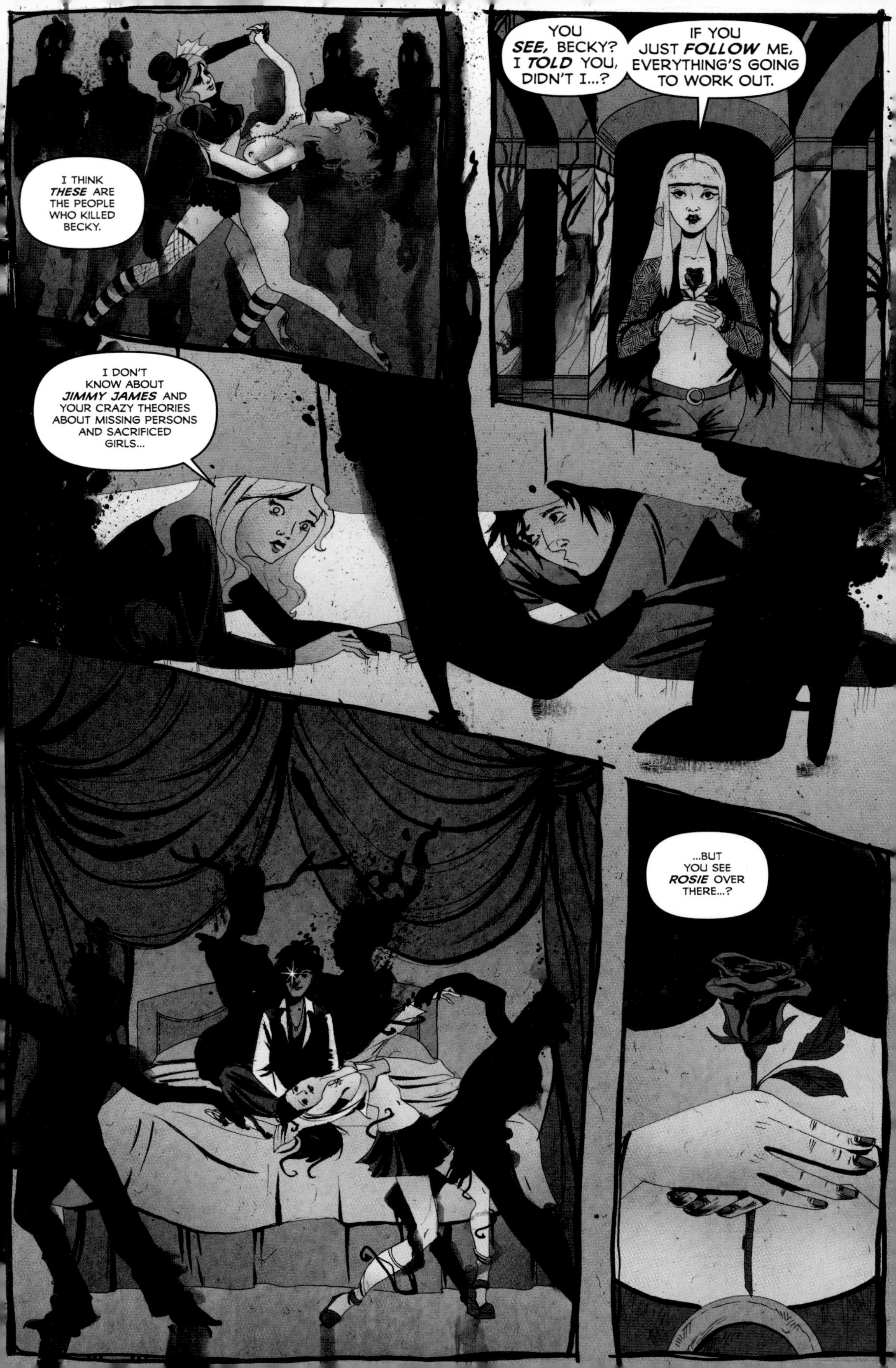
I THINK THESE ARE THE PEOPLE WHO KILLED BECKY.
YOU SEE, BECKY? I TOLD YOU, DIDN'T I...?
IF YOU JUST FOLLOW ME, EVERYTHING'S GOING TO WORK OUT.
I DON'T KNOW ABOUT JIMMY JAMES AND YOUR CRAZY THEORIES ABOUT MISSING PERSONS AND SACRIFICED GIRLS...
...BUT YOU SEE ROSIE OVER THERE...?

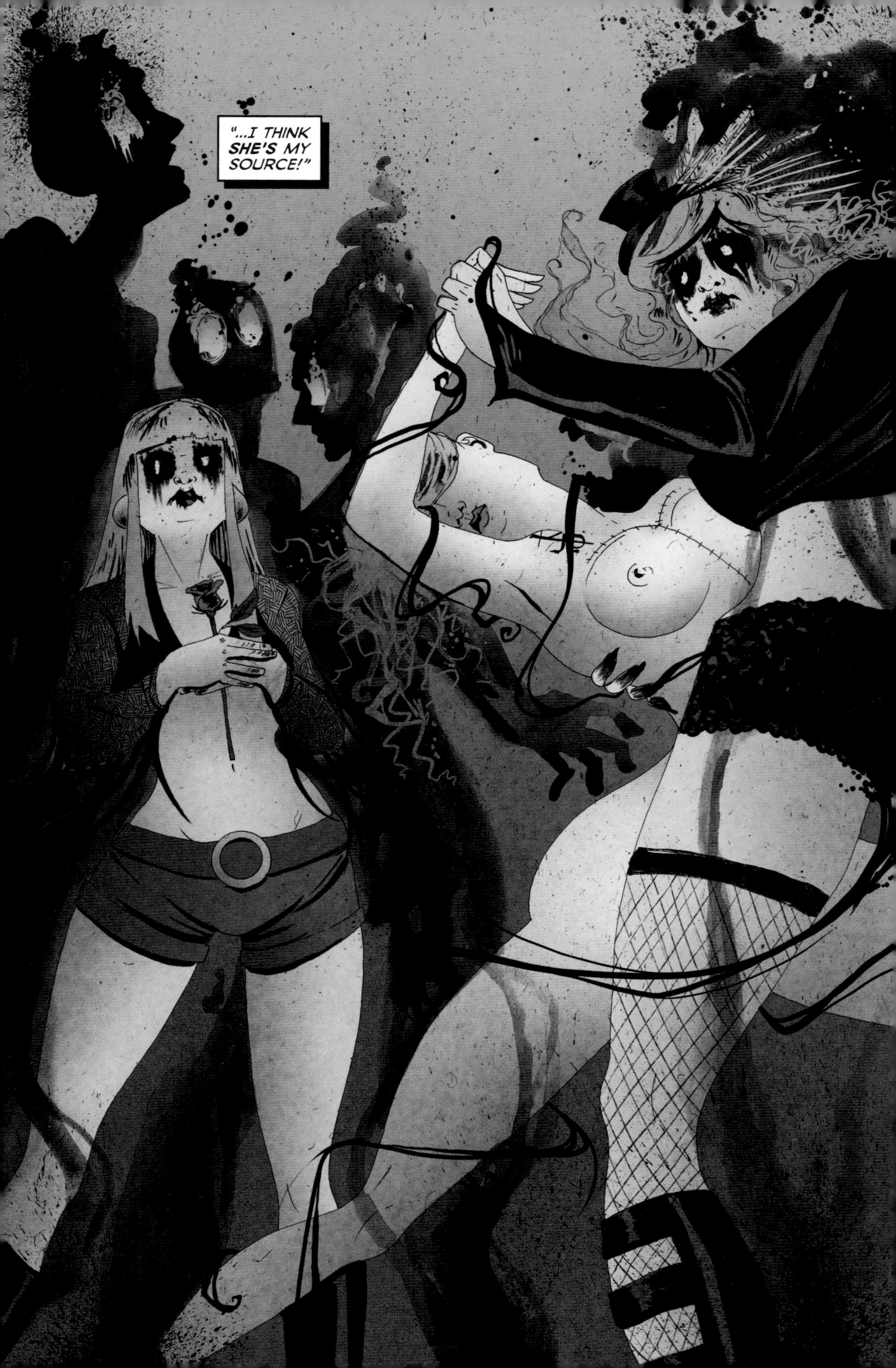
"...I THINK SHE'S MY SOURCE!"

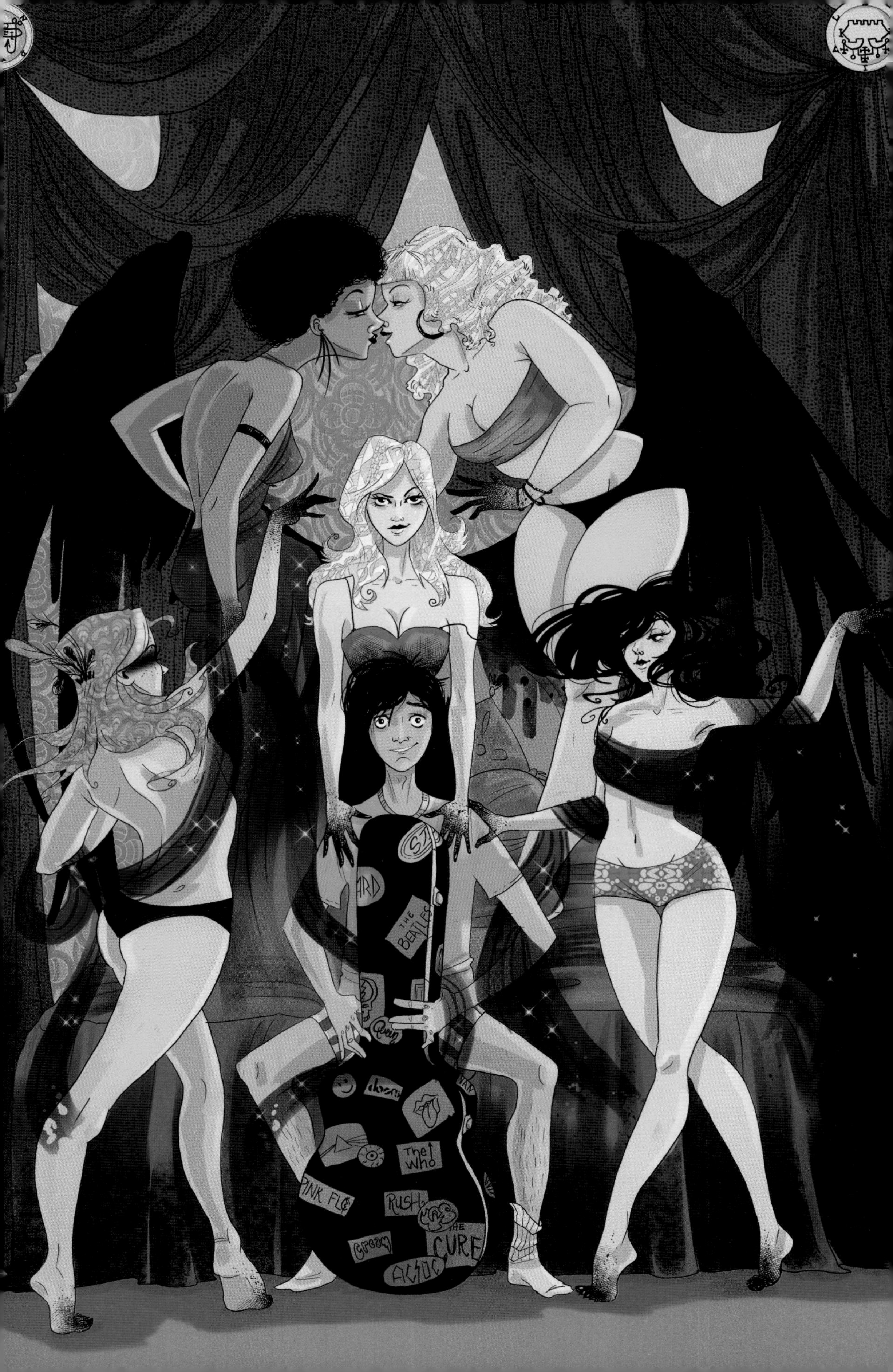
ARD
THE BEATLES
Queen
doors
The who
PINK FLO
RUSH
THE CURE
Cream
AC/DC

ROCKSTARS

Music nerd investigators Jackie Mayer and Dorothy Buell have uncovered one hell of a rock 'n' roll mystery. But if "Rock is Dead," as they say... WHAT WILL THEY DO ABOUT ALL THE GHOSTS, DEMONS AND GHOULS?

SIDE #1
FULL COLOR

Track 2

NATIVITY IN BLACKLIGHT

22

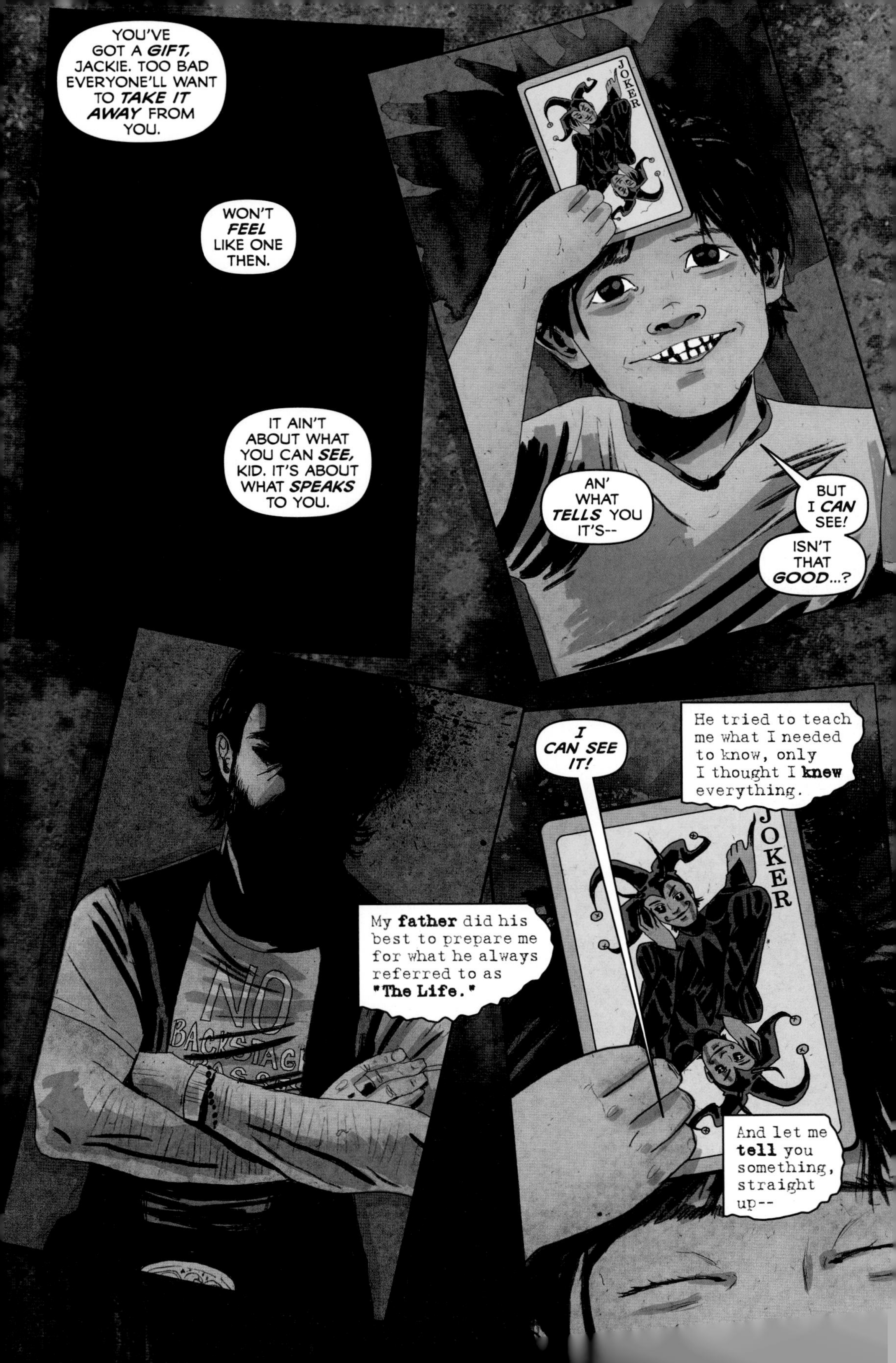
YOU'VE GOT A GIFT, JACKIE. TOO BAD EVERYONE'LL WANT TO TAKE IT AWAY FROM YOU.
JOKER
WON'T FEEL LIKE ONE THEN.
IT AIN'T ABOUT WHAT YOU CAN SEE, KID. IT'S ABOUT WHAT SPEAKS TO YOU.
AN' WHAT TELLS YOU IT'S--
BUT I CAN SEE!
ISN'T THAT GOOD...?
My father did his best to prepare me for what he always referred to as "The Life."
NO BACKSTAGE
I CAN SEE IT!
He tried to teach me what I needed to know, only I thought I knew everything.
JOKER
And let me tell you something, straight up--

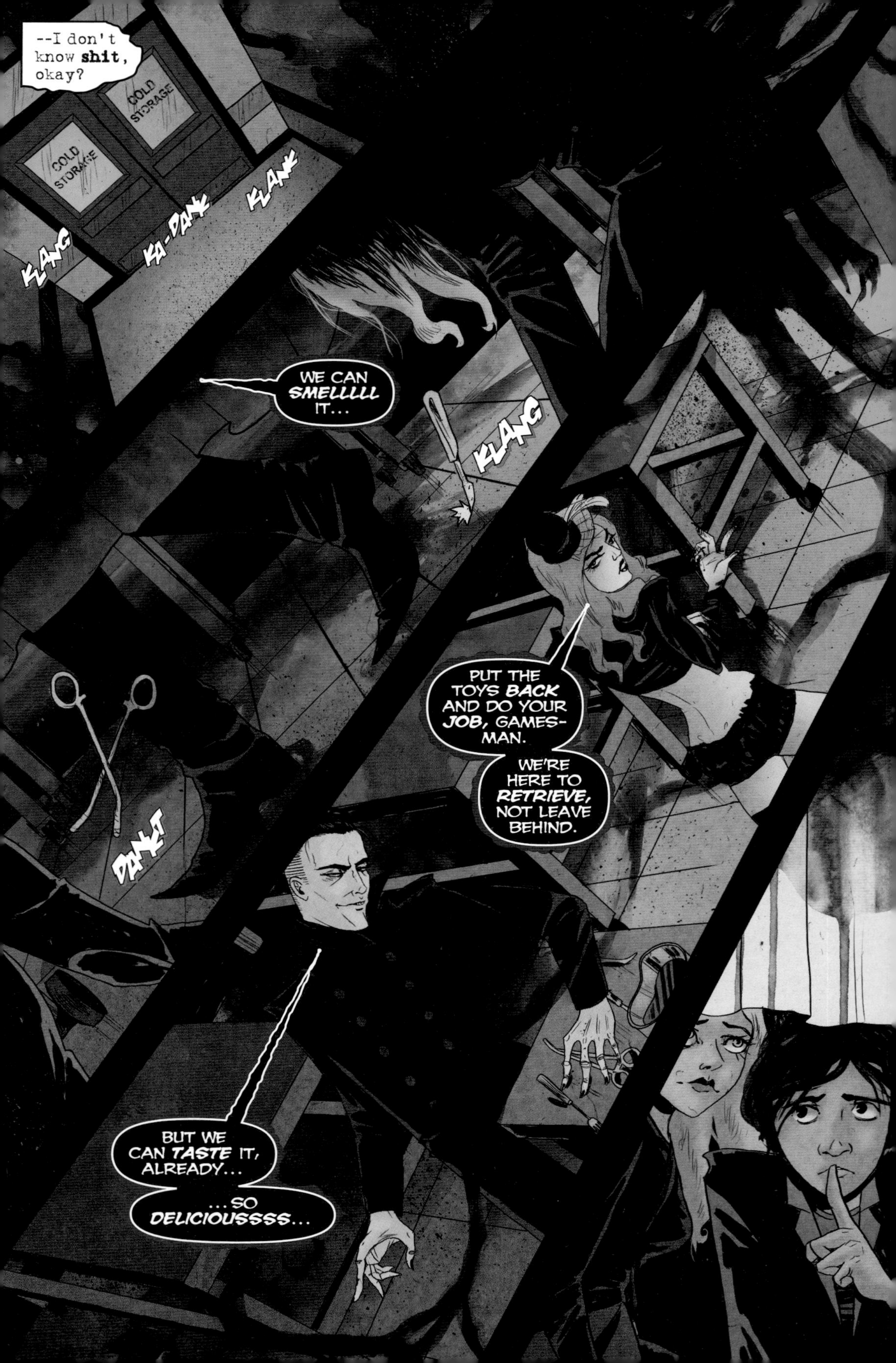
--I don't know **shit**, okay?
COLD STORAGE
COLD STORAGE
KLANG
KA-DANK
KLANK
WE CAN *SMELLLLL* IT...
KLANG
PUT THE TOYS *BACK* AND DO YOUR *JOB,* GAMES-MAN.
WE'RE HERE TO *RETRIEVE,* NOT LEAVE BEHIND.
DANKT
BUT WE CAN *TASTE* IT, ALREADY...
...SO *DELICIOUSSSS*...

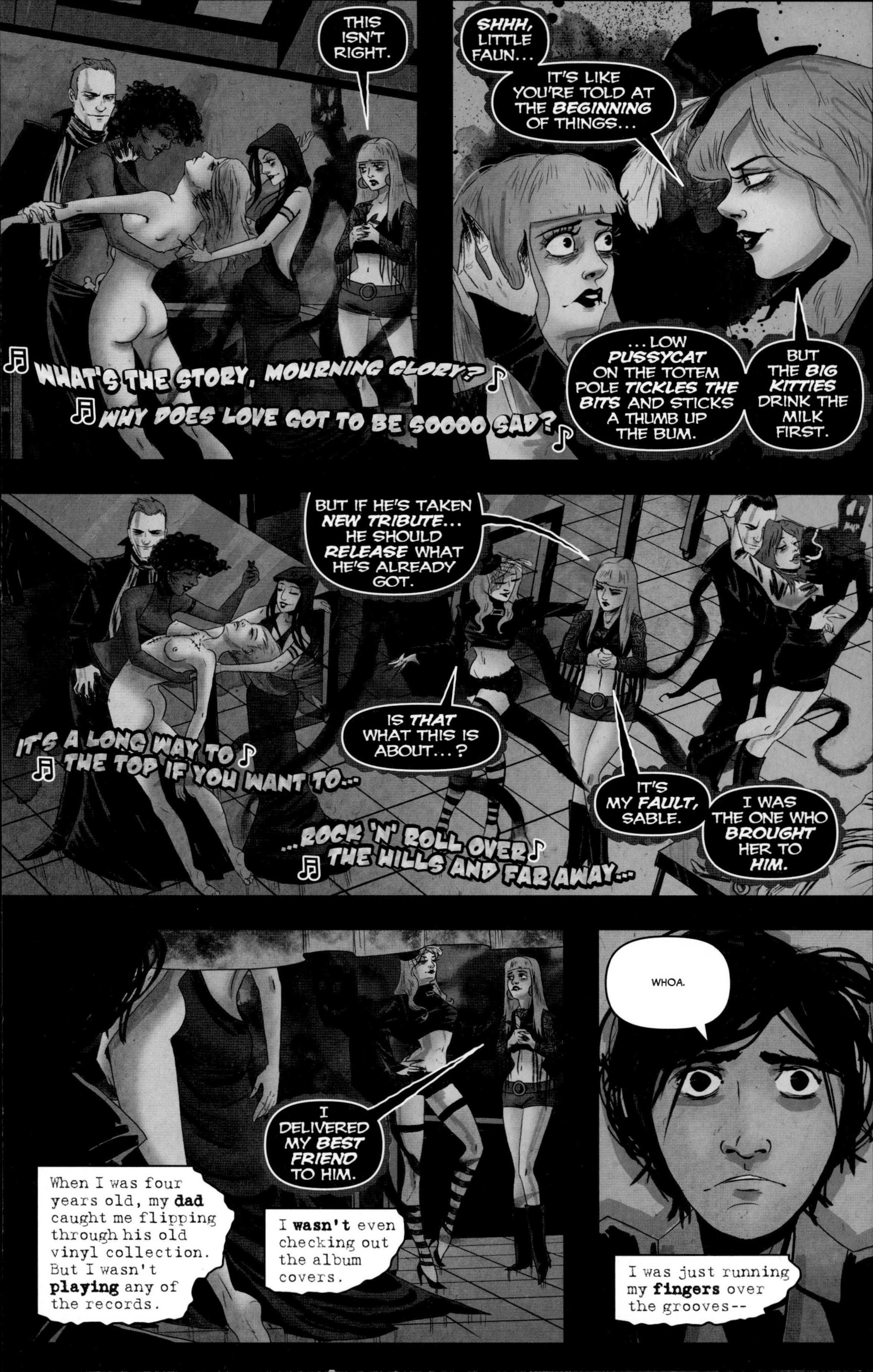
THIS ISN'T RIGHT.
SHHH, LITTLE FAUN...
IT'S LIKE YOU'RE TOLD AT THE BEGINNING OF THINGS...
WHAT'S THE STORY, MOURNING GLORY?
WHY DOES LOVE GOT TO BE SOOOO SAD?
...LOW PUSSYCAT ON THE TOTEM POLE TICKLES THE BITS AND STICKS A THUMB UP THE BUM.
BUT THE BIG KITTIES DRINK THE MILK FIRST.
BUT IF HE'S TAKEN NEW TRIBUTE... HE SHOULD RELEASE WHAT HE'S ALREADY GOT.
IS THAT WHAT THIS IS ABOUT...?
IT'S A LONG WAY TO THE TOP IF YOU WANT TO...
...ROCK 'N' ROLL OVER THE HILLS AND FAR AWAY...
IT'S MY FAULT, SABLE.
I WAS THE ONE WHO BROUGHT HER TO HIM.
I DELIVERED MY BEST FRIEND TO HIM.
When I was four years old, my dad caught me flipping through his old vinyl collection. But I wasn't playing any of the records.
I wasn't even checking out the album covers.
WHOA.
I was just running my fingers over the grooves--

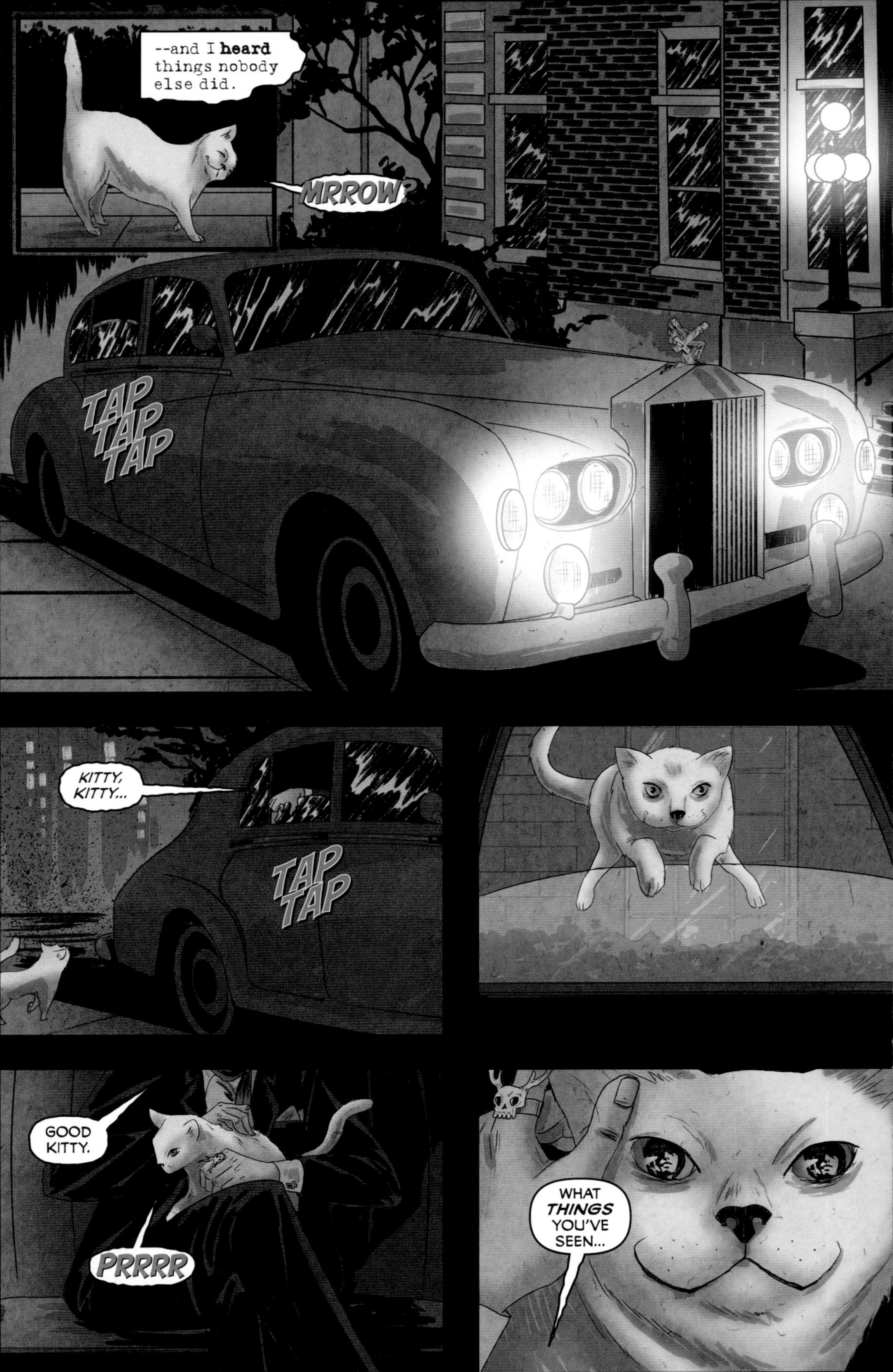
--and I **heard** things nobody else did.
MRROW?
TAP TAP TAP
KITTY, KITTY...
TAP TAP
GOOD KITTY.
PRRRR
WHAT *THINGS* YOU'VE SEEN...

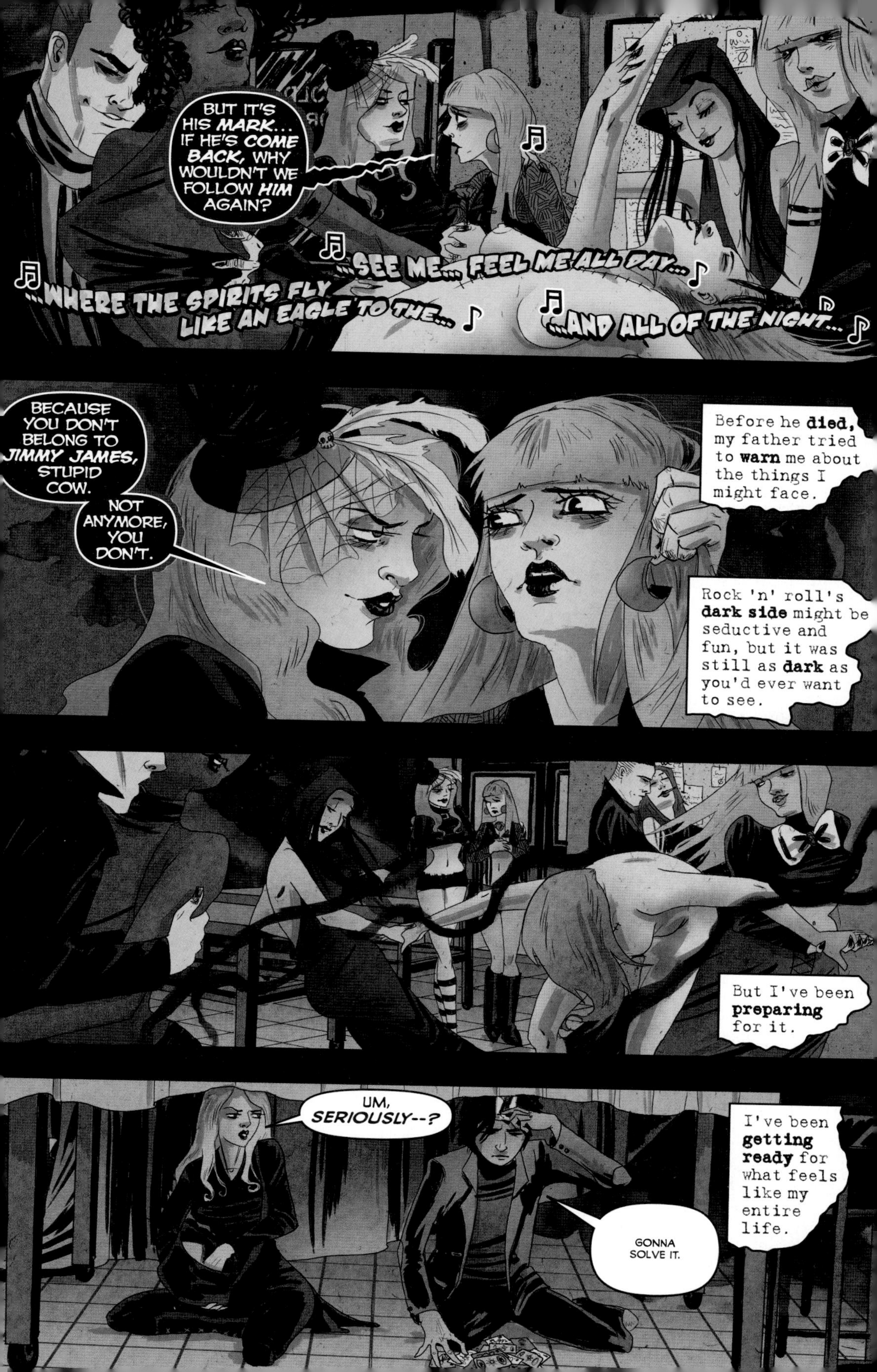

BUT IT'S HIS MARK... IF HE'S COME BACK, WHY WOULDN'T WE FOLLOW HIM AGAIN?
...WHERE THE SPIRITS FLY LIKE AN EAGLE TO THE...
...SEE ME... FEEL ME ALL DAY...
...AND ALL OF THE NIGHT...
BECAUSE YOU DON'T BELONG TO JIMMY JAMES, STUPID COW.
NOT ANYMORE, YOU DON'T.
Before he died, my father tried to warn me about the things I might face.
Rock 'n' roll's dark side might be seductive and fun, but it was still as dark as you'd ever want to see.
But I've been preparing for it.
UM, SERIOUSLY--?
I've been getting ready for what feels like my entire life.
GONNA SOLVE IT.

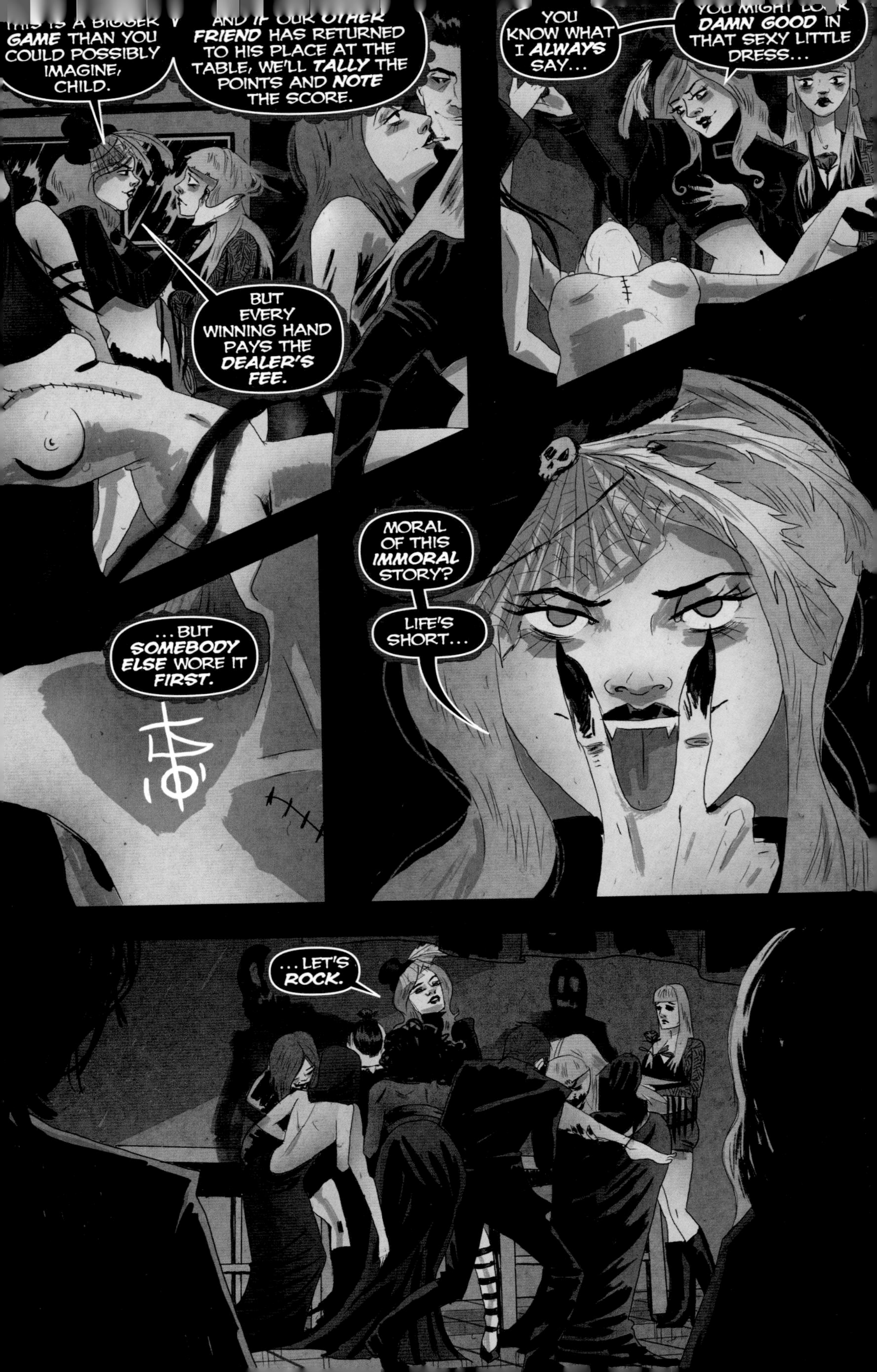
THIS IS A BIGGER GAME THAN YOU COULD POSSIBLY IMAGINE, CHILD.
AND IF OUR OTHER FRIEND HAS RETURNED TO HIS PLACE AT THE TABLE, WE'LL TALLY THE POINTS AND NOTE THE SCORE.
BUT EVERY WINNING HAND PAYS THE DEALER'S FEE.
YOU KNOW WHAT I ALWAYS SAY...
YOU MIGHT
DAMN GOOD IN THAT SEXY LITTLE DRESS...
...BUT SOMEBODY ELSE WORE IT FIRST.
MORAL OF THIS IMMORAL STORY?
LIFE'S SHORT...
...LET'S ROCK.

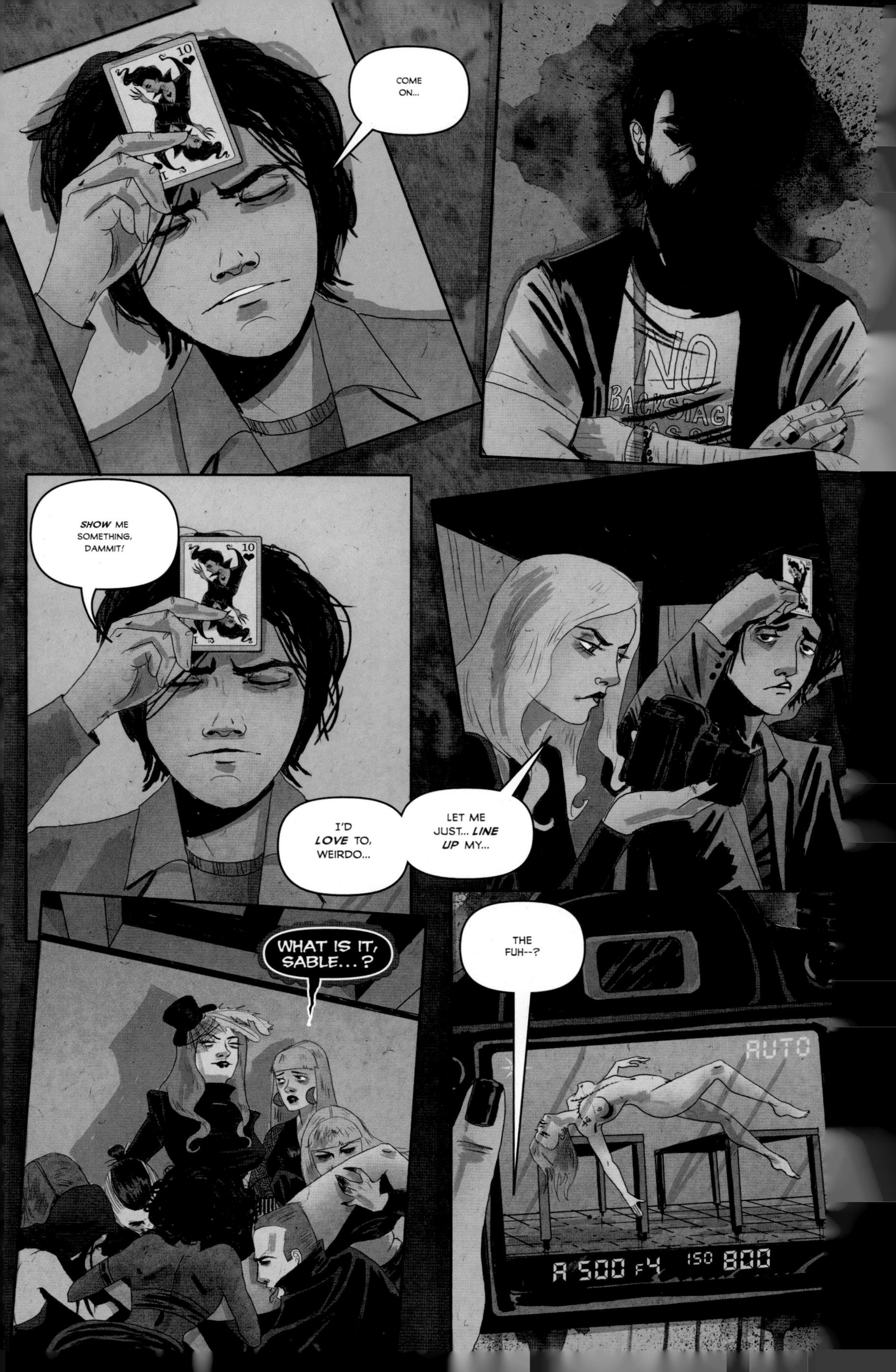
COME ON...
SHOW ME SOMETHING, DAMMIT!
I'D LOVE TO, WEIRDO...
LET ME JUST... LINE UP MY...
WHAT IS IT, SABLE...?
THE FUH--?
AUTO
A 500 F4 ISO 800

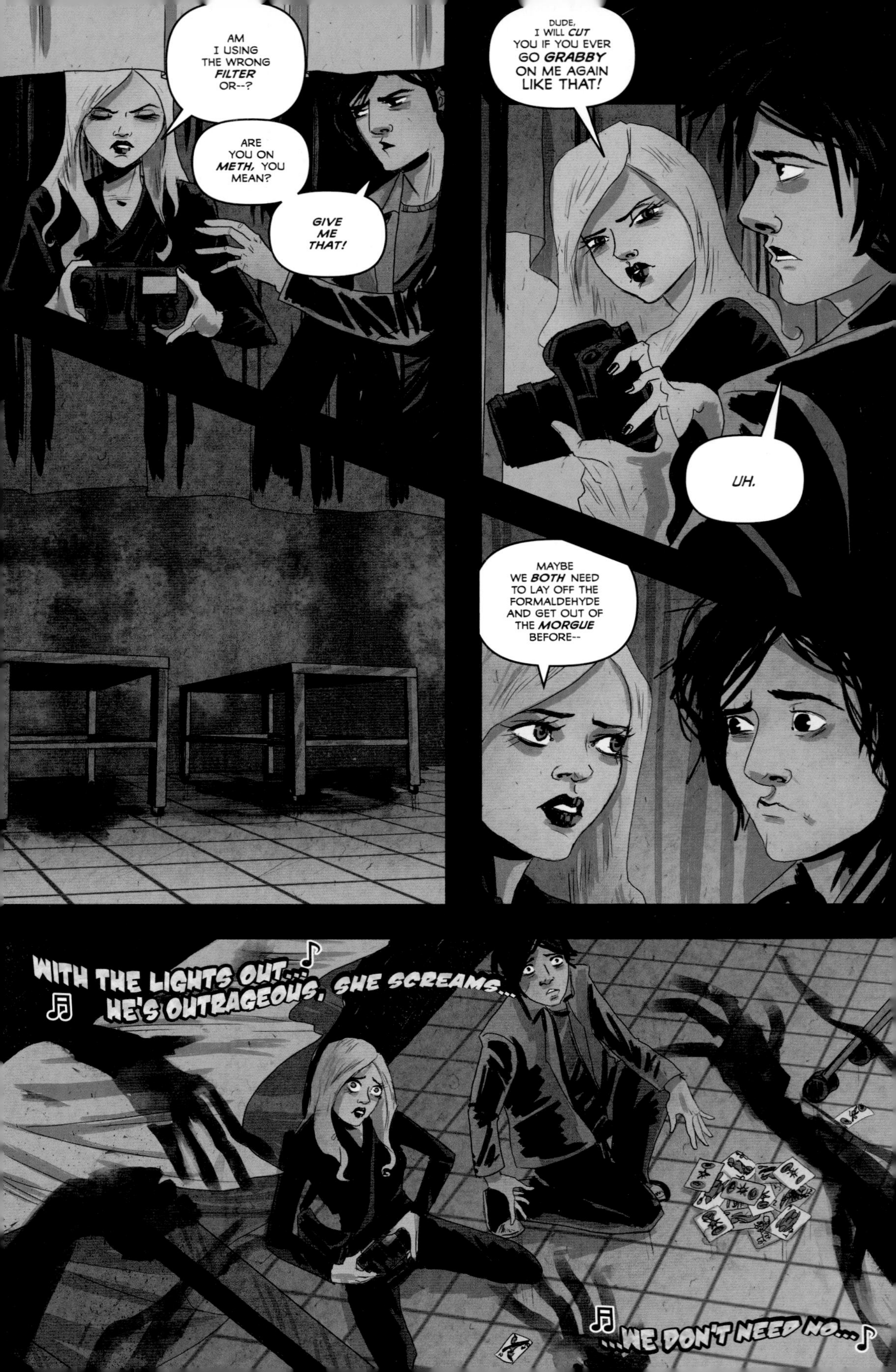
AM I USING THE WRONG FILTER OR--?
ARE YOU ON METH, YOU MEAN?
GIVE ME THAT!
DUDE, I WILL CUT YOU IF YOU EVER GO GRABBY ON ME AGAIN LIKE THAT!
UH.
MAYBE WE BOTH NEED TO LAY OFF THE FORMALDEHYDE AND GET OUT OF THE MORGUE BEFORE--
WITH THE LIGHTS OUT...
HE'S OUTRAGEOUS, SHE SCREAMS...
...WE DON'T NEED NO...

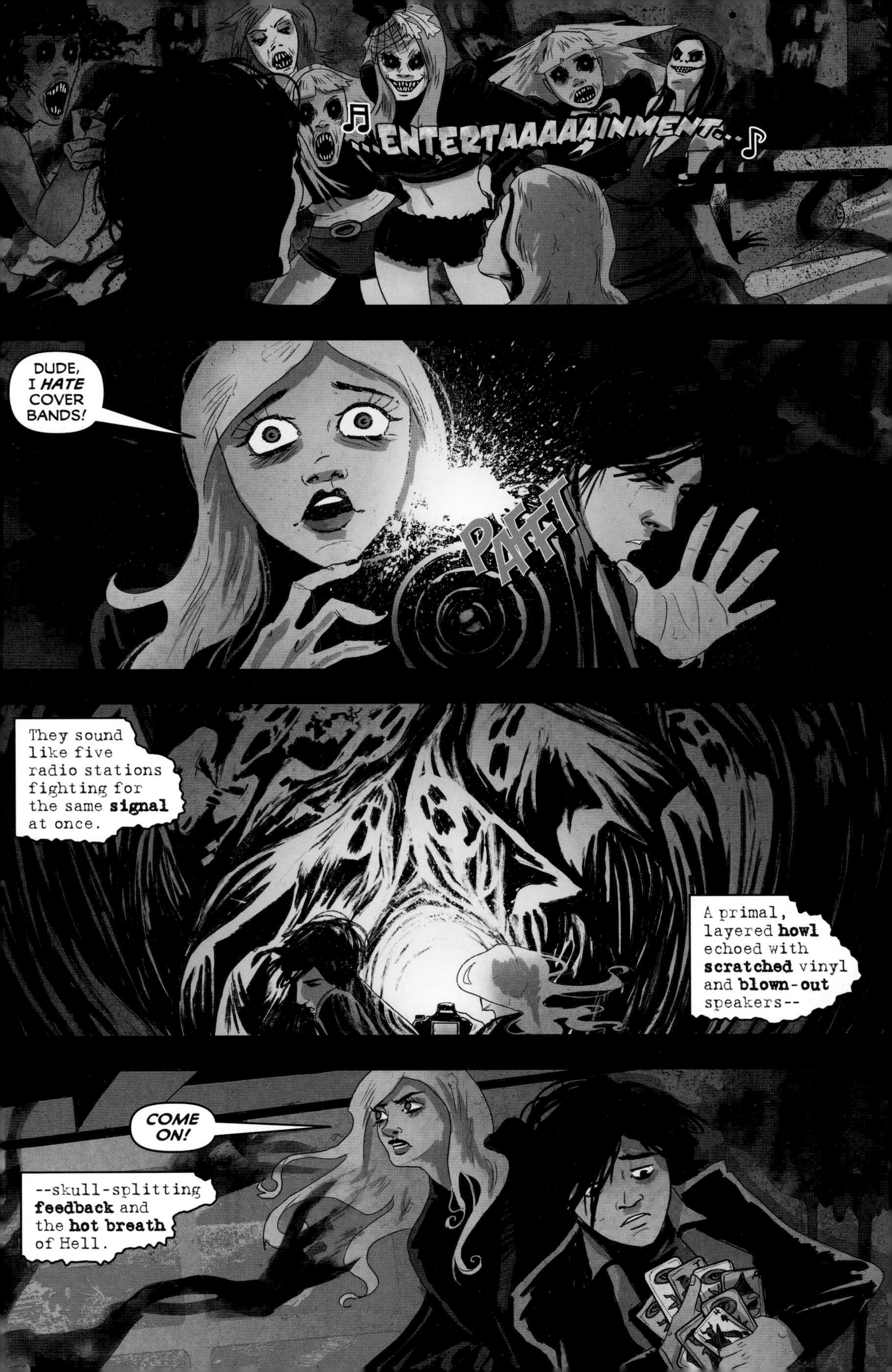
...ENTERTAAAAAINMENT...
DUDE, I HATE COVER BANDS!
PAFFT
They sound like five radio stations fighting for the same signal at once.
A primal, layered howl echoed with scratched vinyl and blown-out speakers--
COME ON!
--skull-splitting feedback and the hot breath of Hell.

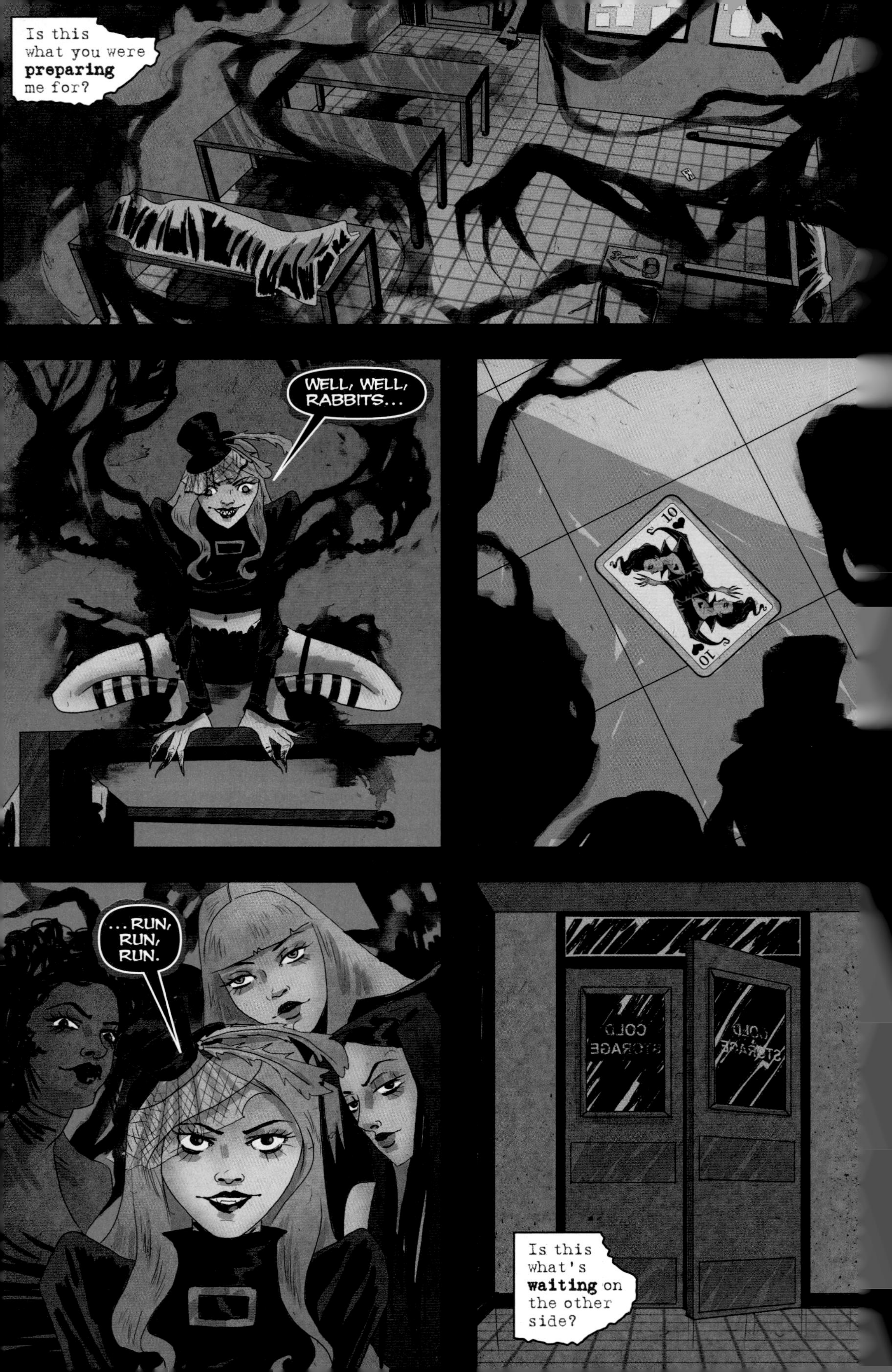
Is this what you were **preparing** me for?
WELL, WELL, RABBITS...
...RUN, RUN, RUN.
COLD STORAGE
COLD STORAGE
Is this what's **waiting** on the other side?

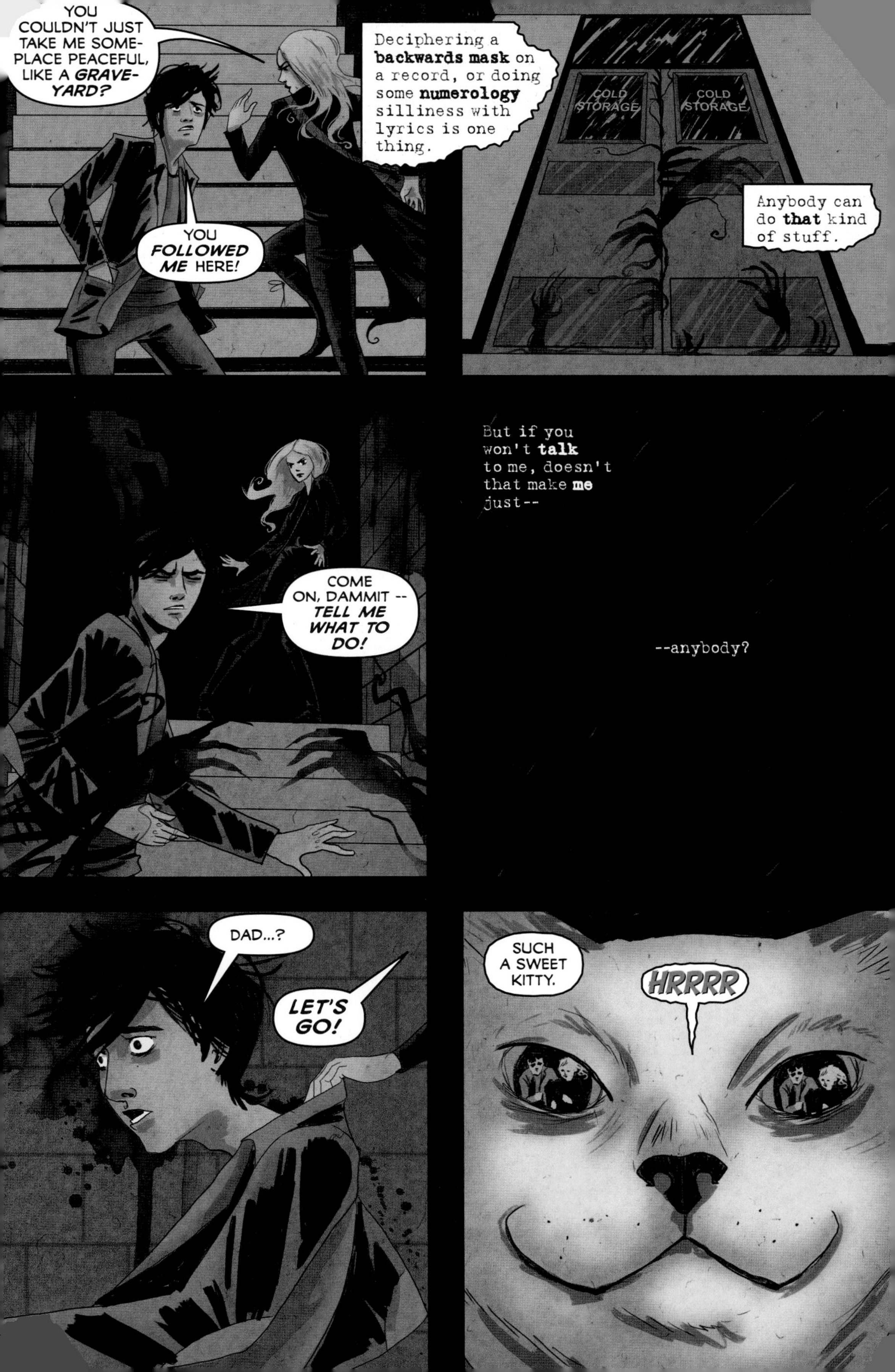

YOU COULDN'T JUST TAKE ME SOME-PLACE PEACEFUL, LIKE A *GRAVE-YARD?*
YOU *FOLLOWED ME* HERE!
Deciphering a **backwards mask** on a record, or doing some **numerology** silliness with lyrics is one thing.
COLD STORAGE
COLD STORAGE
Anybody can do **that** kind of stuff.
COME ON, DAMMIT -- *TELL ME WHAT TO DO!*
But if you won't **talk** to me, doesn't that make **me** just--
--anybody?
DAD...?
LET'S GO!
SUCH A SWEET KITTY.
HRRRR

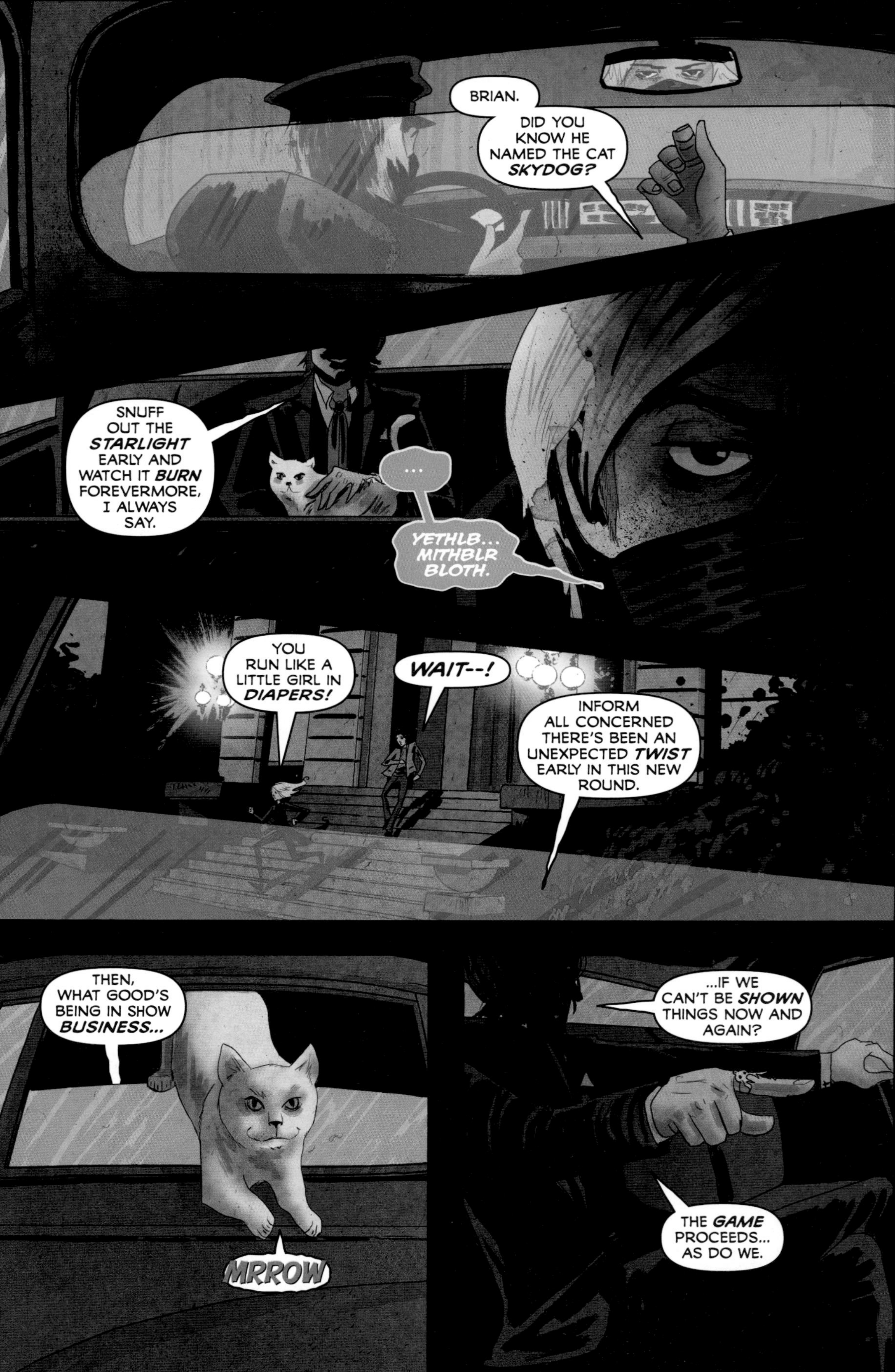
BRIAN.
DID YOU KNOW HE NAMED THE CAT SKYDOG?
SNUFF OUT THE STARLIGHT EARLY AND WATCH IT BURN FOREVERMORE, I ALWAYS SAY.
...
YETHLB... MITHBLR BLOTH.
YOU RUN LIKE A LITTLE GIRL IN DIAPERS!
WAIT--!
INFORM ALL CONCERNED THERE'S BEEN AN UNEXPECTED TWIST EARLY IN THIS NEW ROUND.
THEN, WHAT GOOD'S BEING IN SHOW BUSINESS...
...IF WE CAN'T BE SHOWN THINGS NOW AND AGAIN?
MRROW
THE GAME PROCEEDS... AS DO WE.

ONE *PRODIGAL* RETURNS TO THE FRAY... A *TRUE SON* OF THE *MOST WICKED GAME* IS REVEALED...

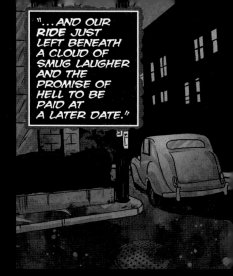

"...AND OUR *RIDE* JUST LEFT BENEATH A CLOUD OF *SMUG LAUGHER* AND THE *PROMISE OF HELL* TO BE PAID AT A LATER DATE."

LOOKS LIKE WE'RE GETTING *ROLLED,* SABLE.

HMMH... EVERY-BODY LOVES A *FRONTRUNNER,* BUT SLOW AND STEADY GETS *ME* READY.

GRASS ON THE FIELD, KITTY-CATS...

...WHAT SAY WE SCRATCH OUR *CLAWS* A LITTLE?

I once had a **dream** that **Kurt Cobain** died.

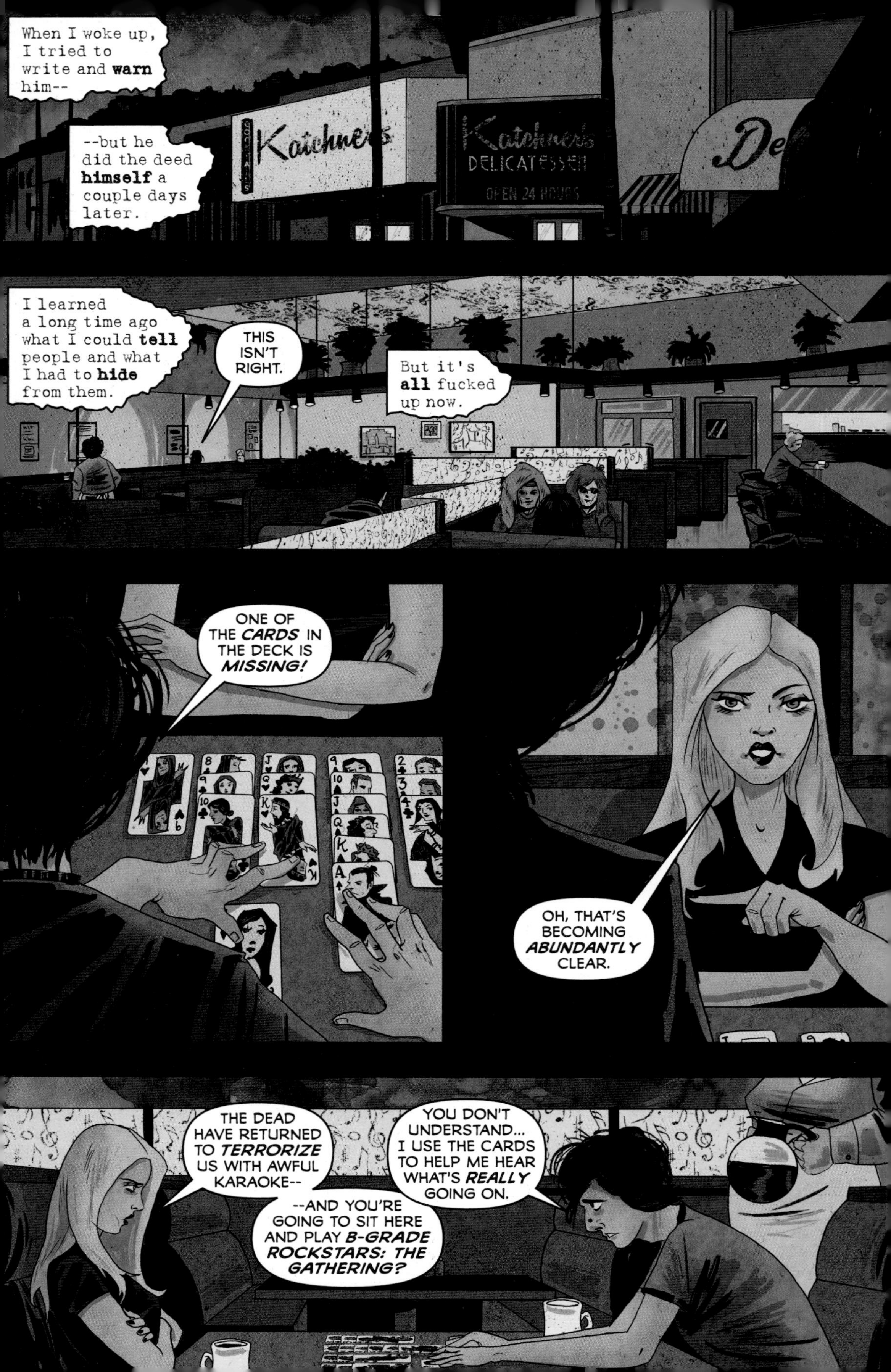
When I woke up, I tried to write and **warn** him--
--but he did the deed **himself** a couple days later.
Katchner's
Katchner's
DELICATESSEN
OPEN 24 HOURS
I learned a long time ago what I could **tell** people and what I had to **hide** from them.
THIS ISN'T RIGHT.
But it's **all** fucked up now.
ONE OF THE *CARDS* IN THE DECK IS *MISSING!*
OH, THAT'S BECOMING *ABUNDANTLY* CLEAR.
THE DEAD HAVE RETURNED TO *TERRORIZE* US WITH AWFUL KARAOKE--
--AND YOU'RE GOING TO SIT HERE AND PLAY *B-GRADE ROCKSTARS: THE GATHERING?*
YOU DON'T UNDERSTAND... I USE THE CARDS TO HELP ME HEAR WHAT'S *REALLY* GOING ON.

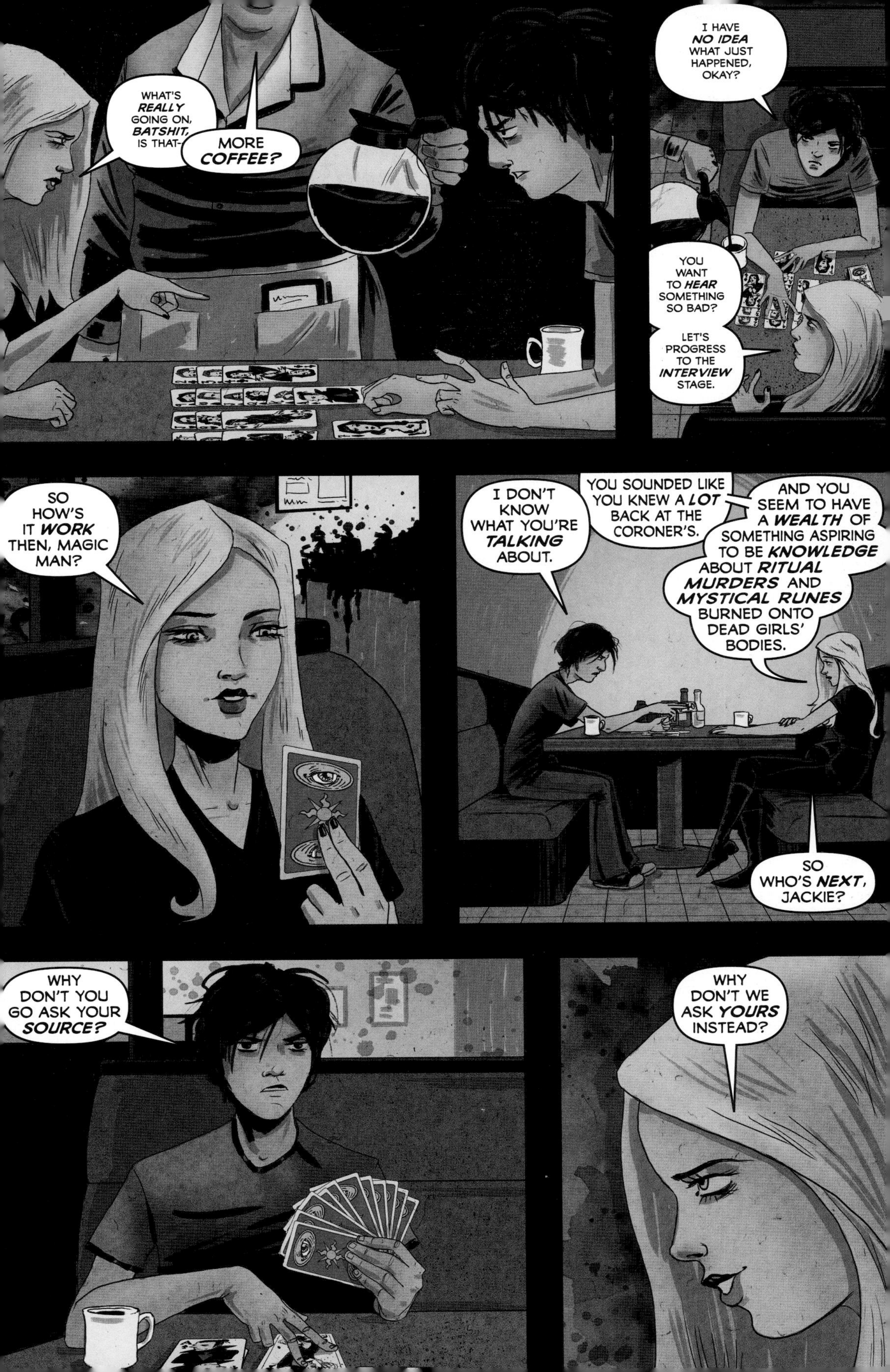
WHAT'S REALLY GOING ON, BATSHIT, IS THAT-
MORE COFFEE?
I HAVE NO IDEA WHAT JUST HAPPENED, OKAY?
YOU WANT TO HEAR SOMETHING SO BAD?
LET'S PROGRESS TO THE INTERVIEW STAGE.
SO HOW'S IT WORK THEN, MAGIC MAN?
I DON'T KNOW WHAT YOU'RE TALKING ABOUT.
YOU SOUNDED LIKE YOU KNEW A LOT BACK AT THE CORONER'S.
AND YOU SEEM TO HAVE A WEALTH OF SOMETHING ASPIRING TO BE KNOWLEDGE ABOUT RITUAL MURDERS AND MYSTICAL RUNES BURNED ONTO DEAD GIRLS' BODIES.
SO WHO'S NEXT, JACKIE?
WHY DON'T YOU GO ASK YOUR SOURCE?
WHY DON'T WE ASK YOURS INSTEAD?

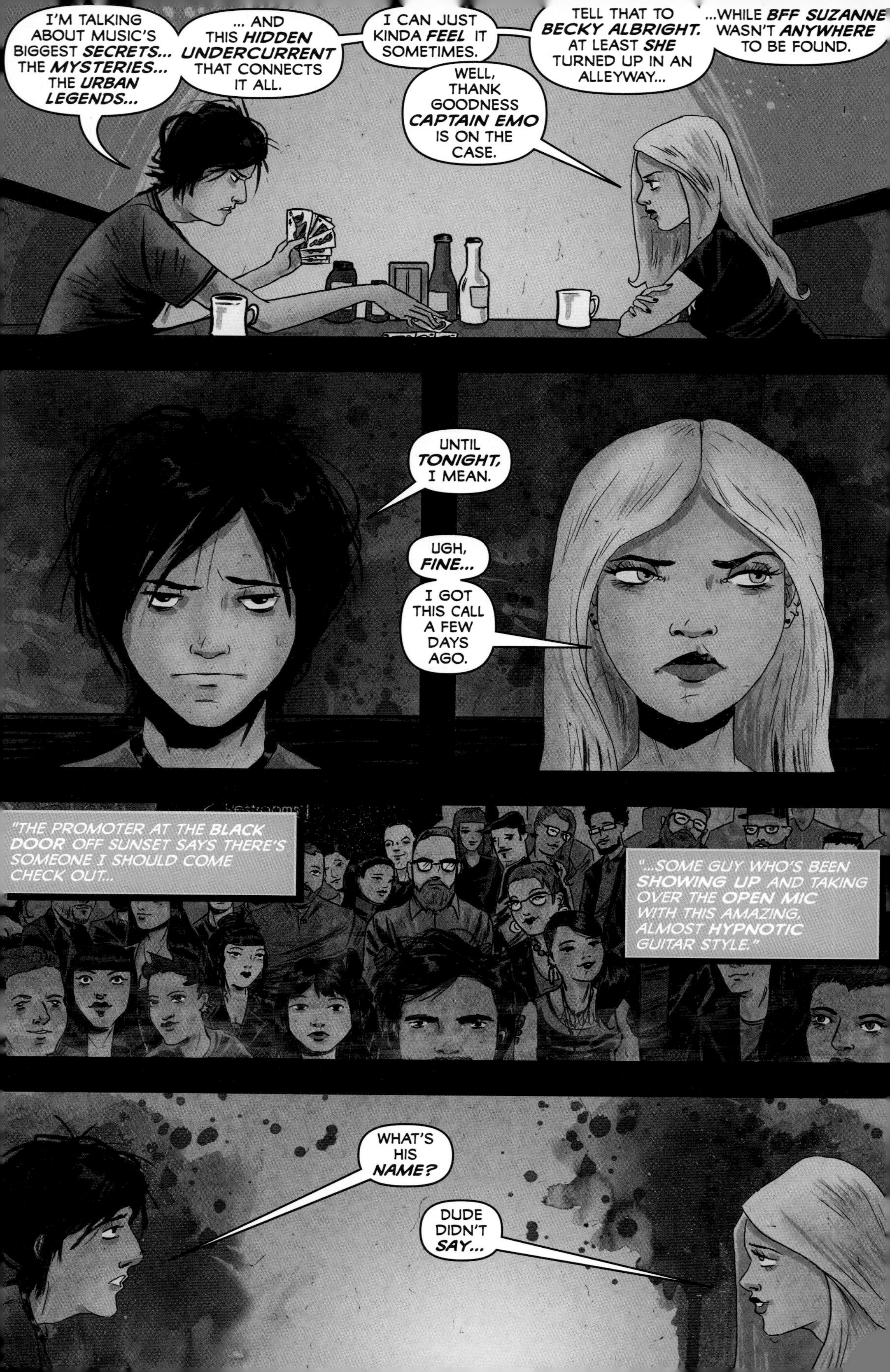
I'M TALKING ABOUT MUSIC'S BIGGEST SECRETS... THE MYSTERIES... THE URBAN LEGENDS...
... AND THIS HIDDEN UNDERCURRENT THAT CONNECTS IT ALL.
I CAN JUST KINDA FEEL IT SOMETIMES.
WELL, THANK GOODNESS CAPTAIN EMO IS ON THE CASE.
TELL THAT TO BECKY ALBRIGHT. AT LEAST SHE TURNED UP IN AN ALLEYWAY...
...WHILE BFF SUZANNE WASN'T ANYWHERE TO BE FOUND.
UNTIL TONIGHT, I MEAN.
UGH, FINE...
I GOT THIS CALL A FEW DAYS AGO.
"THE PROMOTER AT THE BLACK DOOR OFF SUNSET SAYS THERE'S SOMEONE I SHOULD COME CHECK OUT...
"...SOME GUY WHO'S BEEN SHOWING UP AND TAKING OVER THE OPEN MIC WITH THIS AMAZING, ALMOST HYPNOTIC GUITAR STYLE."
WHAT'S HIS NAME?
DUDE DIDN'T SAY...

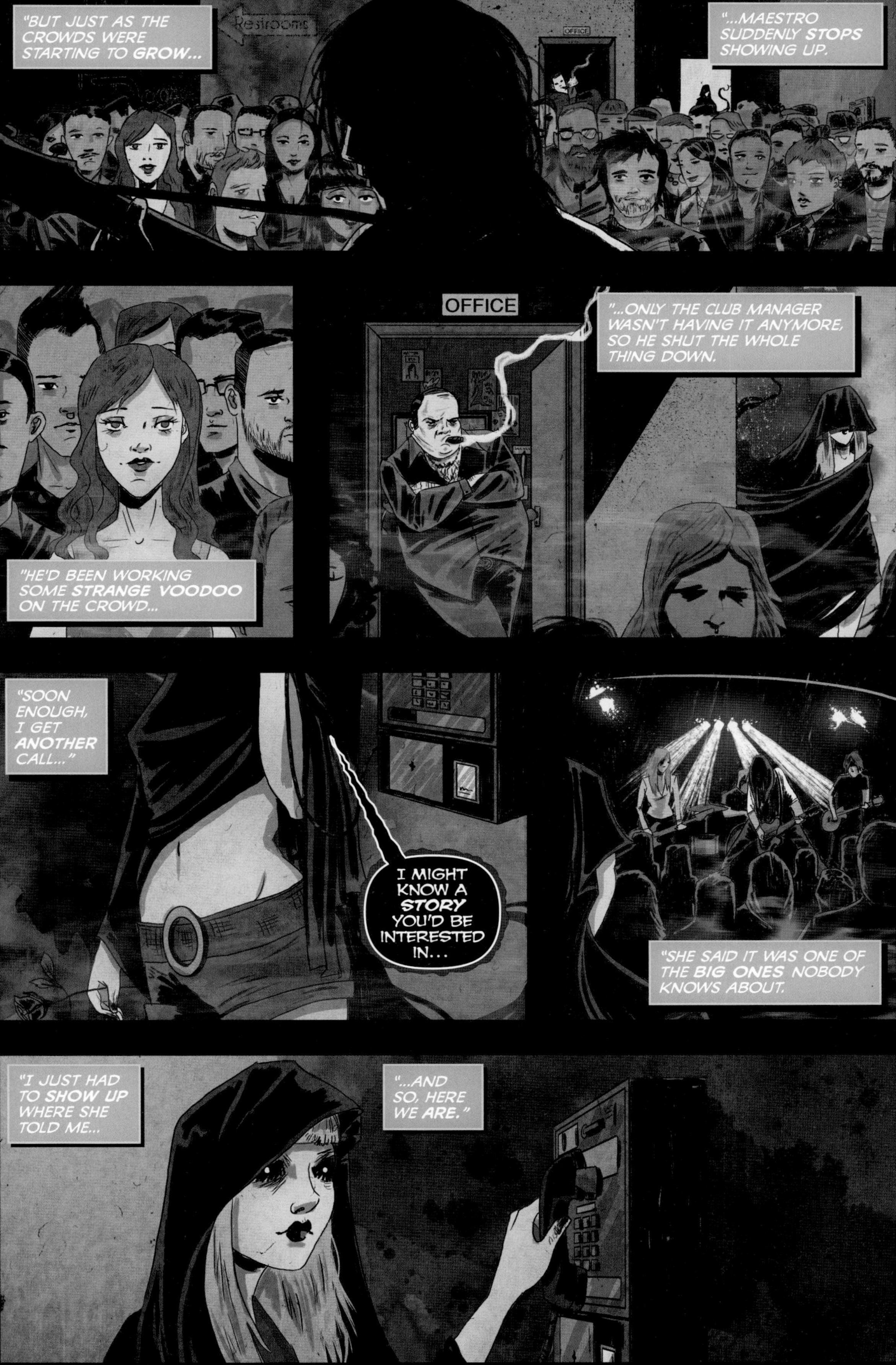
"BUT JUST AS THE CROWDS WERE STARTING TO GROW...
RESTROOMS
OFFICE
"...MAESTRO SUDDENLY STOPS SHOWING UP.
"HE'D BEEN WORKING SOME STRANGE VOODOO ON THE CROWD...
OFFICE
"...ONLY THE CLUB MANAGER WASN'T HAVING IT ANYMORE, SO HE SHUT THE WHOLE THING DOWN.
"SOON ENOUGH, I GET ANOTHER CALL..."
I MIGHT KNOW A STORY YOU'D BE INTERESTED IN...
"SHE SAID IT WAS ONE OF THE BIG ONES NOBODY KNOWS ABOUT.
"I JUST HAD TO SHOW UP WHERE SHE TOLD ME...
"...AND SO, HERE WE ARE."

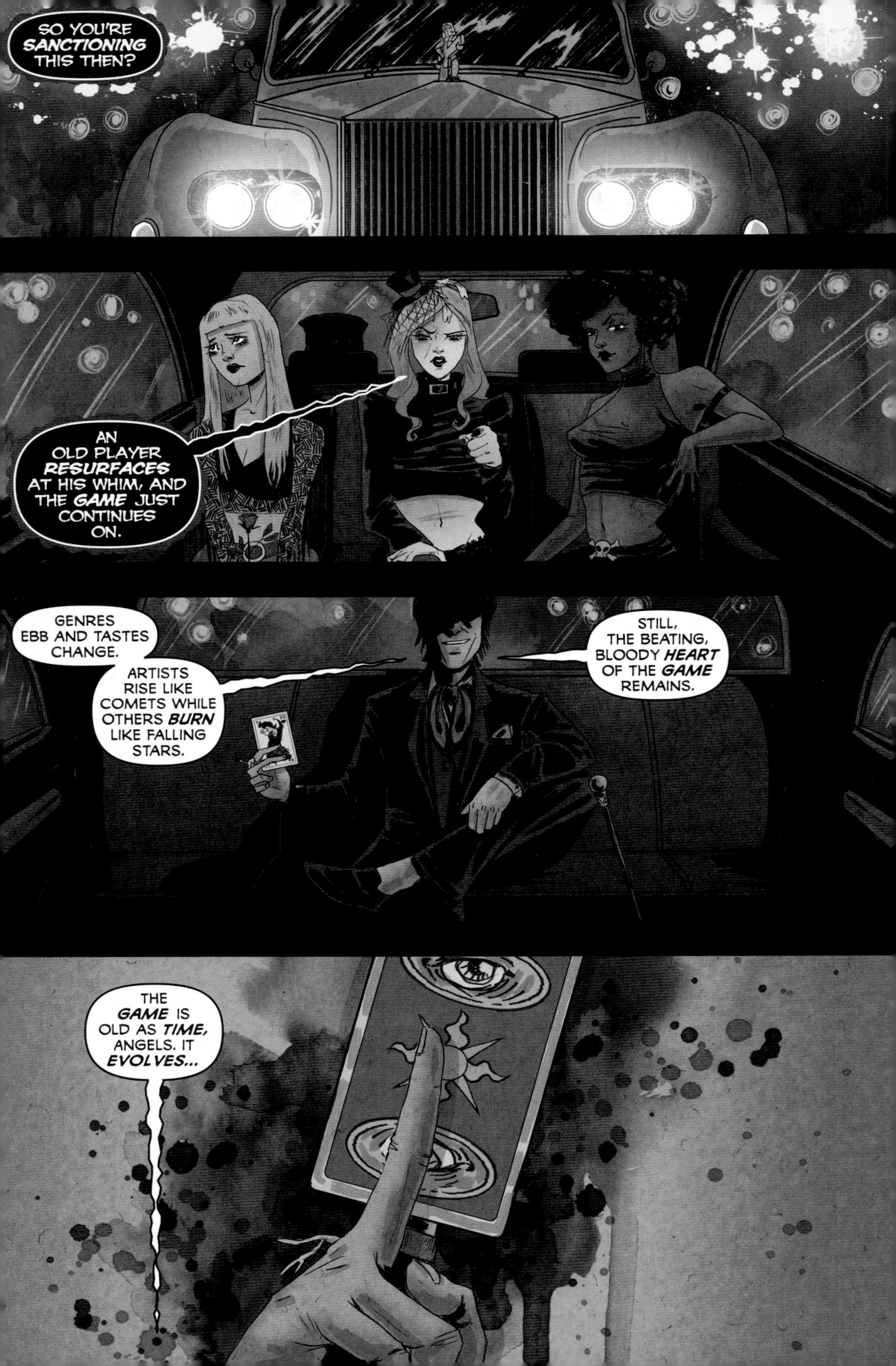
SO YOU'RE SANCTIONING THIS THEN?
AN OLD PLAYER RESURFACES AT HIS WHIM, AND THE GAME JUST CONTINUES ON.
GENRES EBB AND TASTES CHANGE.
ARTISTS RISE LIKE COMETS WHILE OTHERS BURN LIKE FALLING STARS.
STILL, THE BEATING, BLOODY HEART OF THE GAME REMAINS.
THE GAME IS OLD AS TIME, ANGELS. IT EVOLVES...

"OUR ROLES ARE AS VITAL AS EVER, MY MINXES."

LOOKS LIKE *REACH-AROUND ROSIE* WAS ONTO SOMETHING.

SWEET BABY JANE *UNMASKED.*

MISSING

ALLISON MOORE

Known to friends as "Allie"
Missing since Wednesday 4/24
If seen, call 310-555-2477

"WE FACILITATE *DREAMS.*"

"WE IMBUE THE CREATIVE FULFILLMENT."

IT'S A GOOD BET WHOEVER LEFT HER IN THAT *ALLEYWAY* PICKED UP HIS *DANCE PARTNER* HERE.

"WE ADDLE THE EXPERIENCES THAT *INFORM* IT."

DON'T WANDER OFF AGAIN, *SKYDOG.*

"AND WE KEEP A *COUNT* ON ALL THE MISCHIEF, MAYHEM, TRAGEDY AND TRIUMPH THAT *FLOWS* FORTH."

PRRRR

MISSII

ALLISON MOORE

Known to friends as "Allie"
Missing since Wednesday 4/24
If seen, call 310-555-2477

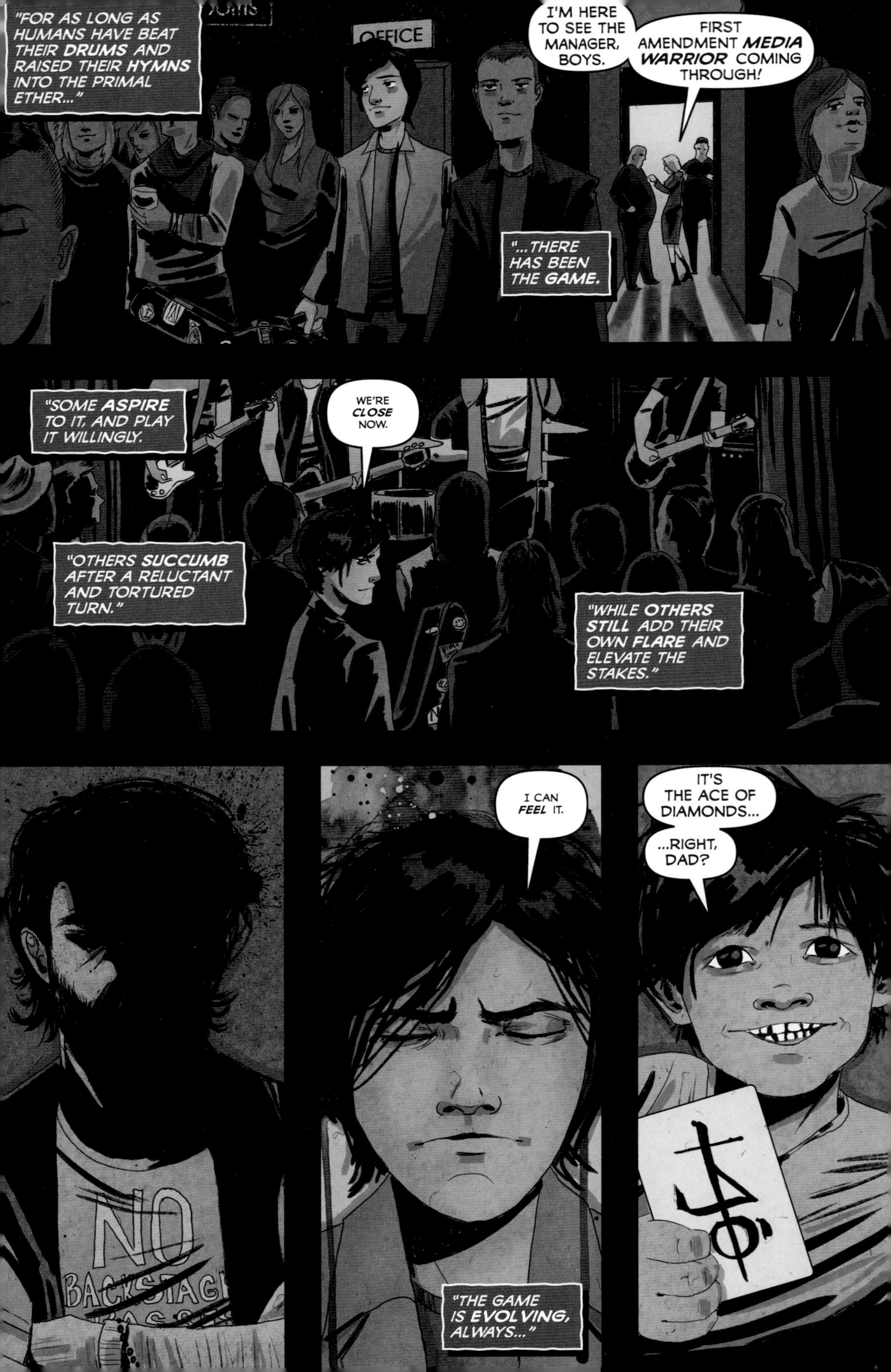
"FOR AS LONG AS HUMANS HAVE BEAT THEIR DRUMS AND RAISED THEIR HYMNS INTO THE PRIMAL ETHER..."
OFFICE
I'M HERE TO SEE THE MANAGER, BOYS.
FIRST AMENDMENT MEDIA WARRIOR COMING THROUGH!
"...THERE HAS BEEN THE GAME.
"SOME ASPIRE TO IT, AND PLAY IT WILLINGLY.
WE'RE CLOSE NOW.
"OTHERS SUCCUMB AFTER A RELUCTANT AND TORTURED TURN."
"WHILE OTHERS STILL ADD THEIR OWN FLARE AND ELEVATE THE STAKES."
NO BACKSTAGE
I CAN FEEL IT.
"THE GAME IS EVOLVING, ALWAYS..."
IT'S THE ACE OF DIAMONDS...
...RIGHT, DAD?

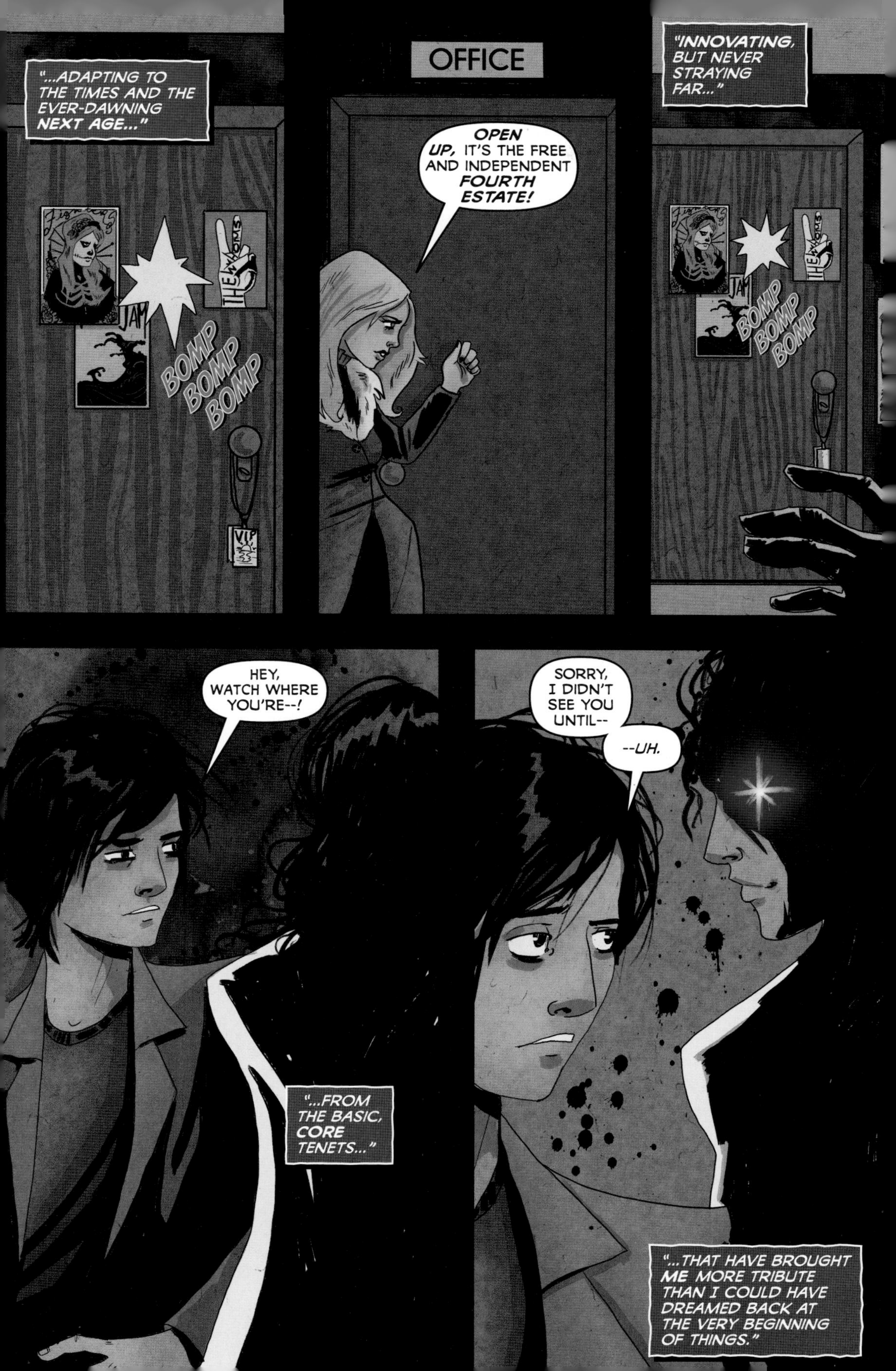
"...ADAPTING TO THE TIMES AND THE EVER-DAWNING NEXT AGE..."
THE WHOMS
JAM
BOMP BOMP BOMP
VIP
OFFICE
OPEN UP, IT'S THE FREE AND INDEPENDENT FOURTH ESTATE!
"INNOVATING, BUT NEVER STRAYING FAR..."
BOMP BOMP BOMP
HEY, WATCH WHERE YOU'RE--!
"...FROM THE BASIC, CORE TENETS..."
SORRY, I DIDN'T SEE YOU UNTIL--
--UH.
"...THAT HAVE BROUGHT ME MORE TRIBUTE THAN I COULD HAVE DREAMED BACK AT THE VERY BEGINNING OF THINGS."

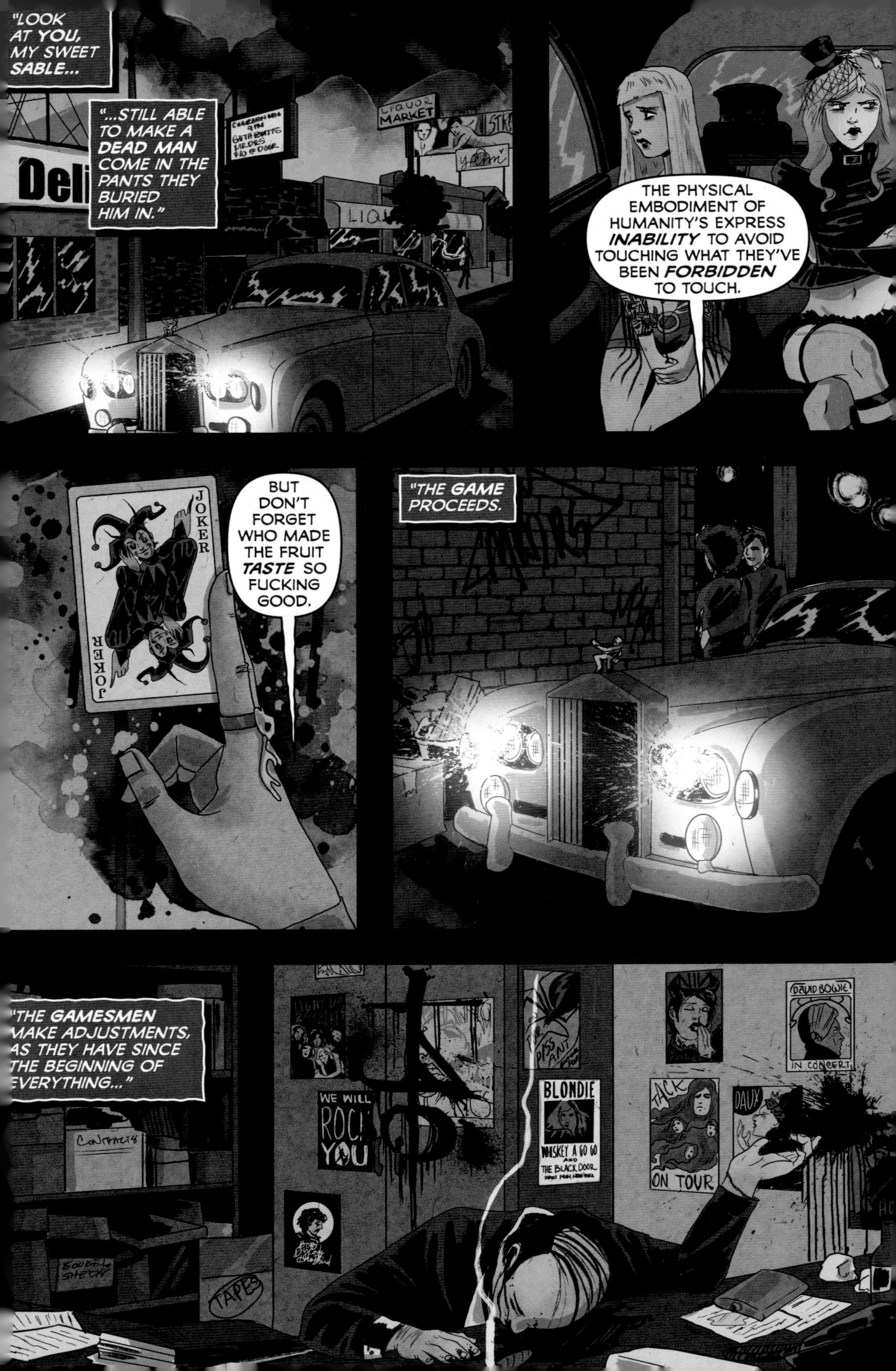

"LOOK AT YOU, MY SWEET SABLE...
"...STILL ABLE TO MAKE A DEAD MAN COME IN THE PANTS THEY BURIED HIM IN."
Deli
LIQUOR MARKET
THE PHYSICAL EMBODIMENT OF HUMANITY'S EXPRESS INABILITY TO AVOID TOUCHING WHAT THEY'VE BEEN FORBIDDEN TO TOUCH.
JOKER
BUT DON'T FORGET WHO MADE THE FRUIT TASTE SO FUCKING GOOD.
"THE GAME PROCEEDS.
"THE GAMESMEN MAKE ADJUSTMENTS, AS THEY HAVE SINCE THE BEGINNING OF EVERYTHING..."
DAVID BOWIE
IN CONCERT
BLONDIE
WHISKEY A GO GO
AND
THE BLACK DOOR
ON TOUR
DAUX
TAPES

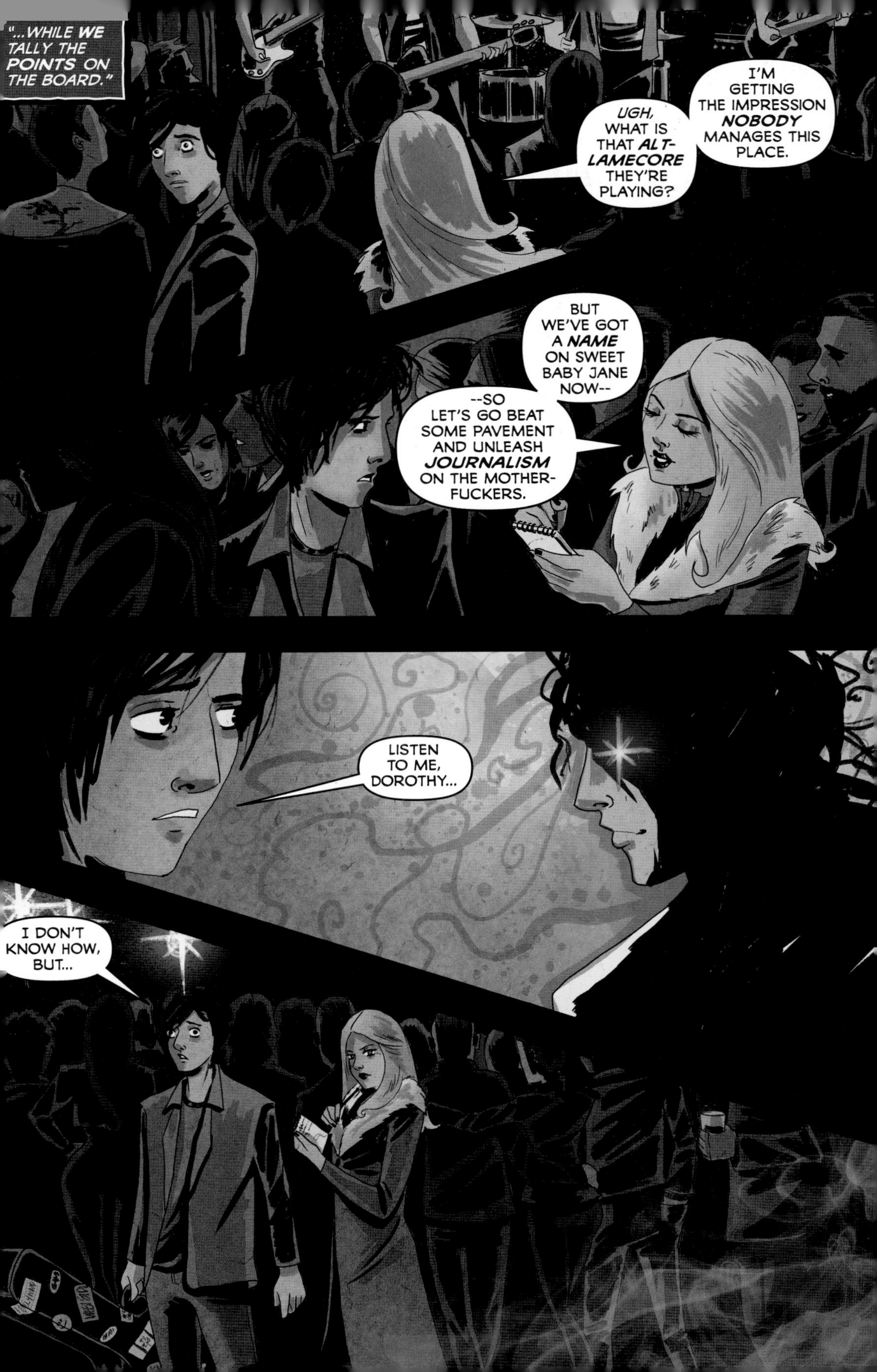
"...WHILE WE TALLY THE POINTS ON THE BOARD."
UGH, WHAT IS THAT ALT-LAMECORE THEY'RE PLAYING?
I'M GETTING THE IMPRESSION NOBODY MANAGES THIS PLACE.
BUT WE'VE GOT A NAME ON SWEET BABY JANE NOW--
--SO LET'S GO BEAT SOME PAVEMENT AND UNLEASH JOURNALISM ON THE MOTHER-FUCKERS.
LISTEN TO ME, DOROTHY...
I DON'T KNOW HOW, BUT...

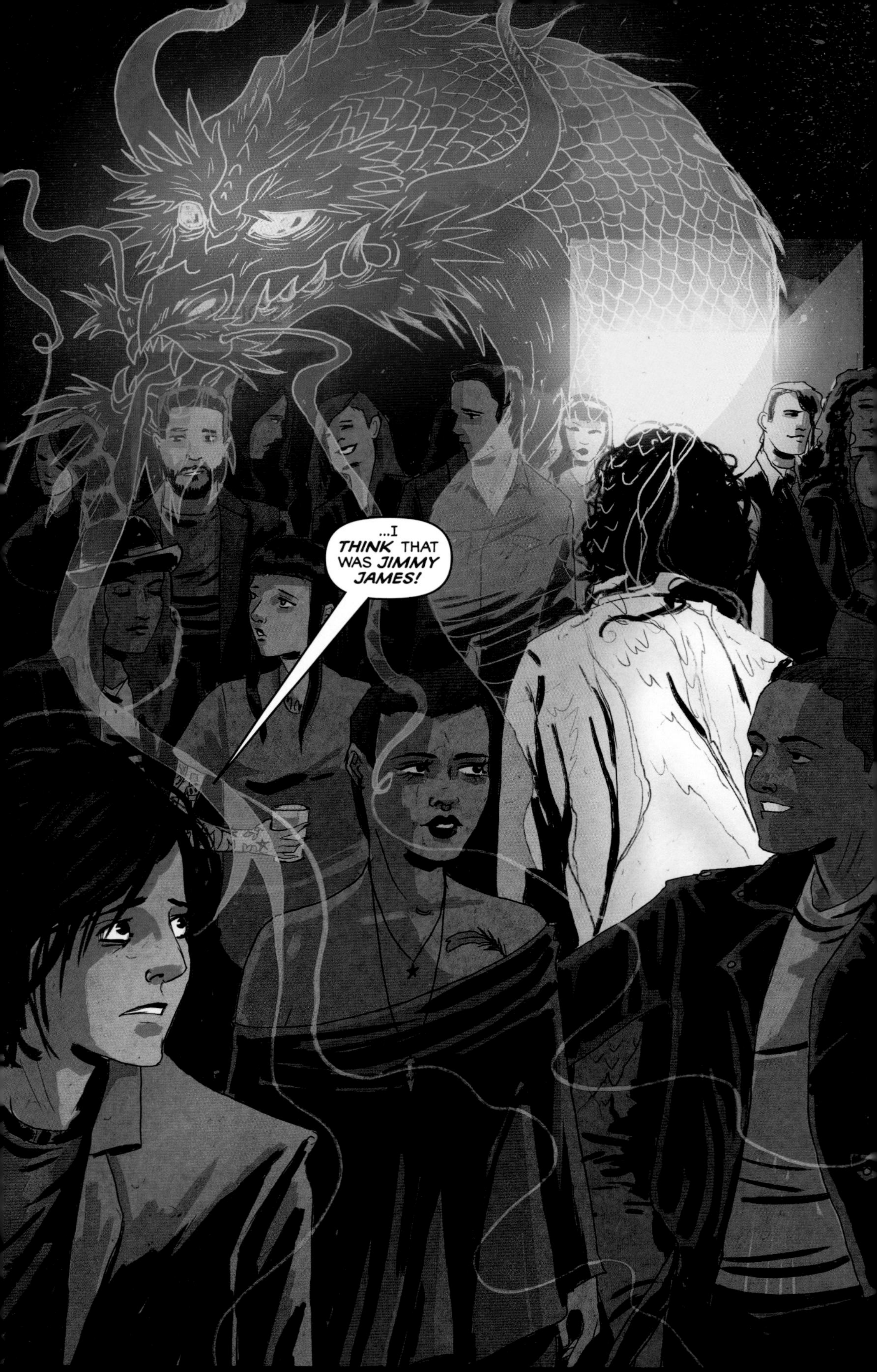
...I THINK THAT WAS JIMMY JAMES!

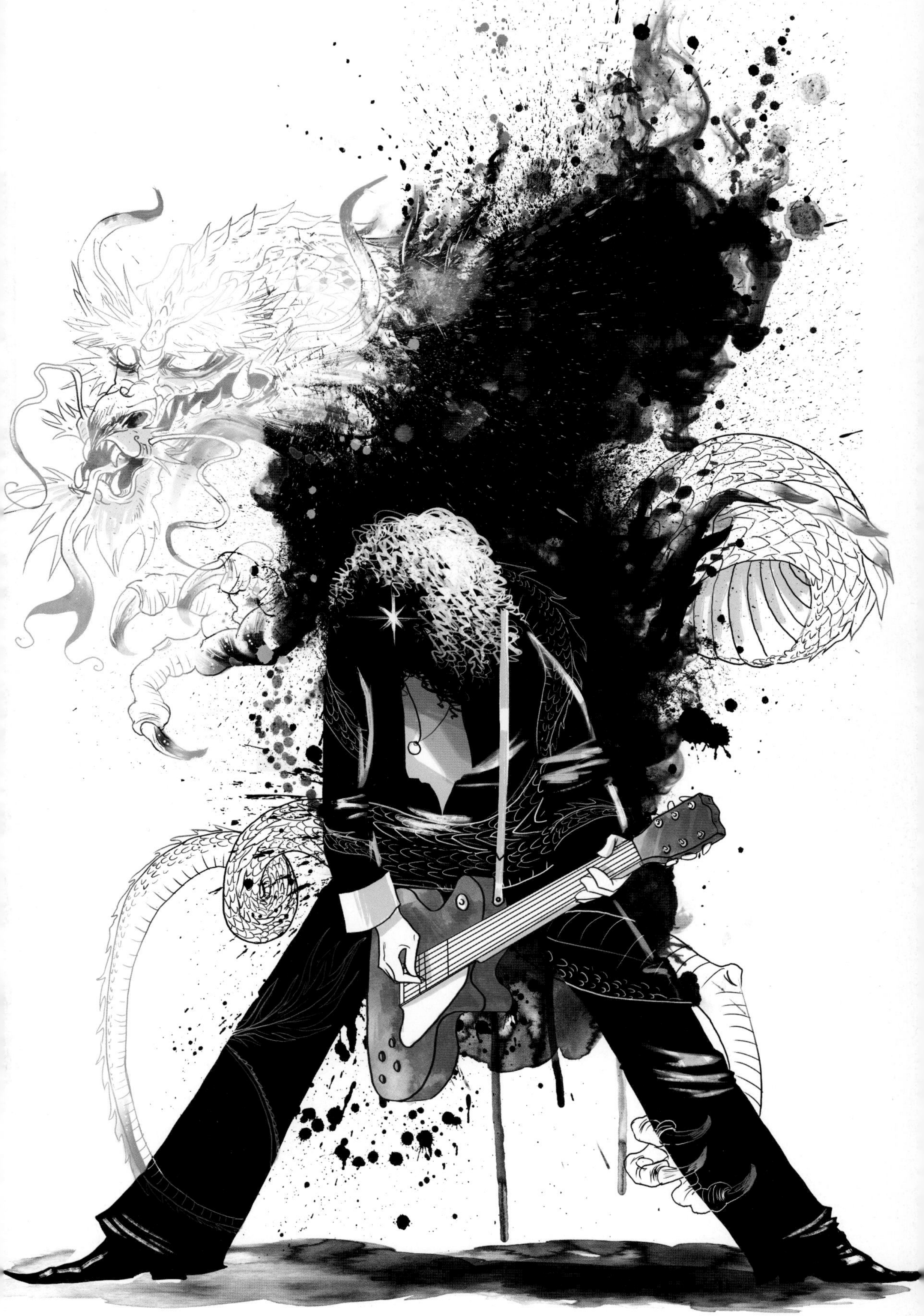

Jimmy James was once the greatest guitar player anybody could name. Together with Blue Rider, they changed music forever-- BUT WHAT HAPPENS AFTER THE MAGIC RUNS OUT?

ROCKSTARS

SIDE # 1 **FULL COLOR**		**Track 3**

NATIVITY IN
BLACKLIGHT

22

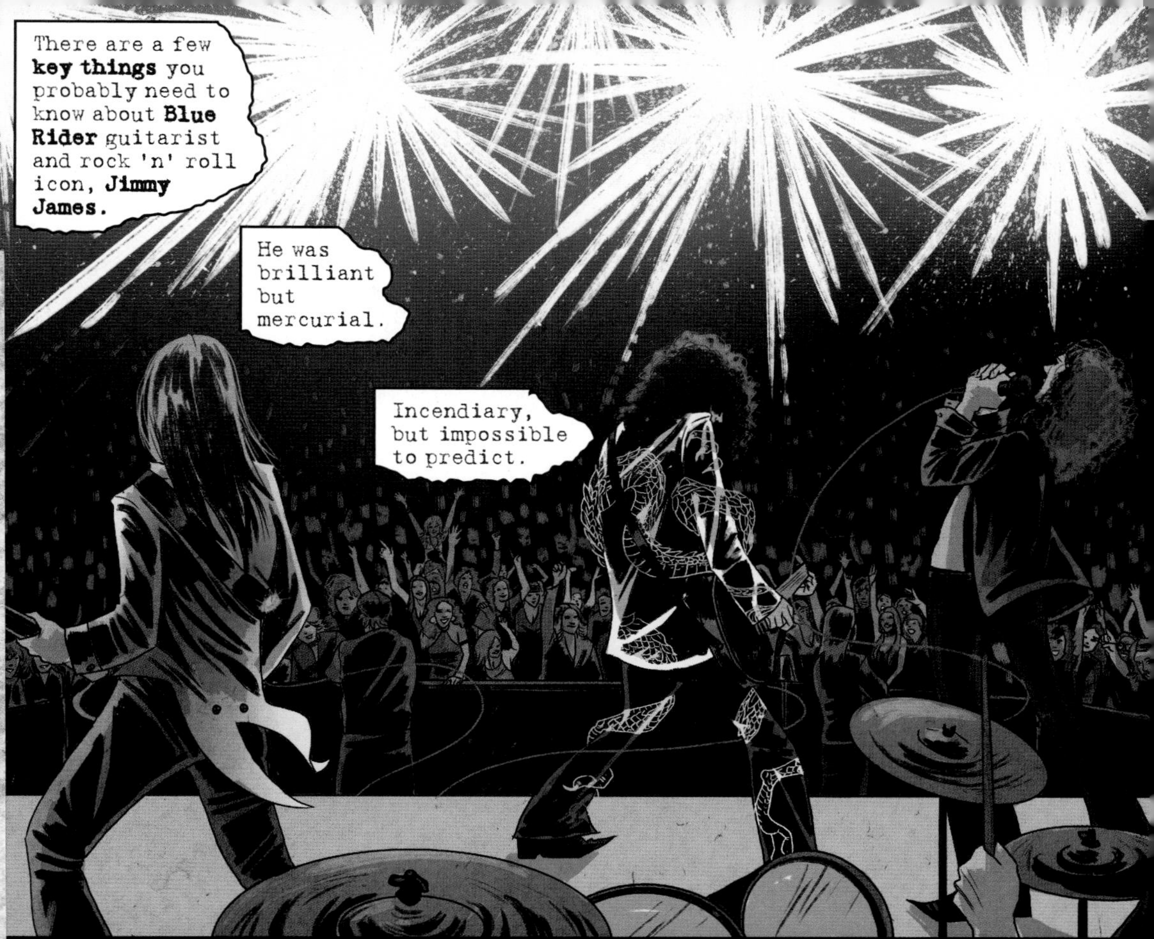
There are a few **key things** you probably need to know about **Blue Rider** guitarist and rock 'n' roll icon, **Jimmy James.**
He was brilliant but mercurial.
Incendiary, but impossible to predict.

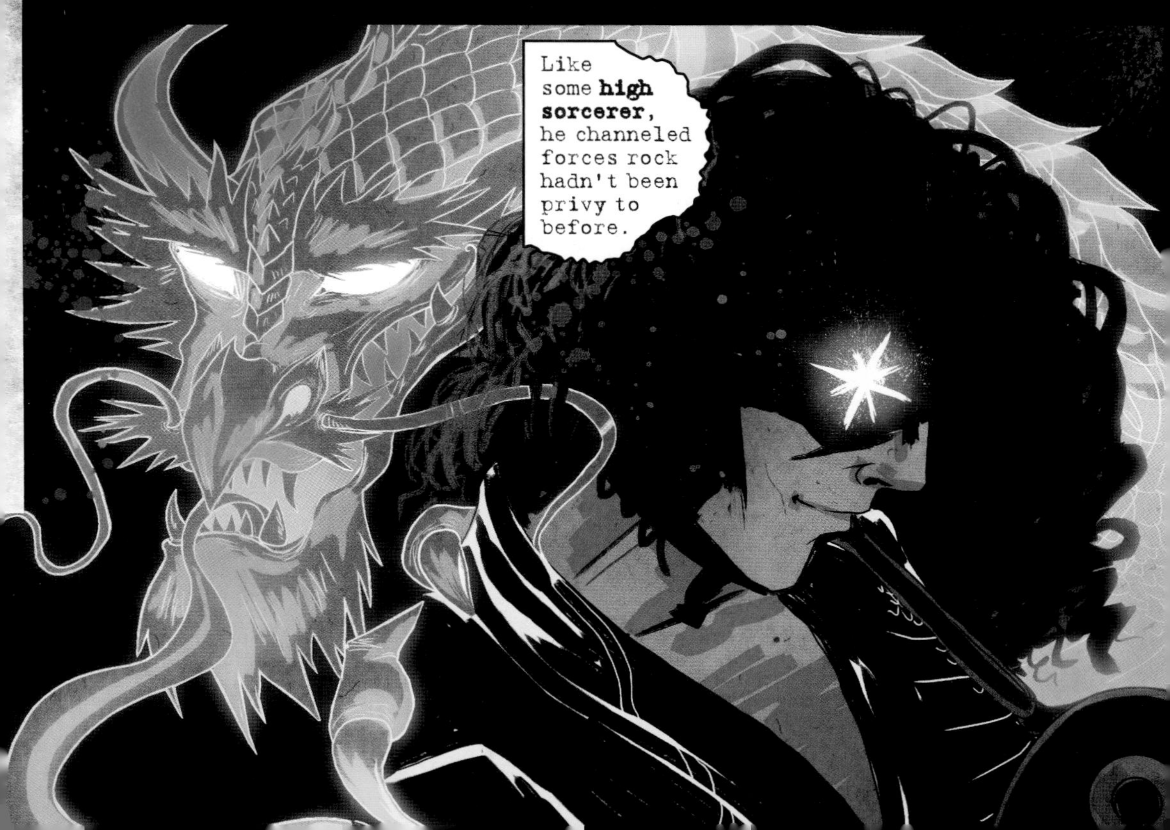
Like some **high sorcerer**, he channeled forces rock hadn't been privy to before.

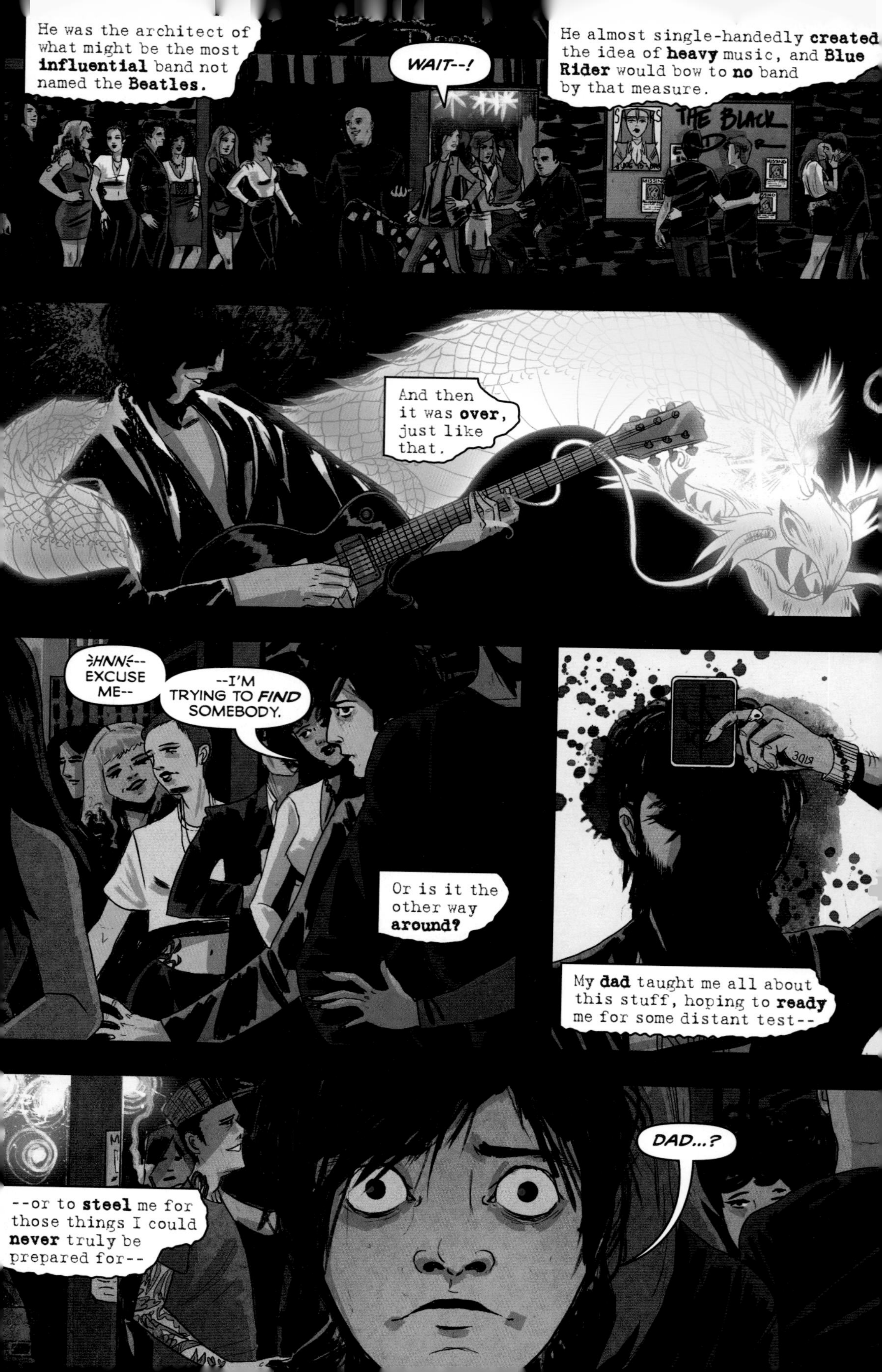
He was the architect of what might be the most influential band not named the Beatles.
WAIT--!
He almost single-handedly created the idea of heavy music, and Blue Rider would bow to no band by that measure.
THE BLACK
MISSING
And then it was over, just like that.
ƷHNNƐ-- EXCUSE ME--
--I'M TRYING TO FIND SOMEBODY.
Or is it the other way around?
My dad taught me all about this stuff, hoping to ready me for some distant test--
DAD...?
--or to steel me for those things I could never truly be prepared for--

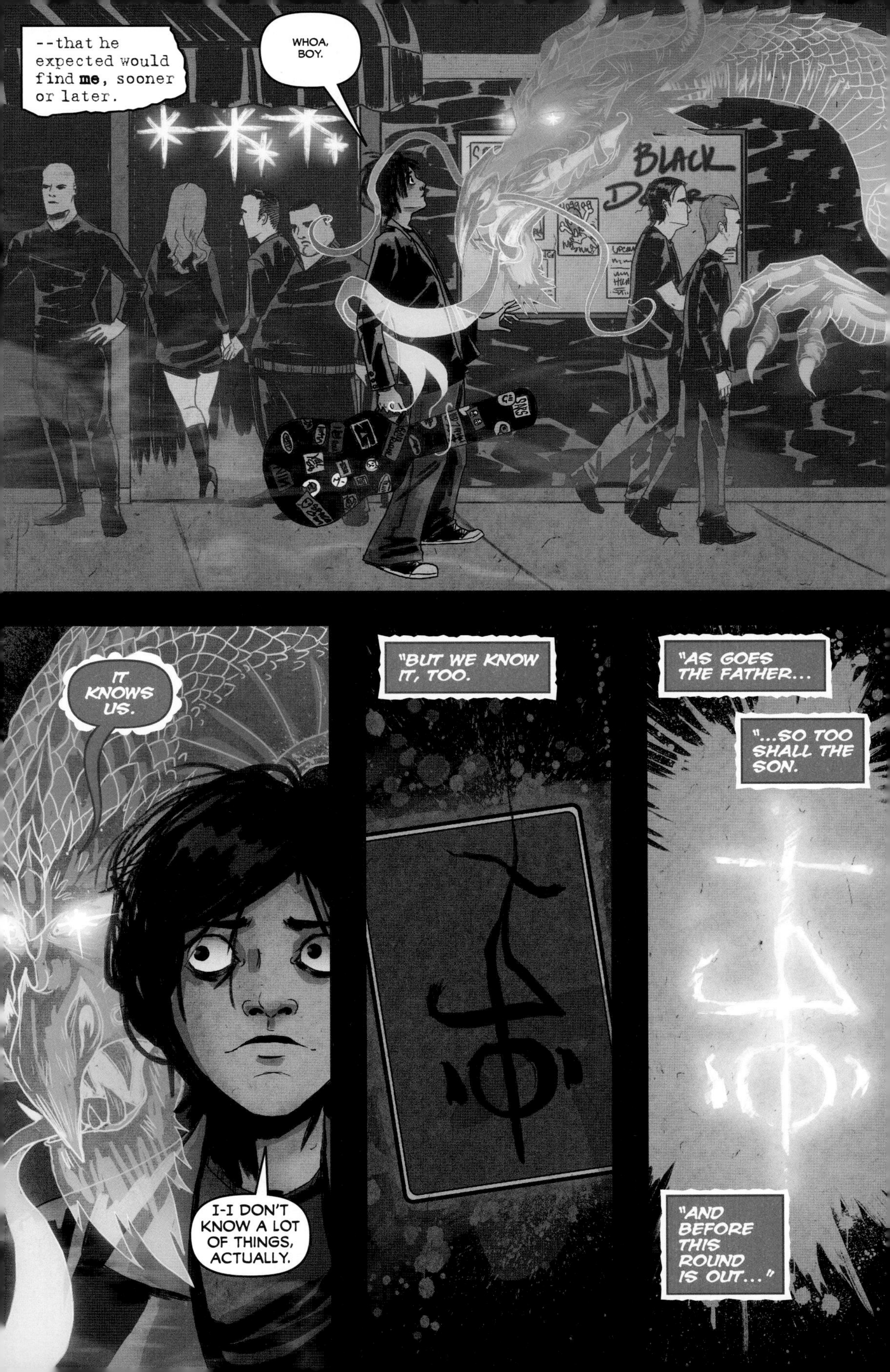
--that he expected would find **me**, sooner or later.
WHOA, BOY.
BLACK
IT KNOWS US.
I-I DON'T KNOW A LOT OF THINGS, ACTUALLY.
"BUT WE KNOW IT, TOO.
"AS GOES THE FATHER...
"...SO TOO SHALL THE SON.
"AND BEFORE THIS ROUND IS OUT..."

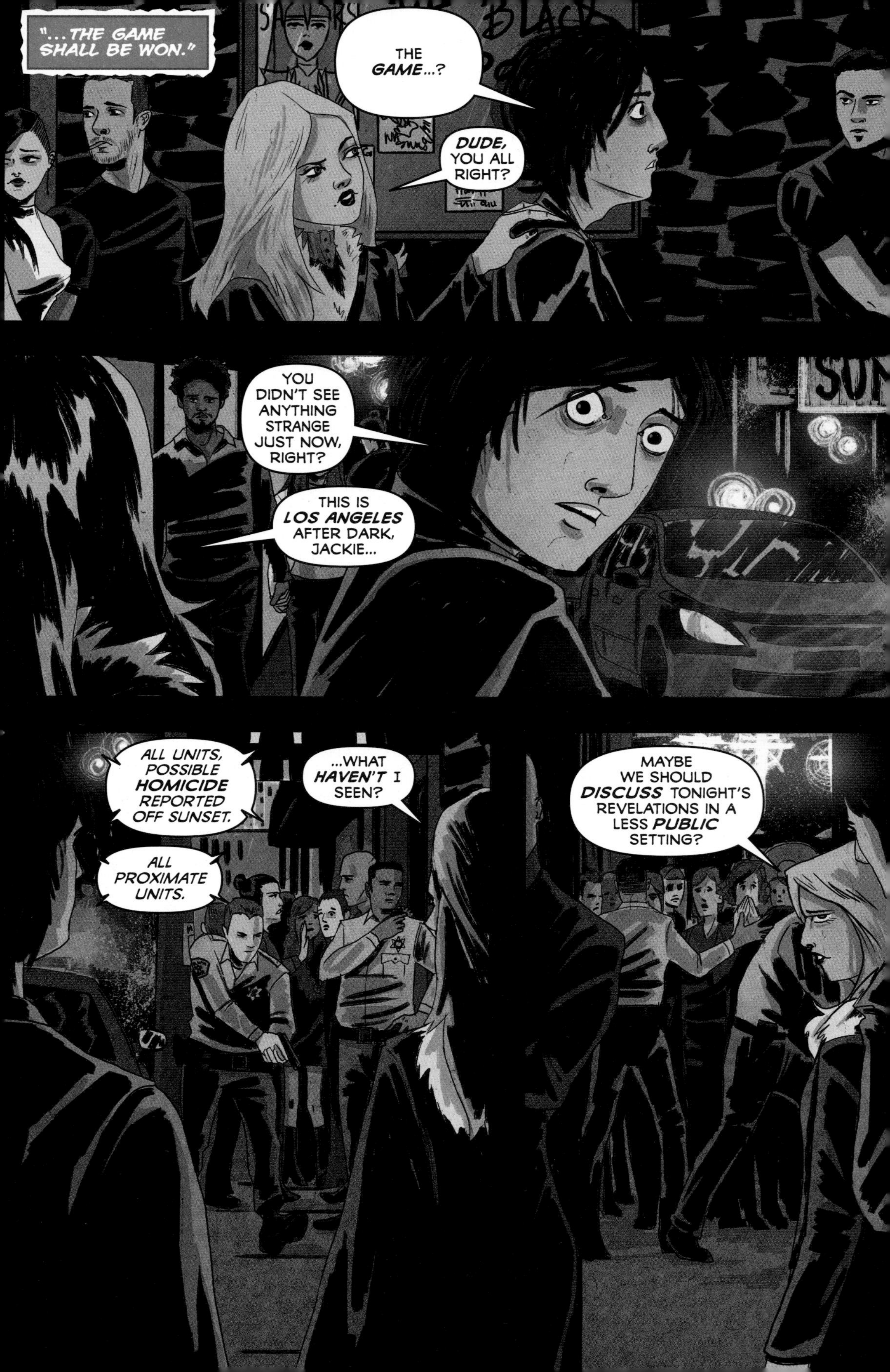
"...THE GAME SHALL BE WON."
THE GAME...?
DUDE, YOU ALL RIGHT?
YOU DIDN'T SEE ANYTHING STRANGE JUST NOW, RIGHT?
THIS IS LOS ANGELES AFTER DARK, JACKIE...
ALL UNITS, POSSIBLE HOMICIDE REPORTED OFF SUNSET.
ALL PROXIMATE UNITS.
...WHAT HAVEN'T I SEEN?
MAYBE WE SHOULD DISCUSS TONIGHT'S REVELATIONS IN A LESS PUBLIC SETTING?

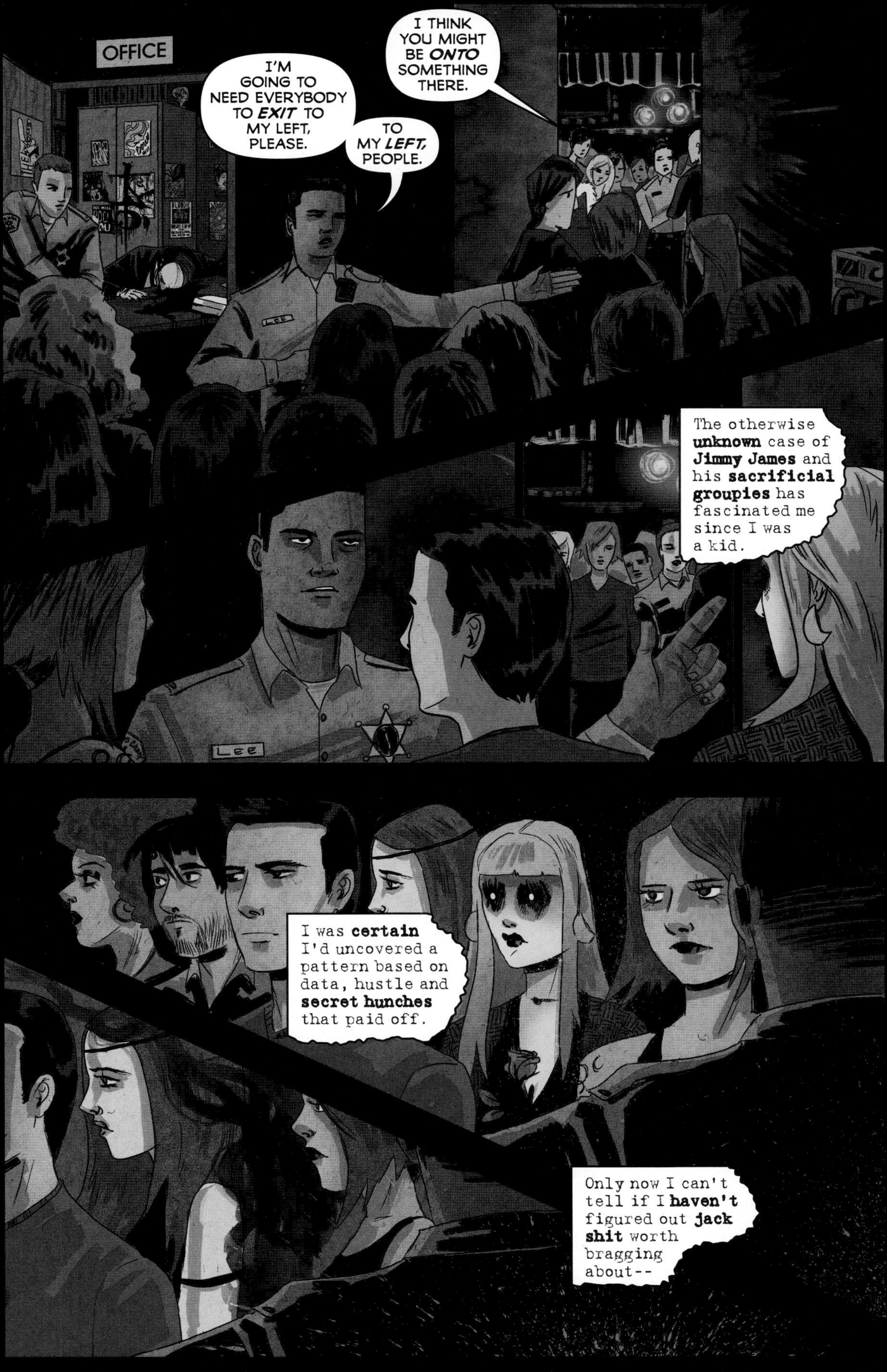
OFFICE
I'M GOING TO NEED EVERYBODY TO EXIT TO MY LEFT, PLEASE.
TO MY LEFT, PEOPLE.
I THINK YOU MIGHT BE ONTO SOMETHING THERE.
LEE
The otherwise unknown case of Jimmy James and his sacrificial groupies has fascinated me since I was a kid.
LEE
I was certain I'd uncovered a pattern based on data, hustle and secret hunches that paid off.
Only now I can't tell if I haven't figured out jack shit worth bragging about--

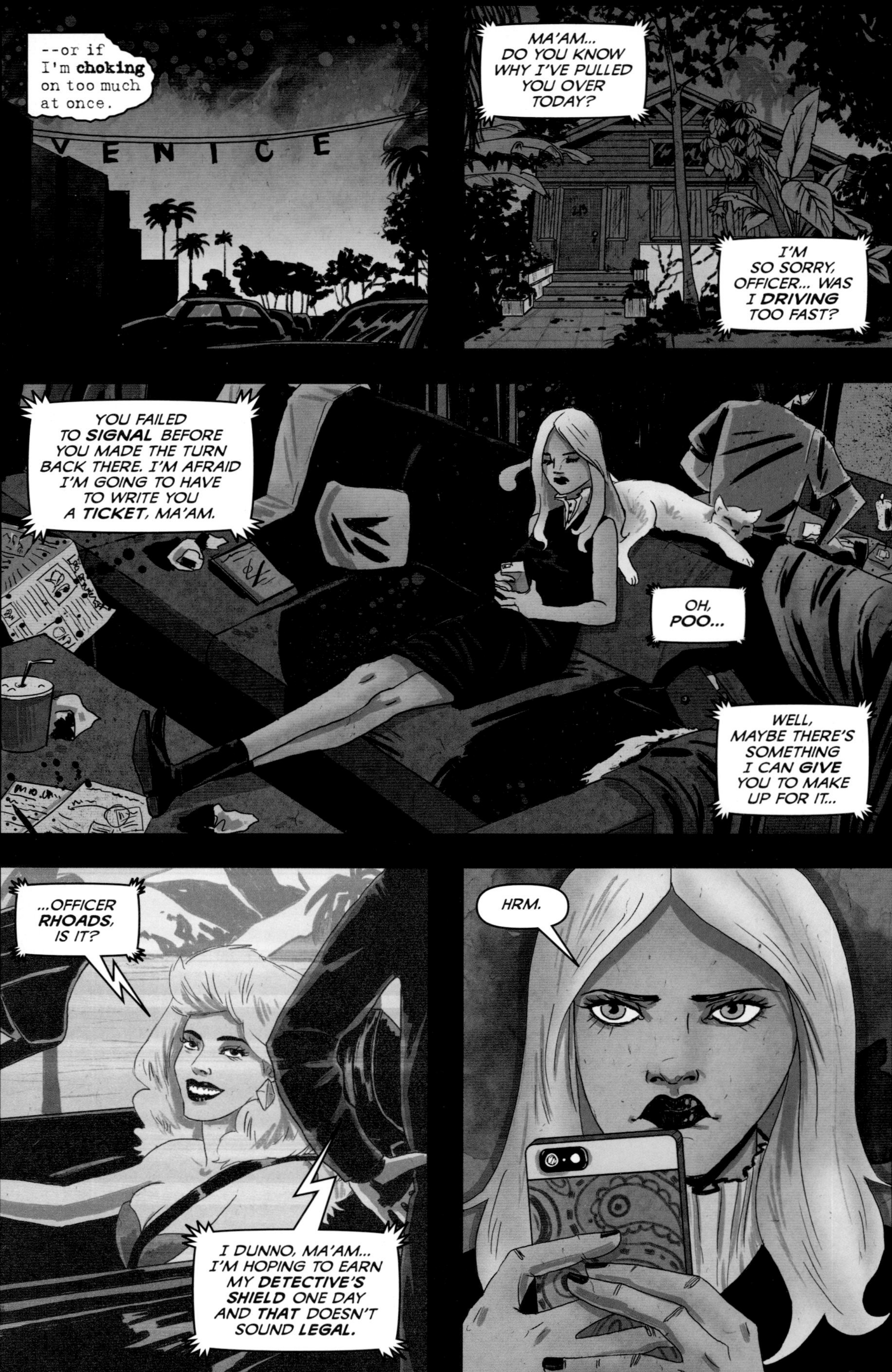
--or if I'm **choking** on too much at once.
VENICE
MA'AM... DO YOU KNOW WHY I'VE PULLED YOU OVER TODAY?
I'M SO SORRY, OFFICER... WAS I **DRIVING** TOO FAST?
YOU FAILED TO **SIGNAL** BEFORE YOU MADE THE TURN BACK THERE. I'M AFRAID I'M GOING TO HAVE TO WRITE YOU A **TICKET**, MA'AM.
OH, **POO**...
WELL, MAYBE THERE'S SOMETHING I CAN **GIVE** YOU TO MAKE UP FOR IT...
...OFFICER **RHOADS**, IS IT?
I DUNNO, MA'AM... I'M HOPING TO EARN MY **DETECTIVE'S SHIELD** ONE DAY AND **THAT** DOESN'T SOUND **LEGAL**.
HRM.

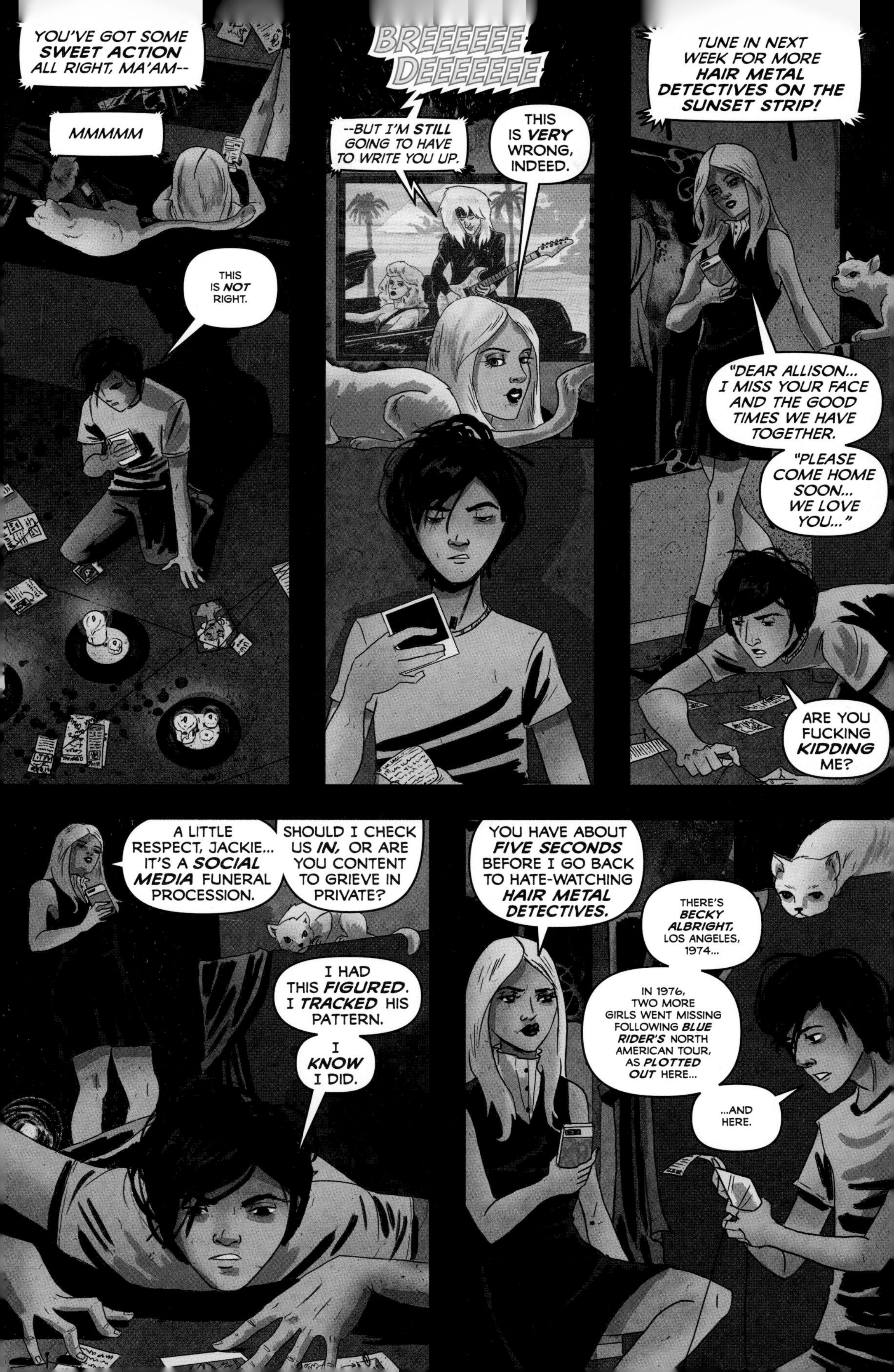
YOU'VE GOT SOME SWEET ACTION ALL RIGHT, MA'AM--
MMMMM
THIS IS NOT RIGHT.
BREEEEEE-DEEEEEEE
--BUT I'M STILL GOING TO HAVE TO WRITE YOU UP.
THIS IS VERY WRONG, INDEED.
TUNE IN NEXT WEEK FOR MORE HAIR METAL DETECTIVES ON THE SUNSET STRIP!
"DEAR ALLISON... I MISS YOUR FACE AND THE GOOD TIMES WE HAVE TOGETHER.
"PLEASE COME HOME SOON... WE LOVE YOU..."
ARE YOU FUCKING KIDDING ME?
A LITTLE RESPECT, JACKIE... IT'S A SOCIAL MEDIA FUNERAL PROCESSION.
SHOULD I CHECK US IN, OR ARE YOU CONTENT TO GRIEVE IN PRIVATE?
I HAD THIS FIGURED. I TRACKED HIS PATTERN.
I KNOW I DID.
YOU HAVE ABOUT FIVE SECONDS BEFORE I GO BACK TO HATE-WATCHING HAIR METAL DETECTIVES.
THERE'S BECKY ALBRIGHT, LOS ANGELES, 1974...
IN 1976, TWO MORE GIRLS WENT MISSING FOLLOWING BLUE RIDER'S NORTH AMERICAN TOUR, AS PLOTTED OUT HERE...
...AND HERE.

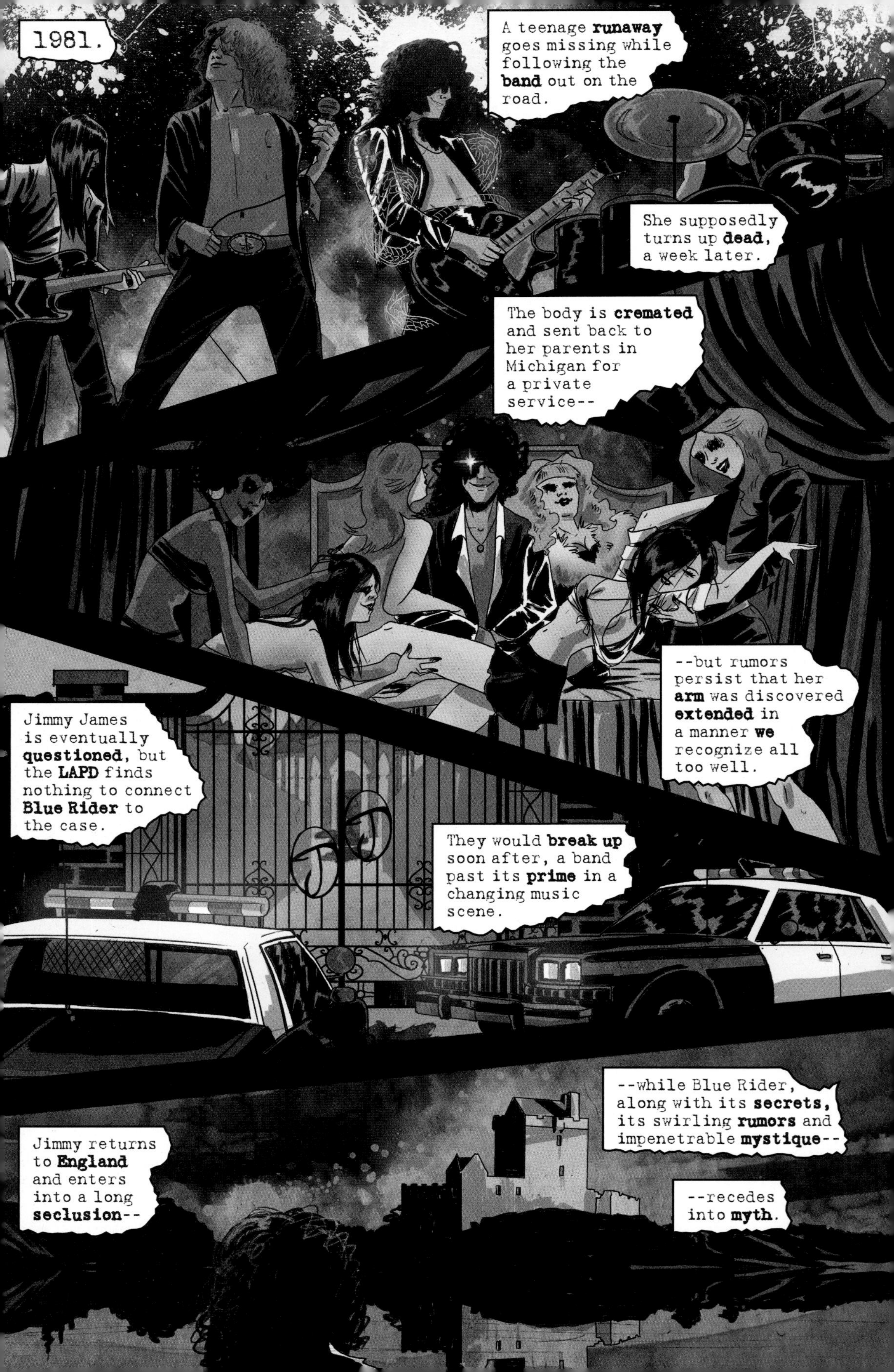
1981.
A teenage runaway goes missing while following the band out on the road.
She supposedly turns up dead, a week later.
The body is cremated and sent back to her parents in Michigan for a private service--
--but rumors persist that her arm was discovered extended in a manner we recognize all too well.
Jimmy James is eventually questioned, but the LAPD finds nothing to connect Blue Rider to the case.
They would break up soon after, a band past its prime in a changing music scene.
--while Blue Rider, along with its secrets, its swirling rumors and impenetrable mystique--
Jimmy returns to England and enters into a long seclusion--
--recedes into myth.

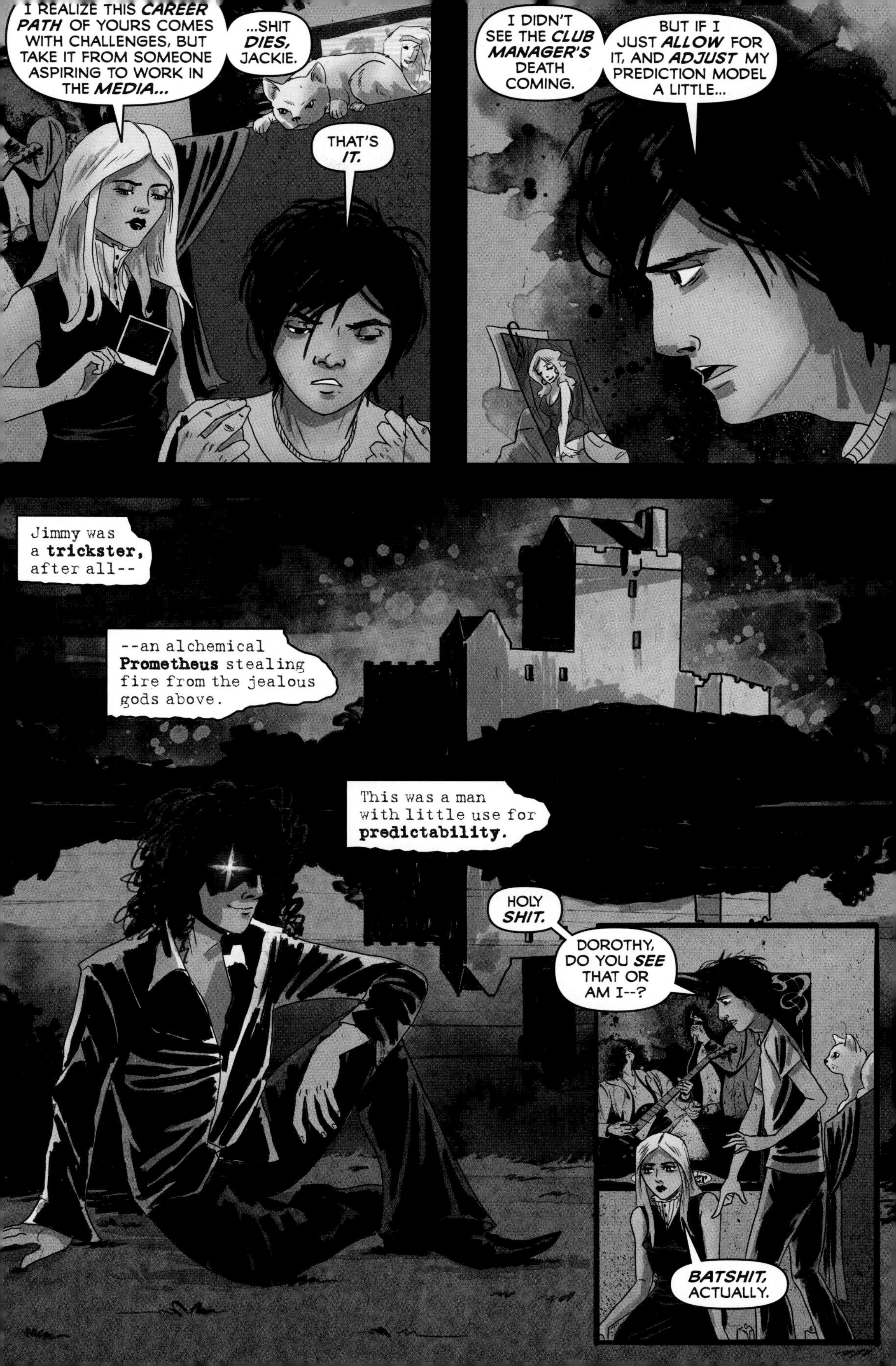

I REALIZE THIS CAREER PATH OF YOURS COMES WITH CHALLENGES, BUT TAKE IT FROM SOMEONE ASPIRING TO WORK IN THE MEDIA...
...SHIT DIES, JACKIE.
THAT'S IT.
I DIDN'T SEE THE CLUB MANAGER'S DEATH COMING.
BUT IF I JUST ALLOW FOR IT, AND ADJUST MY PREDICTION MODEL A LITTLE...
Jimmy was a trickster, after all--
--an alchemical Prometheus stealing fire from the jealous gods above.
This was a man with little use for predictability.
HOLY SHIT.
DOROTHY, DO YOU SEE THAT OR AM I--?
BATSHIT, ACTUALLY.

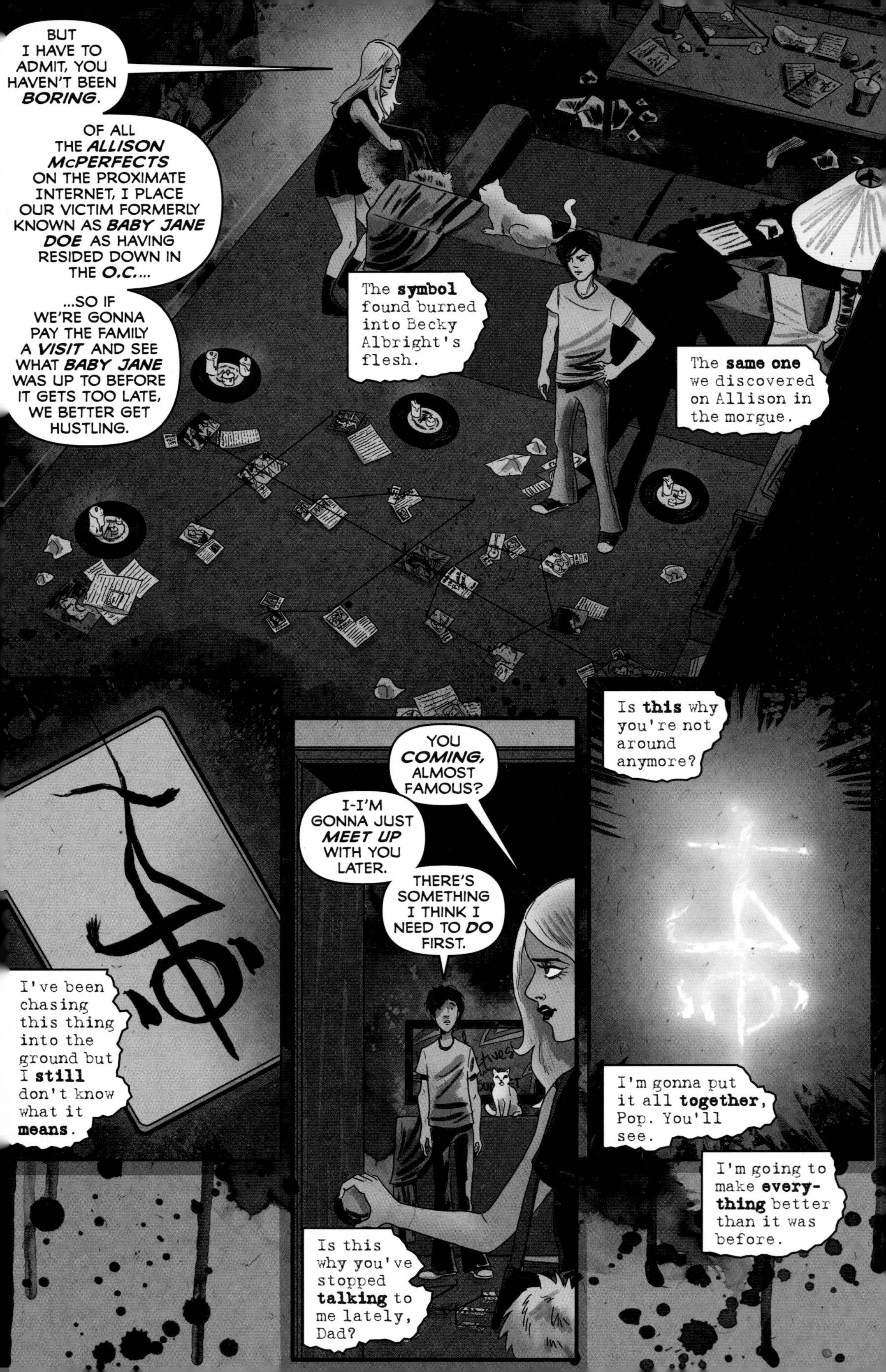

BUT I HAVE TO ADMIT, YOU HAVEN'T BEEN BORING.
OF ALL THE ALLISON McPERFECTS ON THE PROXIMATE INTERNET, I PLACE OUR VICTIM FORMERLY KNOWN AS BABY JANE DOE AS HAVING RESIDED DOWN IN THE O.C....
...SO IF WE'RE GONNA PAY THE FAMILY A VISIT AND SEE WHAT BABY JANE WAS UP TO BEFORE IT GETS TOO LATE, WE BETTER GET HUSTLING.
The symbol found burned into Becky Albright's flesh.
The same one we discovered on Allison in the morgue.
I've been chasing this thing into the ground but I still don't know what it means.
YOU COMING, ALMOST FAMOUS?
I-I'M GONNA JUST MEET UP WITH YOU LATER.
THERE'S SOMETHING I THINK I NEED TO DO FIRST.
Is this why you've stopped talking to me lately, Dad?
Is this why you're not around anymore?
I'm gonna put it all together, Pop. You'll see.
I'm going to make every-thing better than it was before.

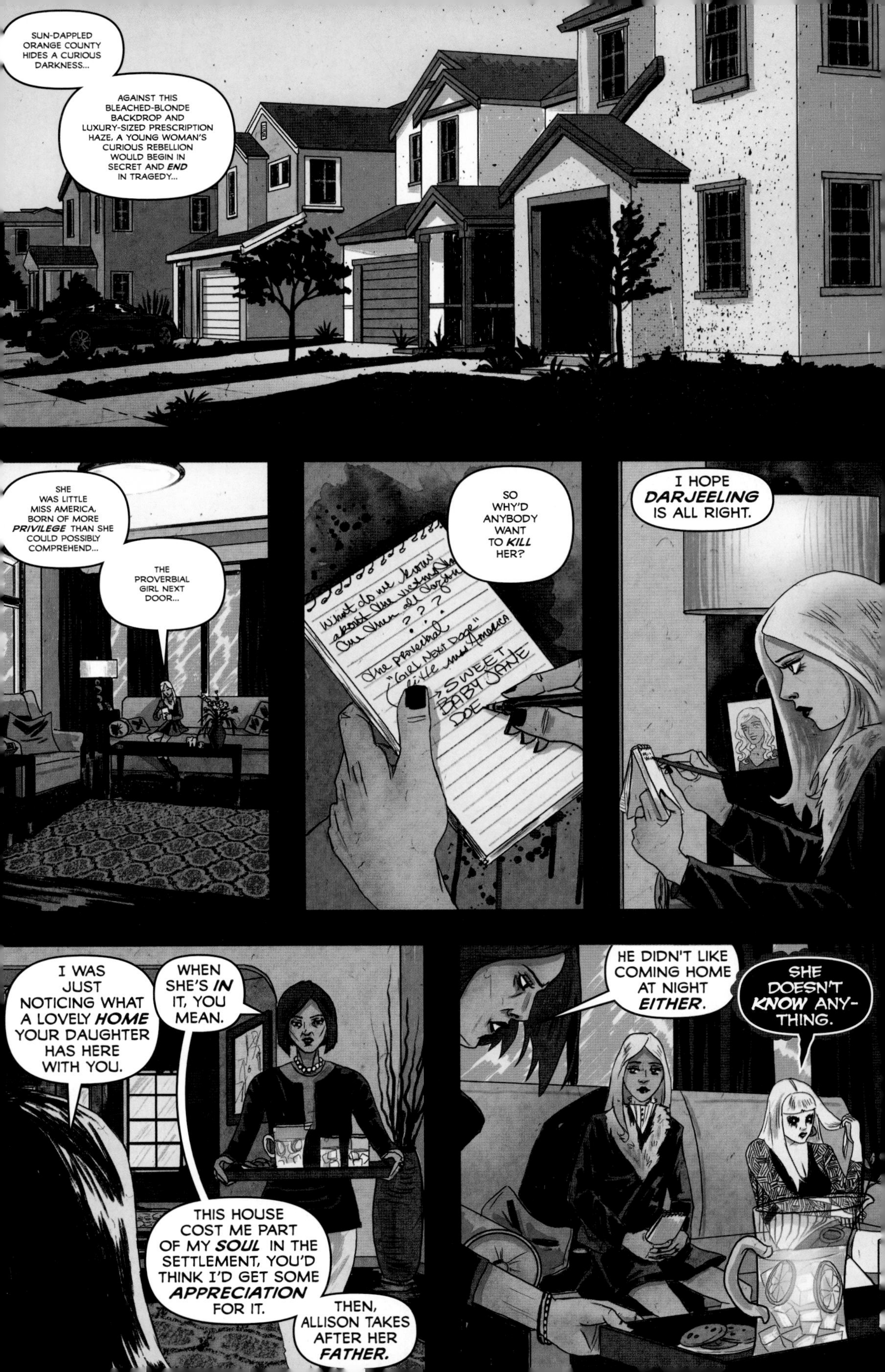
SUN-DAPPLED ORANGE COUNTY HIDES A CURIOUS DARKNESS...
AGAINST THIS BLEACHED-BLONDE BACKDROP AND LUXURY-SIZED PRESCRIPTION HAZE, A YOUNG WOMAN'S CURIOUS REBELLION WOULD BEGIN IN SECRET AND *END* IN TRAGEDY...
SHE WAS LITTLE MISS AMERICA, BORN OF MORE *PRIVILEGE* THAN SHE COULD POSSIBLY COMPREHEND...
THE PROVERBIAL GIRL NEXT DOOR...
SO WHY'D ANYBODY WANT TO *KILL* HER?
SWEET BABY JANE DOE
I HOPE *DARJEELING* IS ALL RIGHT.
I WAS JUST NOTICING WHAT A LOVELY *HOME* YOUR DAUGHTER HAS HERE WITH YOU.
WHEN SHE'S *IN* IT, YOU MEAN.
THIS HOUSE COST ME PART OF MY *SOUL* IN THE SETTLEMENT, YOU'D THINK I'D GET SOME *APPRECIATION* FOR IT.
THEN, ALLISON TAKES AFTER HER *FATHER.*
HE DIDN'T LIKE COMING HOME AT NIGHT *EITHER*.
SHE DOESN'T *KNOW* ANY-THING.

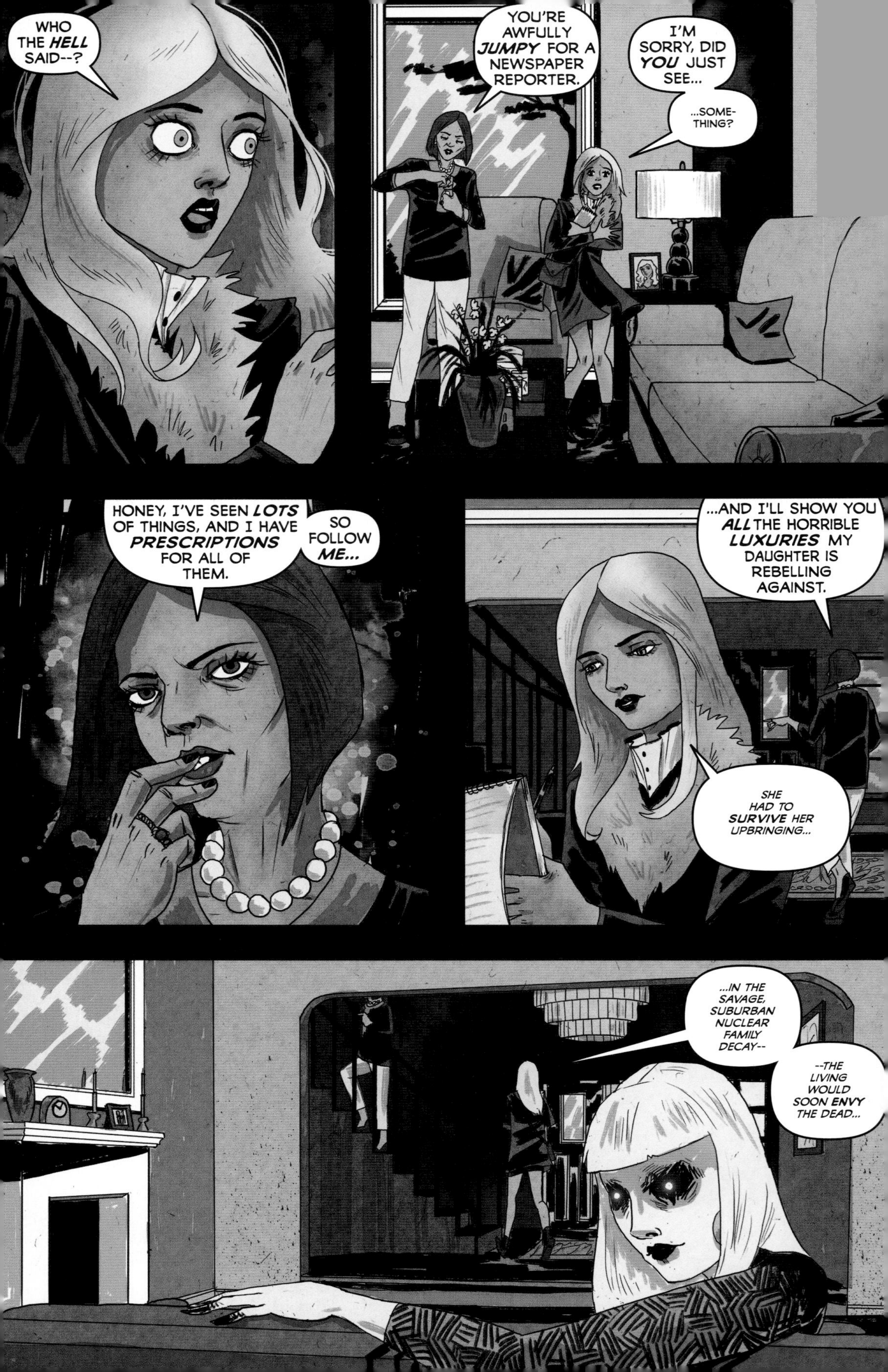
WHO THE HELL SAID--?
YOU'RE AWFULLY JUMPY FOR A NEWSPAPER REPORTER.
I'M SORRY, DID YOU JUST SEE...
...SOME-THING?
HONEY, I'VE SEEN LOTS OF THINGS, AND I HAVE PRESCRIPTIONS FOR ALL OF THEM.
SO FOLLOW ME...
...AND I'LL SHOW YOU ALL THE HORRIBLE LUXURIES MY DAUGHTER IS REBELLING AGAINST.
SHE HAD TO SURVIVE HER UPBRINGING...
...IN THE SAVAGE, SUBURBAN NUCLEAR FAMILY DECAY--
--THE LIVING WOULD SOON ENVY THE DEAD...

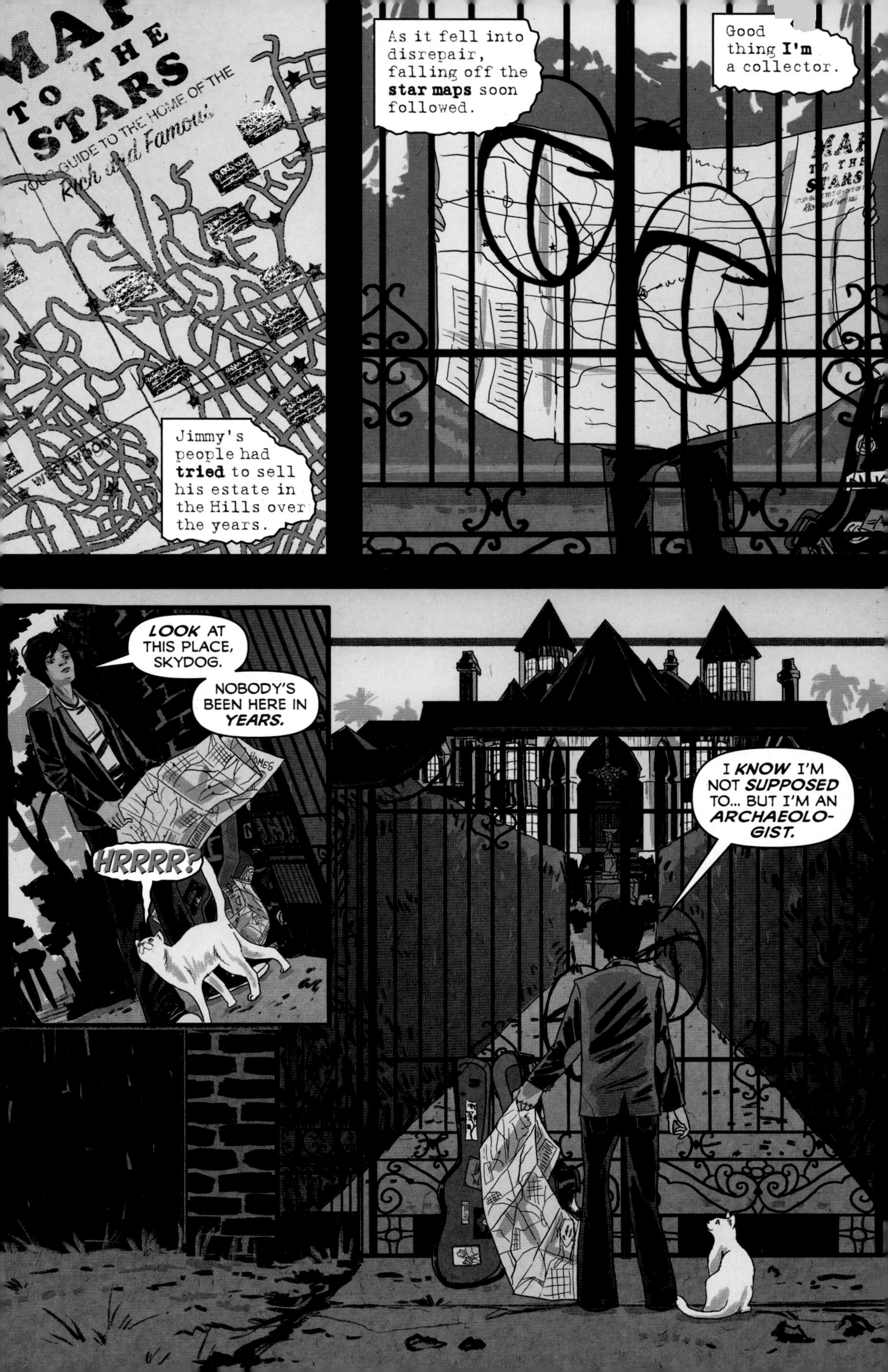
TO THE STARS
YOUR GUIDE TO THE HOME OF THE Rich and Famous
WESTWOOD
Jimmy's people had **tried** to sell his estate in the Hills over the years.
As it fell into disrepair, falling off the **star maps** soon followed.
Good thing **I'm** a collector.
LOOK AT THIS PLACE, SKYDOG.
NOBODY'S BEEN HERE IN *YEARS.*
HOMES
HRRRR?
I *KNOW* I'M NOT *SUPPOSED* TO... BUT I'M AN *ARCHAEOLO-GIST.*

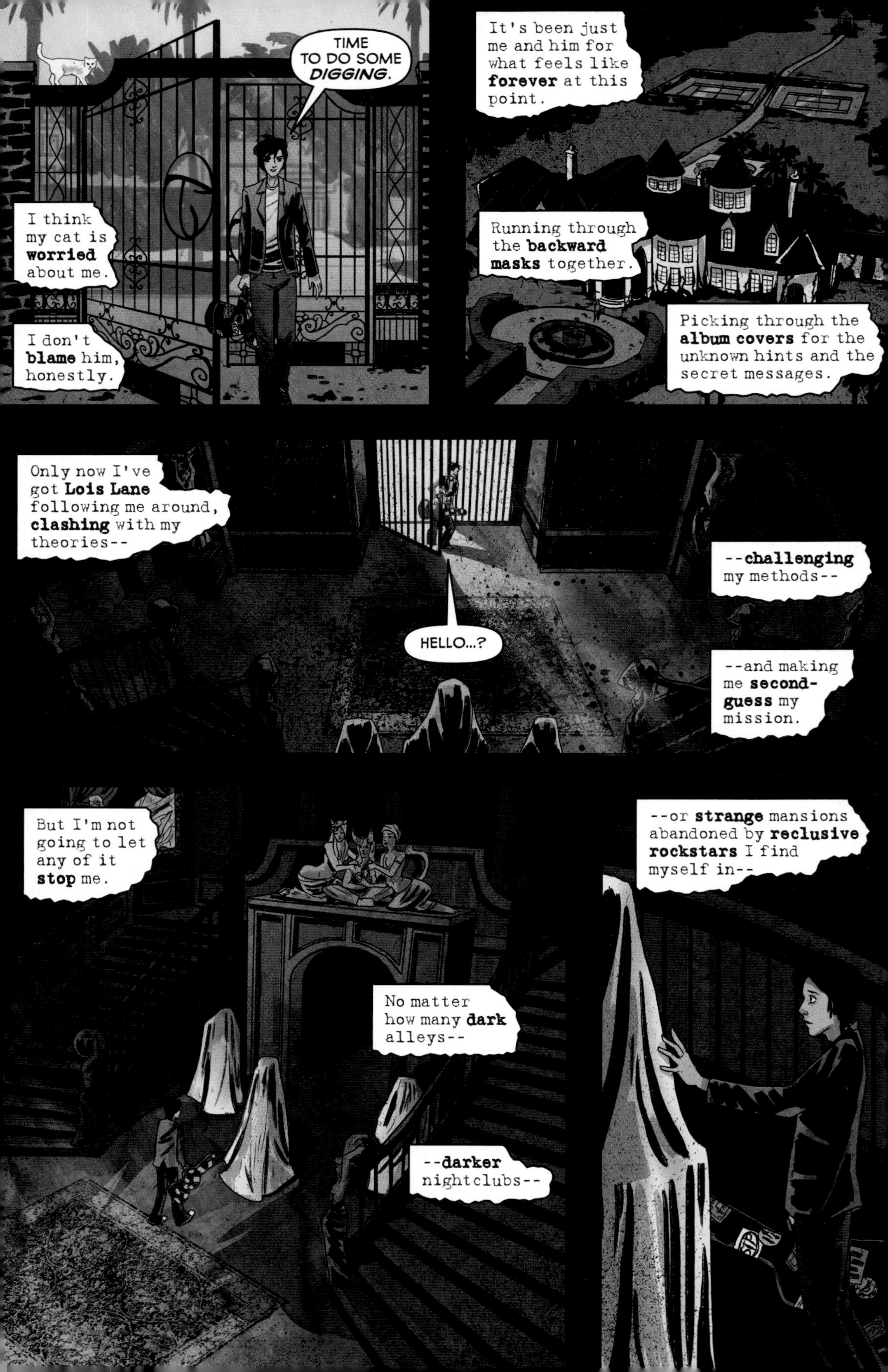
TIME TO DO SOME DIGGING.
I think my cat is worried about me.
I don't blame him, honestly.
It's been just me and him for what feels like forever at this point.
Running through the backward masks together.
Picking through the album covers for the unknown hints and the secret messages.
Only now I've got Lois Lane following me around, clashing with my theories--
--challenging my methods--
HELLO...?
--and making me second-guess my mission.
But I'm not going to let any of it stop me.
No matter how many dark alleys--
--darker nightclubs--
--or strange mansions abandoned by reclusive rockstars I find myself in--

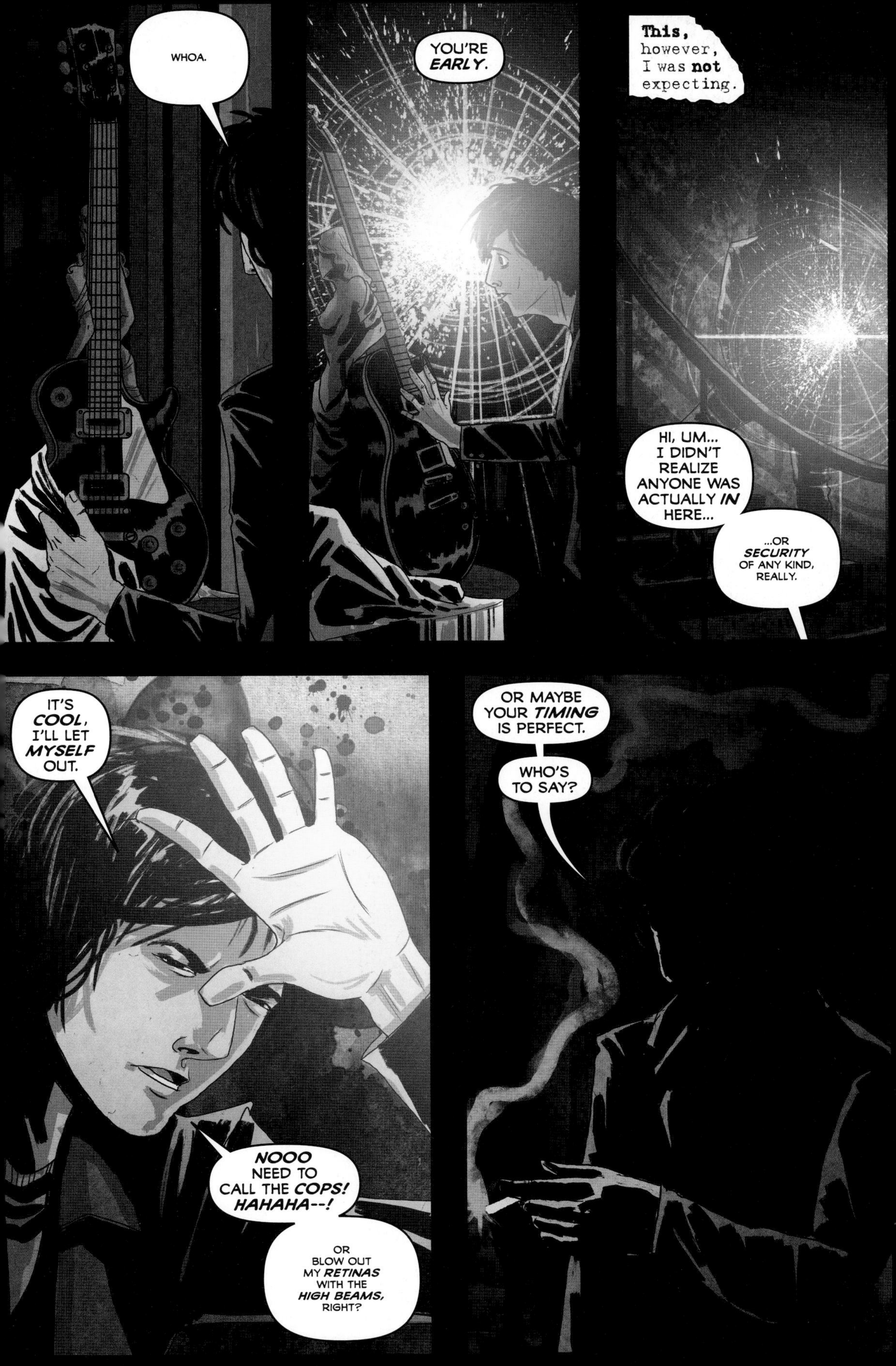
WHOA.
YOU'RE *EARLY*.
This, however, I was **not** expecting.
HI, UM... I DIDN'T REALIZE ANYONE WAS ACTUALLY *IN* HERE...
...OR *SECURITY* OF ANY KIND, REALLY.
IT'S *COOL*, I'LL LET *MYSELF* OUT.
NOOO NEED TO CALL THE *COPS! HAHAHA--!*
OR BLOW OUT MY *RETINAS* WITH THE *HIGH BEAMS,* RIGHT?
OR MAYBE YOUR *TIMING* IS PERFECT.
WHO'S TO SAY?

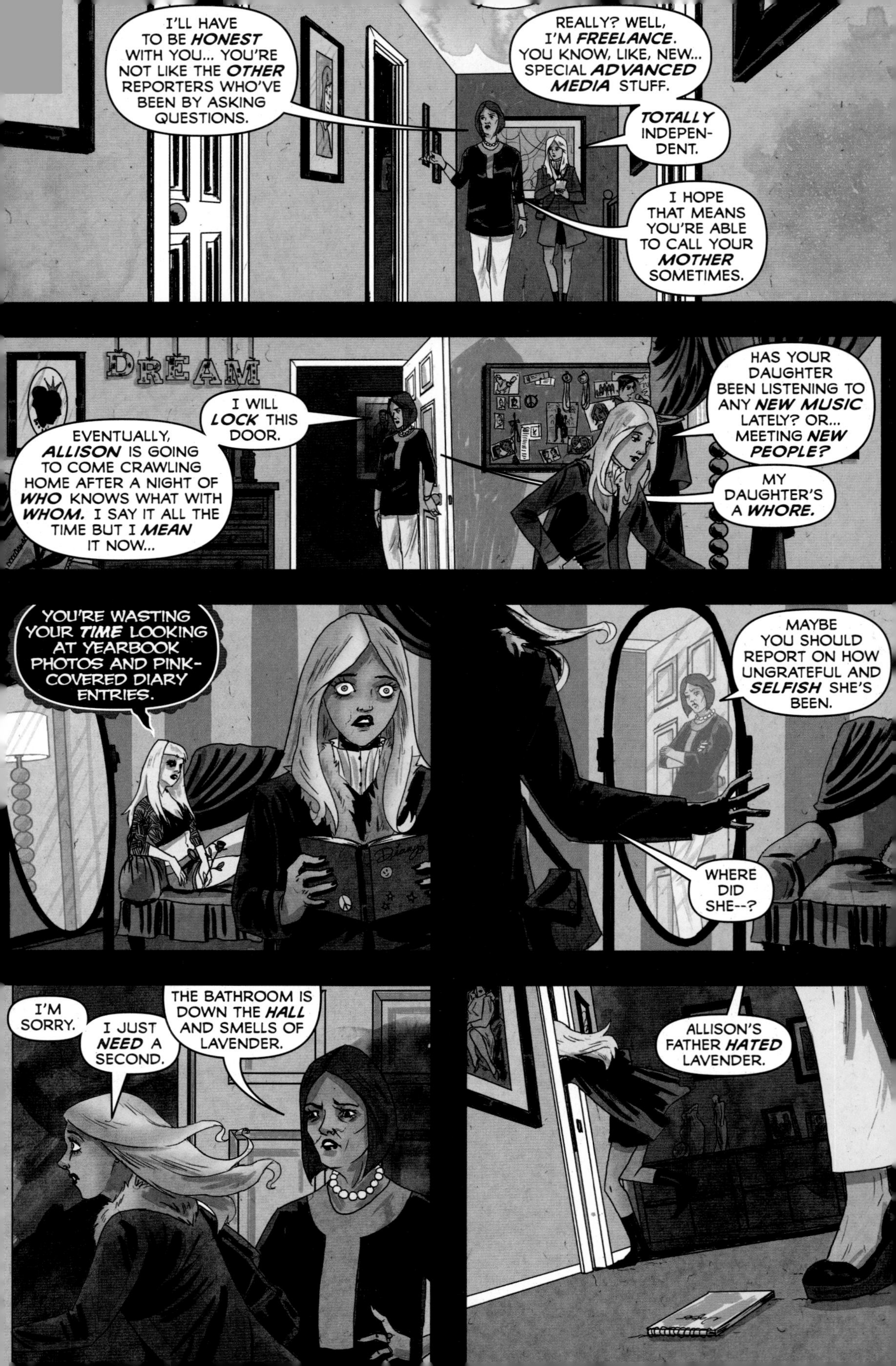
I'LL HAVE TO BE HONEST WITH YOU... YOU'RE NOT LIKE THE OTHER REPORTERS WHO'VE BEEN BY ASKING QUESTIONS.
REALLY? WELL, I'M FREELANCE. YOU KNOW, LIKE, NEW... SPECIAL ADVANCED MEDIA STUFF.
TOTALLY INDEPEN-DENT.
I HOPE THAT MEANS YOU'RE ABLE TO CALL YOUR MOTHER SOMETIMES.
DREAM
HAS YOUR DAUGHTER BEEN LISTENING TO ANY NEW MUSIC LATELY? OR... MEETING NEW PEOPLE?
MY DAUGHTER'S A WHORE.
EVENTUALLY, ALLISON IS GOING TO COME CRAWLING HOME AFTER A NIGHT OF WHO KNOWS WHAT WITH WHOM. I SAY IT ALL THE TIME BUT I MEAN IT NOW...
I WILL LOCK THIS DOOR.
YOU'RE WASTING YOUR TIME LOOKING AT YEARBOOK PHOTOS AND PINK-COVERED DIARY ENTRIES.
MAYBE YOU SHOULD REPORT ON HOW UNGRATEFUL AND SELFISH SHE'S BEEN.
WHERE DID SHE--?
I'M SORRY.
I JUST NEED A SECOND.
THE BATHROOM IS DOWN THE HALL AND SMELLS OF LAVENDER.
ALLISON'S FATHER HATED LAVENDER.

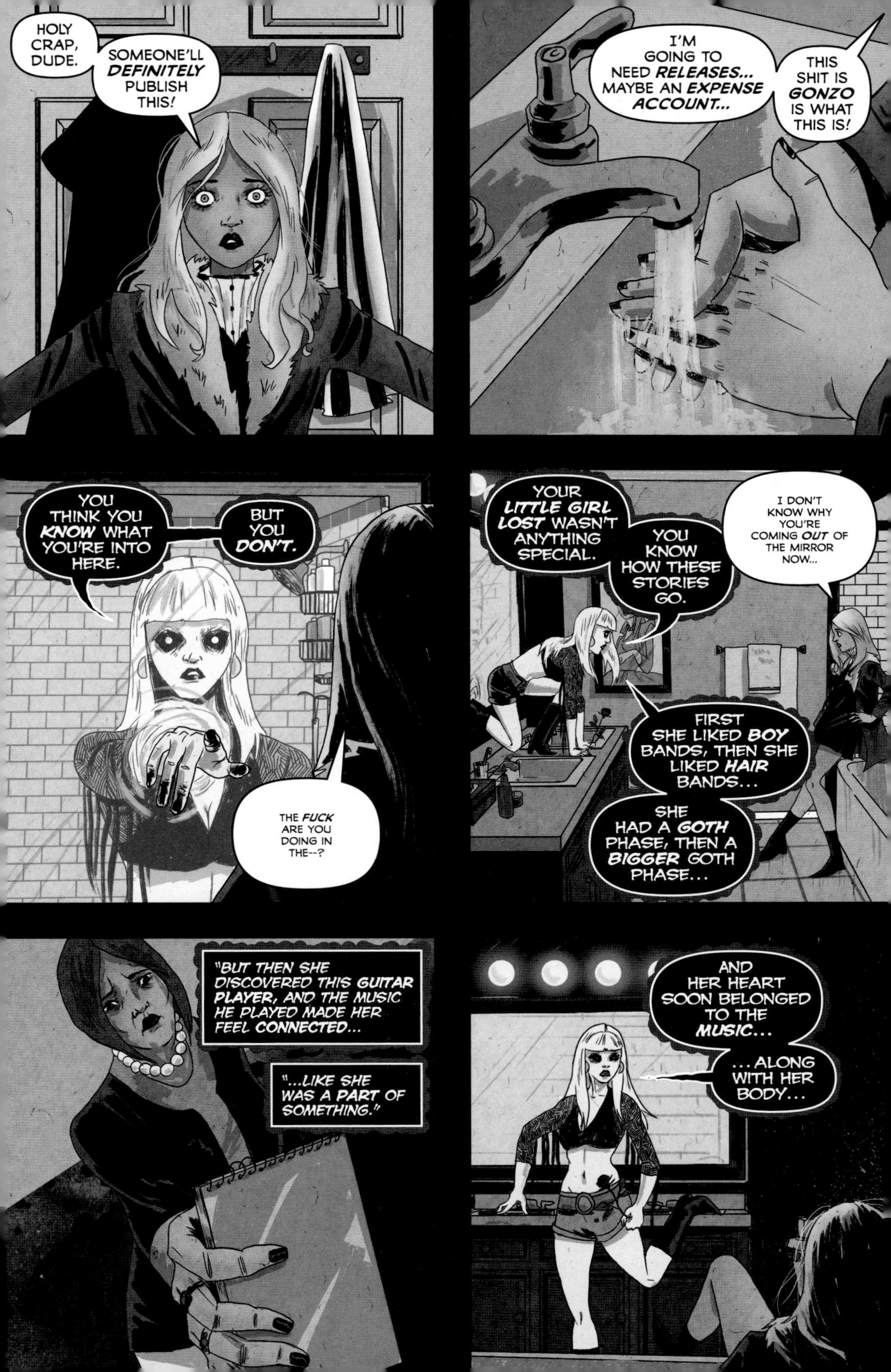

HOLY CRAP, DUDE.
SOMEONE'LL DEFINITELY PUBLISH THIS!
I'M GOING TO NEED RELEASES... MAYBE AN EXPENSE ACCOUNT...
THIS SHIT IS GONZO IS WHAT THIS IS!
YOU THINK YOU KNOW WHAT YOU'RE INTO HERE.
BUT YOU DON'T.
THE FUCK ARE YOU DOING IN THE--?
YOUR LITTLE GIRL LOST WASN'T ANYTHING SPECIAL.
YOU KNOW HOW THESE STORIES GO.
I DON'T KNOW WHY YOU'RE COMING OUT OF THE MIRROR NOW...
FIRST SHE LIKED BOY BANDS, THEN SHE LIKED HAIR BANDS...
SHE HAD A GOTH PHASE, THEN A BIGGER GOTH PHASE...
"BUT THEN SHE DISCOVERED THIS GUITAR PLAYER, AND THE MUSIC HE PLAYED MADE HER FEEL CONNECTED...
"...LIKE SHE WAS A PART OF SOMETHING."
AND HER HEART SOON BELONGED TO THE MUSIC...
...ALONG WITH HER BODY...

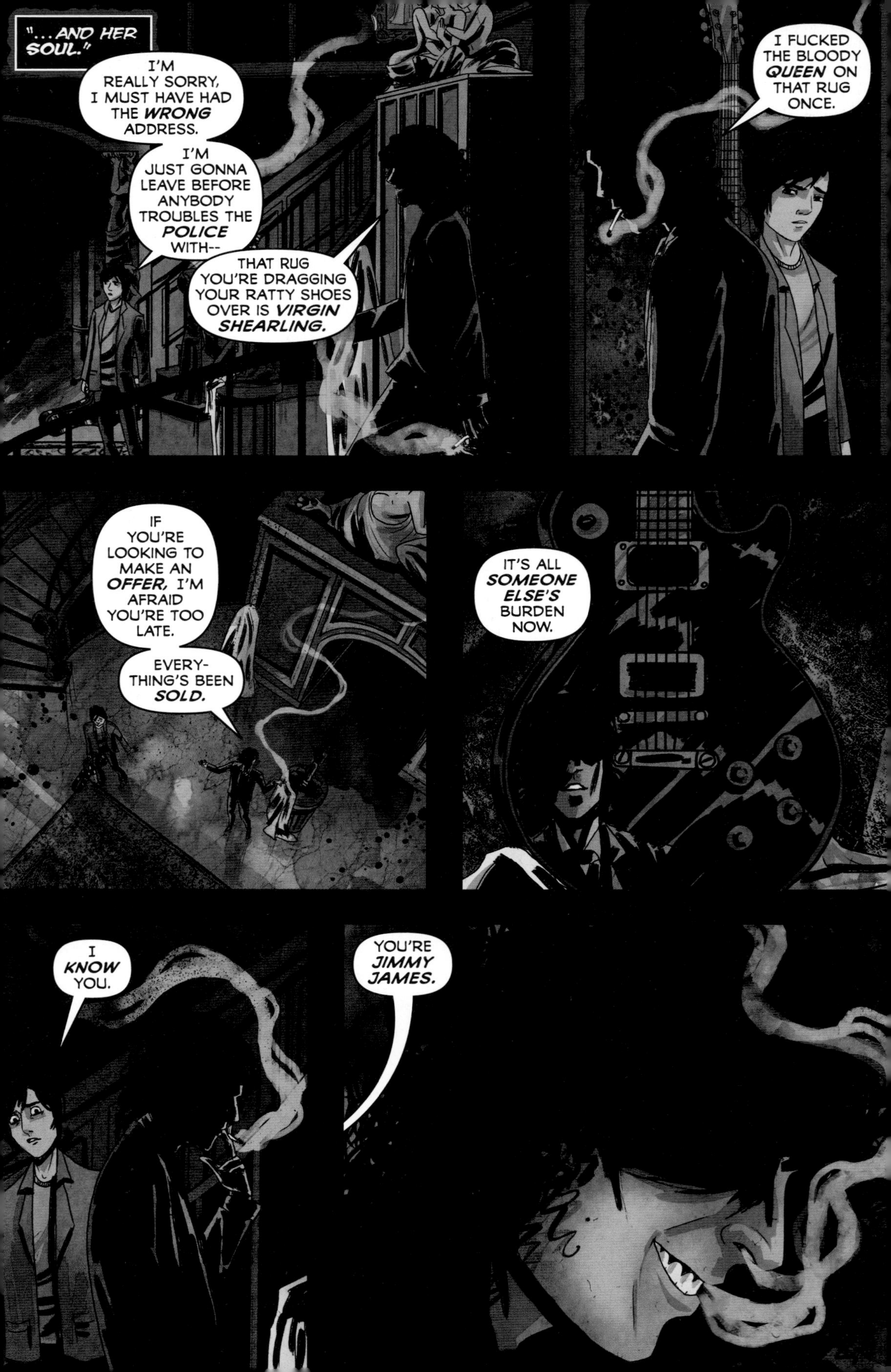
"...AND HER SOUL."
I'M REALLY SORRY, I MUST HAVE HAD THE WRONG ADDRESS.
I'M JUST GONNA LEAVE BEFORE ANYBODY TROUBLES THE POLICE WITH--
THAT RUG YOU'RE DRAGGING YOUR RATTY SHOES OVER IS VIRGIN SHEARLING.
I FUCKED THE BLOODY QUEEN ON THAT RUG ONCE.
IF YOU'RE LOOKING TO MAKE AN OFFER, I'M AFRAID YOU'RE TOO LATE.
EVERY-THING'S BEEN SOLD.
IT'S ALL SOMEONE ELSE'S BURDEN NOW.
I KNOW YOU.
YOU'RE JIMMY JAMES.

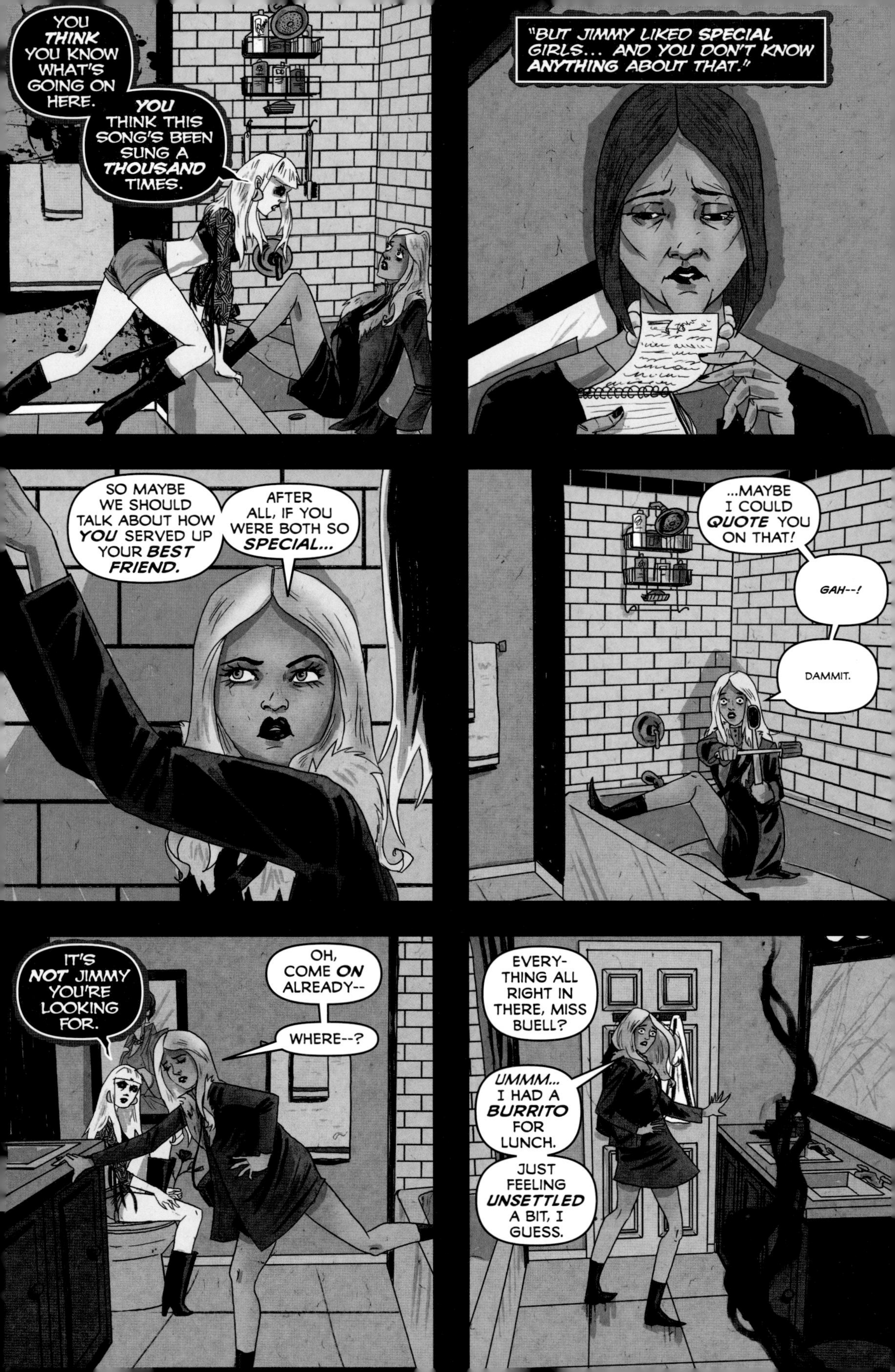
YOU THINK YOU KNOW WHAT'S GOING ON HERE.
YOU THINK THIS SONG'S BEEN SUNG A THOUSAND TIMES.
"BUT JIMMY LIKED SPECIAL GIRLS... AND YOU DON'T KNOW ANYTHING ABOUT THAT."
SO MAYBE WE SHOULD TALK ABOUT HOW YOU SERVED UP YOUR BEST FRIEND.
AFTER ALL, IF YOU WERE BOTH SO SPECIAL...
...MAYBE I COULD QUOTE YOU ON THAT!
GAH--!
DAMMIT.
IT'S NOT JIMMY YOU'RE LOOKING FOR.
OH, COME ON ALREADY--
WHERE--?
EVERY-THING ALL RIGHT IN THERE, MISS BUELL?
UMMM... I HAD A BURRITO FOR LUNCH.
JUST FEELING UNSETTLED A BIT, I GUESS.

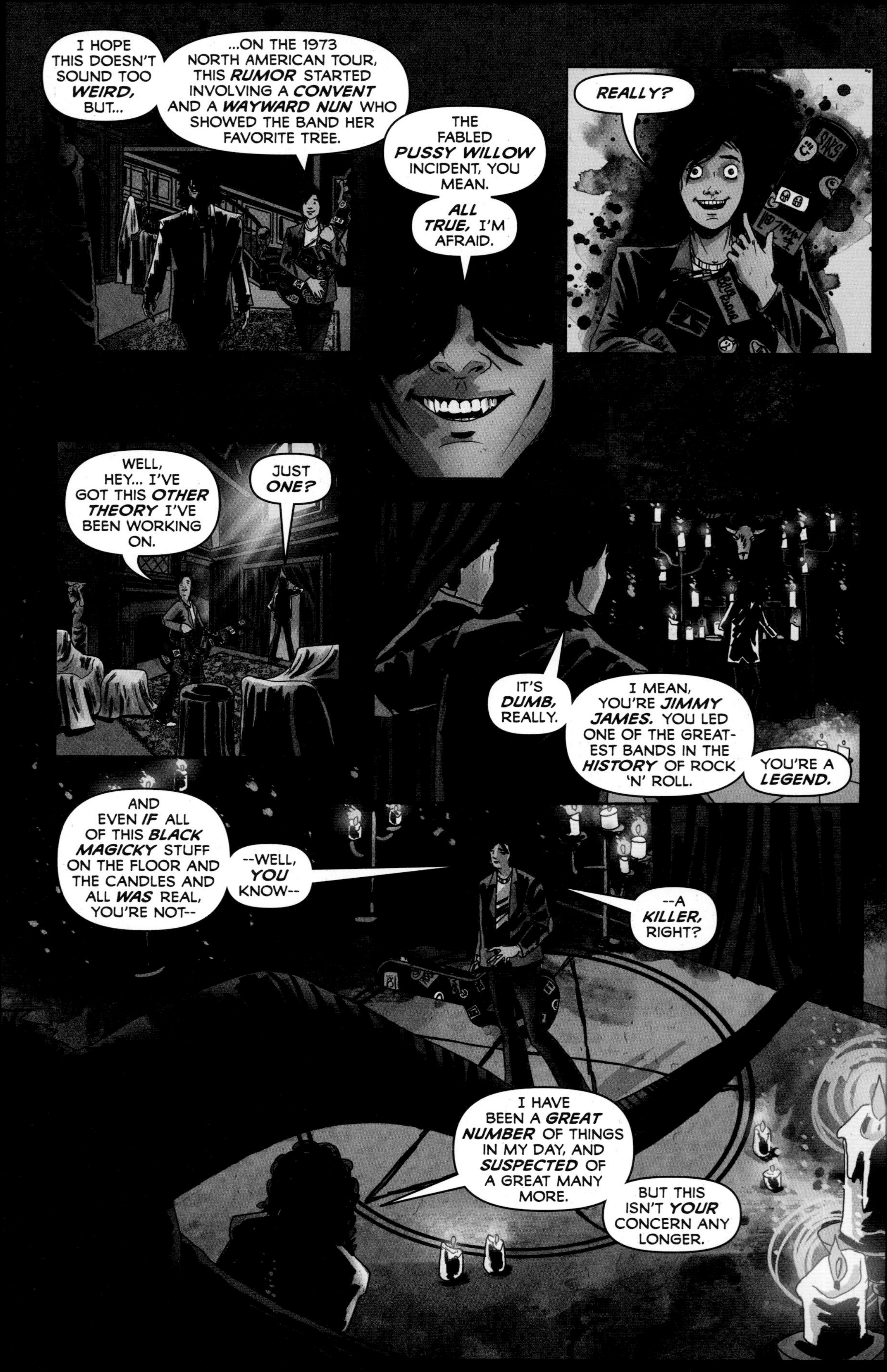
I HOPE THIS DOESN'T SOUND TOO WEIRD, BUT...
...ON THE 1973 NORTH AMERICAN TOUR, THIS RUMOR STARTED INVOLVING A CONVENT AND A WAYWARD NUN WHO SHOWED THE BAND HER FAVORITE TREE.
THE FABLED PUSSY WILLOW INCIDENT, YOU MEAN.
ALL TRUE, I'M AFRAID.
REALLY?
WELL, HEY... I'VE GOT THIS OTHER THEORY I'VE BEEN WORKING ON.
JUST ONE?
IT'S DUMB, REALLY.
I MEAN, YOU'RE JIMMY JAMES. YOU LED ONE OF THE GREAT-EST BANDS IN THE HISTORY OF ROCK 'N' ROLL.
YOU'RE A LEGEND.
AND EVEN IF ALL OF THIS BLACK MAGICKY STUFF ON THE FLOOR AND THE CANDLES AND ALL WAS REAL, YOU'RE NOT--
--WELL, YOU KNOW--
--A KILLER, RIGHT?
I HAVE BEEN A GREAT NUMBER OF THINGS IN MY DAY, AND SUSPECTED OF A GREAT MANY MORE.
BUT THIS ISN'T YOUR CONCERN ANY LONGER.

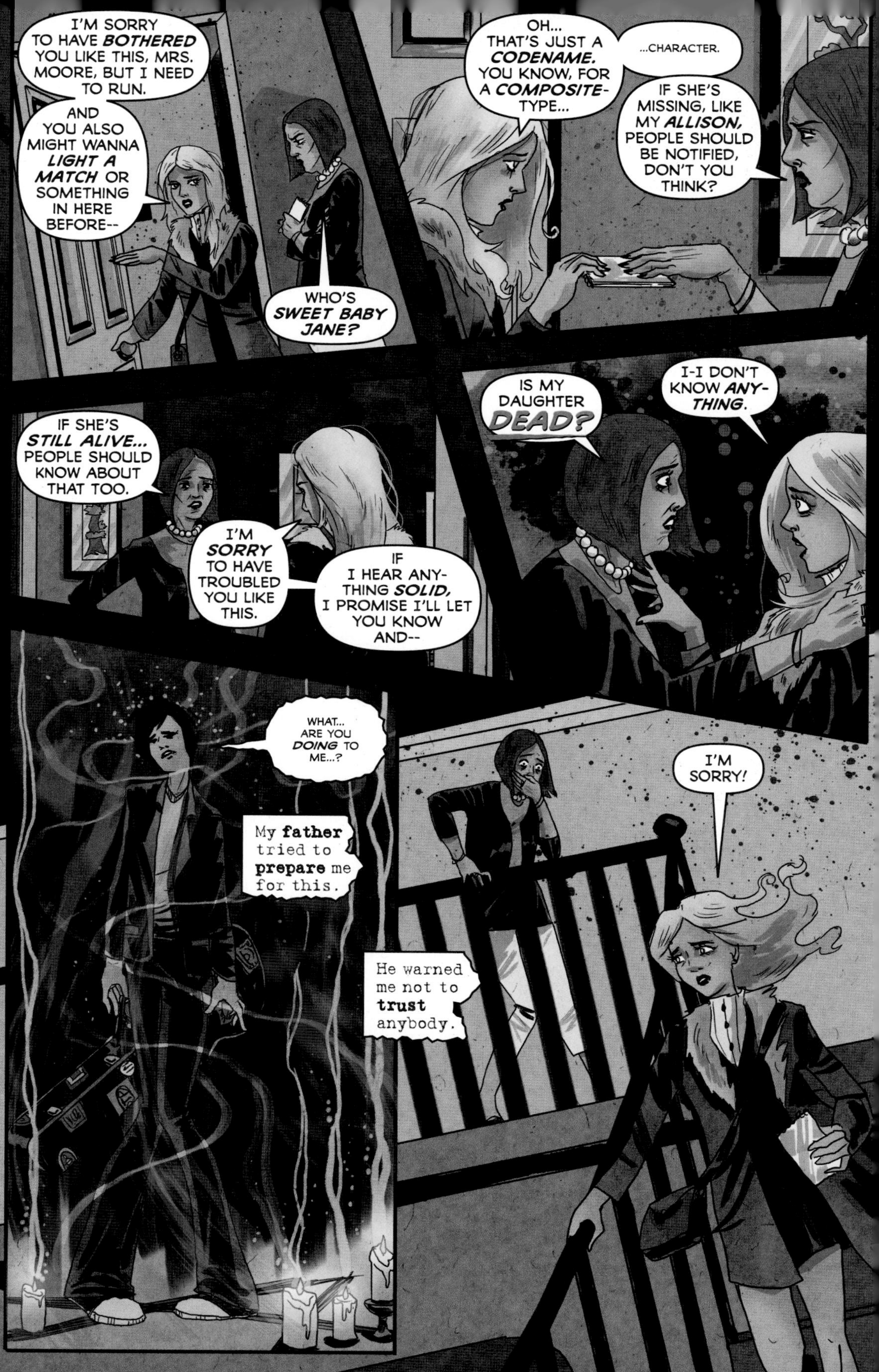
I'M SORRY TO HAVE BOTHERED YOU LIKE THIS, MRS. MOORE, BUT I NEED TO RUN.
AND YOU ALSO MIGHT WANNA LIGHT A MATCH OR SOMETHING IN HERE BEFORE--
WHO'S SWEET BABY JANE?
OH... THAT'S JUST A CODENAME. YOU KNOW, FOR A COMPOSITE-TYPE...
...CHARACTER.
IF SHE'S MISSING, LIKE MY ALLISON, PEOPLE SHOULD BE NOTIFIED, DON'T YOU THINK?
IF SHE'S STILL ALIVE... PEOPLE SHOULD KNOW ABOUT THAT TOO.
I'M SORRY TO HAVE TROUBLED YOU LIKE THIS.
IF I HEAR ANYTHING SOLID, I PROMISE I'LL LET YOU KNOW AND--
IS MY DAUGHTER DEAD?
I-I DON'T KNOW ANYTHING.
WHAT... ARE YOU DOING TO ME...?
My father tried to prepare me for this.
He warned me not to trust anybody.
I'M SORRY!

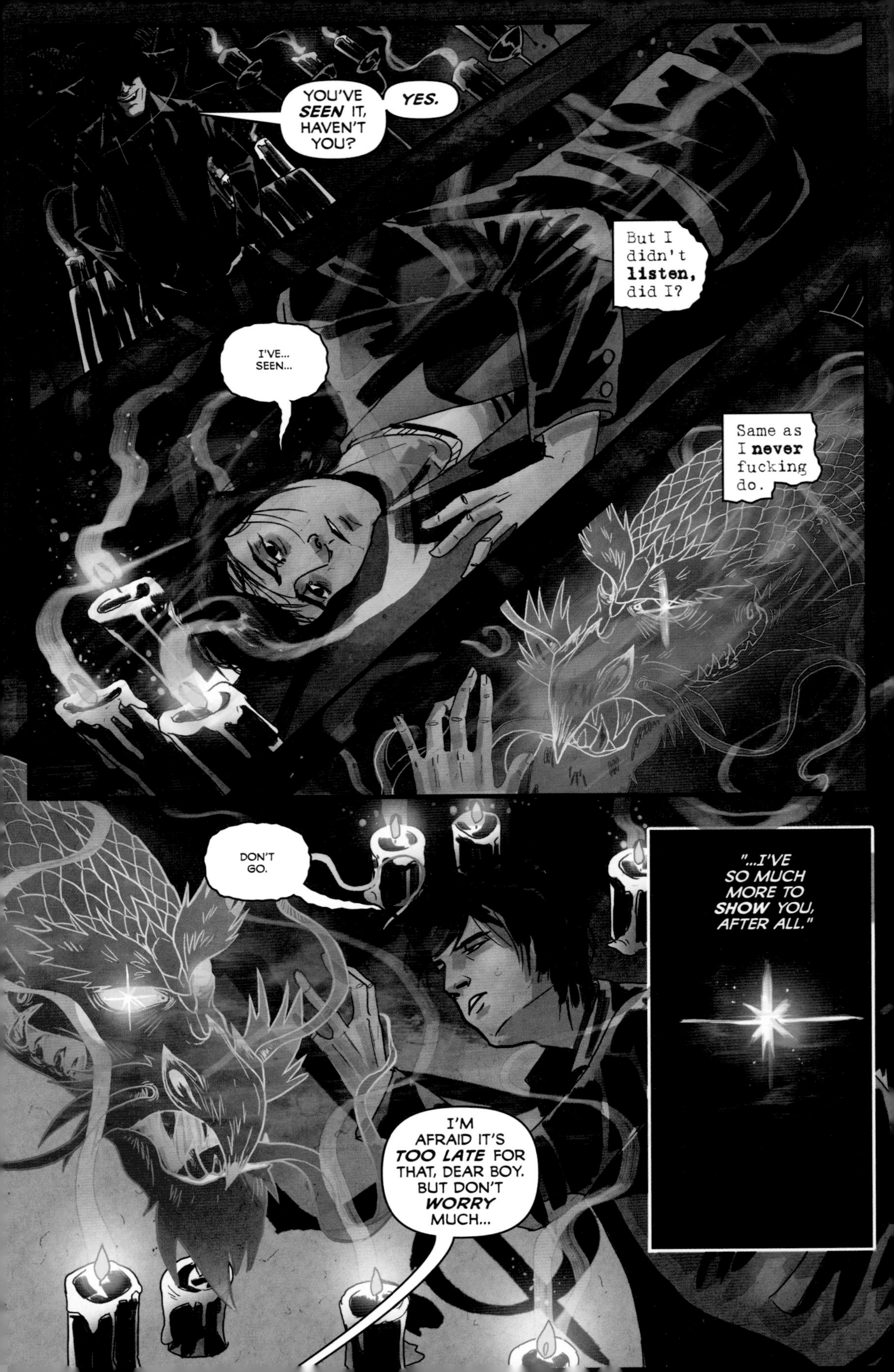
YOU'VE SEEN IT, HAVEN'T YOU?
YES.
But I didn't listen, did I?
I'VE... SEEN...
Same as I never fucking do.
DON'T GO.
"...I'VE SO MUCH MORE TO SHOW YOU, AFTER ALL."
I'M AFRAID IT'S TOO LATE FOR THAT, DEAR BOY. BUT DON'T WORRY MUCH...

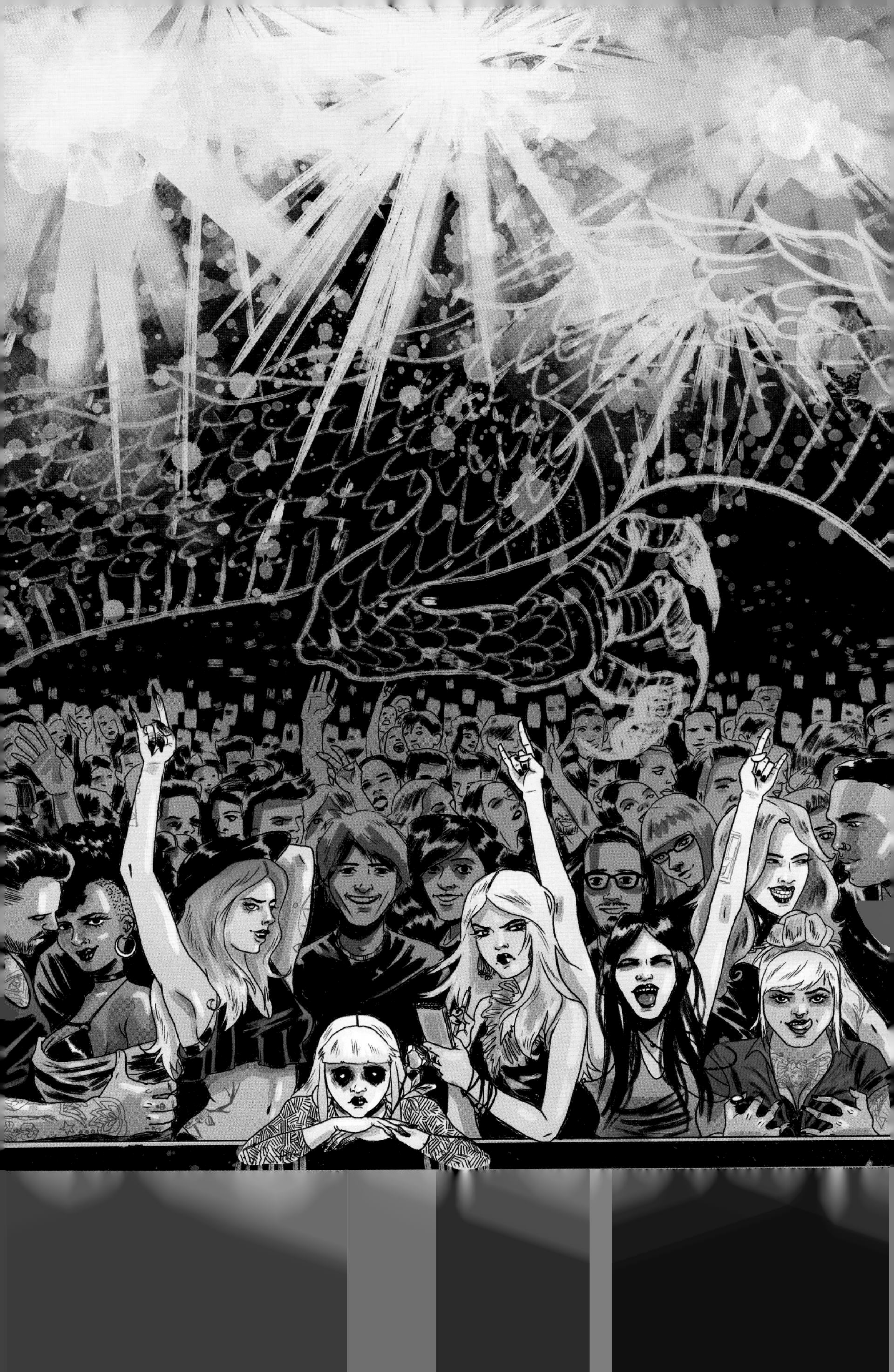

Jimmy James was once the greatest guitar player anybody could name. Together with Blue Rider, they changed music forever... BUT WHAT HAPPENS AFTER THE MAGIC RUNS OUT?

ROCKSTARS

SIDE # 1
FULL COLOR

Track 4

NATIVITY IN
BLACKLIGHT

22

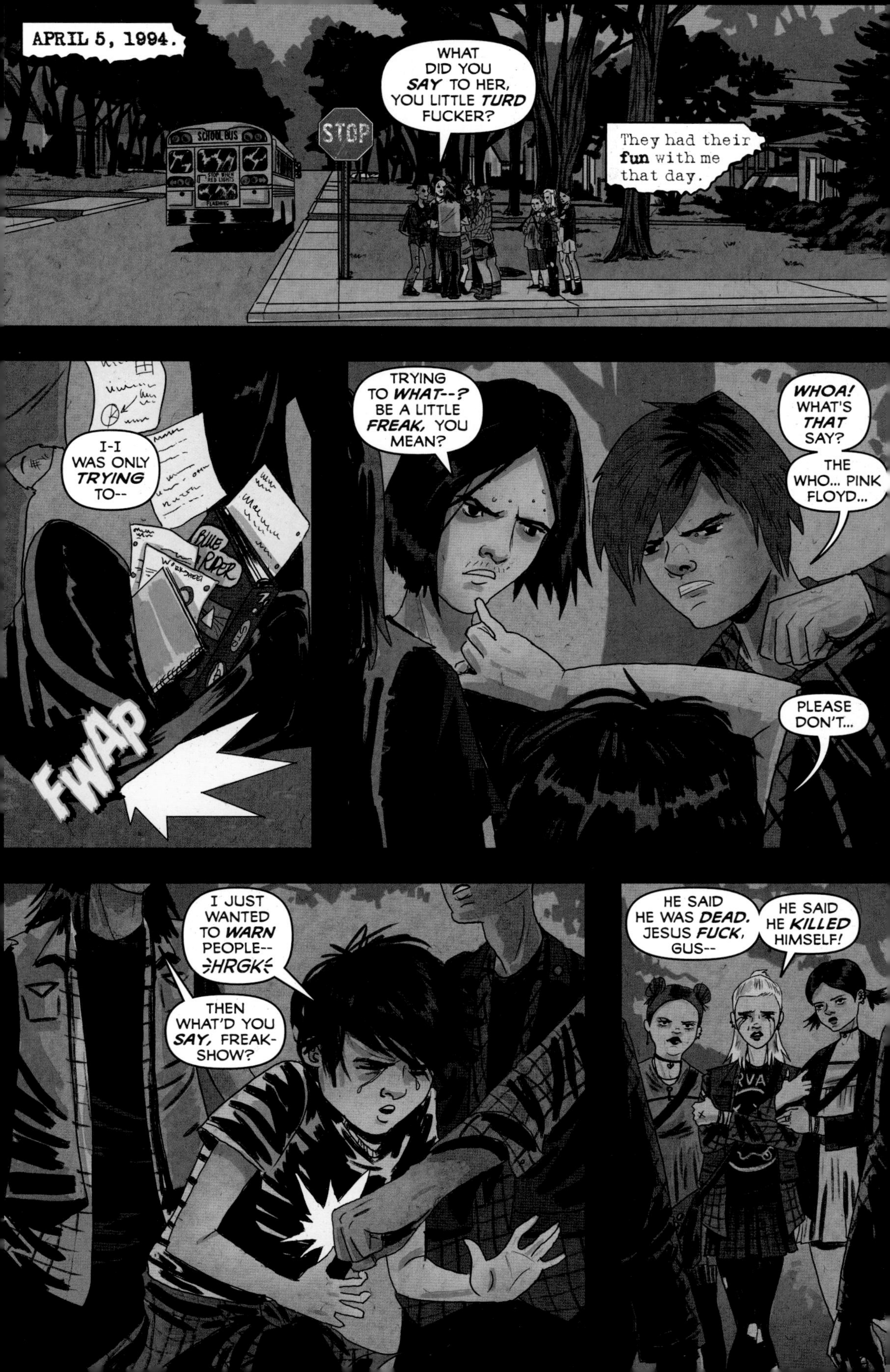
APRIL 5, 1994.
SCHOOL BUS
STOP WHEN RED LIGHTS FLASHING
STOP
WHAT DID YOU SAY TO HER, YOU LITTLE TURD FUCKER?
They had their fun with me that day.
I-I WAS ONLY TRYING TO--
BLUE RIDER
FWAP
TRYING TO WHAT--? BE A LITTLE FREAK, YOU MEAN?
WHOA! WHAT'S THAT SAY?
THE WHO... PINK FLOYD...
PLEASE DON'T...
I JUST WANTED TO WARN PEOPLE-- HRGK
THEN WHAT'D YOU SAY, FREAK-SHOW?
HE SAID HE WAS DEAD. JESUS FUCK, GUS--
HE SAID HE KILLED HIMSELF!

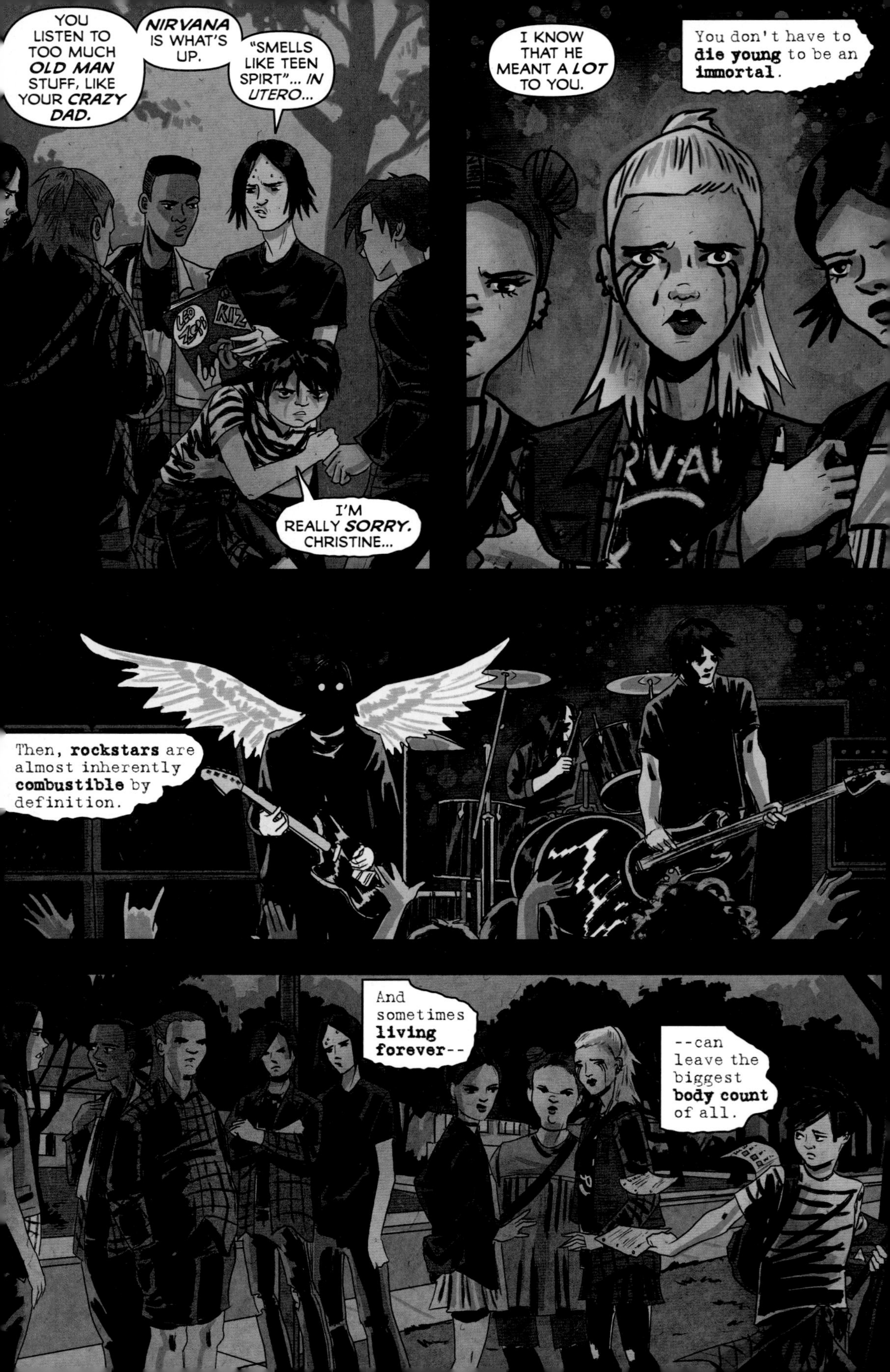
YOU LISTEN TO TOO MUCH OLD MAN STUFF, LIKE YOUR CRAZY DAD.
NIRVANA IS WHAT'S UP.
"SMELLS LIKE TEEN SPIRT"... IN UTERO...
I'M REALLY SORRY. CHRISTINE...
I KNOW THAT HE MEANT A LOT TO YOU.
You don't have to die young to be an immortal.
Then, rockstars are almost inherently combustible by definition.
And sometimes living forever--
--can leave the biggest body count of all.

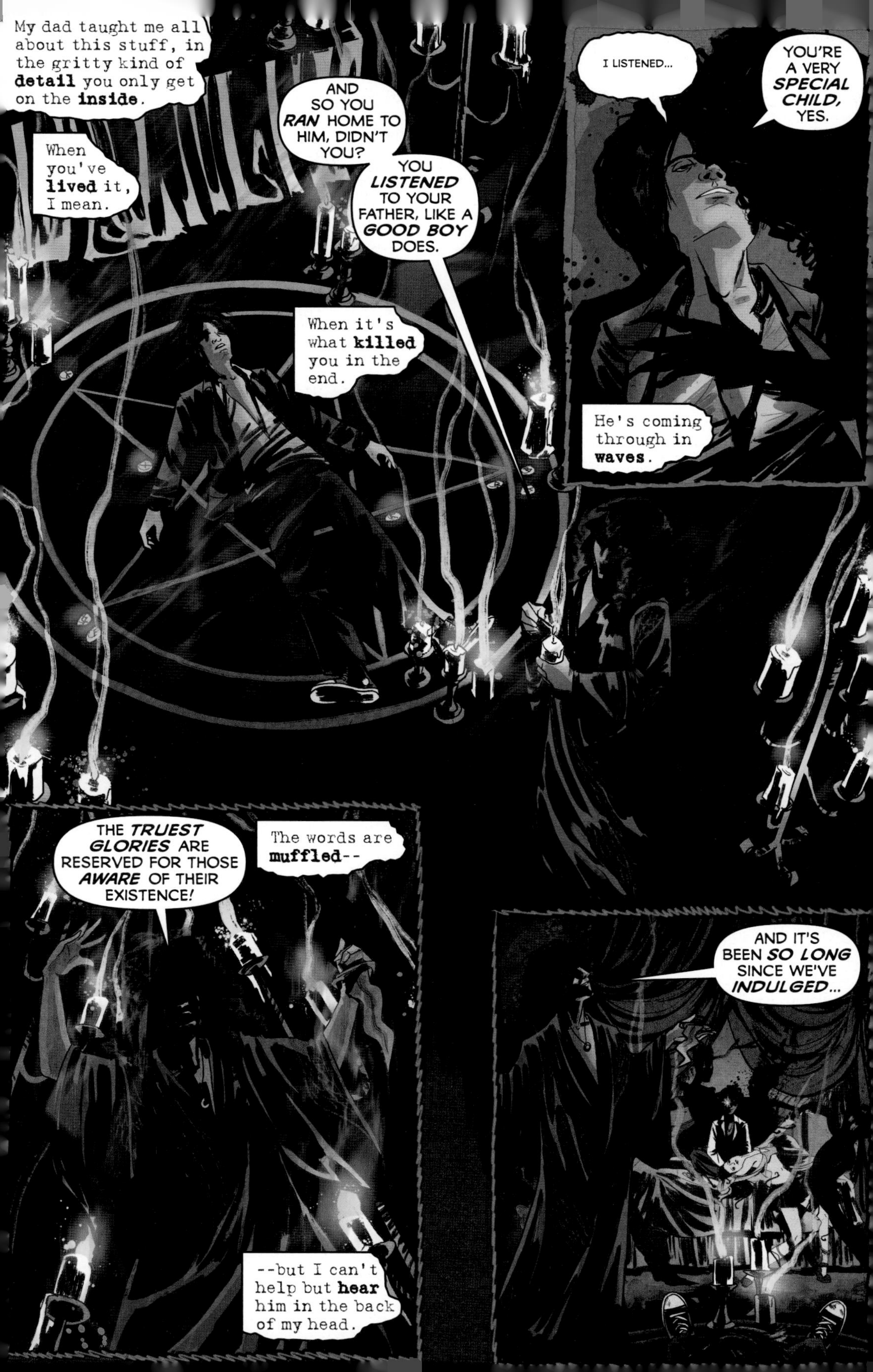
My dad taught me all about this stuff, in the gritty kind of detail you only get on the inside.
When you've lived it, I mean.
AND SO YOU RAN HOME TO HIM, DIDN'T YOU?
YOU LISTENED TO YOUR FATHER, LIKE A GOOD BOY DOES.
When it's what killed you in the end.
I LISTENED...
YOU'RE A VERY SPECIAL CHILD, YES.
He's coming through in waves.
THE TRUEST GLORIES ARE RESERVED FOR THOSE AWARE OF THEIR EXISTENCE!
The words are muffled--
--but I can't help but hear him in the back of my head.
AND IT'S BEEN SO LONG SINCE WE'VE INDULGED...

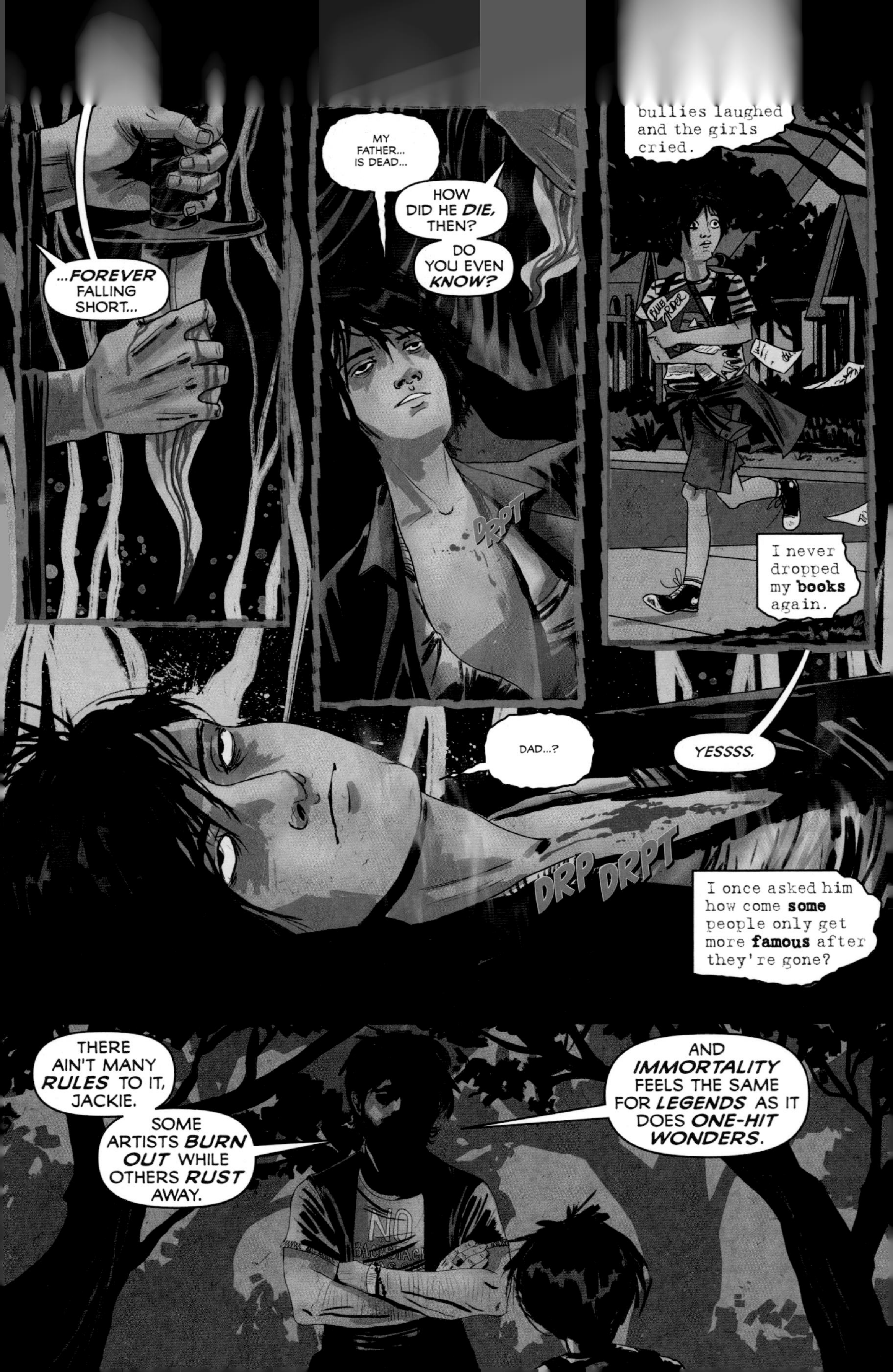
bullies laughed and the girls cried.
...FOREVER FALLING SHORT...
MY FATHER... IS DEAD...
HOW DID HE DIE, THEN?
DO YOU EVEN KNOW?
DRPT
I never dropped my books again.
DAD...?
YESSSS.
DRP DRPT
I once asked him how come some people only get more famous after they're gone?
THERE AIN'T MANY RULES TO IT, JACKIE.
SOME ARTISTS BURN OUT WHILE OTHERS RUST AWAY.
AND IMMORTALITY FEELS THE SAME FOR LEGENDS AS IT DOES ONE-HIT WONDERS.

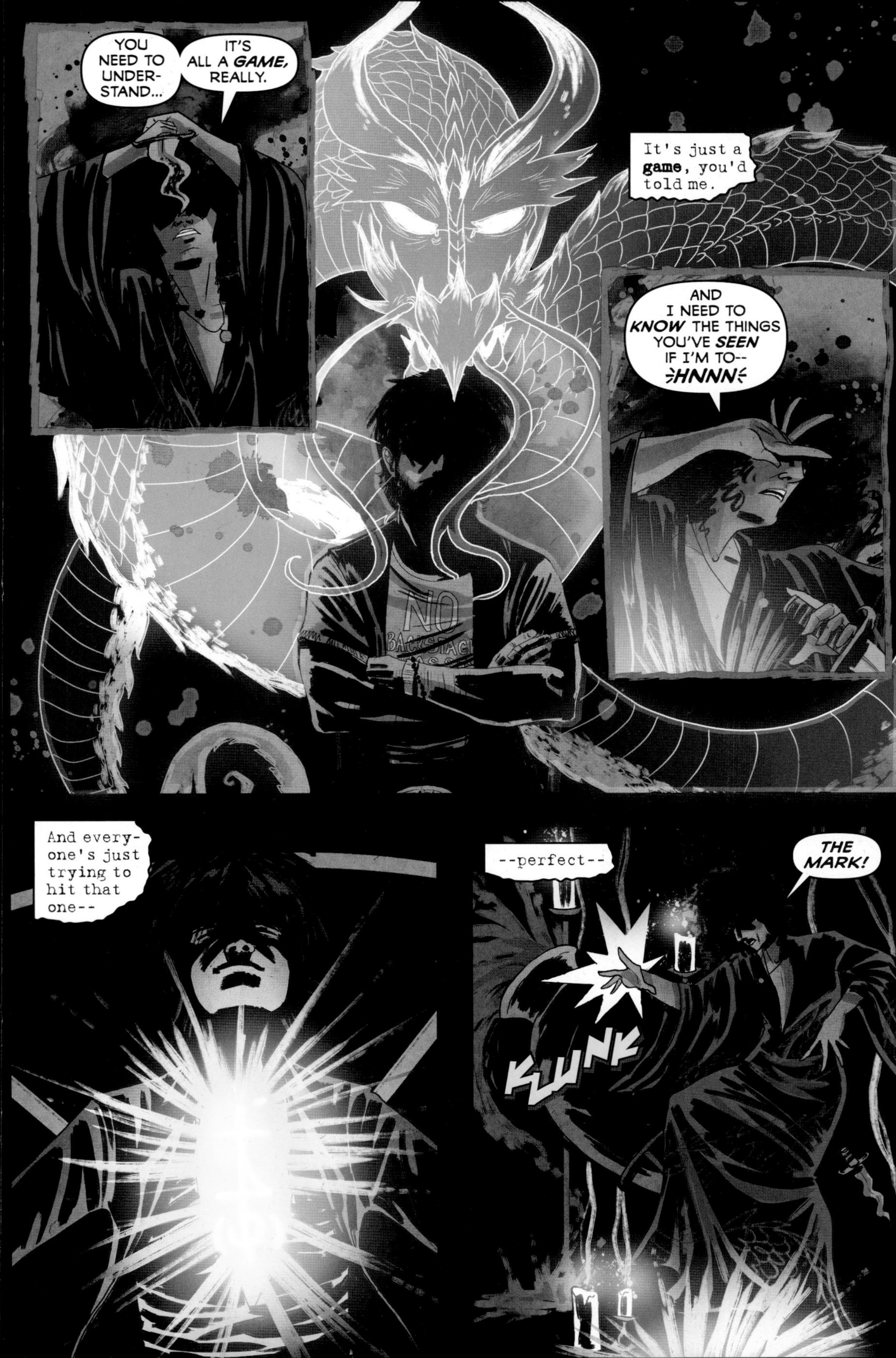
YOU NEED TO UNDER-STAND...
IT'S ALL A GAME, REALLY.
It's just a game, you'd told me.
AND I NEED TO KNOW THE THINGS YOU'VE SEEN IF I'M TO-- HNNN
NO BACKSTAGE PASS
And every-one's just trying to hit that one--
--perfect--
THE MARK!
KLUNK

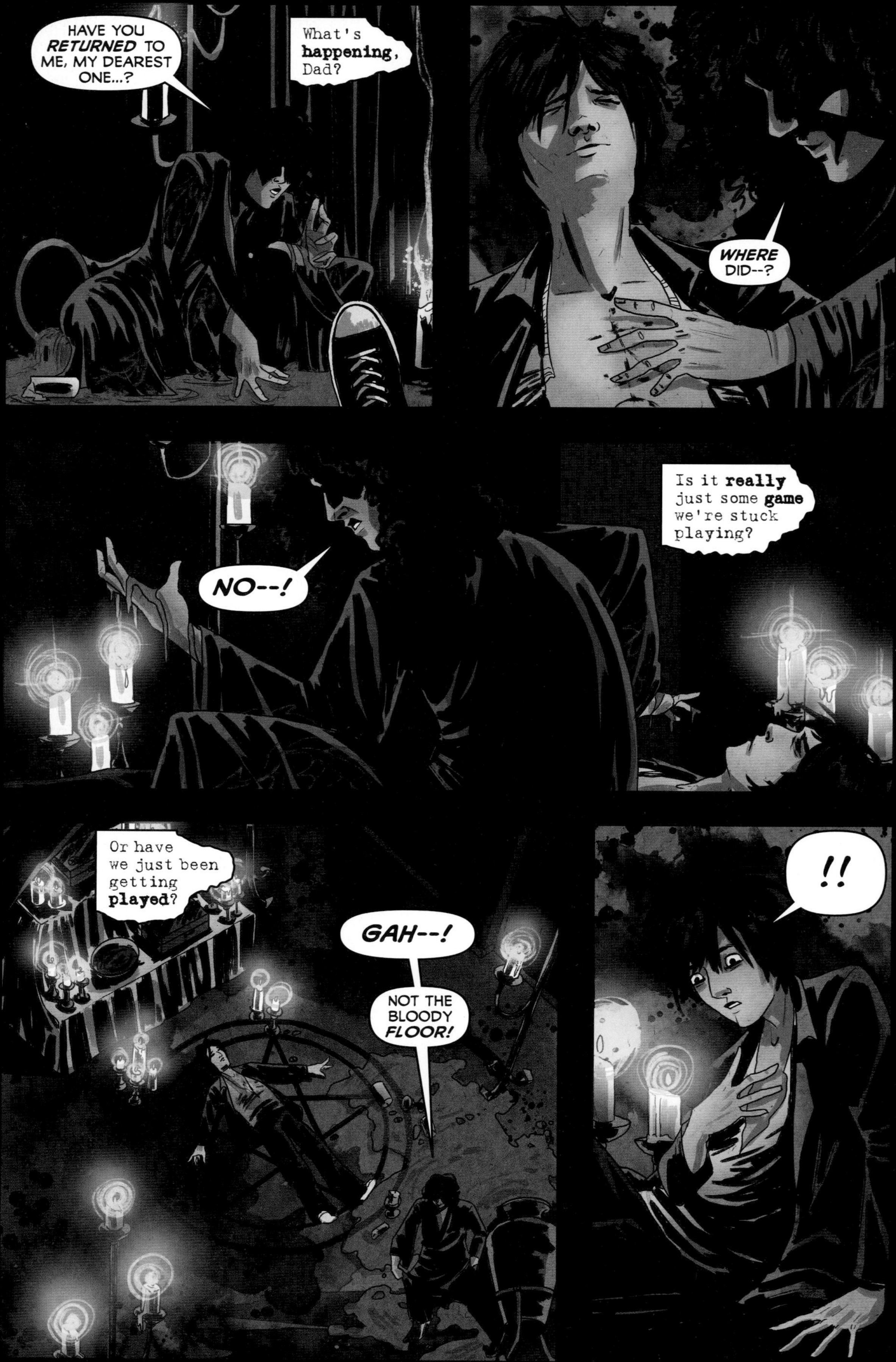
HAVE YOU *RETURNED* TO ME, MY DEAREST ONE...?
What's **happening**, Dad?
WHERE DID--?
NO--!
Is it **really** just some **game** we're stuck playing?
Or have we just been getting **played**?
GAH--!
NOT THE BLOODY *FLOOR!*
!!

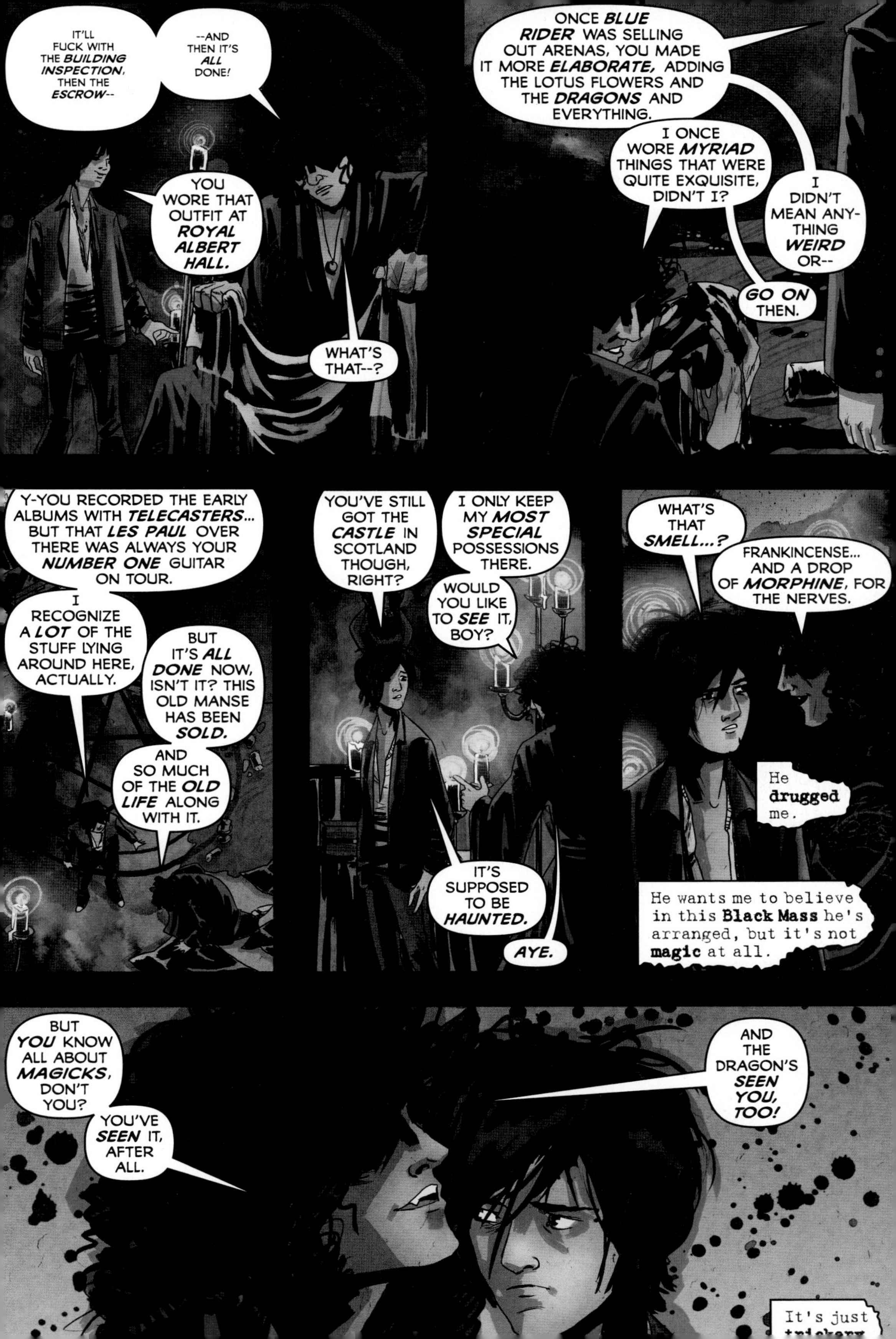
IT'LL FUCK WITH THE BUILDING INSPECTION, THEN THE ESCROW--
--AND THEN IT'S ALL DONE!
YOU WORE THAT OUTFIT AT ROYAL ALBERT HALL.
WHAT'S THAT--?
ONCE BLUE RIDER WAS SELLING OUT ARENAS, YOU MADE IT MORE ELABORATE, ADDING THE LOTUS FLOWERS AND THE DRAGONS AND EVERYTHING.
I ONCE WORE MYRIAD THINGS THAT WERE QUITE EXQUISITE, DIDN'T I?
I DIDN'T MEAN ANY-THING WEIRD OR--
GO ON THEN.
Y-YOU RECORDED THE EARLY ALBUMS WITH TELECASTERS... BUT THAT LES PAUL OVER THERE WAS ALWAYS YOUR NUMBER ONE GUITAR ON TOUR.
I RECOGNIZE A LOT OF THE STUFF LYING AROUND HERE, ACTUALLY.
BUT IT'S ALL DONE NOW, ISN'T IT? THIS OLD MANSE HAS BEEN SOLD.
AND SO MUCH OF THE OLD LIFE ALONG WITH IT.
YOU'VE STILL GOT THE CASTLE IN SCOTLAND THOUGH, RIGHT?
I ONLY KEEP MY MOST SPECIAL POSSESSIONS THERE.
WOULD YOU LIKE TO SEE IT, BOY?
IT'S SUPPOSED TO BE HAUNTED.
AYE.
WHAT'S THAT SMELL...?
FRANKINCENSE... AND A DROP OF MORPHINE, FOR THE NERVES.
He drugged me.
He wants me to believe in this Black Mass he's arranged, but it's not magic at all.
BUT YOU KNOW ALL ABOUT MAGICKS, DON'T YOU?
YOU'VE SEEN IT, AFTER ALL.
AND THE DRAGON'S SEEN YOU, TOO!
It's just

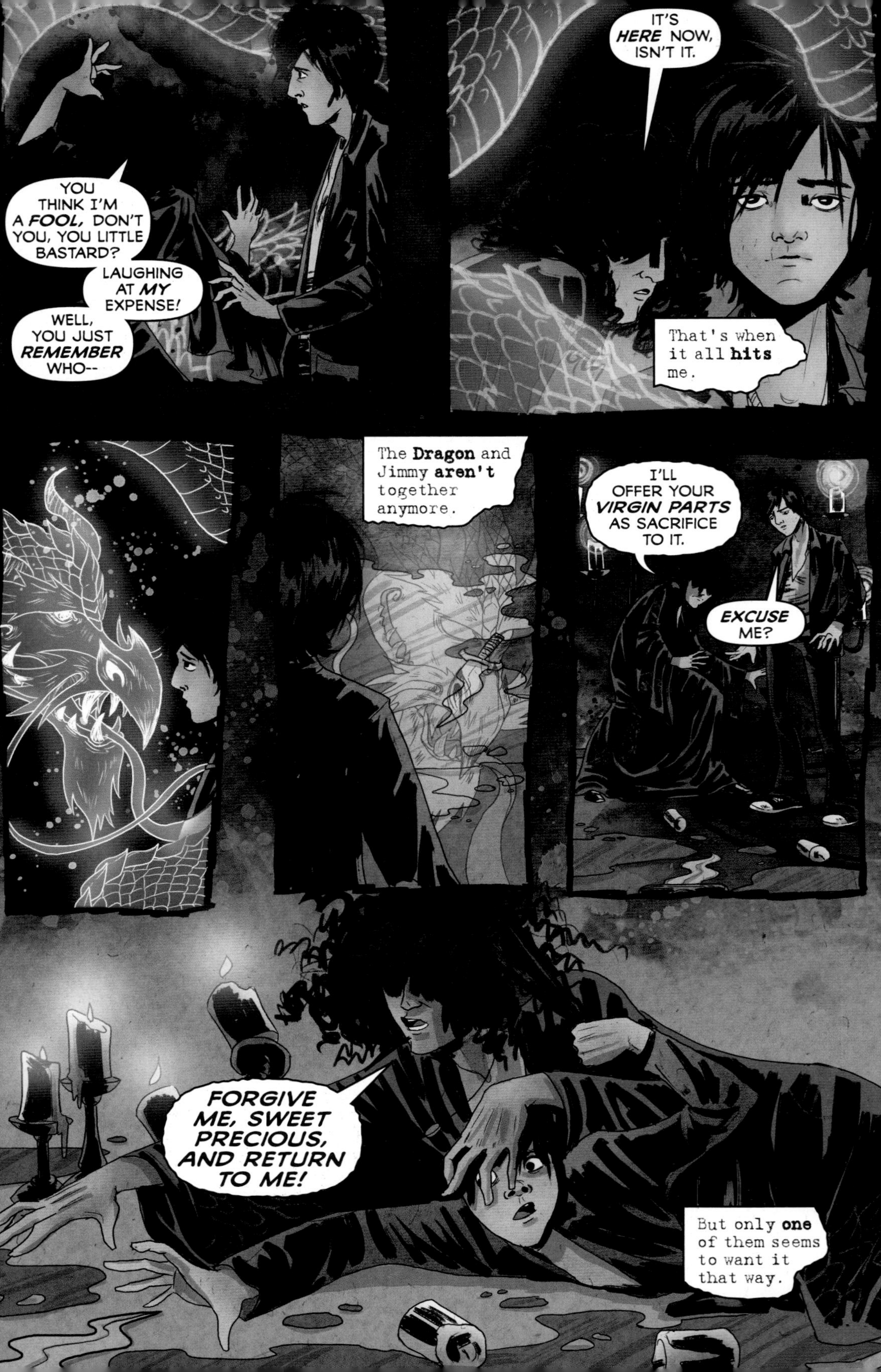
YOU THINK I'M A *FOOL,* DON'T YOU, YOU LITTLE BASTARD?
LAUGHING AT *MY* EXPENSE!
WELL, YOU JUST *REMEMBER* WHO--
IT'S *HERE* NOW, ISN'T IT.
That's when it all **hits** me.
The **Dragon** and Jimmy **aren't** together anymore.
I'LL OFFER YOUR *VIRGIN PARTS* AS SACRIFICE TO IT.
EXCUSE ME?
FORGIVE ME, SWEET PRECIOUS, AND RETURN TO ME!
But only **one** of them seems to want it that way.

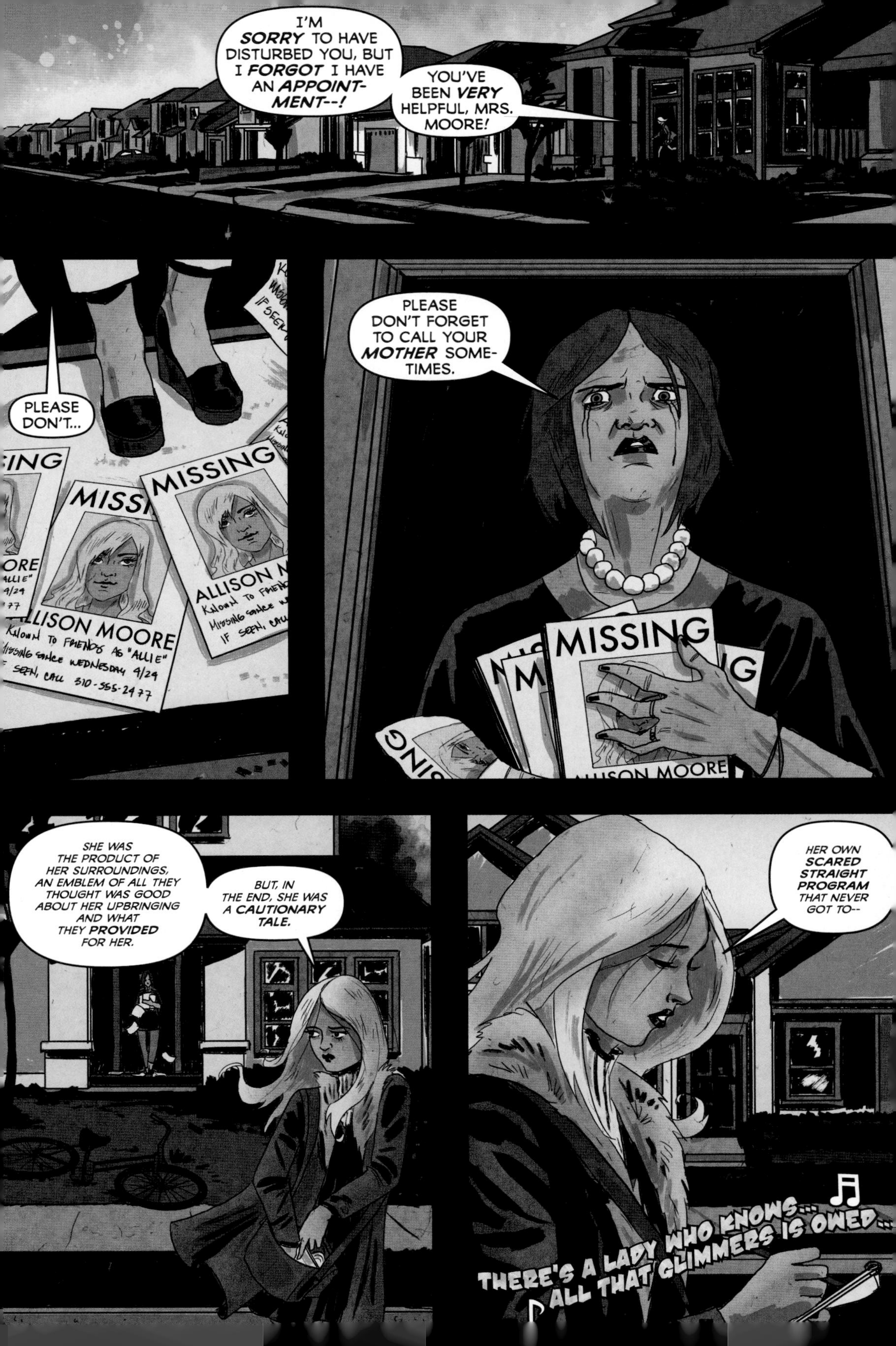
I'M SORRY TO HAVE DISTURBED YOU, BUT I FORGOT I HAVE AN APPOINT-MENT--!
YOU'VE BEEN VERY HELPFUL, MRS. MOORE!
PLEASE DON'T...
MISSING
ALLISON MOORE
KNOWN TO FRIENDS AS "ALLIE"
MISSING SINCE WEDNESDAY 4/24
IF SEEN, CALL 310-555-2477
PLEASE DON'T FORGET TO CALL YOUR MOTHER SOME-TIMES.
MISSING
ALLISON MOORE
SHE WAS THE PRODUCT OF HER SURROUNDINGS, AN EMBLEM OF ALL THEY THOUGHT WAS GOOD ABOUT HER UPBRINGING AND WHAT THEY PROVIDED FOR HER.
BUT, IN THE END, SHE WAS A CAUTIONARY TALE.
HER OWN SCARED STRAIGHT PROGRAM THAT NEVER GOT TO--
THERE'S A LADY WHO KNOWS... ALL THAT GLIMMERS IS OWED...

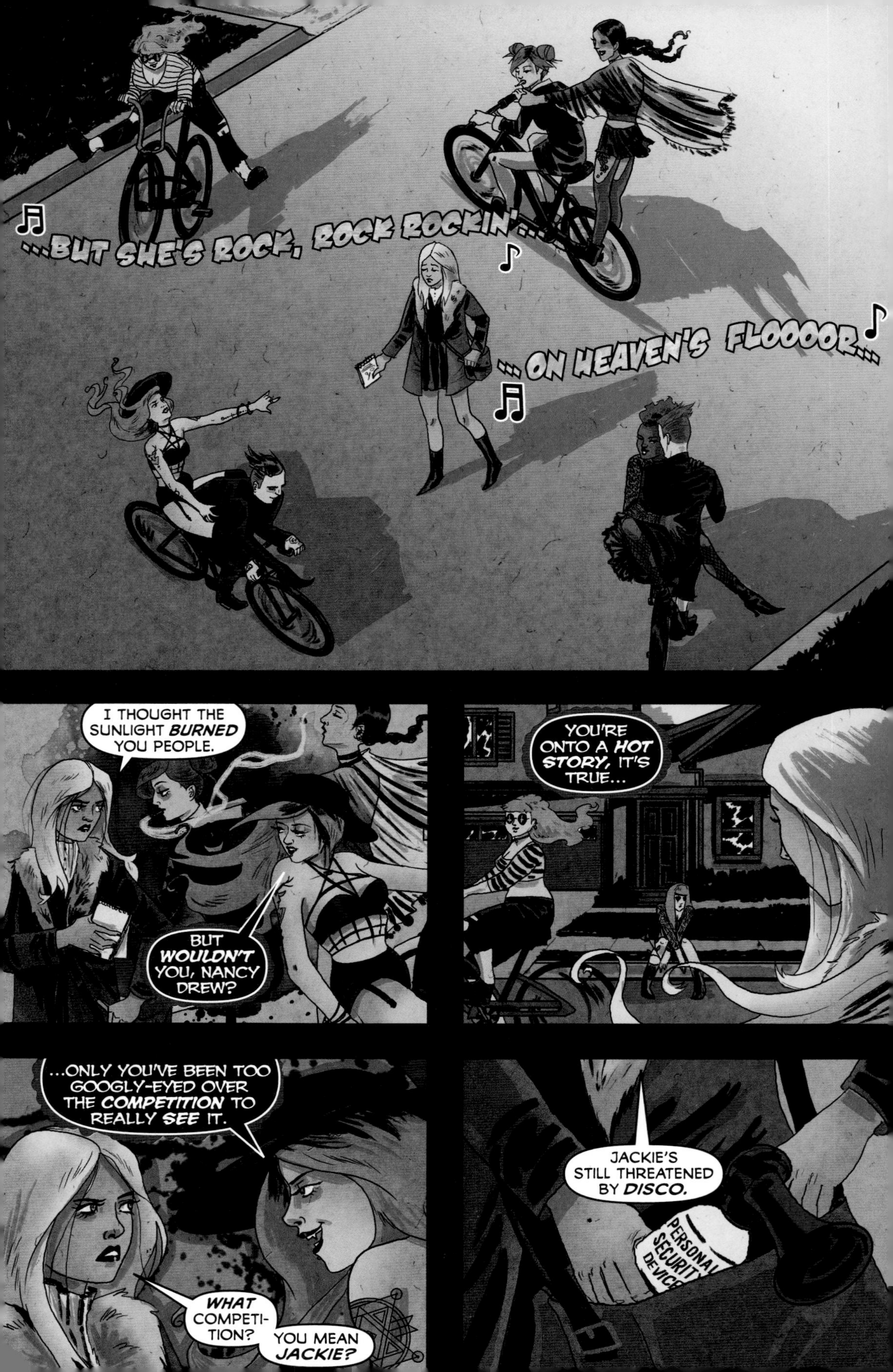
...BUT SHE'S ROCK, ROCK ROCKIN'...
...ON HEAVEN'S FLOOOOR...
I THOUGHT THE SUNLIGHT BURNED YOU PEOPLE.
BUT WOULDN'T YOU, NANCY DREW?
YOU'RE ONTO A HOT STORY, IT'S TRUE...
...ONLY YOU'VE BEEN TOO GOOGLY-EYED OVER THE COMPETITION TO REALLY SEE IT.
WHAT COMPETITION?
YOU MEAN JACKIE?
JACKIE'S STILL THREATENED BY DISCO.
PERSONAL SECURITY DEVICE

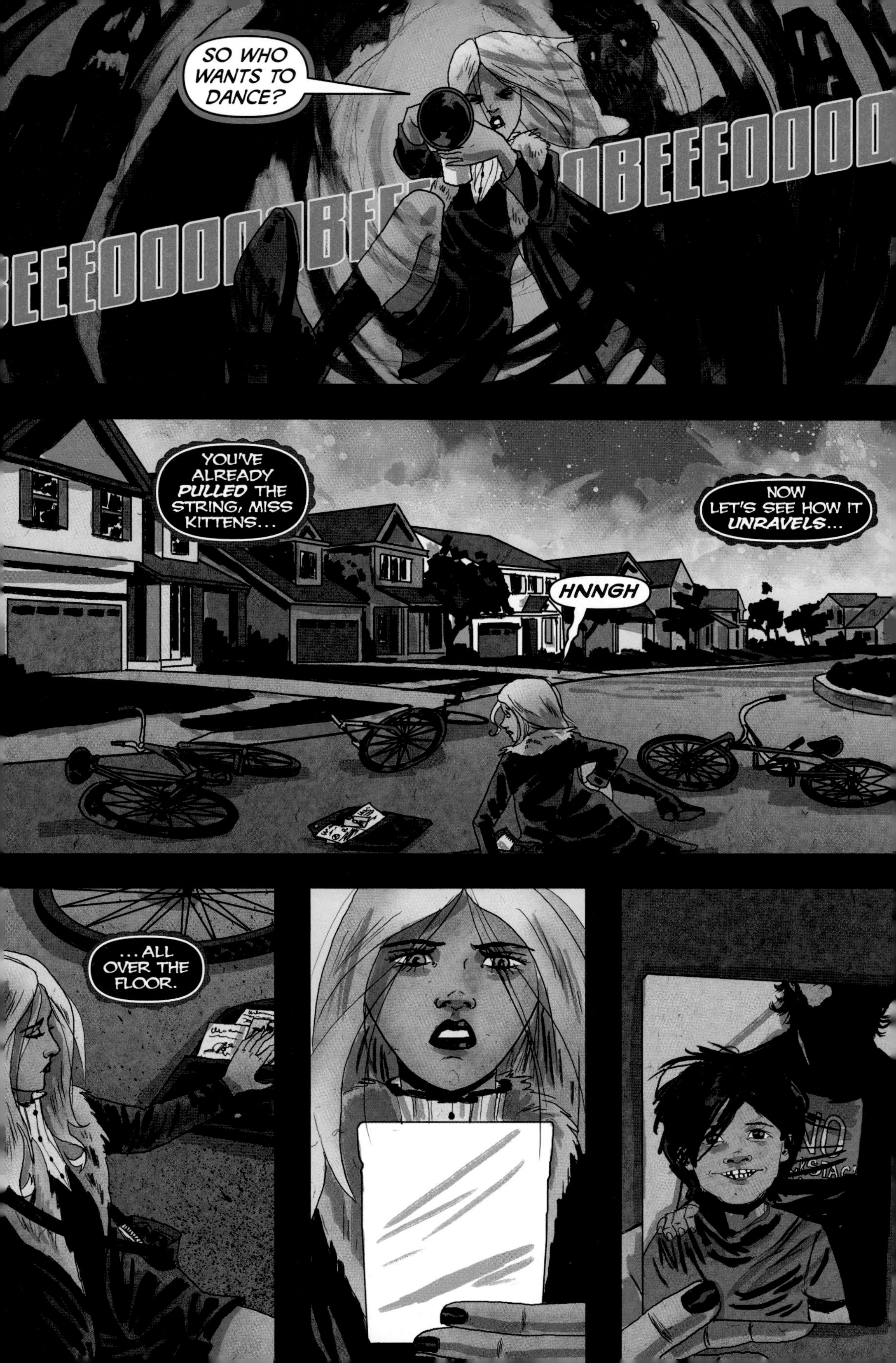
SO WHO WANTS TO DANCE?
YOU'VE ALREADY PULLED THE STRING, MISS KITTENS...
NOW LET'S SEE HOW IT UNRAVELS...
HNNGH
...ALL OVER THE FLOOR.

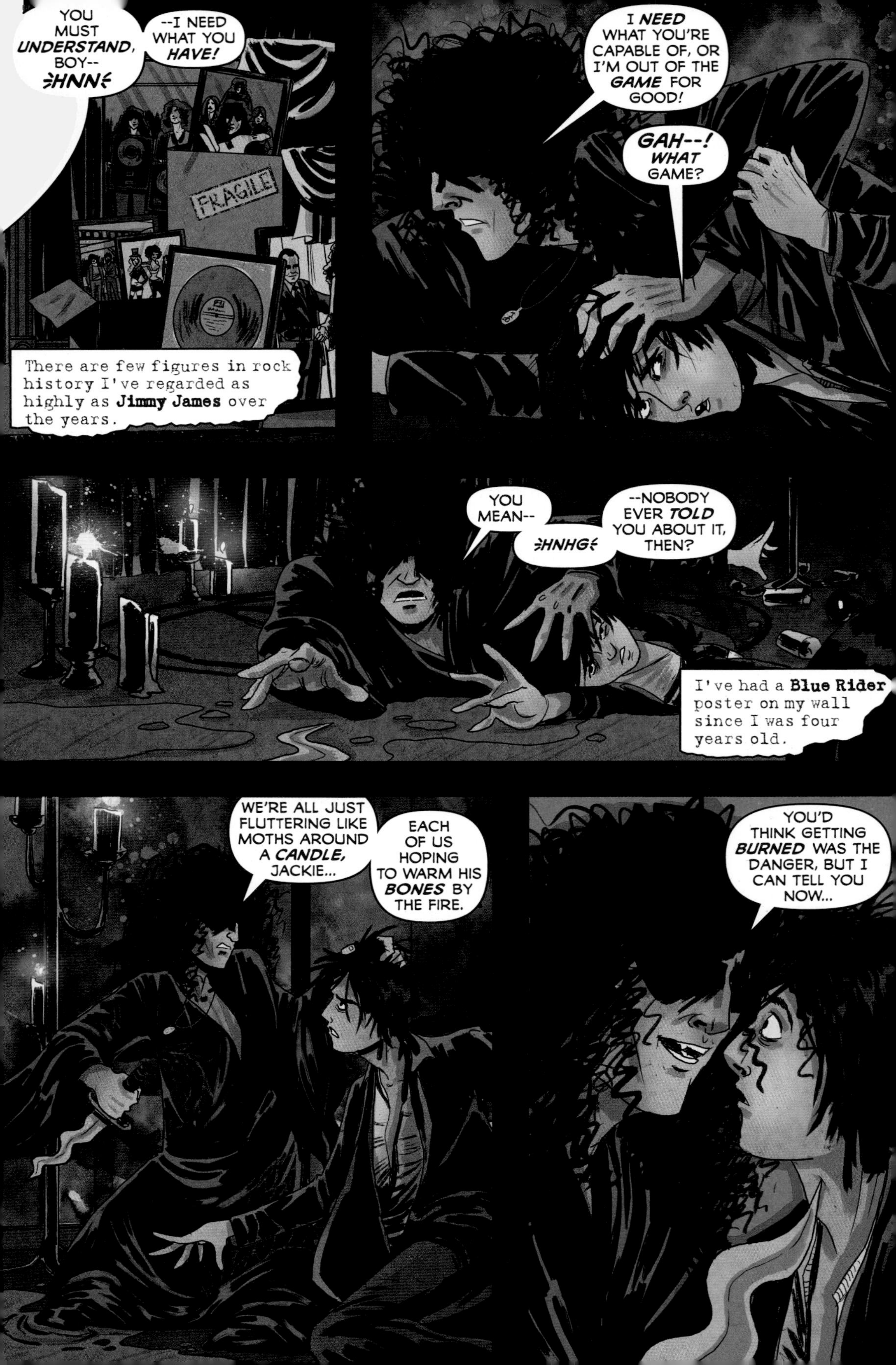
YOU MUST UNDERSTAND, BOY-- ≷HNN≷
--I NEED WHAT YOU HAVE!
FRAGILE
There are few figures in rock history I've regarded as highly as Jimmy James over the years.
I NEED WHAT YOU'RE CAPABLE OF, OR I'M OUT OF THE GAME FOR GOOD!
GAH--! WHAT GAME?
YOU MEAN--
≷HNHG≷
--NOBODY EVER TOLD YOU ABOUT IT, THEN?
I've had a Blue Rider poster on my wall since I was four years old.
WE'RE ALL JUST FLUTTERING LIKE MOTHS AROUND A CANDLE, JACKIE...
EACH OF US HOPING TO WARM HIS BONES BY THE FIRE.
YOU'D THINK GETTING BURNED WAS THE DANGER, BUT I CAN TELL YOU NOW...

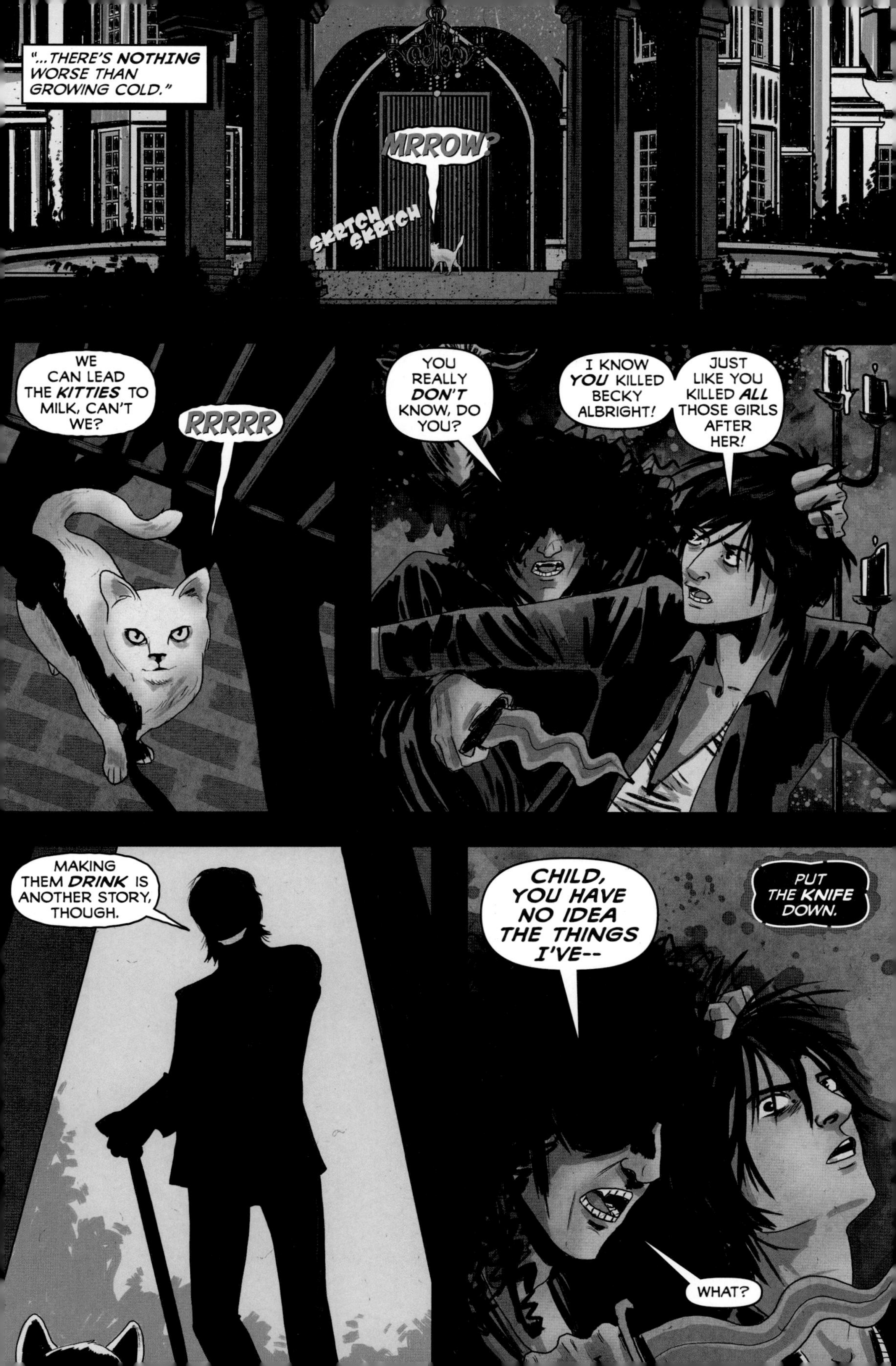
"...THERE'S NOTHING WORSE THAN GROWING COLD."
MRROW?
SKRTCH SKRTCH
WE CAN LEAD THE KITTIES TO MILK, CAN'T WE?
RRRRR
YOU REALLY DON'T KNOW, DO YOU?
I KNOW YOU KILLED BECKY ALBRIGHT!
JUST LIKE YOU KILLED ALL THOSE GIRLS AFTER HER!
MAKING THEM DRINK IS ANOTHER STORY, THOUGH.
CHILD, YOU HAVE NO IDEA THE THINGS I'VE--
PUT THE KNIFE DOWN.
WHAT?

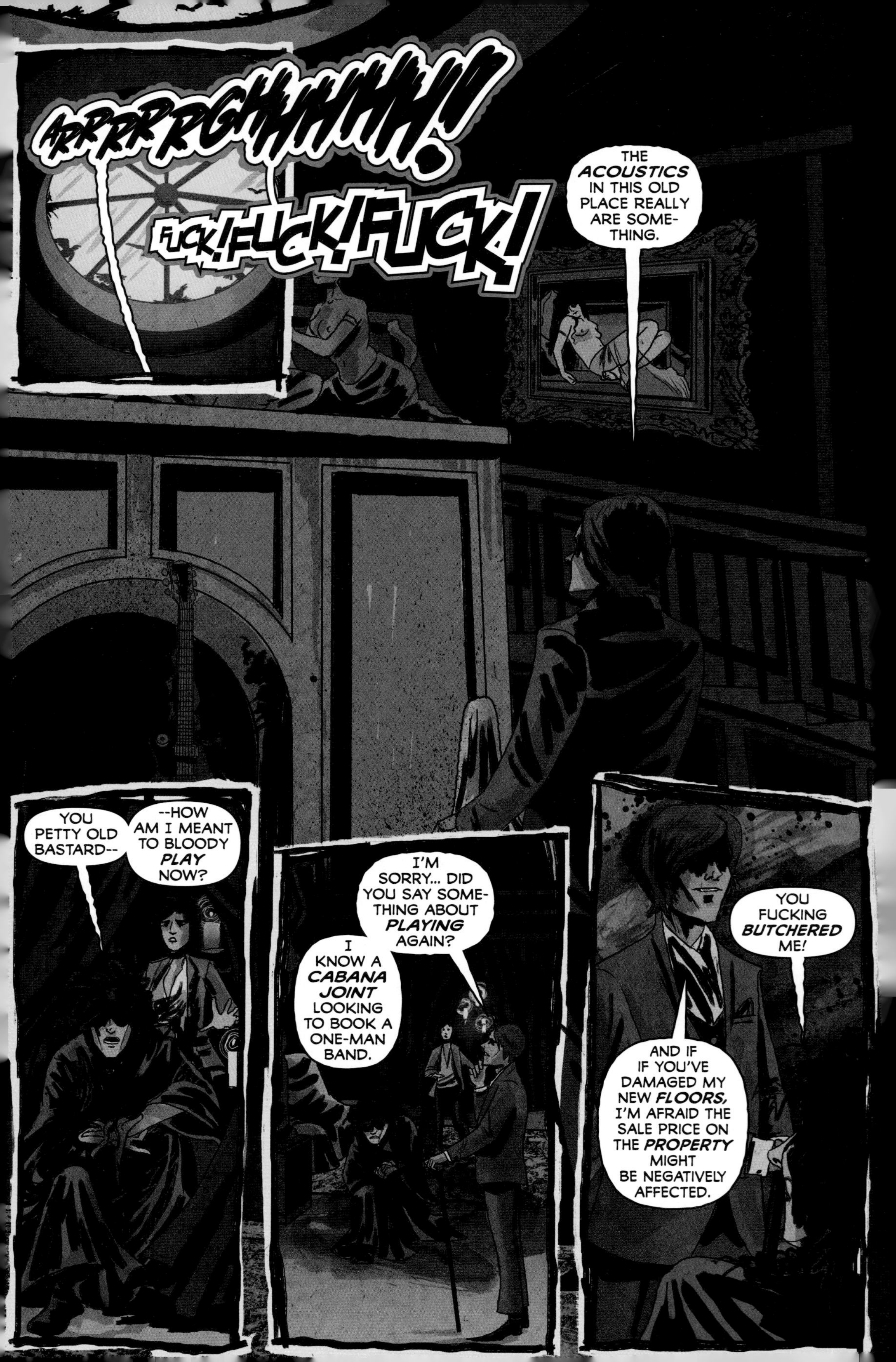
ARRRRRGHHHHHH!
FUCK! FUCK! FUCK!
THE *ACOUSTICS* IN THIS OLD PLACE REALLY ARE SOME-THING.
YOU PETTY OLD BASTARD--
--HOW AM I MEANT TO BLOODY *PLAY* NOW?
I'M SORRY... DID YOU SAY SOME-THING ABOUT *PLAYING* AGAIN?
I KNOW A *CABANA JOINT* LOOKING TO BOOK A ONE-MAN BAND.
YOU FUCKING *BUTCHERED* ME!
AND IF IF YOU'VE DAMAGED MY NEW *FLOORS,* I'M AFRAID THE SALE PRICE ON THE *PROPERTY* MIGHT BE NEGATIVELY AFFECTED.

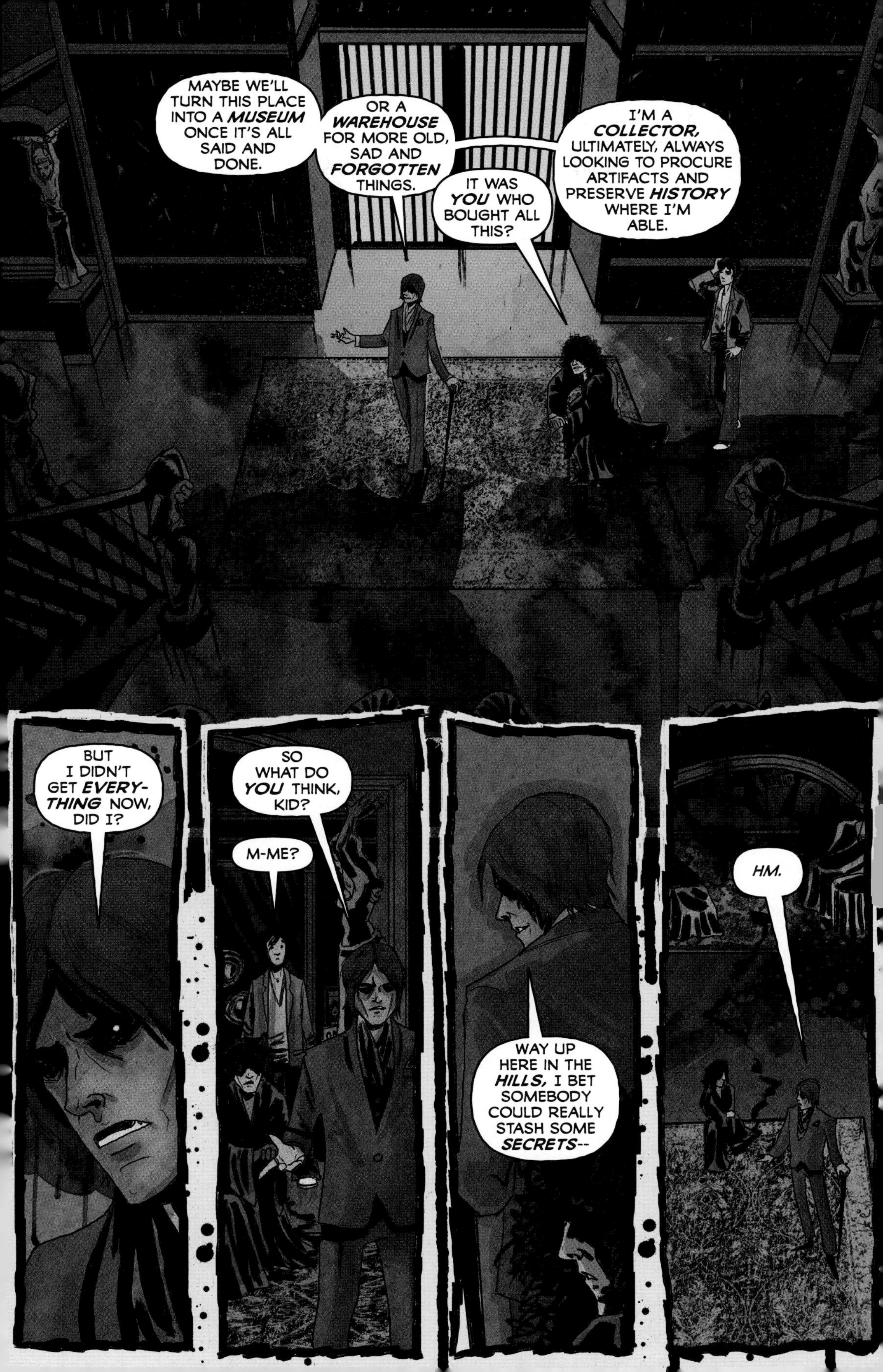
MAYBE WE'LL TURN THIS PLACE INTO A *MUSEUM* ONCE IT'S ALL SAID AND DONE.
OR A *WAREHOUSE* FOR MORE OLD, SAD AND *FORGOTTEN* THINGS.
IT WAS *YOU* WHO BOUGHT ALL THIS?
I'M A *COLLECTOR,* ULTIMATELY, ALWAYS LOOKING TO PROCURE ARTIFACTS AND PRESERVE *HISTORY* WHERE I'M ABLE.
BUT I DIDN'T GET *EVERY-THING* NOW, DID I?
SO WHAT DO *YOU* THINK, KID?
M-ME?
WAY UP HERE IN THE *HILLS,* I BET SOMEBODY COULD REALLY STASH SOME *SECRETS*--
HM.

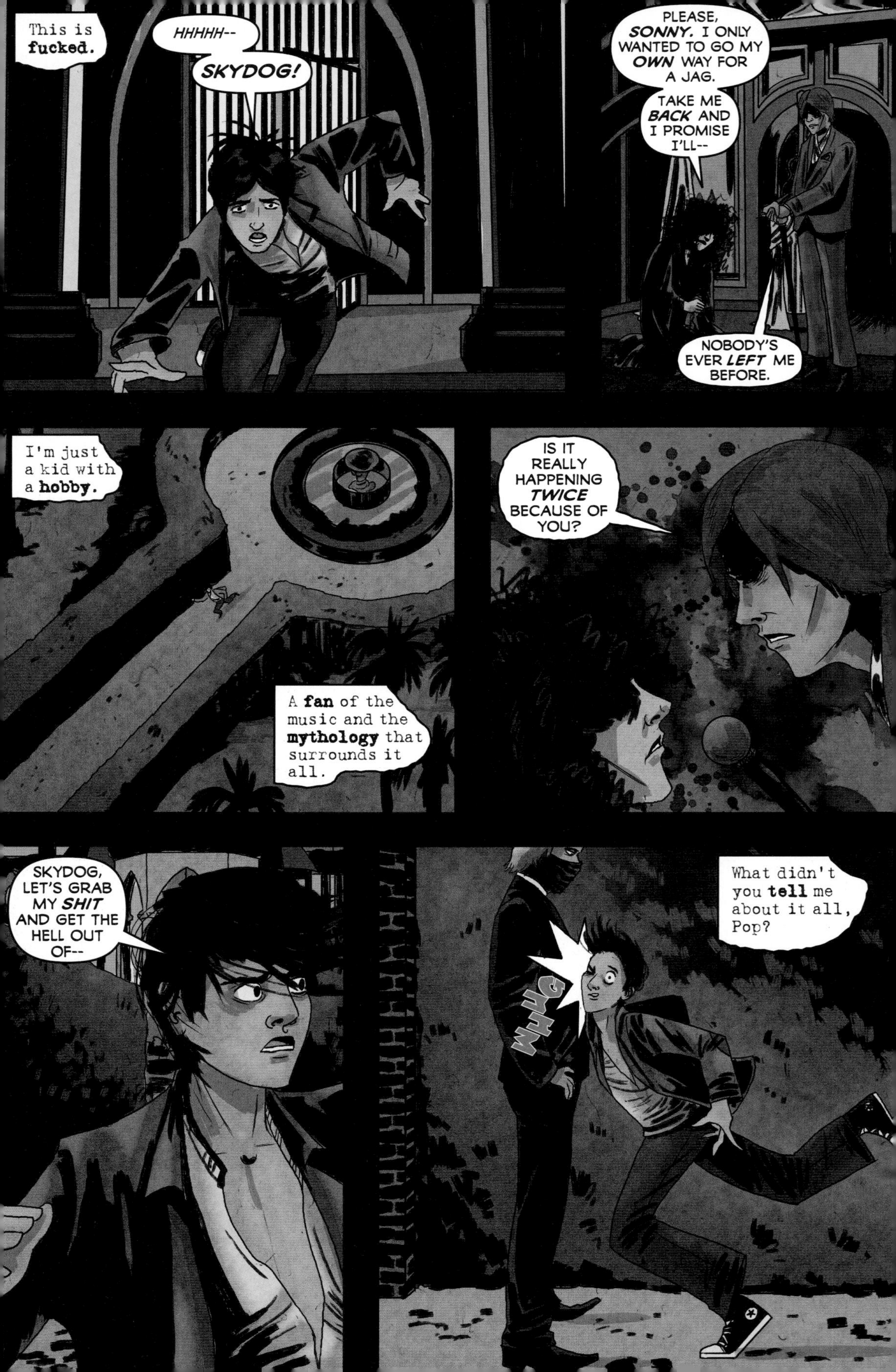
This is **fucked.**
HHHHH--
SKYDOG!
PLEASE, **SONNY.** I ONLY WANTED TO GO MY **OWN** WAY FOR A JAG.
TAKE ME **BACK** AND I PROMISE I'LL--
NOBODY'S EVER **LEFT** ME BEFORE.
I'm just a kid with a **hobby.**
A **fan** of the music and the **mythology** that surrounds it all.
IS IT REALLY HAPPENING **TWICE** BECAUSE OF YOU?
SKYDOG, LET'S GRAB MY **SHIT** AND GET THE HELL OUT OF--
WHUG
What didn't you **tell** me about it all, Pop?

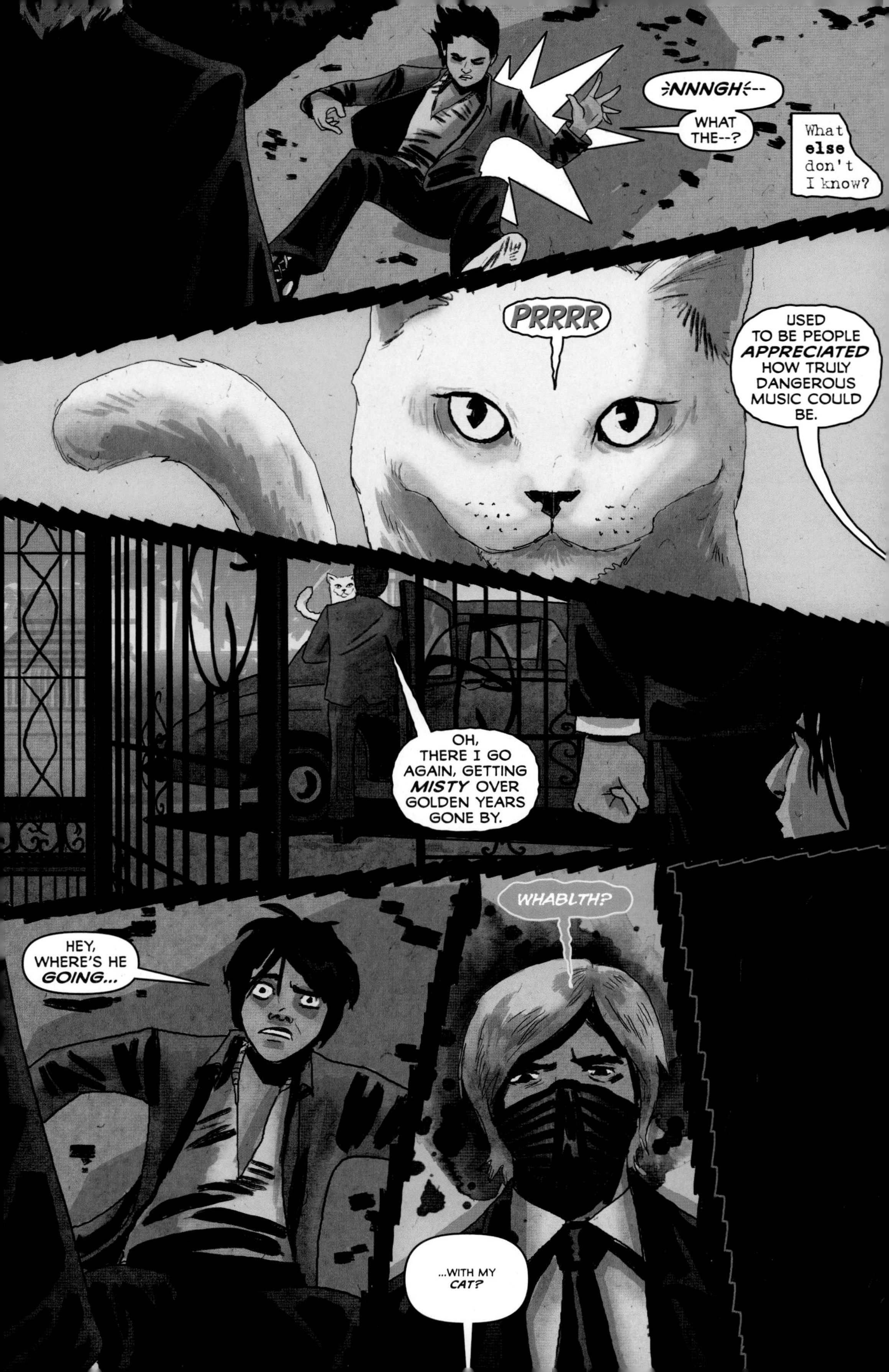
NNNGH--
WHAT THE--?
What else don't I know?
PRRRR
USED TO BE PEOPLE APPRECIATED HOW TRULY DANGEROUS MUSIC COULD BE.
OH, THERE I GO AGAIN, GETTING MISTY OVER GOLDEN YEARS GONE BY.
WHABLTH?
HEY, WHERE'S HE GOING...
...WITH MY CAT?

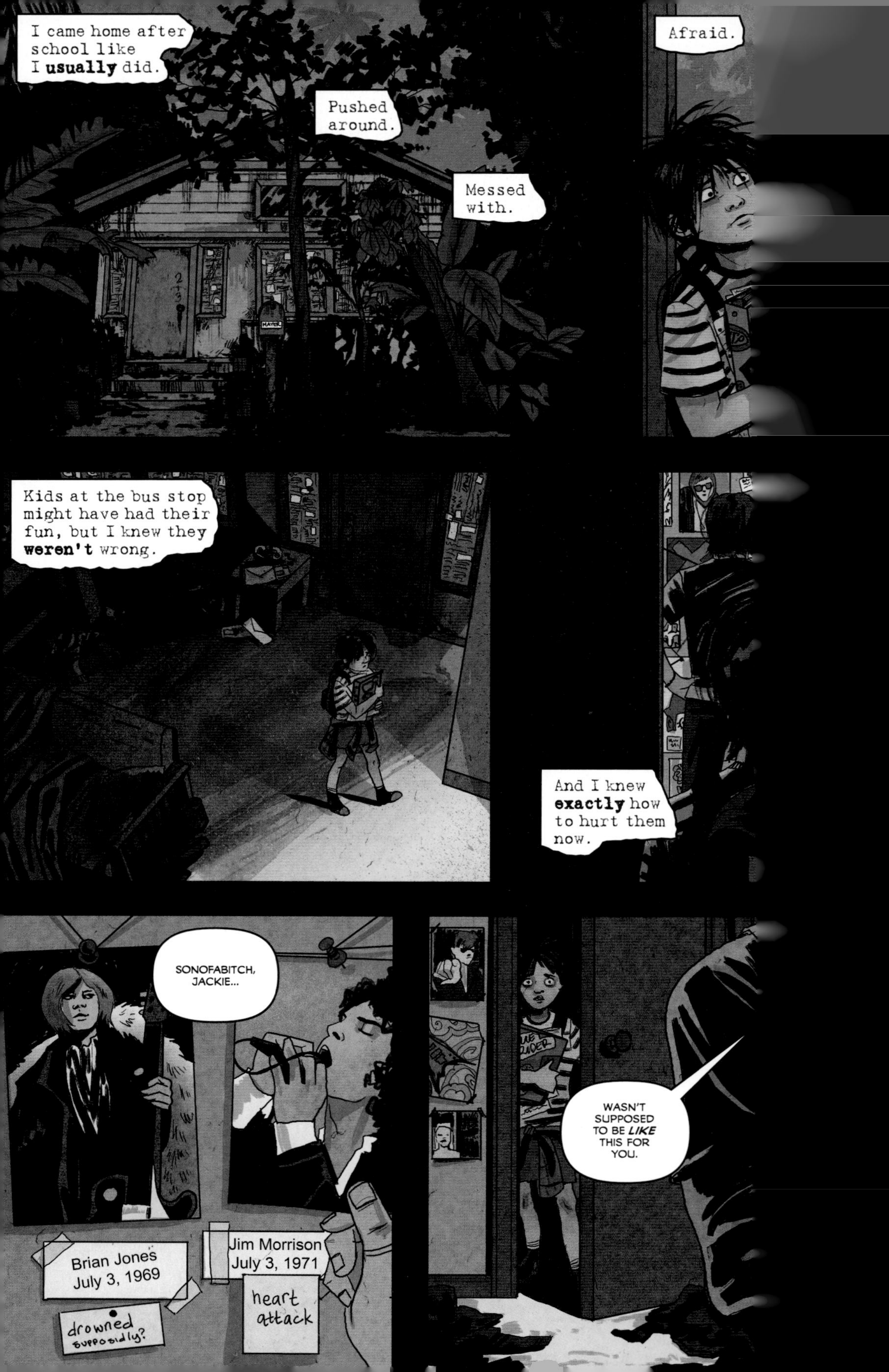
I came home after school like I **usually** did.
Pushed around.
Messed with.
Afraid.
MAYER
Kids at the bus stop might have had their fun, but I knew they **weren't** wrong.
And I knew **exactly** how to hurt them now.
SONOFABITCH, JACKIE...
Brian Jones July 3, 1969
drowned supposidly?
Jim Morrison July 3, 1971
heart attack
WASN'T SUPPOSED TO BE *LIKE* THIS FOR YOU.

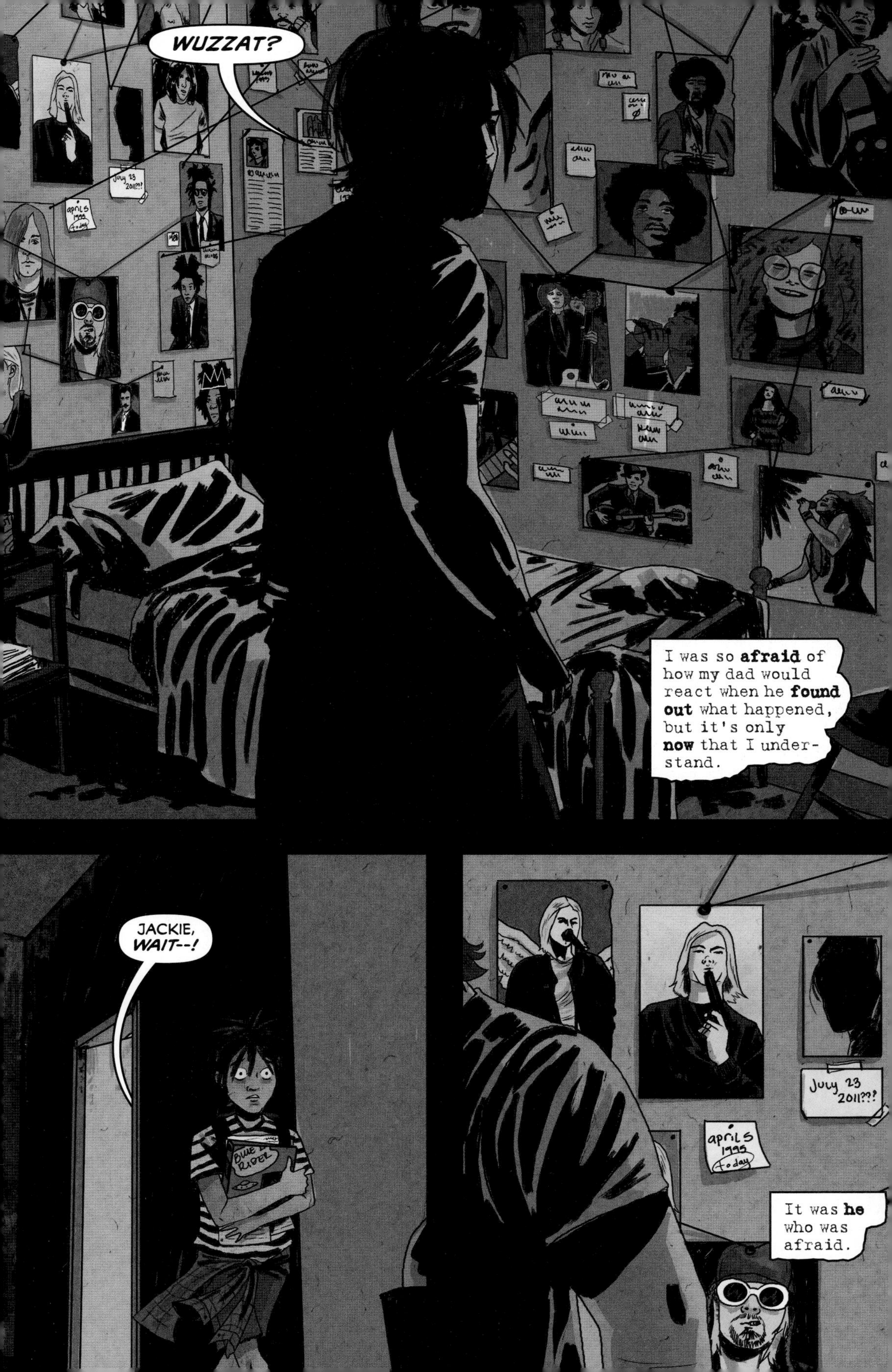
WUZZAT?
I was so **afraid** of how my dad would react when he **found out** what happened, but it's only **now** that I under-stand.
JACKIE, *WAIT--!*
BLUE RIDER
July 23 2011???
april 5 1995 today
It was **he** who was afraid.

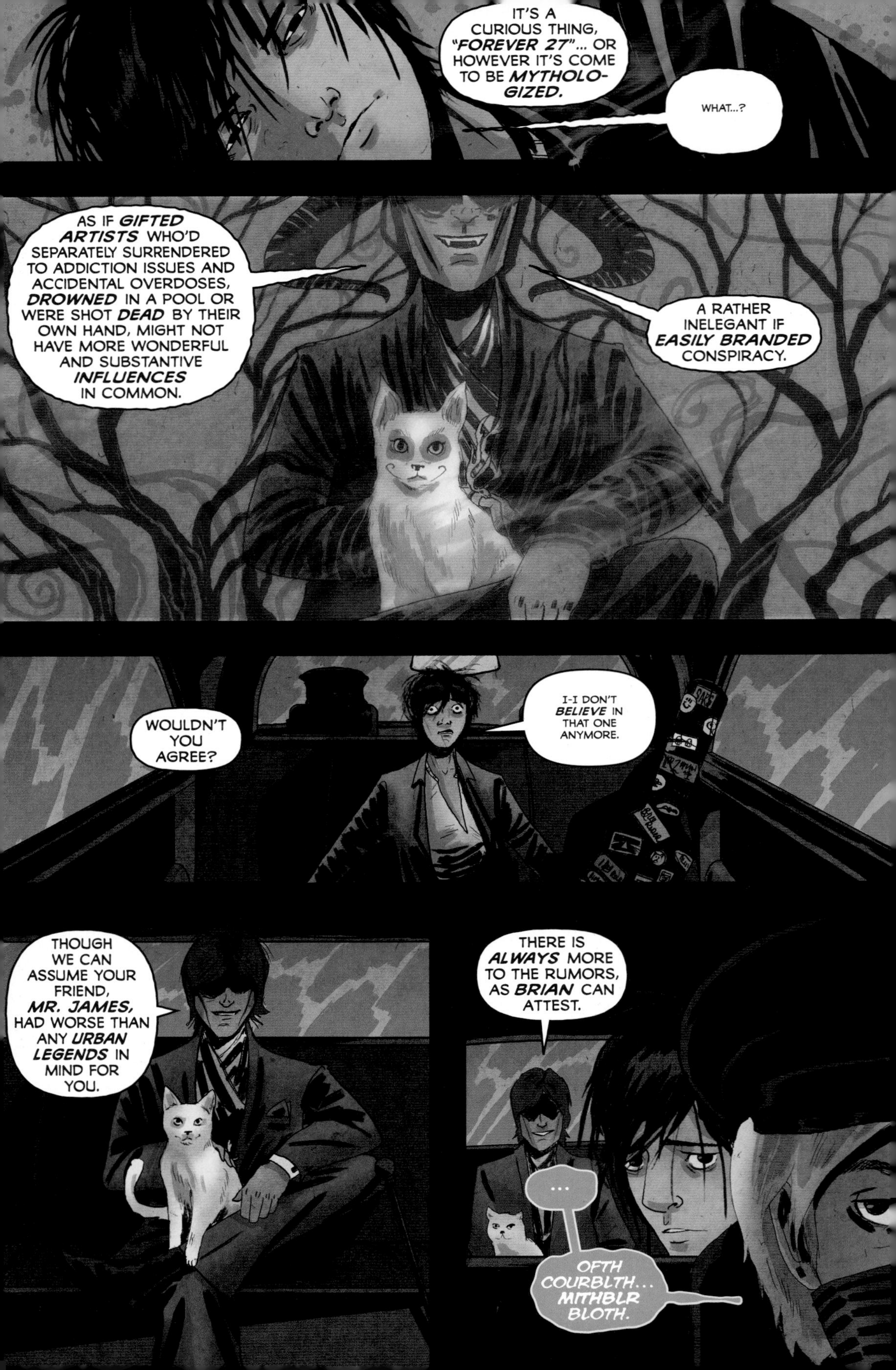
IT'S A CURIOUS THING, "FOREVER 27"... OR HOWEVER IT'S COME TO BE MYTHOLOGIZED.
WHAT...?
AS IF GIFTED ARTISTS WHO'D SEPARATELY SURRENDERED TO ADDICTION ISSUES AND ACCIDENTAL OVERDOSES, DROWNED IN A POOL OR WERE SHOT DEAD BY THEIR OWN HAND, MIGHT NOT HAVE MORE WONDERFUL AND SUBSTANTIVE INFLUENCES IN COMMON.
A RATHER INELEGANT IF EASILY BRANDED CONSPIRACY.
WOULDN'T YOU AGREE?
I-I DON'T BELIEVE IN THAT ONE ANYMORE.
THOUGH WE CAN ASSUME YOUR FRIEND, MR. JAMES, HAD WORSE THAN ANY URBAN LEGENDS IN MIND FOR YOU.
THERE IS ALWAYS MORE TO THE RUMORS, AS BRIAN CAN ATTEST.
...
OFTH COURBLTH... MITHBLR BLOTH.

SOMETHING ABOUT *JIMMY JAMES,* THOUGH.

HE'S A *THIEF.*

I'M JUST A FAN *LOOKING AROUND* FOR STUFF. I DON'T KNOW *ANY-THING* ABOUT ANY--

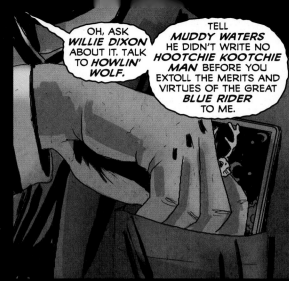

OH, ASK *WILLIE DIXON* ABOUT IT. TALK TO *HOWLIN' WOLF.*

TELL *MUDDY WATERS* HE DIDN'T WRITE NO *HOOTCHIE KOOTCHIE MAN* BEFORE YOU EXTOLL THE MERITS AND VIRTUES OF THE GREAT *BLUE RIDER* TO ME.

THEN, I'VE KNOWN AN *INNUMERABLE* NUMBER OF BRILLIANT ARTISTS WHO WERE *CERTAIN* THEY HAD THE *GAME* ALL FIGURED OUT.

BUT THAT'S HOW THEY *DO* IT, JACKIE.

THEY PLAY *SMALL* GAMES WITH THEMSELVES, ALL THE WHILE LOOKING FOR A *CHEAT.*

I-I *LIKE* BLUE RIDER.

USED TO, I MEAN.

YOU'RE LOOKING FOR A *KILLER* WHO DOESN'T *EXIST...*

...BUT WHOSE *CRIMES* ARE AS REAL, AND RICH AND WILD AS THE *CRAZIEST THEORIES* CAN ONLY CHANCE TO GUESS.

WHO *ARE* YOU?

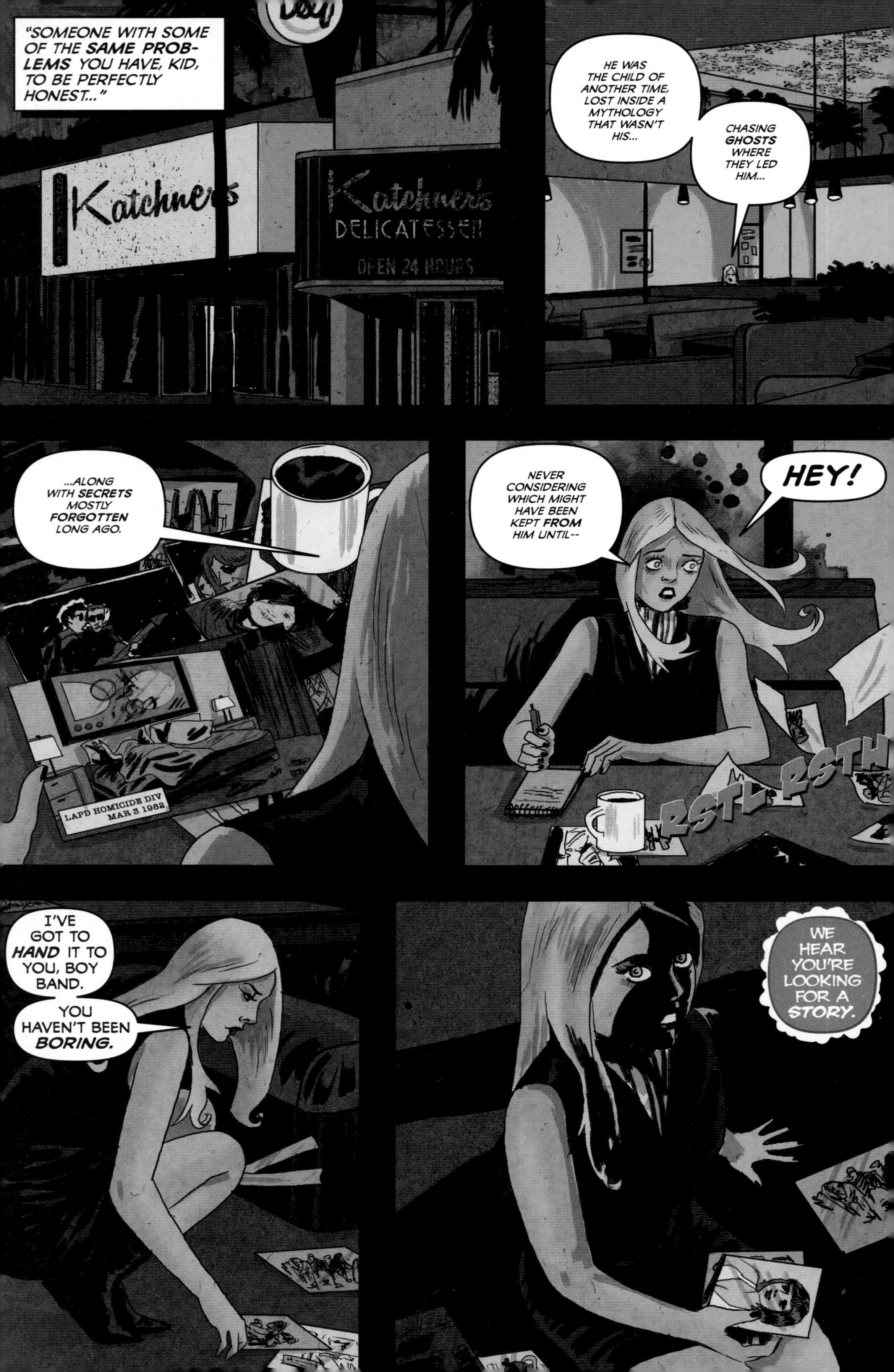
"SOMEONE WITH SOME OF THE SAME PROBLEMS YOU HAVE, KID, TO BE PERFECTLY HONEST..."
Katchner's
Katchner's DELICATESSEN
OPEN 24 HOURS
HE WAS THE CHILD OF ANOTHER TIME, LOST INSIDE A MYTHOLOGY THAT WASN'T HIS...
CHASING GHOSTS WHERE THEY LED HIM...
...ALONG WITH SECRETS MOSTLY FORGOTTEN LONG AGO.
LAPD HOMICIDE DIV MAR 3 1982
NEVER CONSIDERING WHICH MIGHT HAVE BEEN KEPT FROM HIM UNTIL--
HEY!
RSTL RSTH
I'VE GOT TO HAND IT TO YOU, BOY BAND.
YOU HAVEN'T BEEN BORING.
WE HEAR YOU'RE LOOKING FOR A STORY.

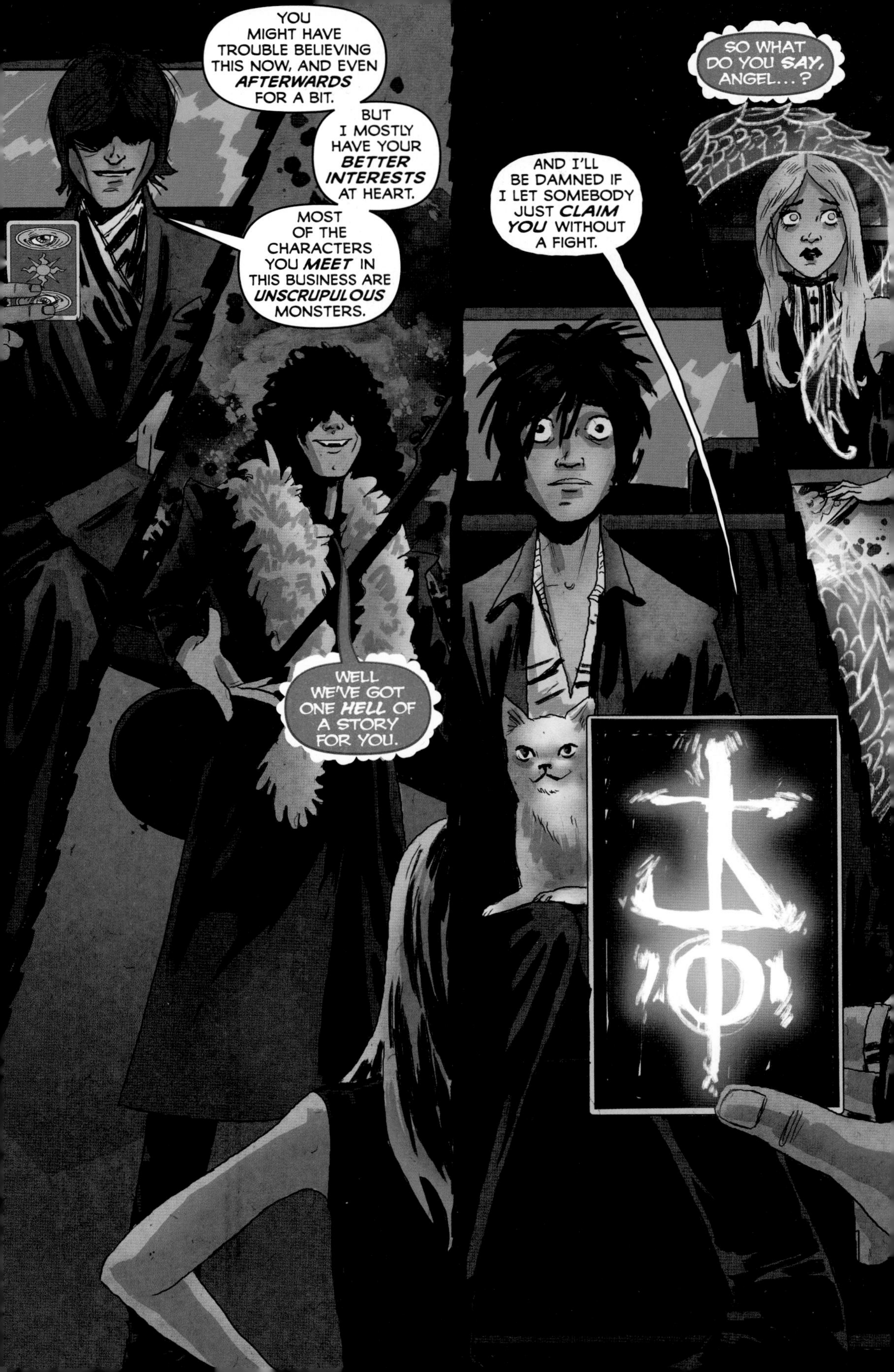
YOU MIGHT HAVE TROUBLE BELIEVING THIS NOW, AND EVEN AFTERWARDS FOR A BIT.
BUT I MOSTLY HAVE YOUR BETTER INTERESTS AT HEART.
MOST OF THE CHARACTERS YOU MEET IN THIS BUSINESS ARE UNSCRUPULOUS MONSTERS.
WELL WE'VE GOT ONE HELL OF A STORY FOR YOU.
AND I'LL BE DAMNED IF I LET SOMEBODY JUST CLAIM YOU WITHOUT A FIGHT.
SO WHAT DO YOU SAY, ANGEL...?

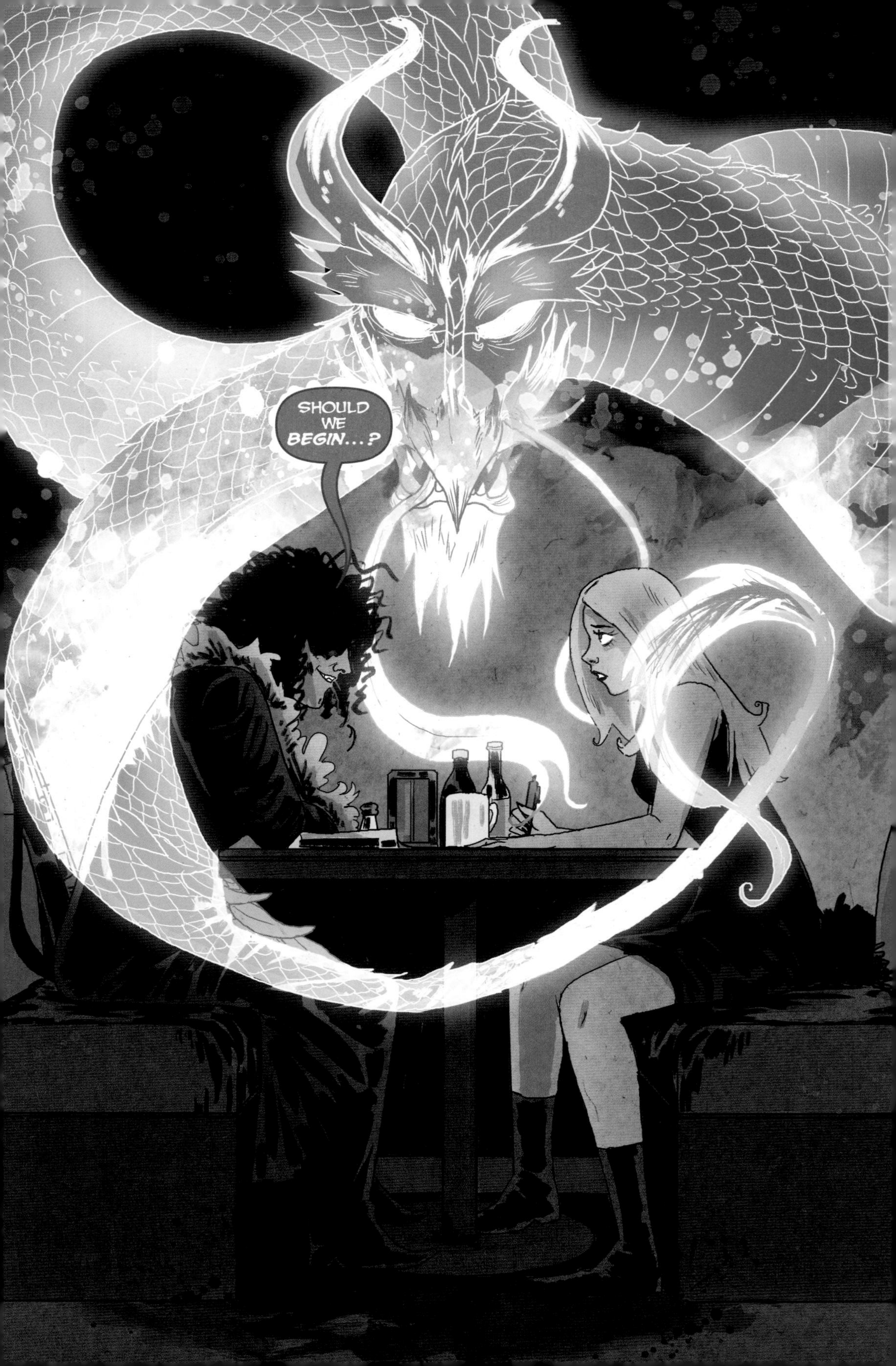
SHOULD WE BEGIN...?

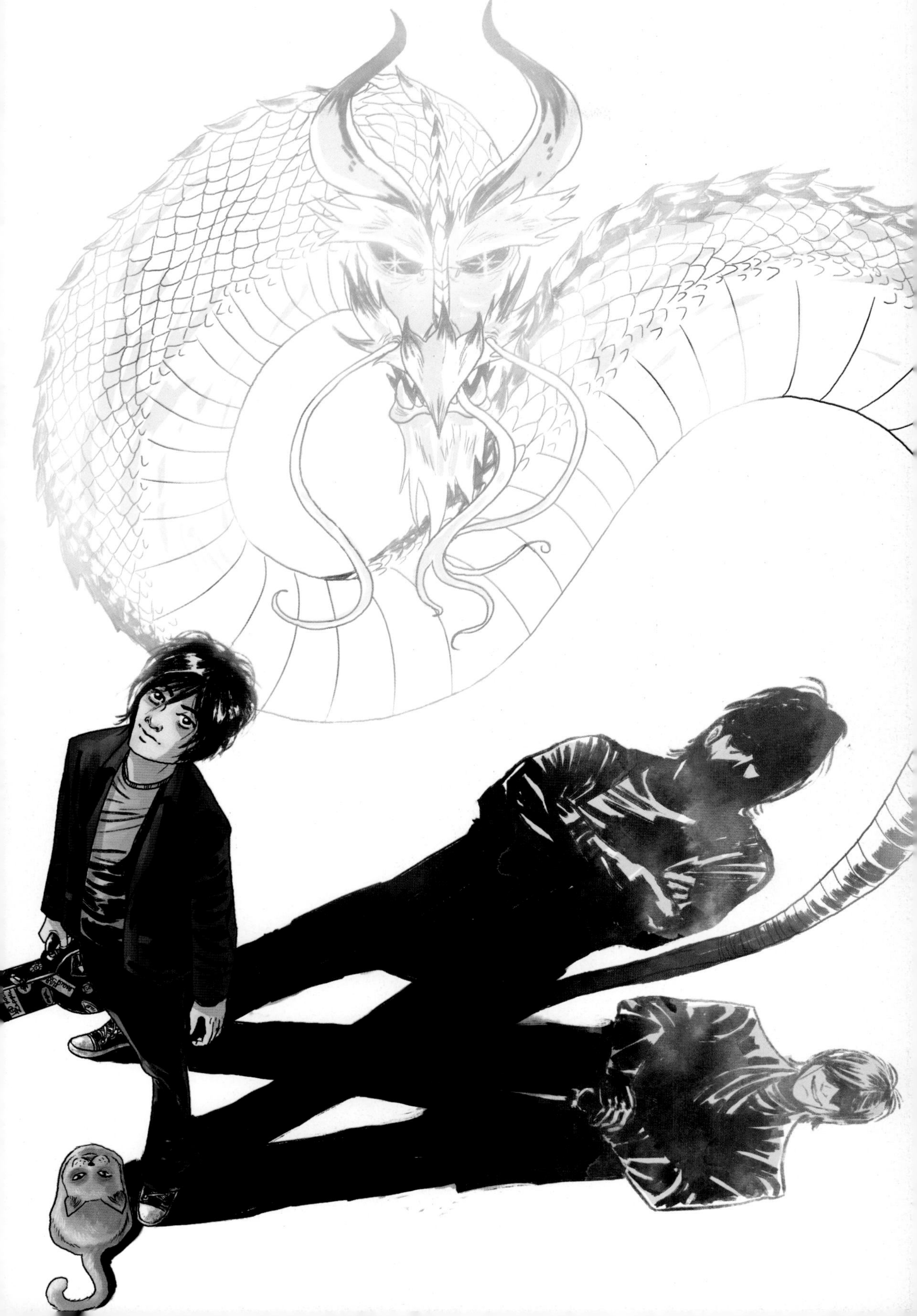

Dorothy takes tea with the Dragon, while the Devil himself calls the tune. And it seems everybody wants a piece of Jackie, but Jackie's gone to pieces. Are they playing the Game... OR ARE THEY GETTING PLAYED?

ROCKSTARS

SIDE # 1 **FULL COLOR**		**Track 5**

NATIVITY IN
BLACKLIGHT

22

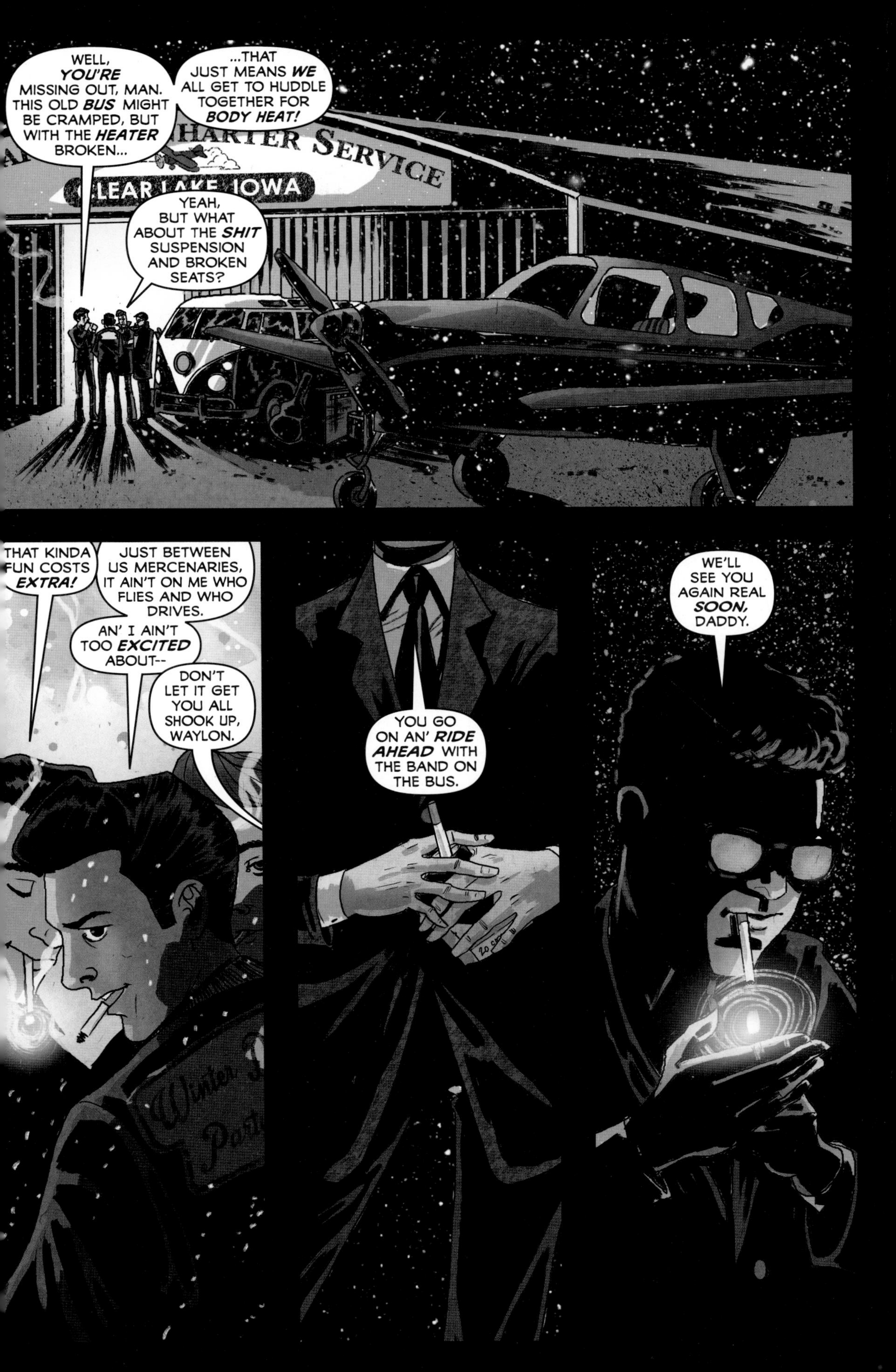

WELL, YOU'RE MISSING OUT, MAN. THIS OLD BUS MIGHT BE CRAMPED, BUT WITH THE HEATER BROKEN...
...THAT JUST MEANS WE ALL GET TO HUDDLE TOGETHER FOR BODY HEAT!
HARTER SERVICE
CLEAR LAKE IOWA
YEAH, BUT WHAT ABOUT THE SHIT SUSPENSION AND BROKEN SEATS?
THAT KINDA FUN COSTS EXTRA!
JUST BETWEEN US MERCENARIES, IT AIN'T ON ME WHO FLIES AND WHO DRIVES.
AN' I AIN'T TOO EXCITED ABOUT--
DON'T LET IT GET YOU ALL SHOOK UP, WAYLON.
YOU GO ON AN' RIDE AHEAD WITH THE BAND ON THE BUS.
WE'LL SEE YOU AGAIN REAL SOON, DADDY.

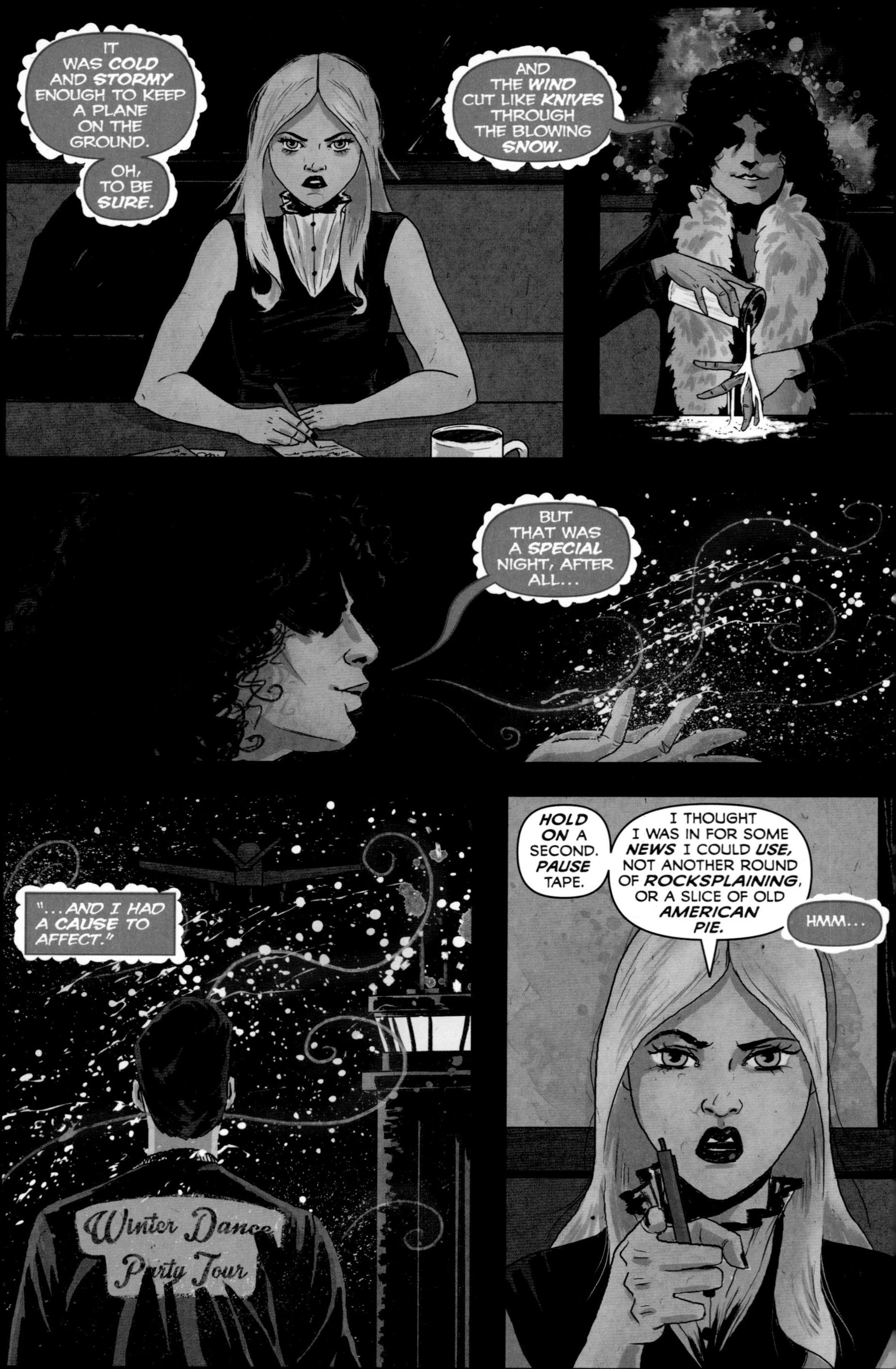
IT WAS COLD AND STORMY ENOUGH TO KEEP A PLANE ON THE GROUND.
OH, TO BE SURE.
AND THE WIND CUT LIKE KNIVES THROUGH THE BLOWING SNOW.
BUT THAT WAS A SPECIAL NIGHT, AFTER ALL...
"...AND I HAD A CAUSE TO AFFECT."
Winter Dance Party Tour
HOLD ON A SECOND. PAUSE TAPE.
I THOUGHT I WAS IN FOR SOME NEWS I COULD USE, NOT ANOTHER ROUND OF ROCKSPLAINING, OR A SLICE OF OLD AMERICAN PIE.
HMM...

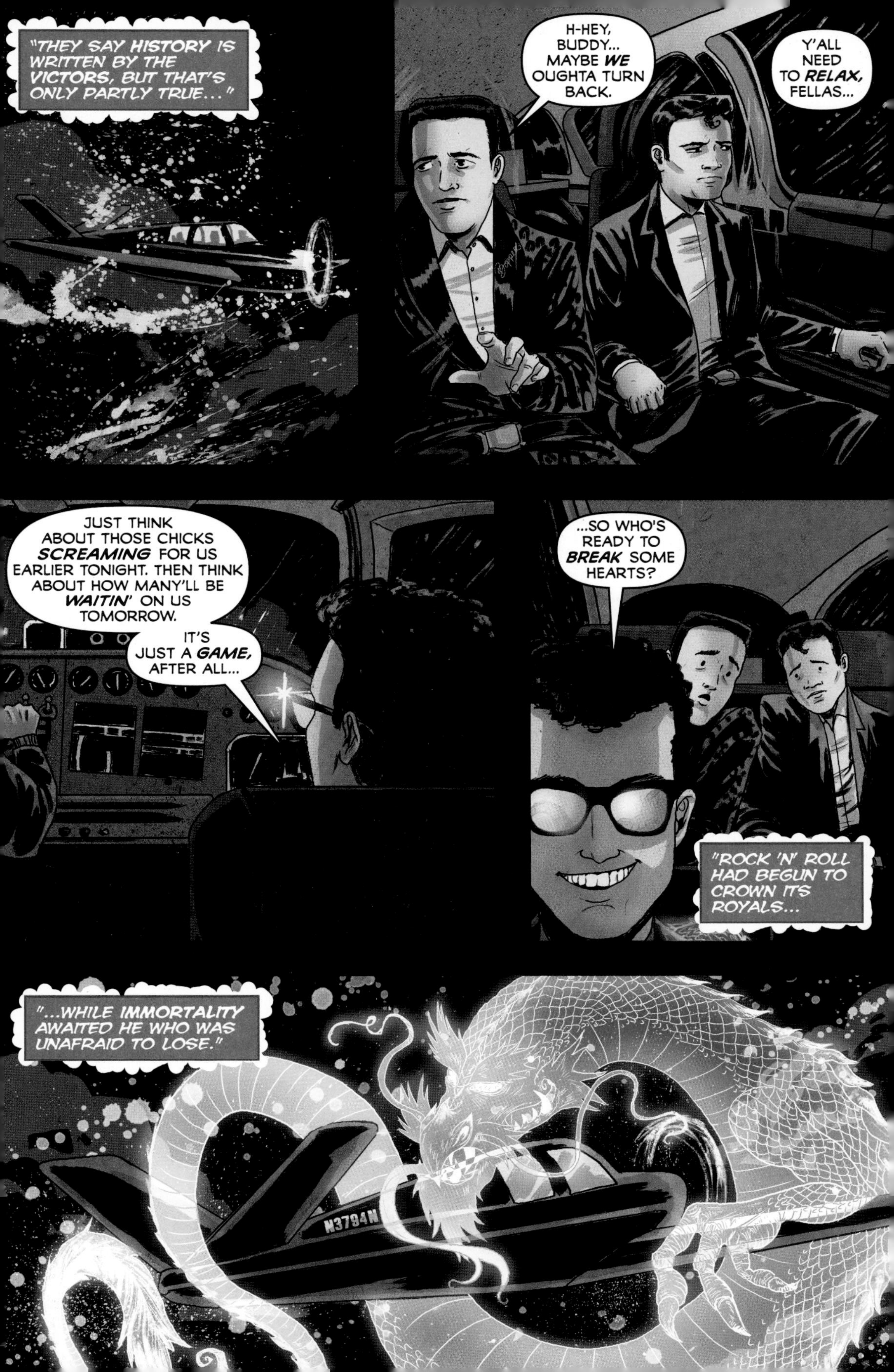
"THEY SAY HISTORY IS WRITTEN BY THE VICTORS, BUT THAT'S ONLY PARTLY TRUE..."
H-HEY, BUDDY... MAYBE WE OUGHTA TURN BACK.
Y'ALL NEED TO RELAX, FELLAS...
JUST THINK ABOUT THOSE CHICKS SCREAMING FOR US EARLIER TONIGHT. THEN THINK ABOUT HOW MANY'LL BE WAITIN' ON US TOMORROW.
IT'S JUST A GAME, AFTER ALL...
...SO WHO'S READY TO BREAK SOME HEARTS?
"ROCK 'N' ROLL HAD BEGUN TO CROWN ITS ROYALS...
"...WHILE IMMORTALITY AWAITED HE WHO WAS UNAFRAID TO LOSE."
N3794N

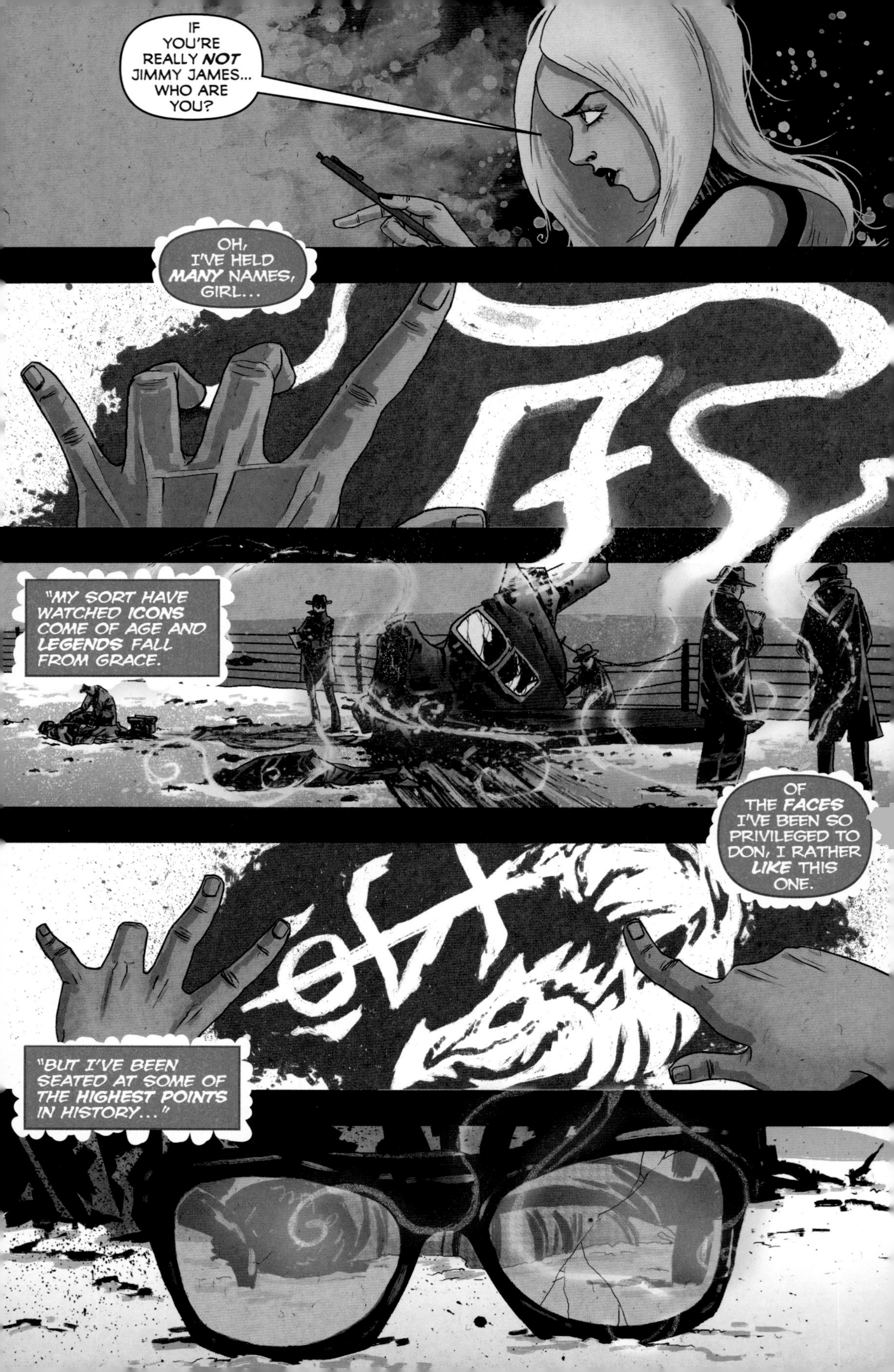
IF YOU'RE REALLY NOT JIMMY JAMES... WHO ARE YOU?
OH, I'VE HELD MANY NAMES, GIRL...
"MY SORT HAVE WATCHED ICONS COME OF AGE AND LEGENDS FALL FROM GRACE.
OF THE FACES I'VE BEEN SO PRIVILEGED TO DON, I RATHER LIKE THIS ONE.
"BUT I'VE BEEN SEATED AT SOME OF THE HIGHEST POINTS IN HISTORY..."

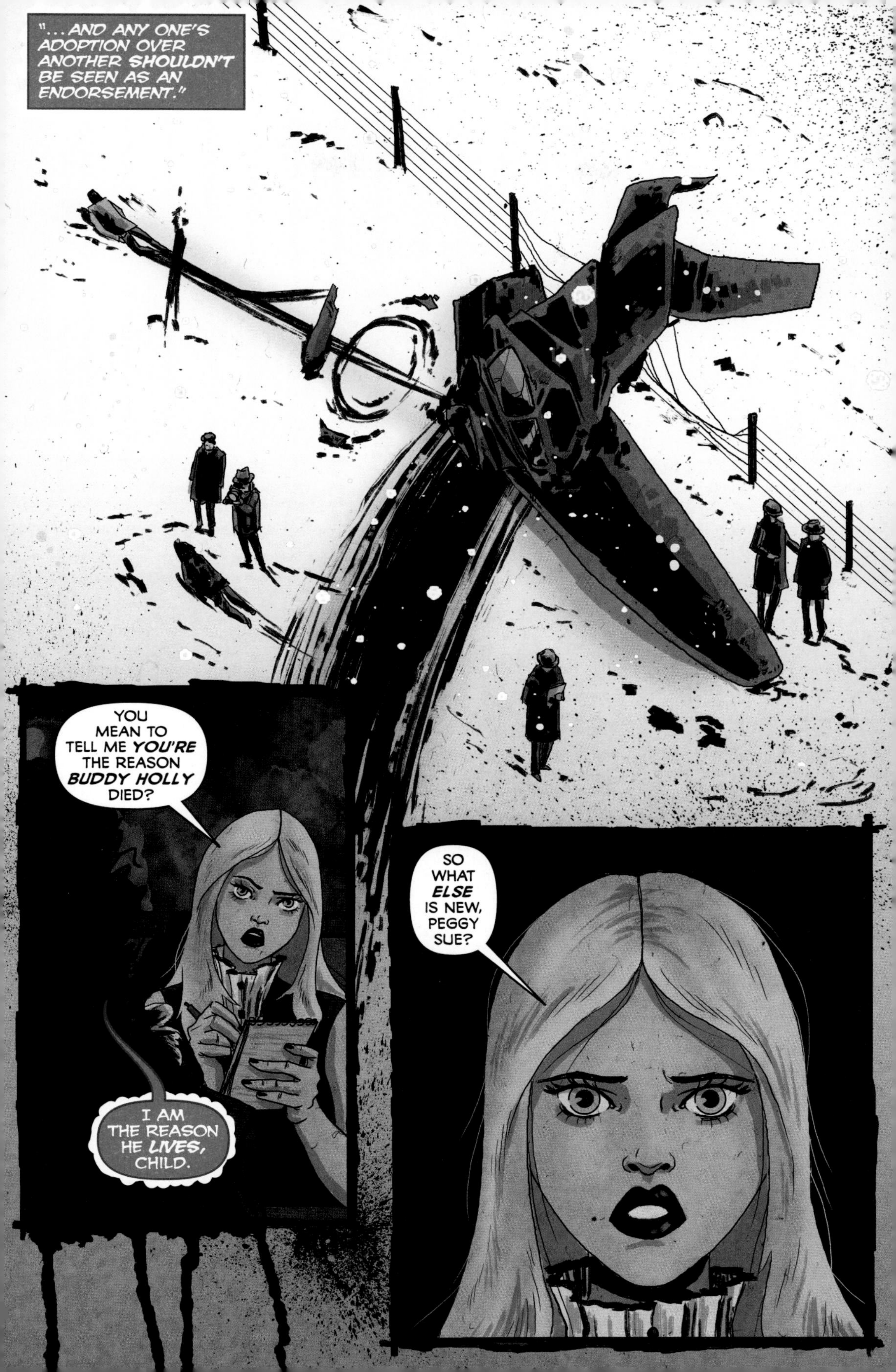
"...AND ANY ONE'S ADOPTION OVER ANOTHER SHOULDN'T BE SEEN AS AN ENDORSEMENT."
YOU MEAN TO TELL ME YOU'RE THE REASON BUDDY HOLLY DIED?
I AM THE REASON HE LIVES, CHILD.
SO WHAT ELSE IS NEW, PEGGY SUE?

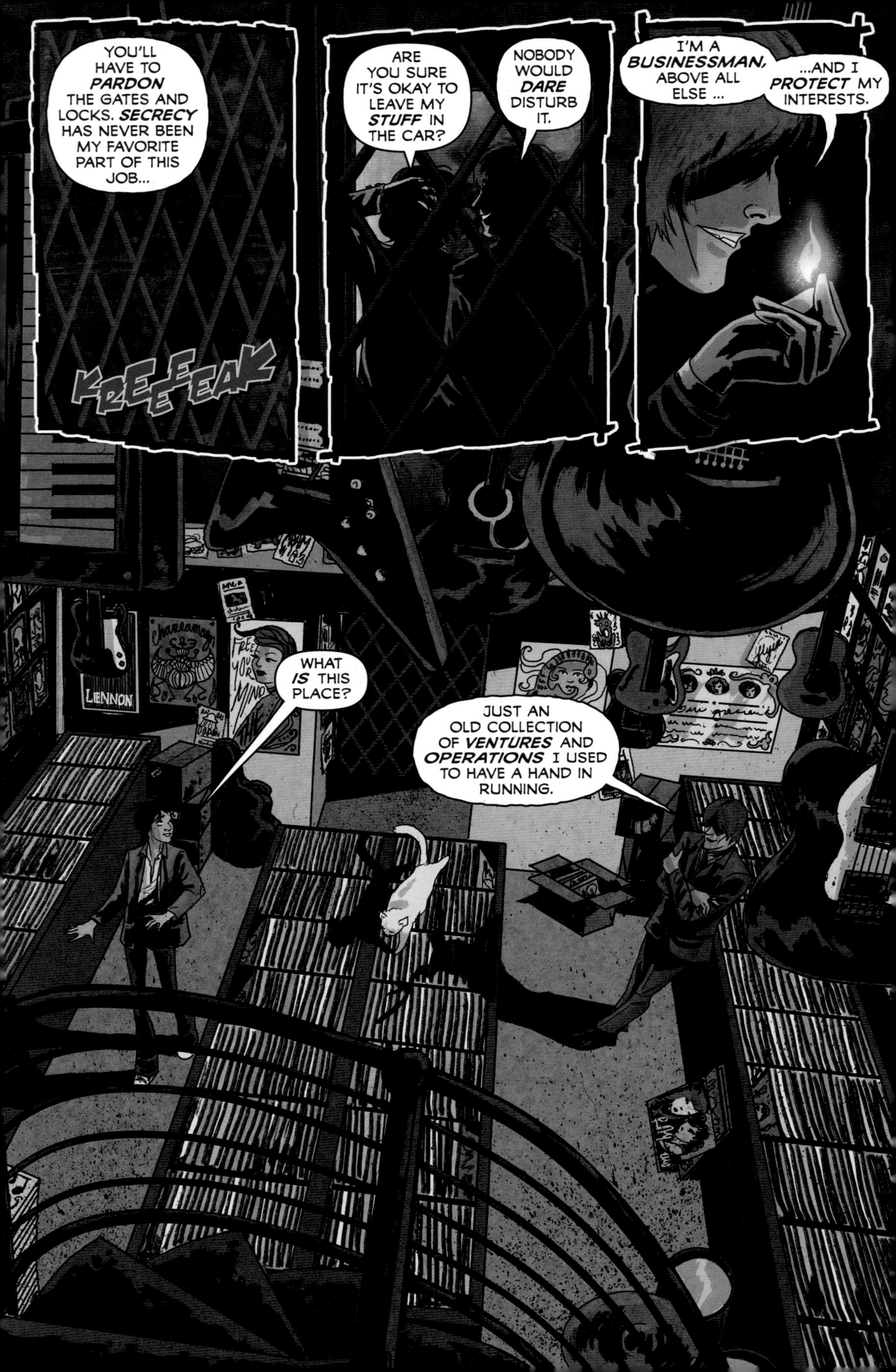
YOU'LL HAVE TO PARDON THE GATES AND LOCKS. SECRECY HAS NEVER BEEN MY FAVORITE PART OF THIS JOB...
KREEEEAK
ARE YOU SURE IT'S OKAY TO LEAVE MY STUFF IN THE CAR?
NOBODY WOULD DARE DISTURB IT.
I'M A BUSINESSMAN, ABOVE ALL ELSE ...
...AND I PROTECT MY INTERESTS.
LENNON
WHAT IS THIS PLACE?
JUST AN OLD COLLECTION OF VENTURES AND OPERATIONS I USED TO HAVE A HAND IN RUNNING.

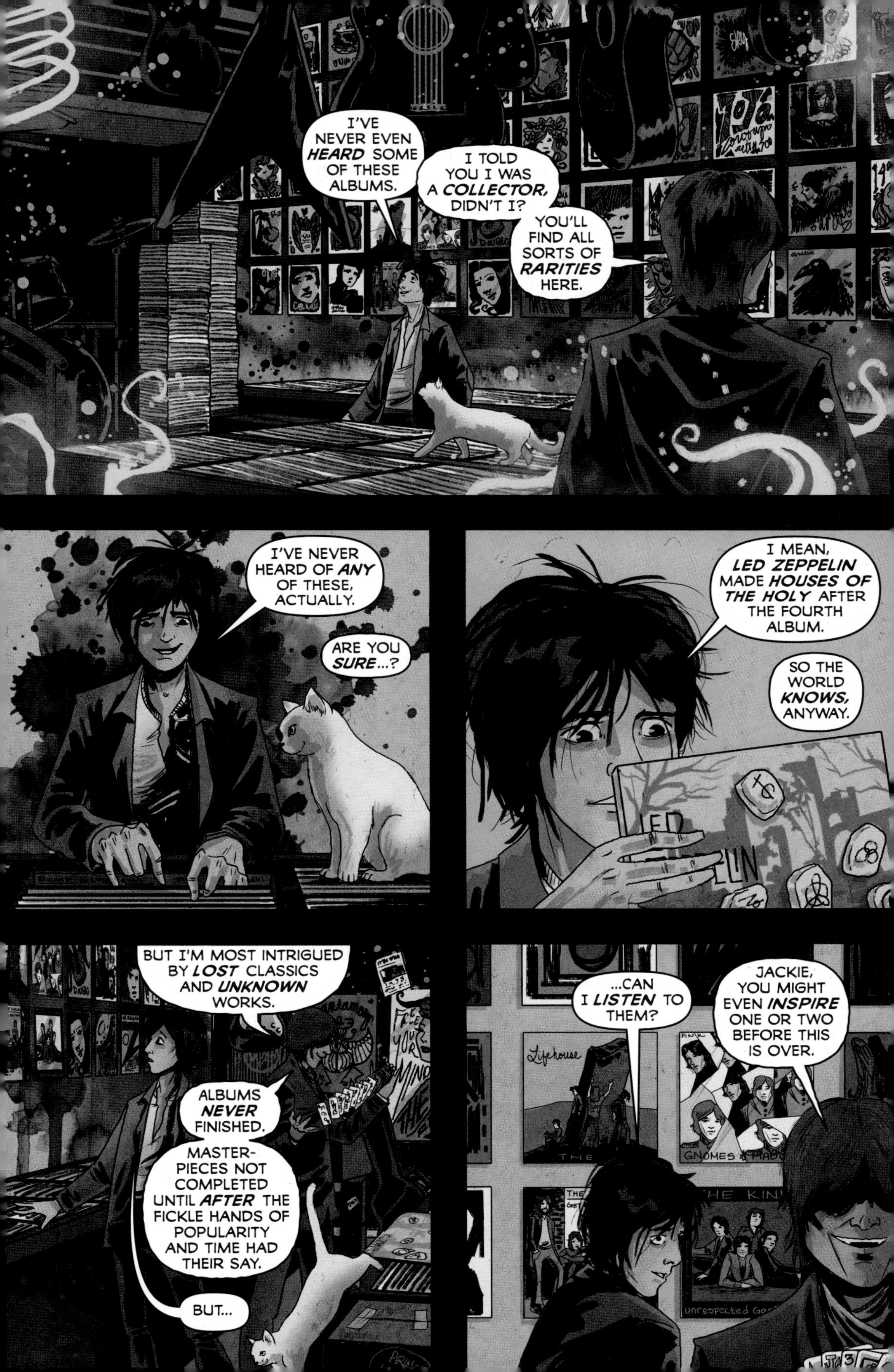
I'VE NEVER EVEN HEARD SOME OF THESE ALBUMS.
I TOLD YOU I WAS A COLLECTOR, DIDN'T I?
YOU'LL FIND ALL SORTS OF RARITIES HERE.
I'VE NEVER HEARD OF ANY OF THESE, ACTUALLY.
ARE YOU SURE...?
I MEAN, LED ZEPPELIN MADE HOUSES OF THE HOLY AFTER THE FOURTH ALBUM.
SO THE WORLD KNOWS, ANYWAY.
BUT I'M MOST INTRIGUED BY LOST CLASSICS AND UNKNOWN WORKS.
ALBUMS NEVER FINISHED.
MASTER-PIECES NOT COMPLETED UNTIL AFTER THE FICKLE HANDS OF POPULARITY AND TIME HAD THEIR SAY.
BUT...
...CAN I LISTEN TO THEM?
JACKIE, YOU MIGHT EVEN INSPIRE ONE OR TWO BEFORE THIS IS OVER.
Lifehouse
Unrespected Gods

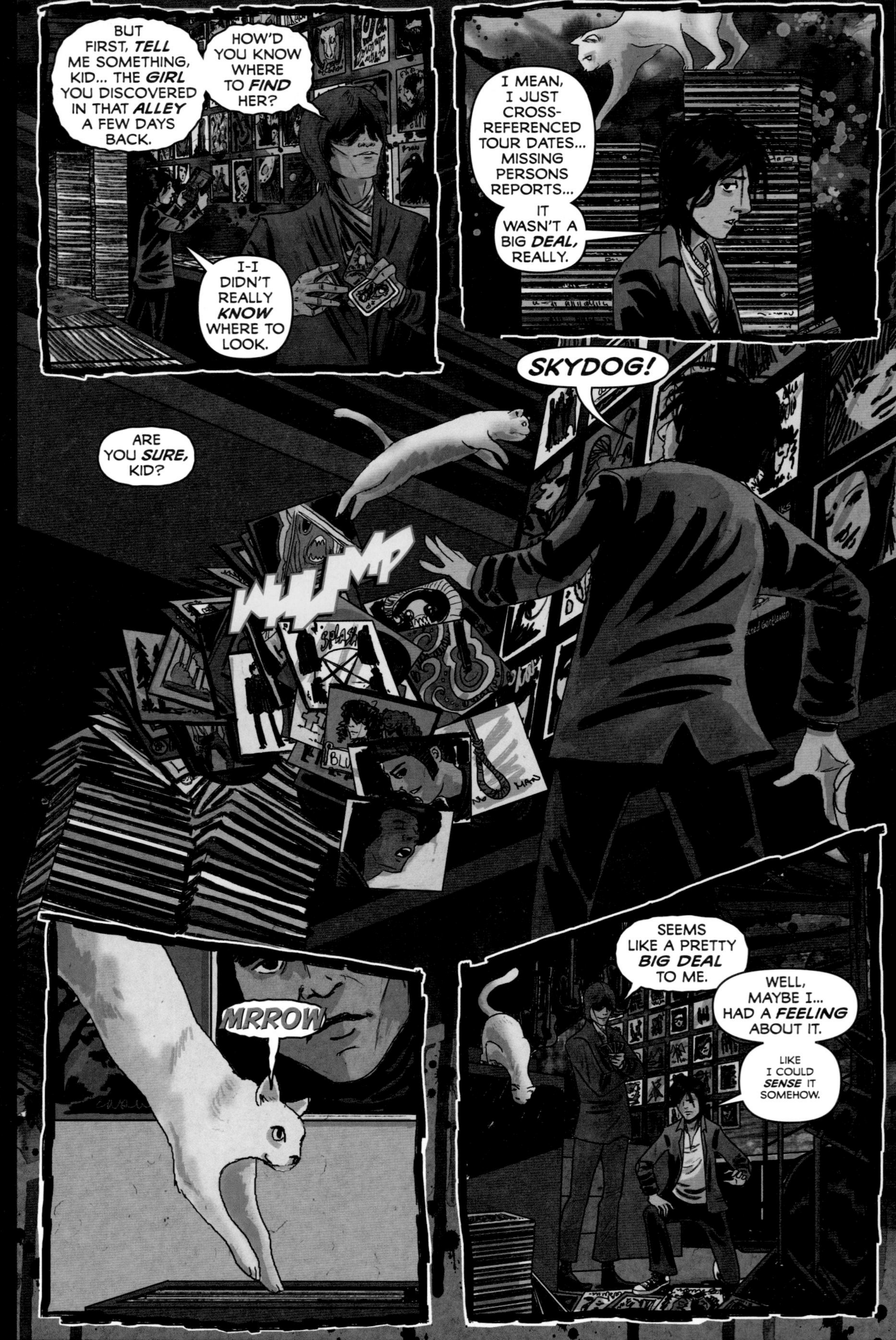
BUT FIRST, TELL ME SOMETHING, KID... THE GIRL YOU DISCOVERED IN THAT ALLEY A FEW DAYS BACK.
HOW'D YOU KNOW WHERE TO FIND HER?
I-I DIDN'T REALLY KNOW WHERE TO LOOK.
I MEAN, I JUST CROSS-REFERENCED TOUR DATES... MISSING PERSONS REPORTS...
IT WASN'T A BIG DEAL, REALLY.
SKYDOG!
ARE YOU SURE, KID?
WHUMP
MRROW
SEEMS LIKE A PRETTY BIG DEAL TO ME.
WELL, MAYBE I... HAD A FEELING ABOUT IT.
LIKE I COULD SENSE IT SOMEHOW.

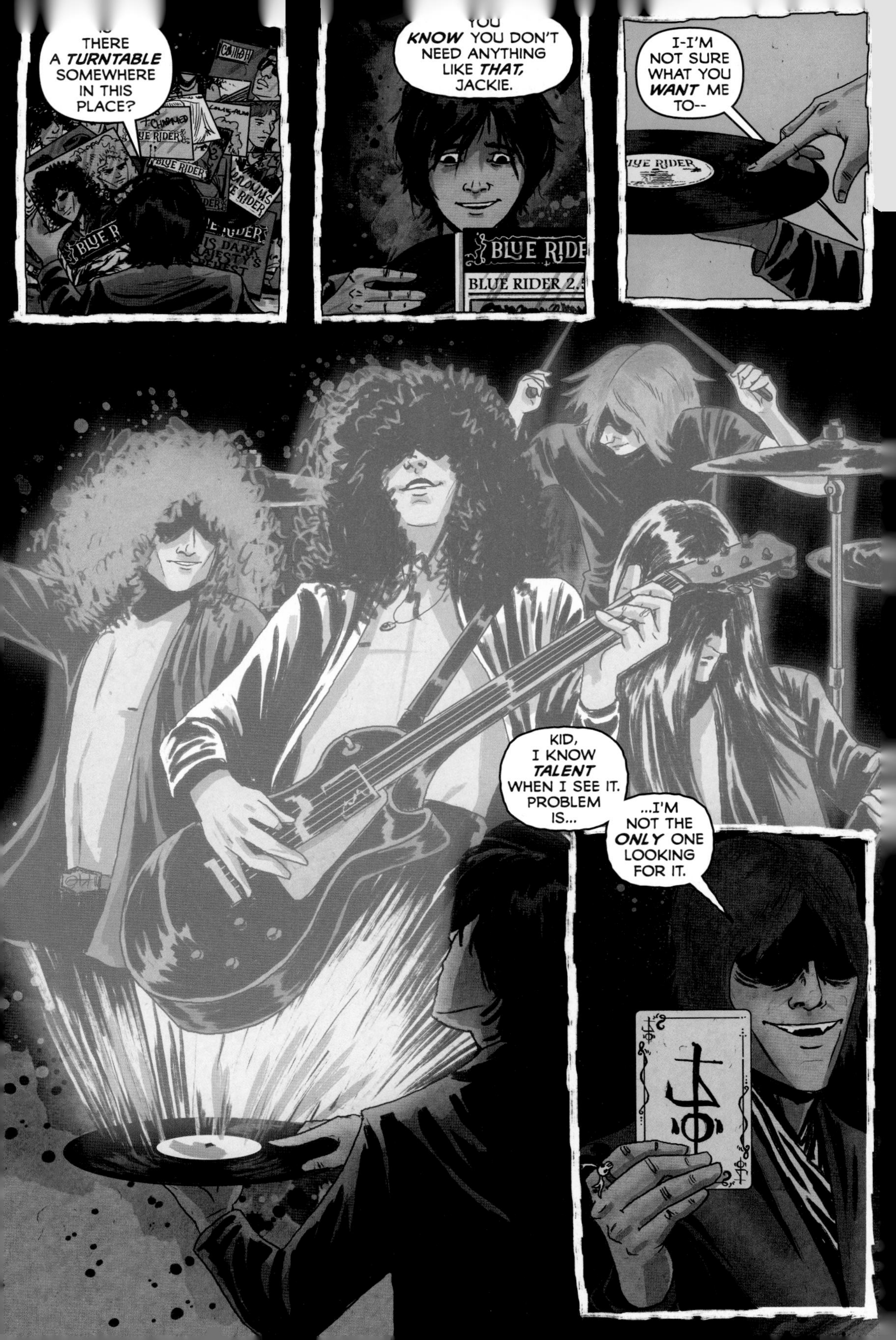

THERE A *TURNTABLE* SOMEWHERE IN THIS PLACE?
BLUE RIDER
YOU *KNOW* YOU DON'T NEED ANYTHING LIKE *THAT,* JACKIE.
I-I'M NOT SURE WHAT YOU *WANT* ME TO--
KID, I KNOW *TALENT* WHEN I SEE IT. PROBLEM IS...
...I'M NOT THE *ONLY* ONE LOOKING FOR IT.

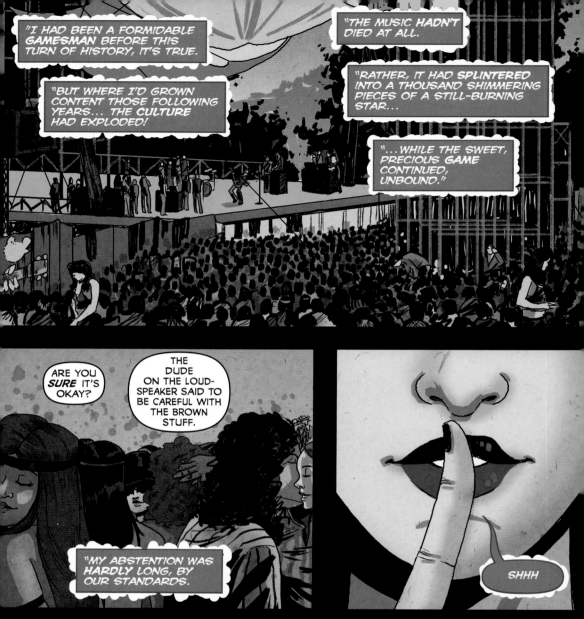

"I HAD BEEN A FORMIDABLE GAMESMAN BEFORE THIS TURN OF HISTORY, IT'S TRUE.

"THE MUSIC HADN'T DIED AT ALL.

"BUT WHERE I'D GROWN CONTENT THOSE FOLLOWING YEARS... THE CULTURE HAD EXPLODED!

"RATHER, IT HAD SPLINTERED INTO A THOUSAND SHIMMERING PIECES OF A STILL-BURNING STAR...

"...WHILE THE SWEET, PRECIOUS GAME CONTINUED, UNBOUND."

ARE YOU SURE IT'S OKAY?

THE DUDE ON THE LOUD-SPEAKER SAID TO BE CAREFUL WITH THE BROWN STUFF.

"MY ABSTENTION WAS HARDLY LONG, BY OUR STANDARDS.

SHHH

"AND I'D STILL FOUND WAYS TO STAY INVOLVED."

I THINK I'M FEELIN' IT!

"BUT THE TRUTH WAS THAT I'D GROWN SOFT."

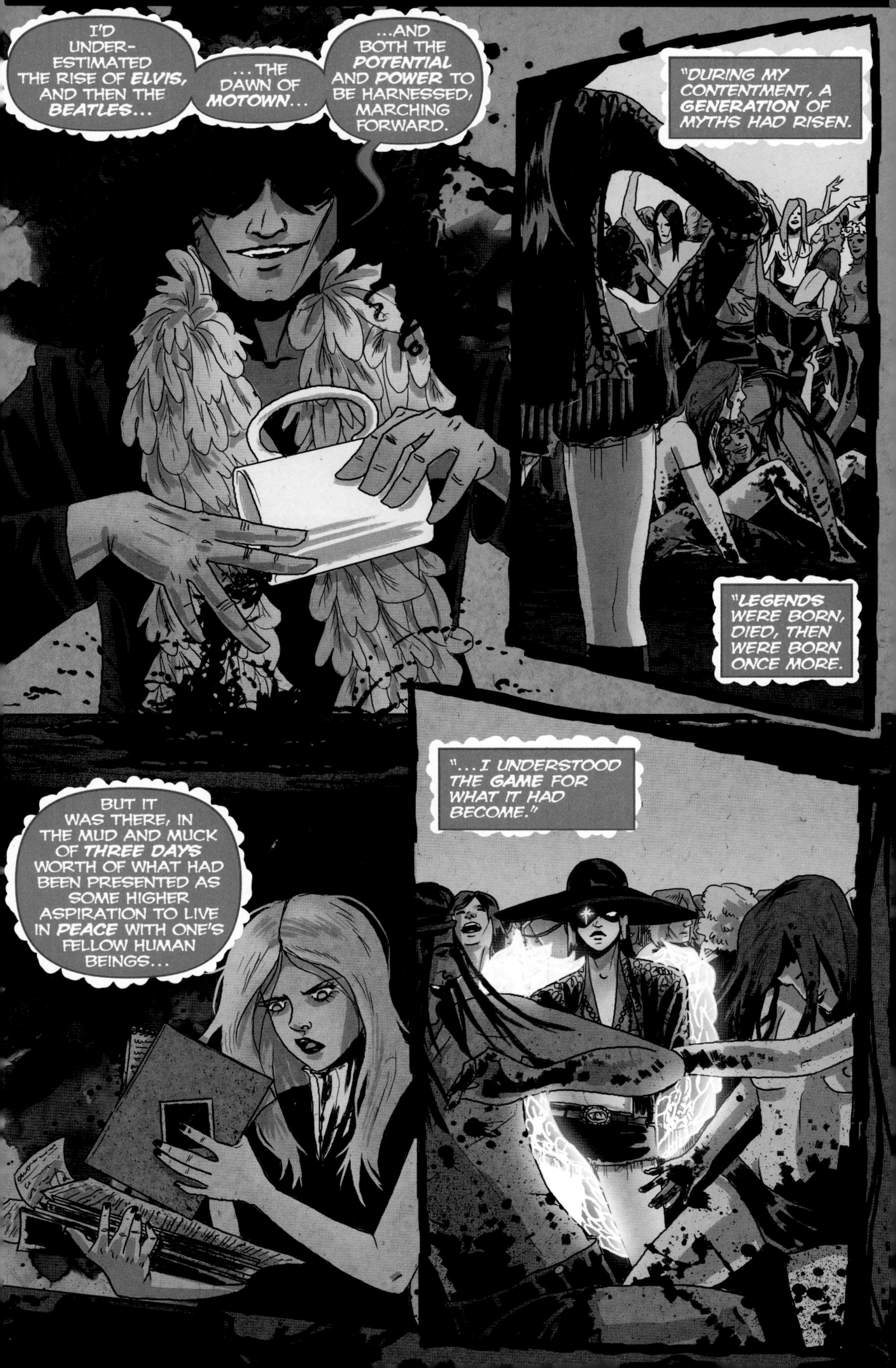
I'D UNDER-ESTIMATED THE RISE OF ELVIS, AND THEN THE BEATLES...
...THE DAWN OF MOTOWN...
...AND BOTH THE POTENTIAL AND POWER TO BE HARNESSED, MARCHING FORWARD.
"DURING MY CONTENTMENT, A GENERATION OF MYTHS HAD RISEN.
"LEGENDS WERE BORN, DIED, THEN WERE BORN ONCE MORE.
BUT IT WAS THERE, IN THE MUD AND MUCK OF THREE DAYS WORTH OF WHAT HAD BEEN PRESENTED AS SOME HIGHER ASPIRATION TO LIVE IN PEACE WITH ONE'S FELLOW HUMAN BEINGS...
"...I UNDERSTOOD THE GAME FOR WHAT IT HAD BECOME."

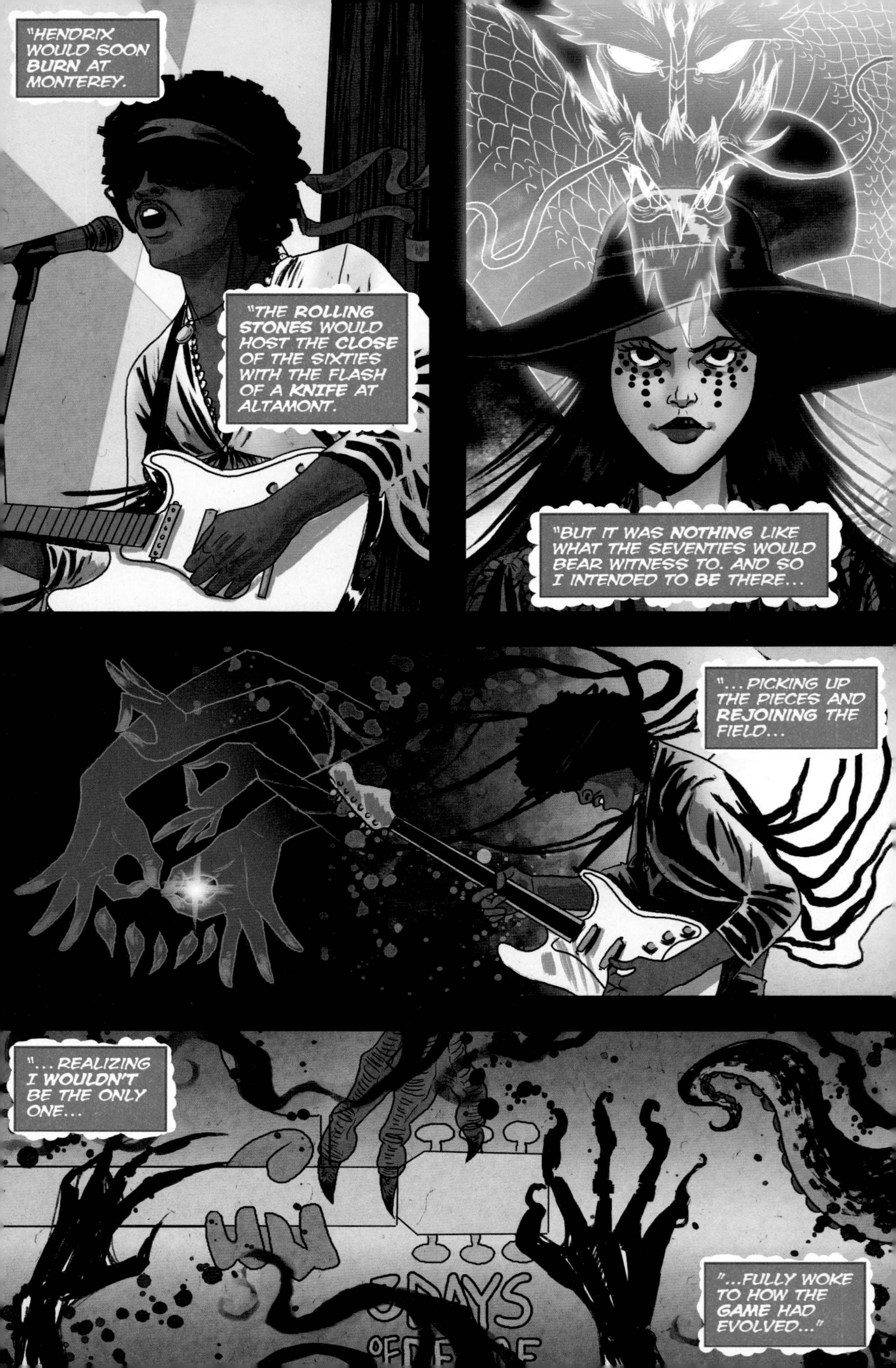
"HENDRIX WOULD SOON BURN AT MONTEREY.
"THE ROLLING STONES WOULD HOST THE CLOSE OF THE SIXTIES WITH THE FLASH OF A KNIFE AT ALTAMONT.
"BUT IT WAS NOTHING LIKE WHAT THE SEVENTIES WOULD BEAR WITNESS TO. AND SO I INTENDED TO BE THERE...
"...PICKING UP THE PIECES AND REJOINING THE FIELD...
"...REALIZING I WOULDN'T BE THE ONLY ONE...
"...FULLY WOKE TO HOW THE GAME HAD EVOLVED..."

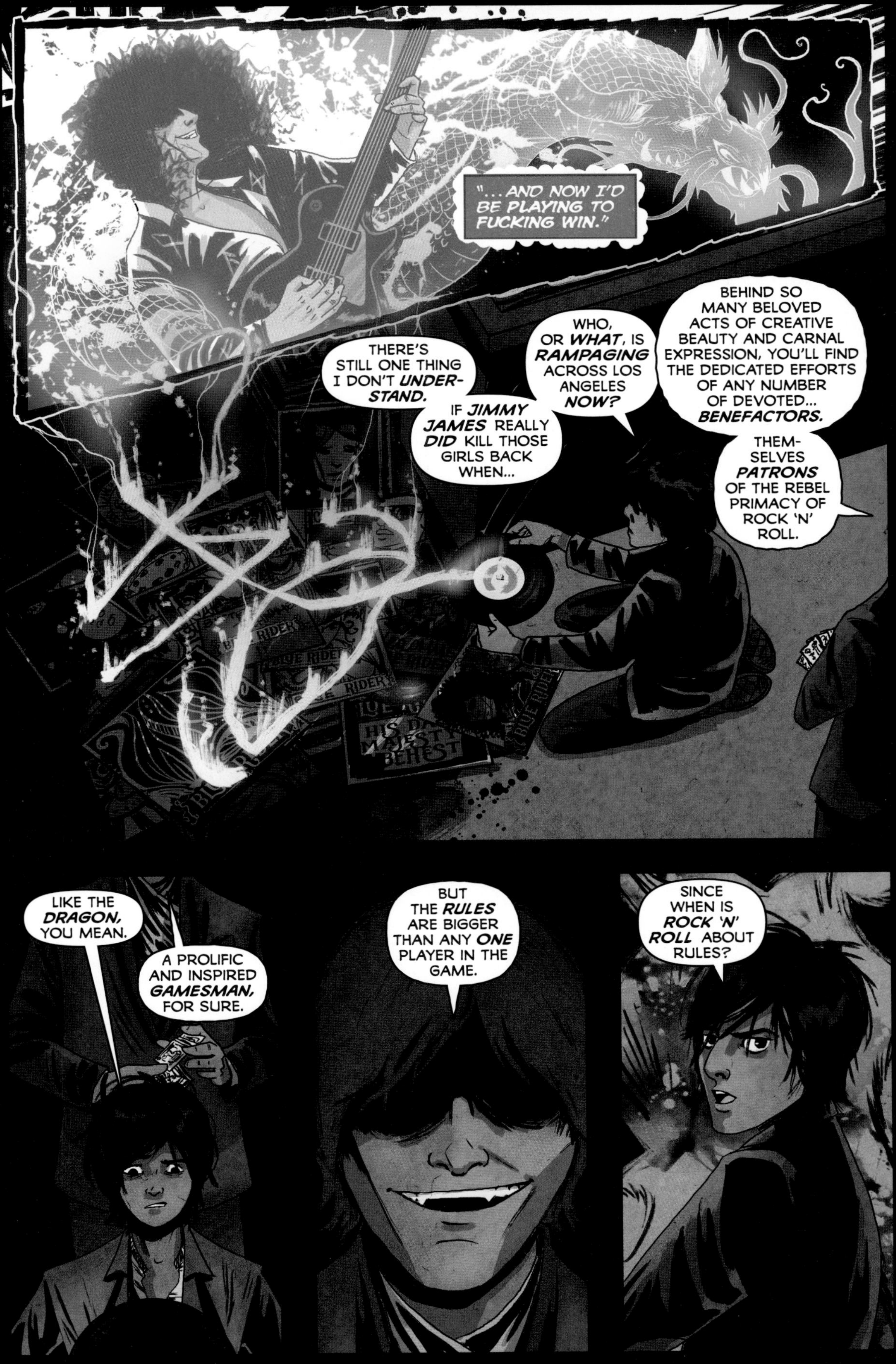
"...AND NOW I'D BE PLAYING TO FUCKING WIN."
THERE'S STILL ONE THING I DON'T UNDER-STAND.
IF JIMMY JAMES REALLY DID KILL THOSE GIRLS BACK WHEN...
WHO, OR WHAT, IS RAMPAGING ACROSS LOS ANGELES NOW?
BEHIND SO MANY BELOVED ACTS OF CREATIVE BEAUTY AND CARNAL EXPRESSION, YOU'LL FIND THE DEDICATED EFFORTS OF ANY NUMBER OF DEVOTED... BENEFACTORS.
THEM-SELVES PATRONS OF THE REBEL PRIMACY OF ROCK 'N' ROLL.
BLUE RIDER
LIKE THE DRAGON, YOU MEAN.
A PROLIFIC AND INSPIRED GAMESMAN, FOR SURE.
BUT THE RULES ARE BIGGER THAN ANY ONE PLAYER IN THE GAME.
SINCE WHEN IS ROCK 'N' ROLL ABOUT RULES?

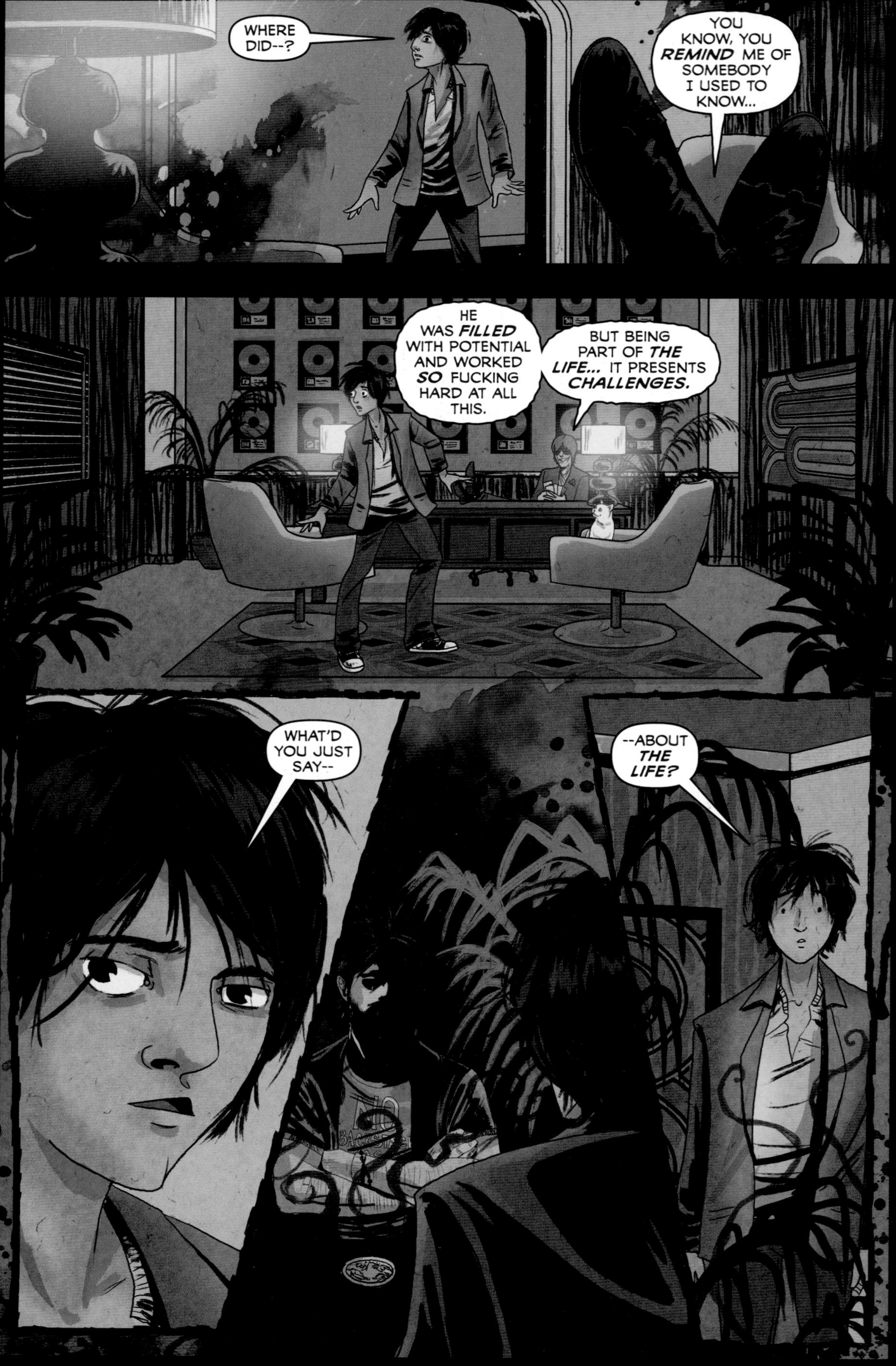
WHERE DID--?
YOU KNOW, YOU *REMIND* ME OF SOMEBODY I USED TO KNOW...
HE WAS *FILLED* WITH POTENTIAL AND WORKED *SO* FUCKING HARD AT ALL THIS.
BUT BEING PART OF *THE LIFE...* IT PRESENTS *CHALLENGES.*
WHAT'D YOU JUST SAY--
--ABOUT *THE LIFE?*

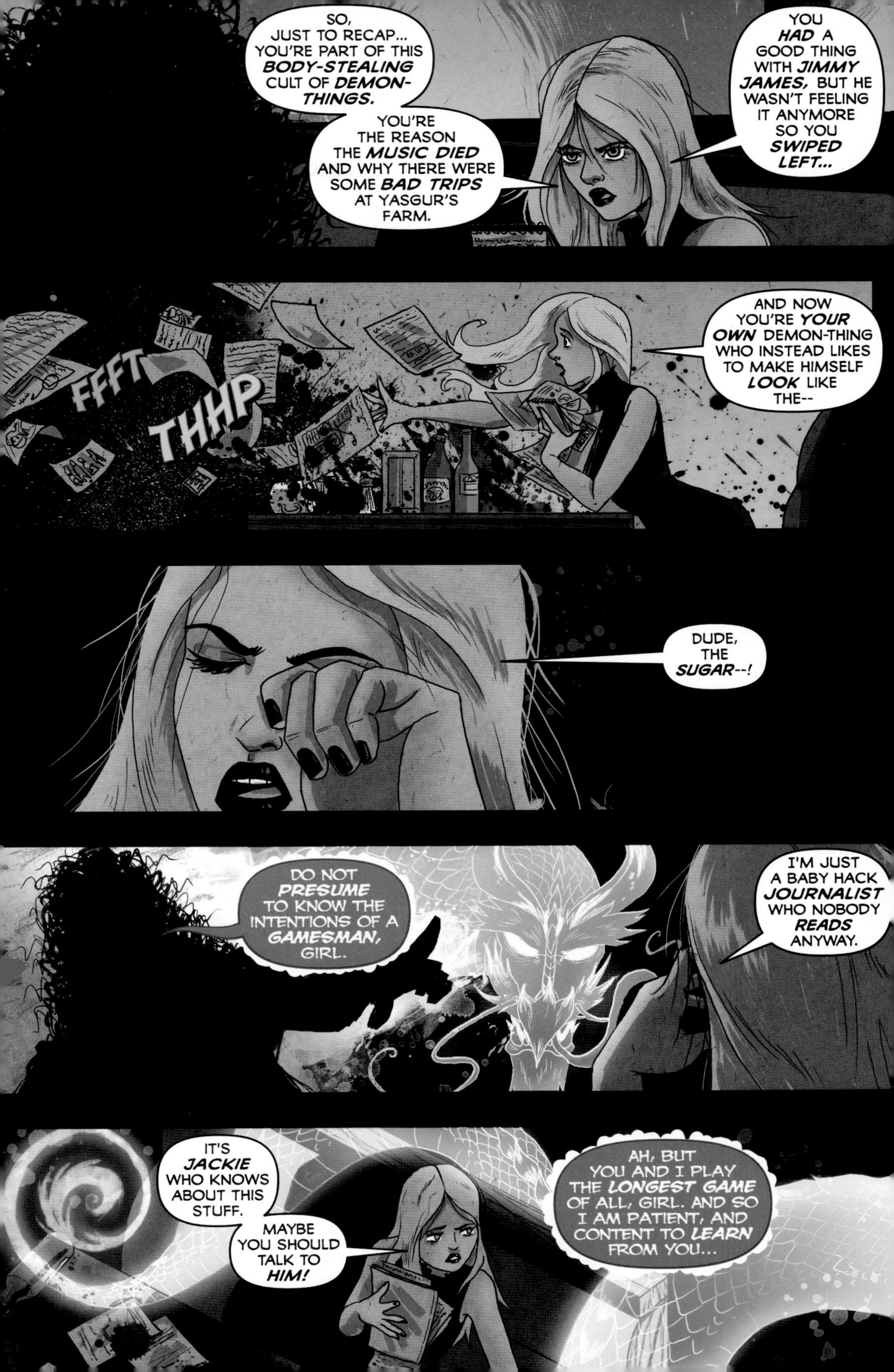
SO, JUST TO RECAP... YOU'RE PART OF THIS BODY-STEALING CULT OF DEMON-THINGS.
YOU'RE THE REASON THE MUSIC DIED AND WHY THERE WERE SOME BAD TRIPS AT YASGUR'S FARM.
YOU HAD A GOOD THING WITH JIMMY JAMES, BUT HE WASN'T FEELING IT ANYMORE SO YOU SWIPED LEFT...
FFFT
THHP
AND NOW YOU'RE YOUR OWN DEMON-THING WHO INSTEAD LIKES TO MAKE HIMSELF LOOK LIKE THE--
DUDE, THE SUGAR--!
DO NOT PRESUME TO KNOW THE INTENTIONS OF A GAMESMAN, GIRL.
I'M JUST A BABY HACK JOURNALIST WHO NOBODY READS ANYWAY.
IT'S JACKIE WHO KNOWS ABOUT THIS STUFF.
MAYBE YOU SHOULD TALK TO HIM!
AH, BUT YOU AND I PLAY THE LONGEST GAME OF ALL, GIRL. AND SO I AM PATIENT, AND CONTENT TO LEARN FROM YOU...

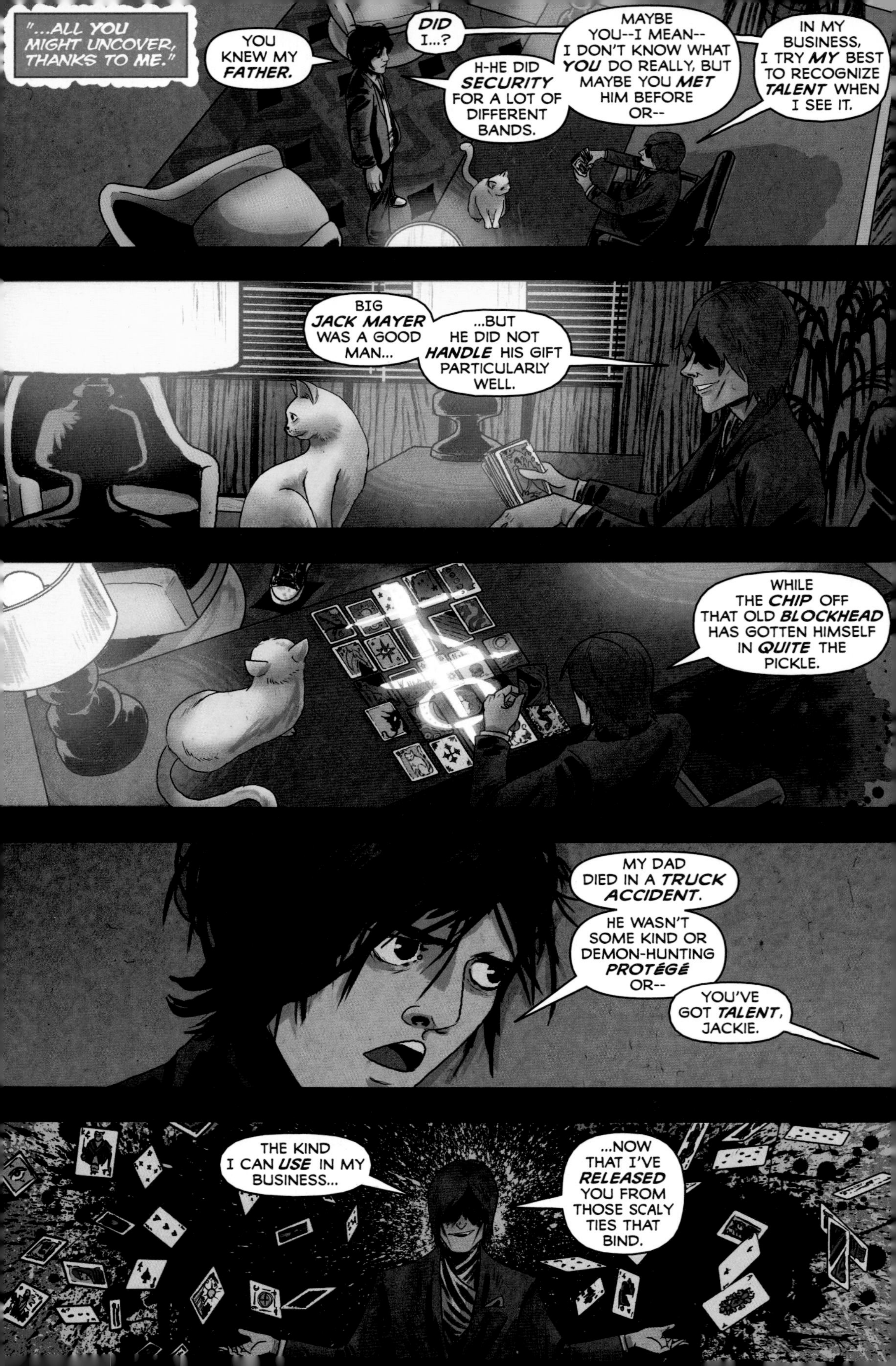
"...ALL YOU MIGHT UNCOVER, THANKS TO ME."
YOU KNEW MY FATHER.
DID I...?
H-HE DID SECURITY FOR A LOT OF DIFFERENT BANDS.
MAYBE YOU--I MEAN-- I DON'T KNOW WHAT YOU DO REALLY, BUT MAYBE YOU MET HIM BEFORE OR--
IN MY BUSINESS, I TRY MY BEST TO RECOGNIZE TALENT WHEN I SEE IT.
BIG JACK MAYER WAS A GOOD MAN...
...BUT HE DID NOT HANDLE HIS GIFT PARTICULARLY WELL.
WHILE THE CHIP OFF THAT OLD BLOCKHEAD HAS GOTTEN HIMSELF IN QUITE THE PICKLE.
MY DAD DIED IN A TRUCK ACCIDENT.
HE WASN'T SOME KIND OR DEMON-HUNTING PROTÉGÉ OR--
YOU'VE GOT TALENT, JACKIE.
THE KIND I CAN USE IN MY BUSINESS...
...NOW THAT I'VE RELEASED YOU FROM THOSE SCALY TIES THAT BIND.

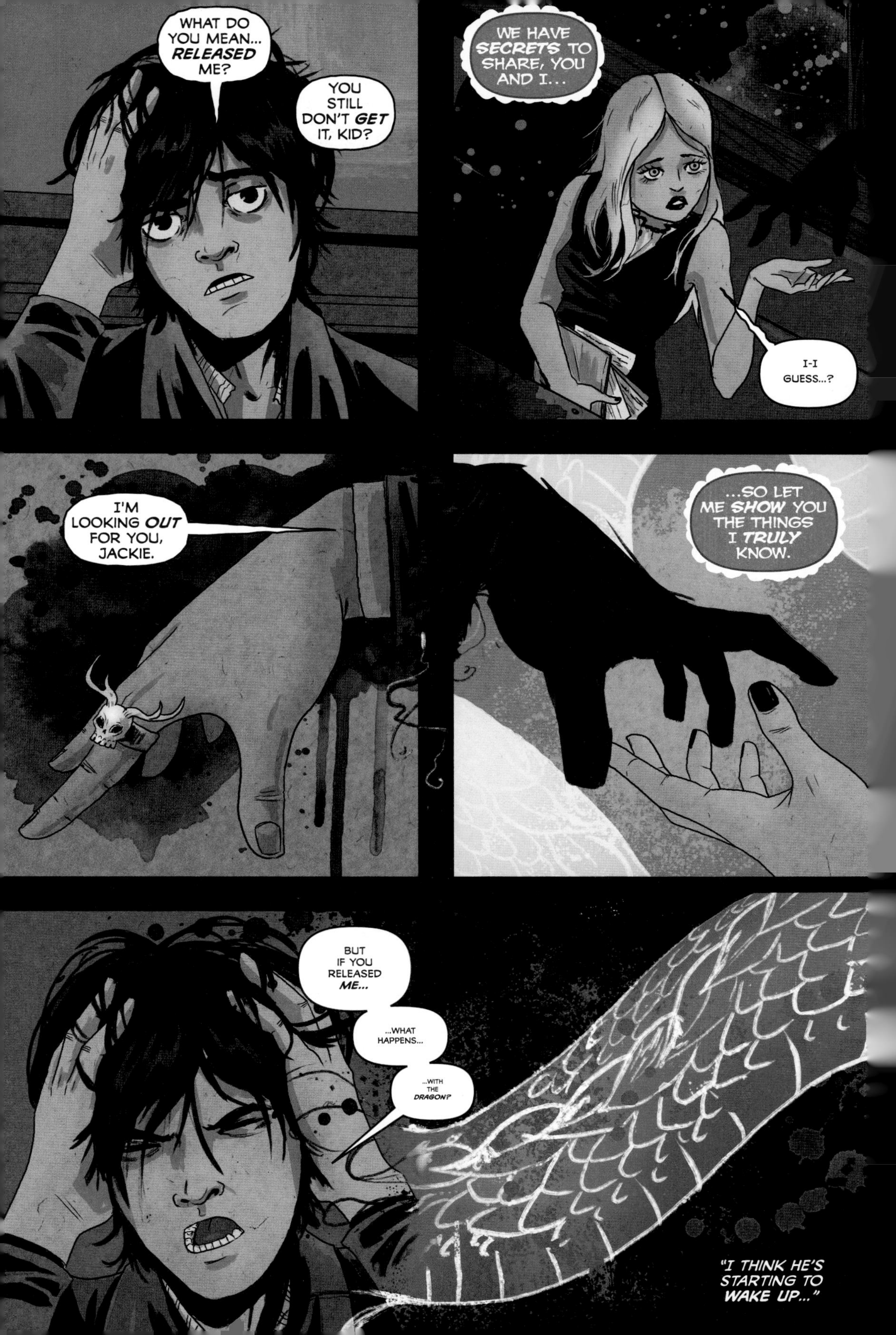
WHAT DO YOU MEAN... RELEASED ME?
YOU STILL DON'T GET IT, KID?
WE HAVE SECRETS TO SHARE, YOU AND I...
I-I GUESS...?
I'M LOOKING OUT FOR YOU, JACKIE.
...SO LET ME SHOW YOU THE THINGS I TRULY KNOW.
BUT IF YOU RELEASED ME...
...WHAT HAPPENS...
...WITH THE DRAGON?
"I THINK HE'S STARTING TO WAKE UP..."

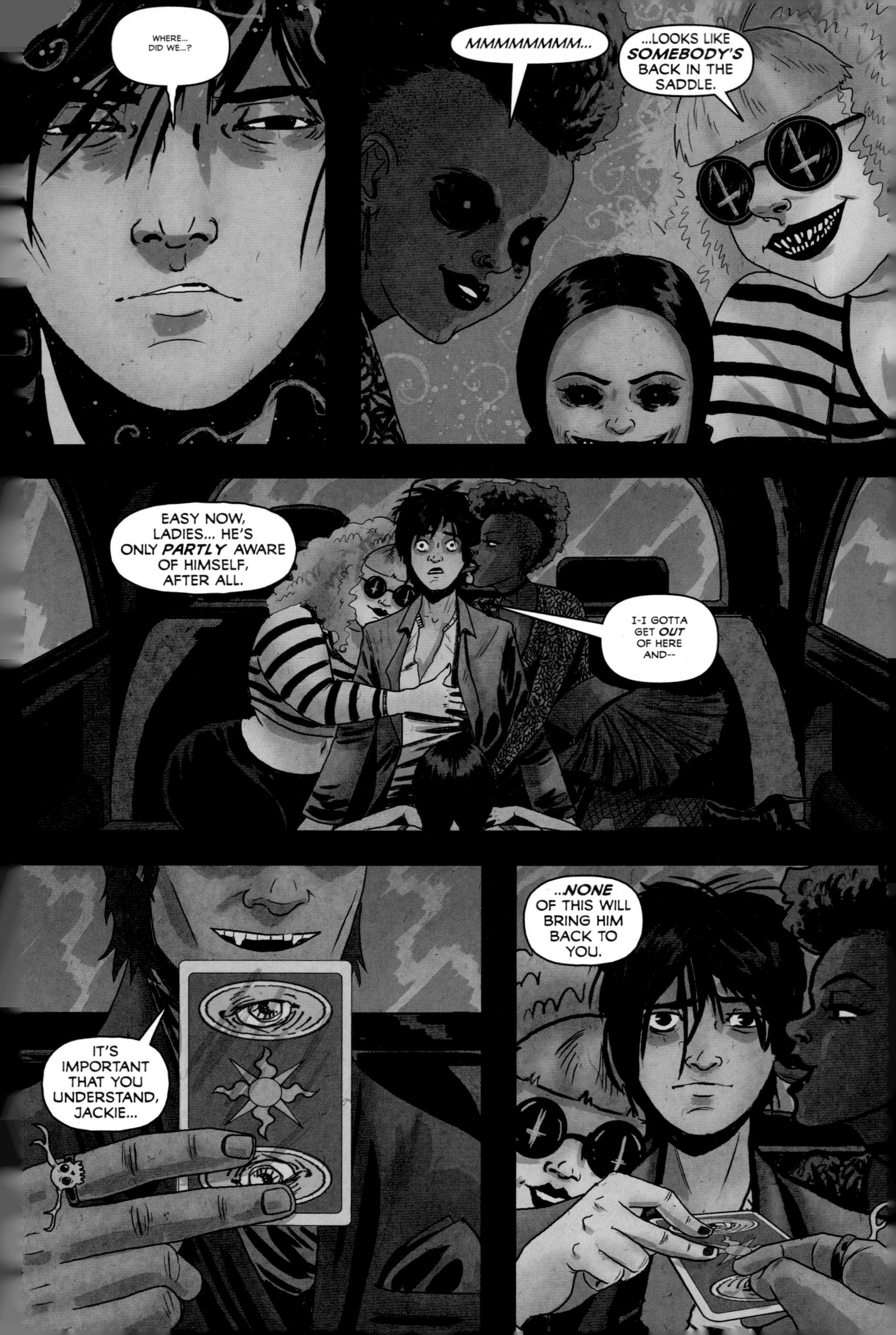
WHERE... DID WE...?
MMMMMMMM...
...LOOKS LIKE SOMEBODY'S BACK IN THE SADDLE.
EASY NOW, LADIES... HE'S ONLY PARTLY AWARE OF HIMSELF, AFTER ALL.
I-I GOTTA GET OUT OF HERE AND--
IT'S IMPORTANT THAT YOU UNDERSTAND, JACKIE...
...NONE OF THIS WILL BRING HIM BACK TO YOU.

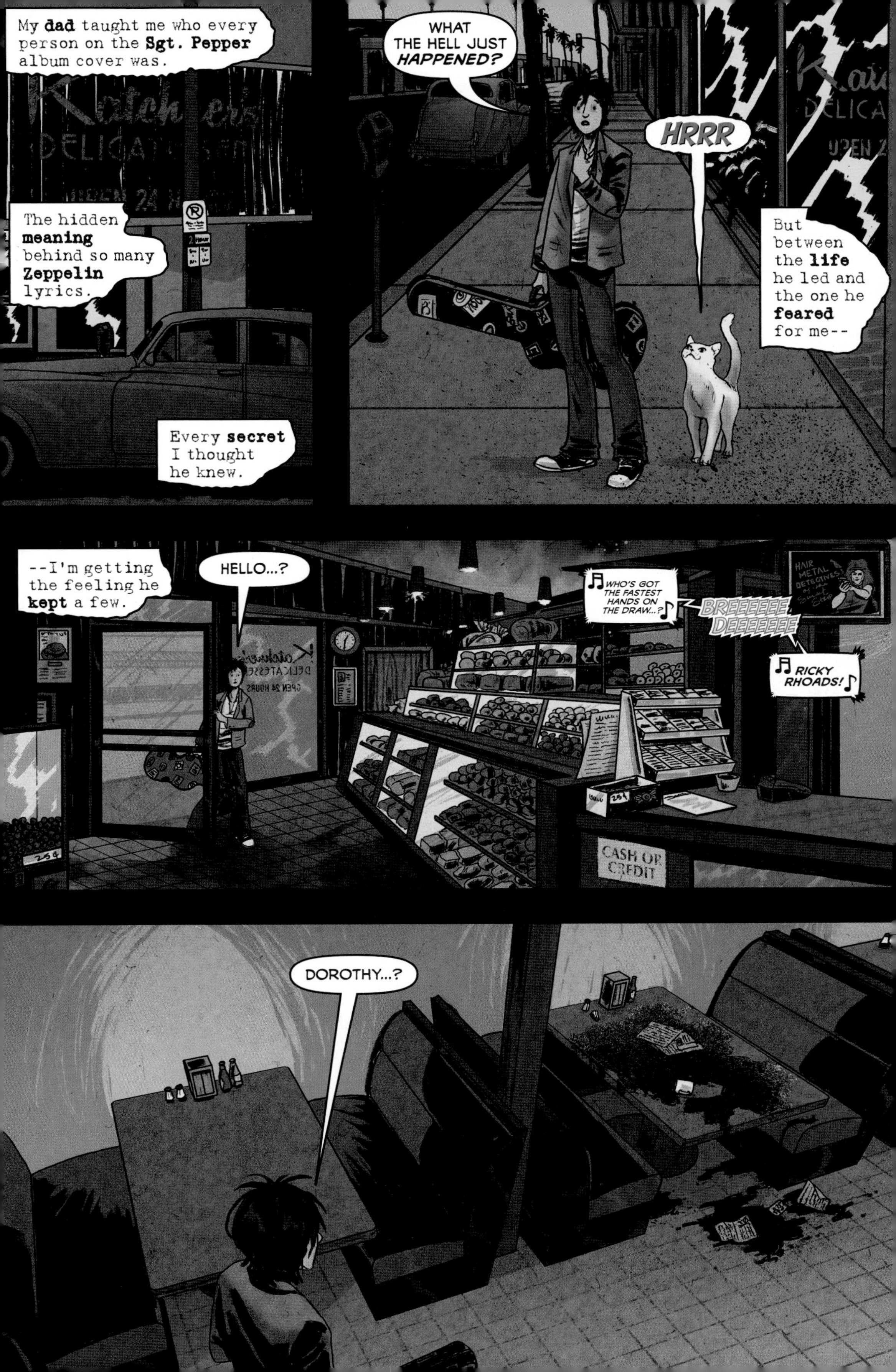

My **dad** taught me who every person on the **Sgt. Pepper** album cover was.
The hidden **meaning** behind so many **Zeppelin** lyrics.
Every **secret** I thought he knew.
WHAT THE HELL JUST *HAPPENED?*
HRRR
But between the **life** he led and the one he **feared** for me--
--I'm getting the feeling he **kept** a few.
HELLO...?
♫ WHO'S GOT THE FASTEST HANDS ON THE DRAW...? ♪
BREEEEEE DEEEEEEE
♫ RICKY RHOADS! ♪
CASH OR CREDIT
DOROTHY...?

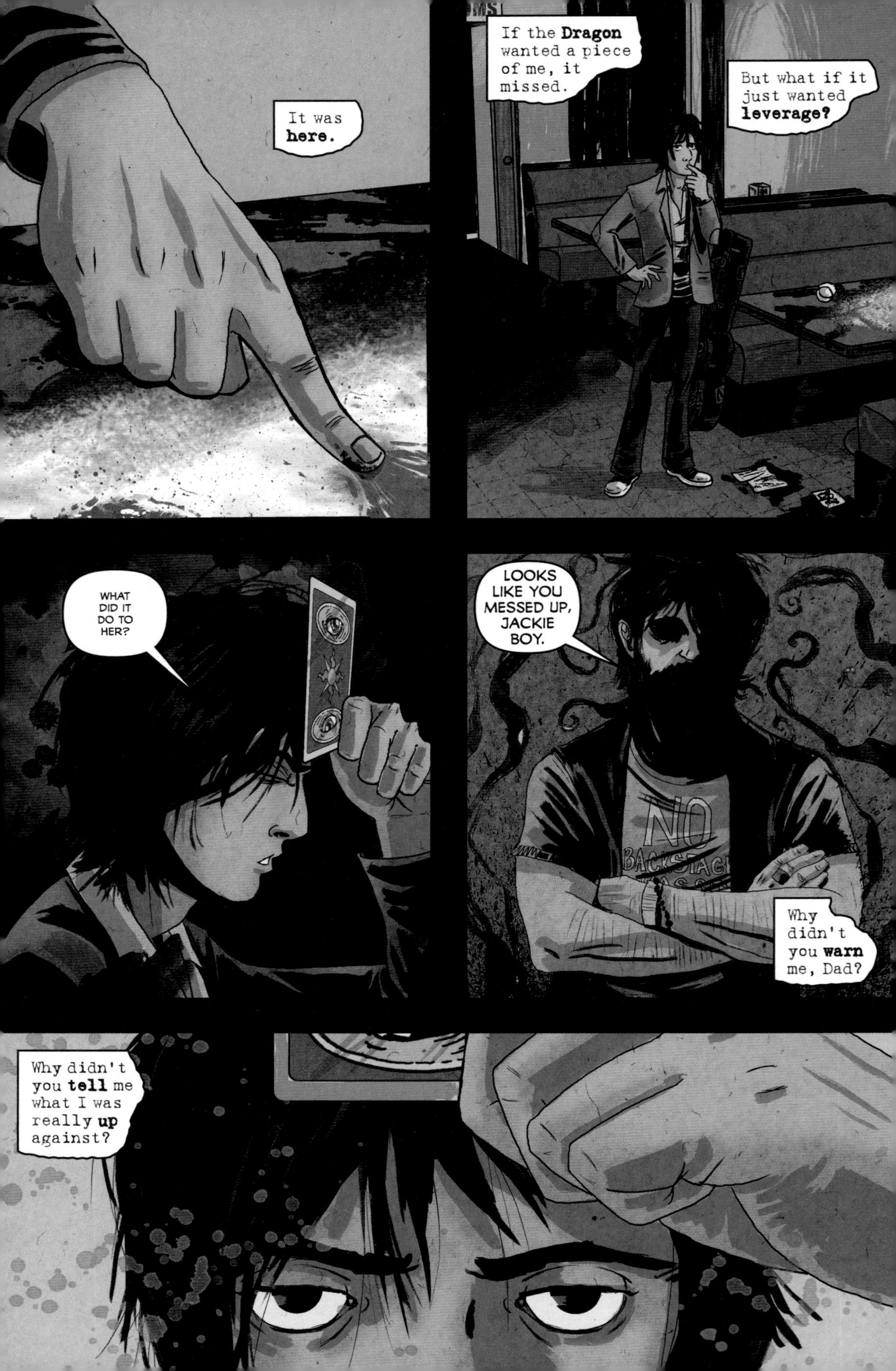

It was **here.**
If the **Dragon** wanted a piece of me, it missed.
But what **if** it just wanted **leverage?**
WHAT DID IT DO TO HER?
LOOKS LIKE YOU MESSED UP, JACKIE BOY.
Why didn't you **warn** me, Dad?
Why didn't you **tell** me what I was really **up** against?

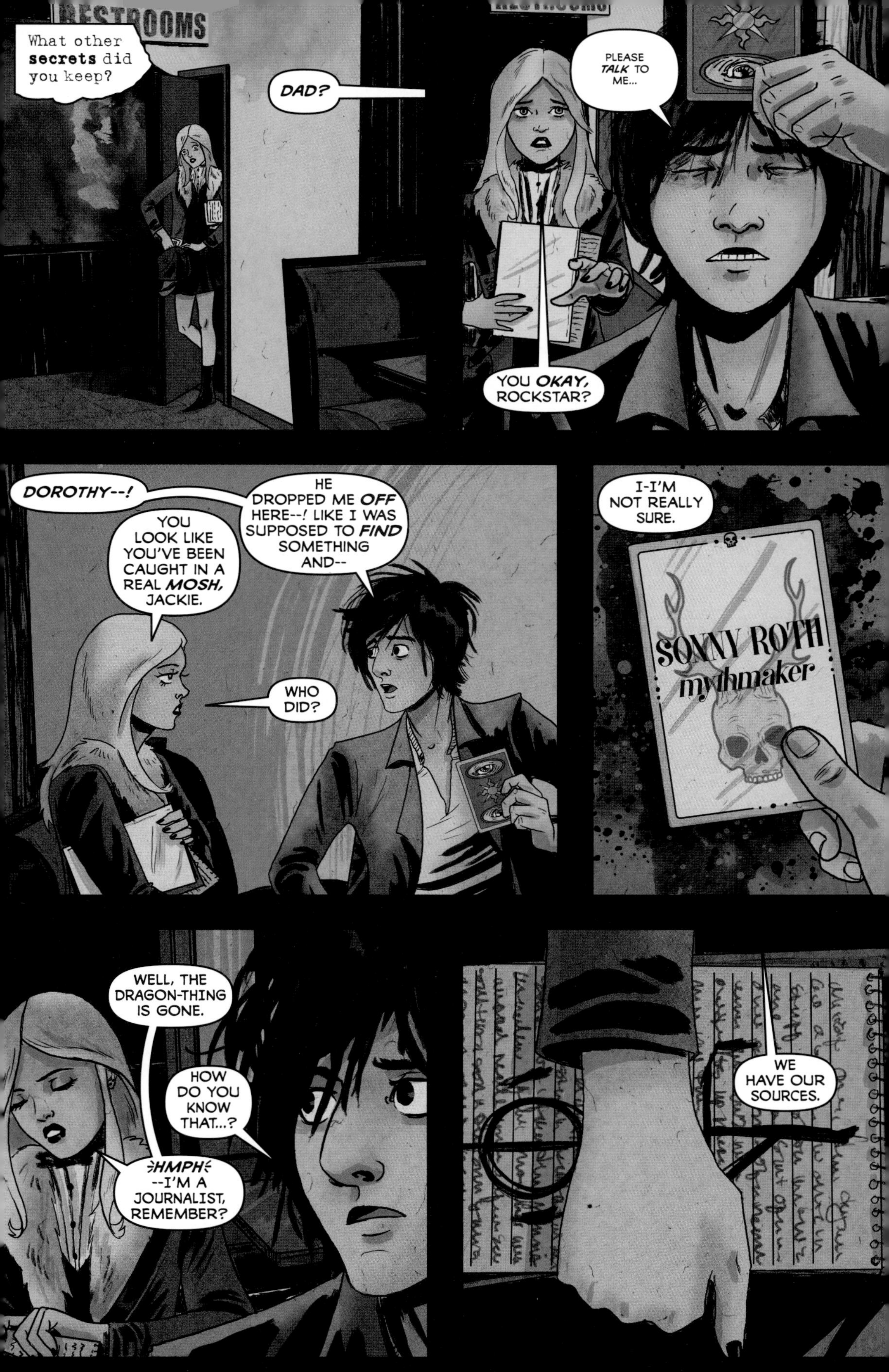
RESTROOMS
What other secrets did you keep?
DAD?
PLEASE TALK TO ME...
YOU OKAY, ROCKSTAR?
DOROTHY--!
HE DROPPED ME OFF HERE--! LIKE I WAS SUPPOSED TO FIND SOMETHING AND--
YOU LOOK LIKE YOU'VE BEEN CAUGHT IN A REAL MOSH, JACKIE.
WHO DID?
I-I'M NOT REALLY SURE.
SONNY ROTH mythmaker
WELL, THE DRAGON-THING IS GONE.
HOW DO YOU KNOW THAT...?
HMPH --I'M A JOURNALIST, REMEMBER?
WE HAVE OUR SOURCES.

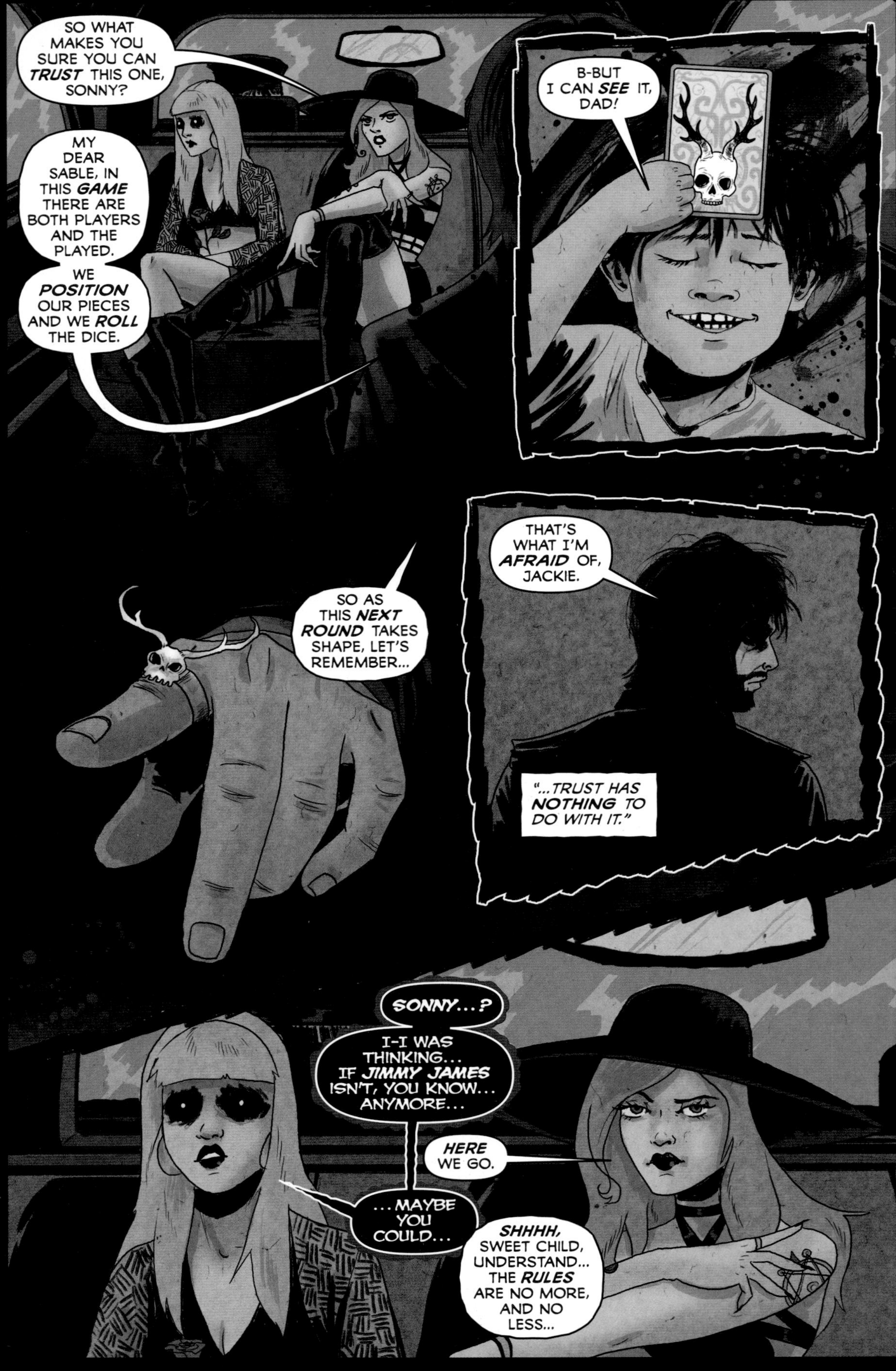

SO WHAT MAKES YOU SURE YOU CAN TRUST THIS ONE, SONNY?
MY DEAR SABLE, IN THIS GAME THERE ARE BOTH PLAYERS AND THE PLAYED.
WE POSITION OUR PIECES AND WE ROLL THE DICE.
B-BUT I CAN SEE IT, DAD!
SO AS THIS NEXT ROUND TAKES SHAPE, LET'S REMEMBER...
THAT'S WHAT I'M AFRAID OF, JACKIE.
"...TRUST HAS NOTHING TO DO WITH IT."
SONNY...?
I-I WAS THINKING... IF JIMMY JAMES ISN'T, YOU KNOW... ANYMORE...
HERE WE GO.
...MAYBE YOU COULD...
SHHHH, SWEET CHILD, UNDERSTAND... THE RULES ARE NO MORE, AND NO LESS...

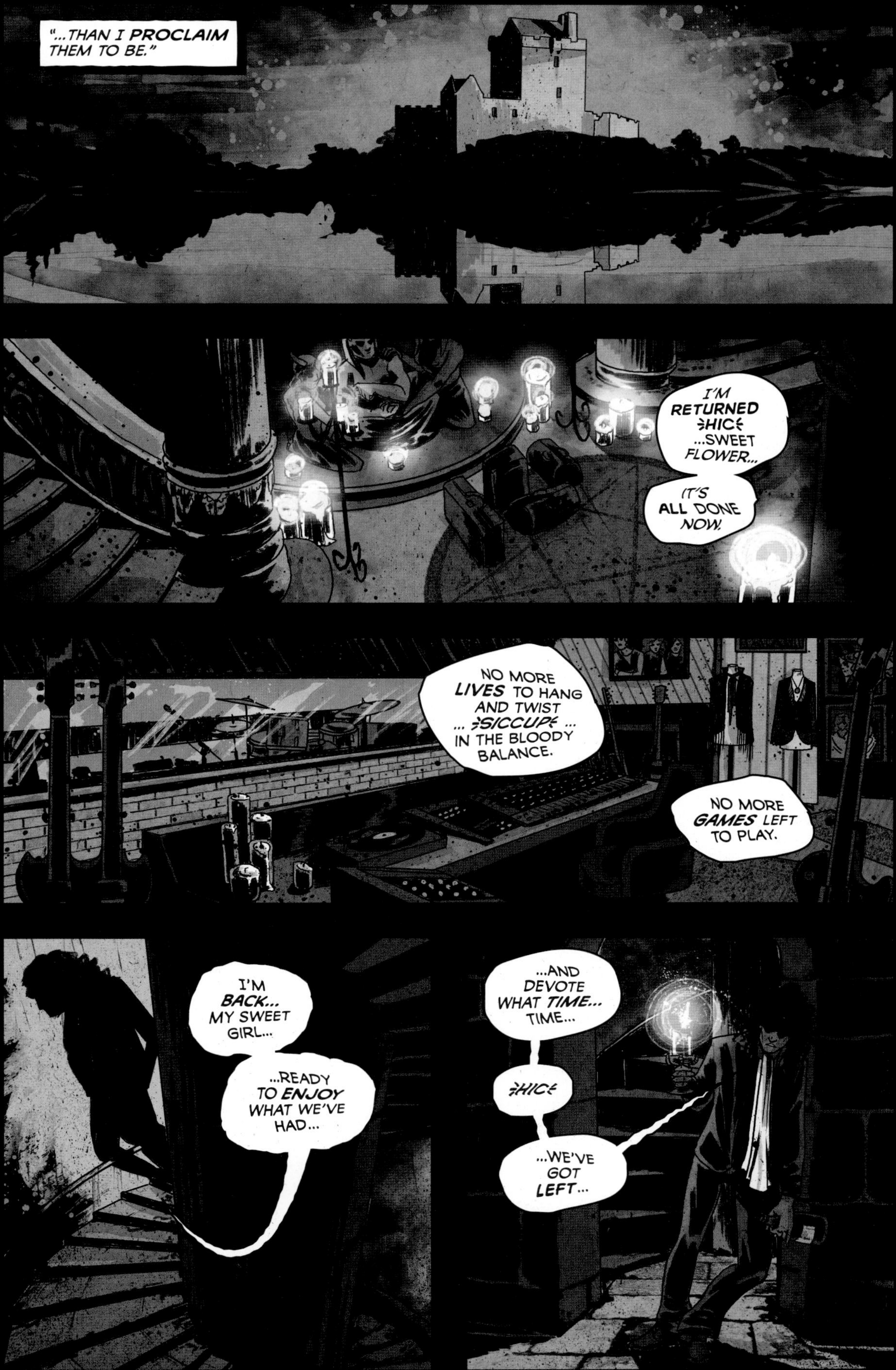
"...THAN I PROCLAIM THEM TO BE."
I'M RETURNED ≠HIC≠ ...SWEET FLOWER...
IT'S ALL DONE NOW.
NO MORE LIVES TO HANG AND TWIST ... ≠SICCUP≠ ... IN THE BLOODY BALANCE.
NO MORE GAMES LEFT TO PLAY.
I'M BACK... MY SWEET GIRL...
...READY TO ENJOY WHAT WE'VE HAD...
...AND DEVOTE WHAT TIME... TIME...
≠HIC≠
...WE'VE GOT LEFT...

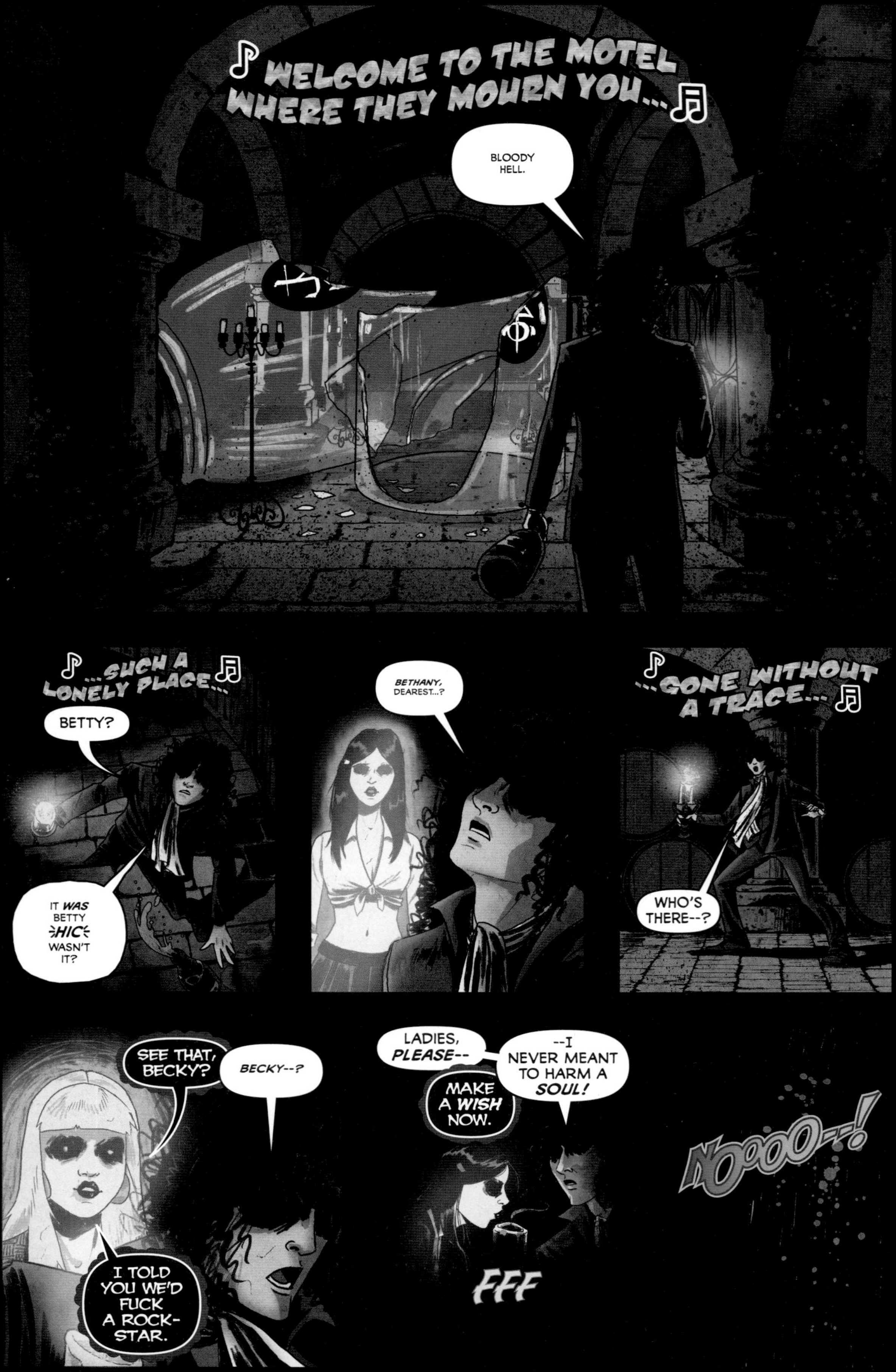
WELCOME TO THE MOTEL WHERE THEY MOURN YOU...
BLOODY HELL.
...SUCH A LONELY PLACE...
BETTY?
IT WAS BETTY HIC WASN'T IT?
BETHANY, DEAREST...?
...GONE WITHOUT A TRACE...
WHO'S THERE--?
SEE THAT, BECKY?
BECKY--?
I TOLD YOU WE'D FUCK A ROCK-STAR.
LADIES, PLEASE--
MAKE A WISH NOW.
--I NEVER MEANT TO HARM A SOUL!
FFF
NOOOO--!

BLUE RIDER

ANNOUNCING
1974 WORLD TOUR

DATES+TICKETS SOON

Portrait by Black Em

JOE HARRIS
WRITER

Joe Harris is the writer and co-creator of the Image Comics titles, *Snowfall* and *Great Pacific*; along with the supernatural thriller series, *Ghost Projekt* and *Spontaneous*, and the original graphic novel, *Wars In Toyland*, for Oni Press. A horror screenwriter and filmmaker, Harris conceived and co-wrote *Darkness Falls* for Sony Pictures—after his short film, *Tooth Fairy* was acquired by Revolution Studios—as well as the politically farcical slasher movie, *The Tripper* for FOX. Since 2013, Joe has penned the fan-favorite, officially licensed line of *The X-Files* comics published by IDW to the enjoyment of fans around the world. A native New Yorker, he lives in Manhattan with his treasured vinyl reissues of the Led Zeppelin catalogue and his vintage Martin D-28 guitar. His high school band, Dream Web, still plays good, honest rock 'n' roll to sold-out bars, clubs and arenas in the comfortably numbed recesses of his mind.

MEGAN HUTCHISON
ARTIST

Portrait by Black Em

After working in the film industry for 10+ years as an art director and production designer, Megan was given the opportunity to illustrate her first graphic novel, An Aurora Grimeon Story: *Will O' the Wisp*, which was published by Archaia Entertainment. She has drawn covers for Boom! Studios, Valiant Entertainment, Image, and Black Mask Studios. Her recently completed OGN, *Vesna*, will debut in 2017. Although her favorite band is The Cure, her go-to karaoke act is Britney Spears.

Portrait by Black Em

KELLY FITZPATRICK
COLORIST

Kelly Fitzpatrick was born in San Antonio, Texas in the spring of 1988. She earned a BFA in Illustration/minor in Photography and Digital Imaging from the Ringling College of Art and Design in Sarasota, FL in 2010 and has worked on hundreds of comics since 2013 with publishers such as Aftershock, Archie, Boom, Dark Horse, DC, Dynamite, Image, Oni, and Young Animal.

TOM MULLER
DESIGNER

Portrait by Black Em

Tom Muller is an Eisner and Harvey Award-nominated Belgian graphic designer and creative director who works with technology startups, movie studios, publishers, media producers, ad agencies, and filmmakers. In comics he's best know for his design work on Ashley Wood's *Popbot*, his numerous projects at Image Comics, including Tori Amos' *Comic Book Tattoo*, *Viking*, *Zero*, *Drifter*, *Wolf*, *Motor Crush*, *Noah*, *The Violent*, *Snowfall*, and *Black Cloud*; his covers and logos for Valiant Comics for *Divinity*, *Generation Zero*, and *X-O Manowar*; and his logos for DC and Vertigo Comics: *Robin*, *Unfollow*, *Constantine*, *Savage Things*, and *Suicide Squad*.

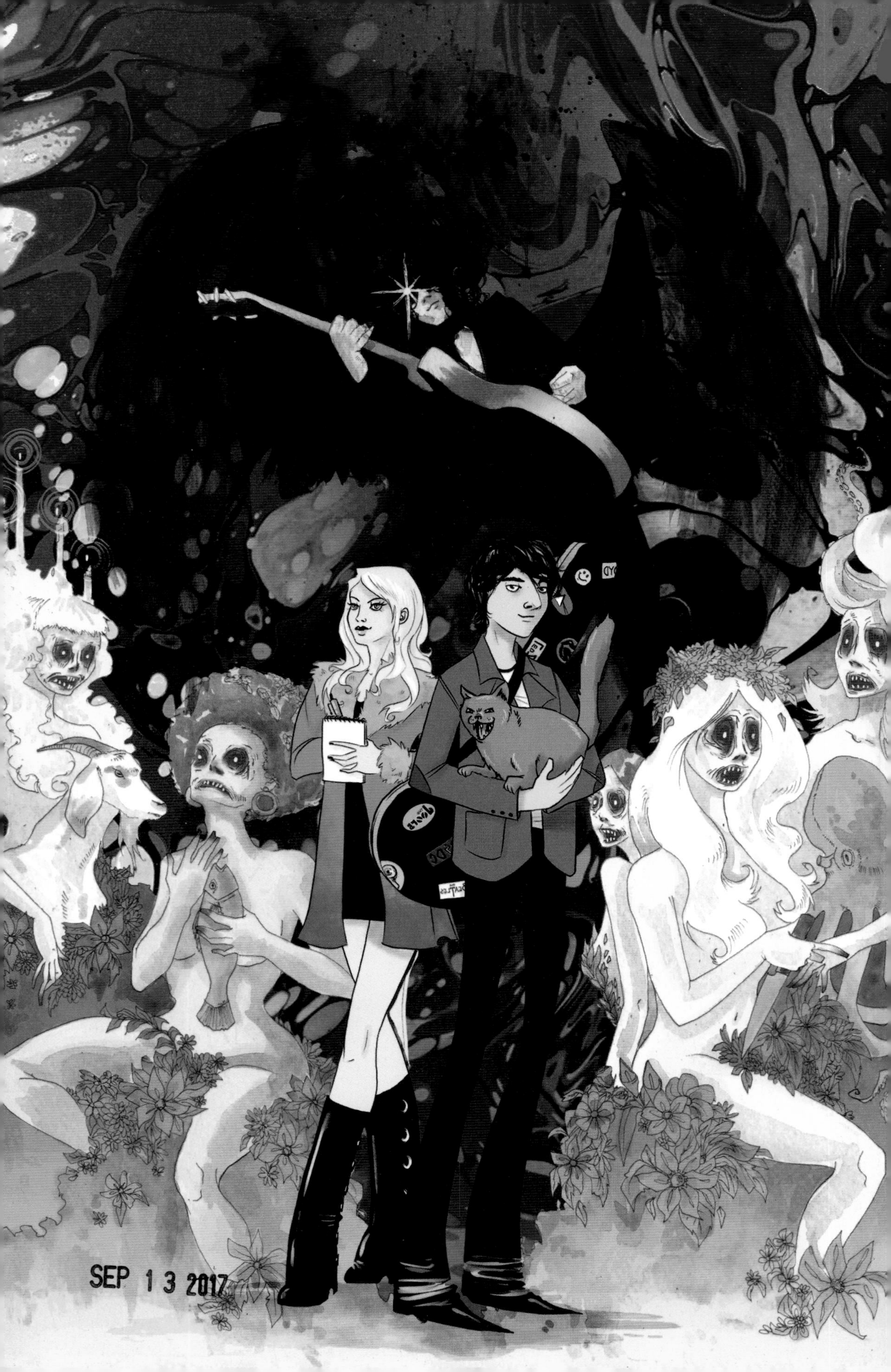